PUCKING STRONG

Emily Rath is a *New York Times* and internationally bestselling author whose chart-topping, sex-positive, queer-inclusive fantasy and romance novels include the Second Sons Regency romances, the Tuonela Duet fantasy novels, and the "why choose" sensation, the Jacksonville Rays Hockey Romances. A former university professor, she holds PhDs in Political Science and Peace Studies. Emily was born in Florida, raised in Kentucky, and now lives in the Pacific Northwest.

ALSO BY EMILY RATH

PUCKING STRONG

EMILY RATH

PENGUIN BOOKS

PENGUIN BOOKS

UK | USA | Canada | Ireland | Australia
India | New Zealand | South Africa

Penguin Books is part of the Penguin Random House group of companies
whose addresses can be found at global.penguinrandomhouse.com

Penguin Random House UK,
One Embassy Gardens, 8 Viaduct Gardens, London SW11 7BW

penguin.co.uk

Penguin
Random House
UK

First published in the United States of America by Kensington Books 2025
First published in Great Britain by Penguin Books 2025

003

Images courtesy of Shutterstock
Printed and bound in Great Britain by Clays Ltd, Elcograf S.p.A.

The authorized representative in the EEA is Penguin Random House Ireland,
Morrison Chambers, 32 Nassau Street, Dublin D02 YH68

A CIP catalogue record for this book is available from the British Library

ISBN: 978-1-405-97120-1

Penguin Random House is committed to a sustainable future
for our business, our readers and our planet. This book is made from
Forest Stewardship Council® certified paper

MIX
Paper | Supporting
responsible forestry
FSC® C018179

This is for everyone who has ever been told you're too much. That you feel too much, talk too much, need too much. No, you don't. You're perfect just as you are.

And this is for Aaron. In high school, you asked me if I had a problem with you being gay. I told you I respected you as a friend but disagreed with your lifestyle. Watching your face fall shattered me. Your quiet disappointment screamed so loud. It set me on my path to accepting my own queerness. Please know I regretted my words the moment they were spoken. And know you're perfect too.

Content Warnings

This book contains themes that may be distressing to readers, including death of a family member (off page), traumatic grief/loss, and brief thoughts of suicidal ideation. A child is injured (off page) and experiences physical pain/distress as they heal (on page). A family struggles from the effects of a parent living with dementia. A character briefly suffers from night terrors.

As an interracial gay couple, the main characters encounter homophobia and racism, this includes microaggressions, like dirty looks and rude comments. A main character is demisexual and struggles to give voice to that. As he works through owning this label for himself, he experiences moments of frustration, even self-loathing. More than once, he refers to himself as "broken." With better education, he comes to understand that sexuality is a spectrum, and he accepts himself for who he is.

Aside from the above, this book contains detailed explicit sex scenes that include elements of oral sex, anal sex, rimming, choking, edging, cum play, toy play, impact play, and public sex.

Author's Note

This is the fourth book in the Jacksonville Rays hockey romance series. Book One, *Pucking Around*, is Rachel's story. Book Two, *Pucking Wild*, is Tess's story. Book Three, *Pucking Sweet*, is Poppy's story. At long last, it's time to fall in love with Teddy!

I know Teddy has had a small role to play in the Jax Rays universe so far, but he's always loomed large in my heart. From the first moment I wrote him as that shy intern, I knew I'd be giving him his own book. Sweet Teddy came to me so clearly formed, from his freckled nose to his nervous smile. I just knew I had to give him a happily ever after.

Readers should be warned that this book will have a much slower burn than previous books. I'm not saying there's no spice. Sweet lord in heaven, there is spice in this book. These two are gonna sizzle your fuzzy pink socks off . . . but we have to earn it first. Buckle in for some deliciously slow-burning angst and gut-wrenching pining. Ohmygod, the pining.

You ready? Turn the page, and let's go.

XO,

E Roth

Meet the Rays

PLAYERS
*Compton/Price, Jake (#42): defenseman, captain
Boucher, Michael "Bouch" (#80): forward
DeGraw, Hunter (#1): starting goalie
Fields, Ethan (#94): forward
Gordon, Sam "Flash" (#18): forward
Hanner, Paul "Paulie" (#24): defenseman
Karlsson, Henrik (#17): forward
Langley, Ryan "Langers" (#20): forward, assistant captain
Lindberg, Christian "Lindy" (#38): center
Novikov, Lukas "Novy" (#22): defenseman, assistant captain
Perry, David "DJ" (#13): forward
Tremblay, Robert "Tremors" (#9): forward
Walsh, Cade (#10): forward
West, Connor "Westie" (#25): forward
Woodson, Chris "Woody" (#51): defenseman

COACHES
Andrews, Brody: assistant coach (defense)
Denison, Nick: assistant coach (offense)
Johnson, Harold "Hodge": head coach
Tomlin, Eric: goalie coach

TEAM SUPPORT
Jones, Cody: Assistant equipment manager
*Sanford/Price, Caleb: head equipment manager

MEDICAL SUPPORT
Avery, Todd: former head physical therapist
Brady, Brad: head physical therapist (interim)
Evers, Dustin: head athletic trainer
O'Connor, Teddy: assistant physical therapist
Price, Rachel: head physical therapist (on maternity leave)
Tyler, Scott: primary care physician

OPERATIONS/MANAGEMENT
Francis, Vicki: operations manager
Singh, Arjan: manager of team services
St. James, Poppy: public relations director
Talbot, Mark: team owner
Varma, Roshni: hockey analytics
Weiss, John: general manager

*Jake and Caleb are listed with their unmarried and married names. Ilmari is retired. Colton Morrow is also retired.

STAR SIGNS
Teddy: Pisces (water): imaginative, empathetic, insecure
Henrik: Capricorn (earth): disciplined, responsible, cold

Useful Swedish Words & Phrases

Du är min man | You are my husband
Du är min nu | You are mine now
Du är så vacker | You are so beautiful
Du betyder allt för mig | You mean everything to me
Du gör mig galen | You drive me crazy
Ett rent hjärta | A pure heart
Fan i helvete | Fucking hell
Gud, hjälpe mig | God, help me
Hallongrotta | Swedish thumbprint cookies, usually filled with
raspberry jam
Hej snygging | Hey, handsome
Jag älskar dig | I love you
Jag är din och du är min | I am yours and you are mine
Jag behöver hjälp | I need help
Jag saknar Mamma | I miss Mommy
Jag vill ha dig | I want you
Kanelbulle | Cinnamon buns, usually dusted with pärlsocker (pearl
sugar)
Min kärlek | My love
Min man | My husband
Mitt allt | My everything
Mitt hjärta | My heart
Mitt liv | My life
Mitt livs kärlek | Love of my life
Morbror | Maternal uncle
Mormor | Maternal grandmother

HELAN GÅR (POPULAR SWEDISH DRINKING SONG)

Helan går
Sjung hopp faderallan lallan lej
Helan går
Sjung hopp faderallan lej
Och den som inte helan tar

Han heller inte halvan får
Helan går
(Drink)
Sjung hopp faderallan lej

Playlist

Crush | Campsite Dream
Money Maker (featuring Pharrell Williams) | Ludacris
Down Bad | Taylor Swift
if you only knew | Alexander Stewart
Turn Me On | Norah Jones
THE LONELIEST | Måneskin
Bleeding Love | Leona Lewis
No Scrubs | TLC
That's What I Like | Bruno Mars
No Plan | Hozier
Lost Without You | Freya Ridings
Unbroken Promise | Erick Baker
feel it all | sød ven
King Of My Heart | Taylor Swift
I Wanna Know (Acoustic) | Will Gittens & Rome Flynn
Beautiful Things | Benson Boone
Somebody Should Kiss You | Teddy Swims
Make It To Me | Sam Smith
I Was Made For Lovin' You | Kiss
The Nearness Of You | Norah Jones

PUCKING STRONG

1

TEDDY

Six Years Ago

Is it possible to lose your job before you even start it? Because if I don't get my coffee in the next *two* fucking seconds, I'm officially gonna be late to my first day of work. It's a busy Monday morning, and this coffee shop is slammed. People are pouring in through both doors like bees into a hive.

"Americano for Evan," shouts a lavender-haired barista.

An insurance salesman–looking guy elbows me as he passes. Cursing under my breath, I step back. In this cramped space, I don't see the dog on the floor behind me. He sure lets me know he's there when I step on his tail and he howls.

"Hey," his owner cries. "Did you just step on my dog?"

I raise both hands. "I'm sorry! I didn't see him, I swear."

The woman and her dog both give me death glares as she tugs him away.

Yeah, I don't think I have what it takes to frequent the Bright Bean. No caffeine jolt is worth this hassle. Groaning, I bounce on the balls of my feet, trying not to check my phone again. I know what time it is. I know exactly how late I am. "Fuck, come on."

One could say this is all my fault. I'm the one who hit snooze twice on my alarm this morning. *I* forgot to stock my mini fridge with canned cold brews. *I* got lost driving in this confusing down-town full of one-ways and detours.

In my defense, I only found out I was selected for this internship, like, two weeks ago. I tried for it back in the spring. All my friends matched, but I didn't. Imagine my surprise when, months later, I got an email from my advisor saying I matched with an NHL team in Jacksonville, Florida. And—oh, by the way—could I start in two weeks? I didn't even know there was an NHL team in Jacksonville. Turns out this is the Rays' first year in the League.

They had two open internship positions for their brand-new PT program, and I snagged one. But that meant I had less than two weeks to change all my plans. Instead of moving back to my university, I moved into temporary housing at the local Jacksonville community college three days ago. I'm rooming with my friend Colin, who matched with the Jacksonville Jaguars.

"Iced latte for Teddy!"

Rushing forward, I claim my coffee with a hurried "thanks." I clutch the cup in both hands like a dragon with his egg. This isn't just an iced latte. It's an iced oat-milk honey latte with a double shot of espresso and vanilla-sweet-cream cold foam with a drizzle of caramel on top. It's basically an orgasm in a cup.

Elbows out, I barrel my way towards the exit, all but stumbling into the free air. It's a muggy September morning, already eighty degrees. But I was born and raised in the South. I can do heat and humidity all day.

I'm still two blocks away from the practice center. Thank god I'm in amazing shape, because I'm about to Usain Bolt my way down this damn sidewalk. I break into a jog, ducking around a couple headed for the coffee shop. Traffic is busy with everyone going to work. Up and down the street, trucks stand open as workers unload morning deliveries. I slink past a guy walking two corgis, trying to cross the street, but the pedestrian light is already flashing in warning.

Fuck, I'm not gonna make it.

The red hand glows bright, and I'm forced to stop. I'm still one block away. I can see the corner of the building beckoning to me. Huffing for breath, I take a sip of my coffee. The flavors hit my tongue like a sweet, creamy kiss. It's soft and cool, with just a hint of nutty espresso. I let out a contented sigh. "God, that's good."

If I lose my job, at least I'll have this drink to savor.

Waiting for the light to change, I pull my phone from my pocket. My phone has been buzzing nonstop from my family group chat. Not surprising, seeing as I have three sisters. Three *older* sisters. Three nosy, noisy, very needy sisters. They're always in my business. Always offering advice whether I want it or not. But that's family. And I've got a damn good one.

SHAE: Good morning, Teddy!
JAYLA: Happy first day of work!
SHAE: Don't you be late. You're always late.
NATALIE: I wanna see those hot hockey boys. Take pics for us.
JAYLA: Wait, he's working for a hockey team?
SHAE: Where you been, Jay? *laughing emoji*
JAYLA: I thought he was working for the Jags. That's football, right? I got myself a jersey and everything. Show me those season tickets, bay-bay!
NATALIE: NHL is hockey. Not football.
JAYLA: Well, then you've lost my interest *wave emoji*

I smile into my coffee as I scroll through the rest of the messages. Apparently, Jayla now expects me to pay for the Jags jersey she can't return. And Shae wants me to get tickets for her whole family to come to the first home game.

The pedestrian light flashes. "Walk sign, Third Street," the robotic traffic voice chirps.

Slipping my phone back in my pocket, I step off the curb. Then a few things happen all at once. First, my entire life flashes before my fucking eyes as a blue pickup truck blasts through the pedestrian walkway. Slamming on his horn, the driver runs the red light, nearly turning me into mashed potatoes.

I'm only saved by the second thing. A pair of strong arms wrap around my chest from behind and jerks me back just in time. "Look out," says a gruff voice in my ear.

Then I'm falling. All I see is sky as I drop back in slow motion, those firm arms locked around my chest. My perfect cup of coffee goes flying from my hand as I land on my savior. He grunts, absorbing our impact as he hits the ground first. My coffee lands next to us with a *splat*. I cry out as I watch it leak all over the sidewalk. "My orgasm!"

The hands on me tighten as the man beneath me groans, rolling me to the side.

Oh my god, I just had a near-death experience. I literally almost just died.

My savior shifts out from under me. "Are you alright?"

I blink twice. Holy fuck, this is the most beautiful man I've ever seen. He's young and white. His eyes are a deep blue, almost navy. They're wide with concern now. A wave of dark blond hair sweeps across his brow. His cheeks are bearded, like sand on the beach, all faded yellow, flecked with brown. He speaks, but there's a ringing in my ears. "What?"

"I said, are you alright?" he asks again.

Fuck me, I think he has an accent. Is he European? I sit up, and he drops his hand away. Suddenly, I want to die all over again. He was touching me and now he's not? Make that make sense.

"Should we call an ambulance?" an older lady asks, clutching her chest as she peers down the street.

My beautiful savior has eyes only for me. "No, I think he's alright. Just startled."

Startled feels like the wrong word to describe how I'm feeling right now. God just threw me into the arms of his most perfect creation. I should introduce myself, right? Maybe tattoo his angelic face on my bicep. At the very least, I should offer to pay him for his trouble. I mean, he *did* just save my life. But I'm a starving college kid. My wasted coffee was already an extravagance. I point to where it's pooling on the ground. "You spilled my orgasm."

"What?"

"My coffee," I correct. "It spilled. I think we're sitting in it."

He shrugs. "It's just coffee. Your life is more important, no?" Then he stands, unbothered by the coffee soaking the side of his shirt. "Can you stand?"

I take his hand, and he pulls me to my feet before quickly dropping his hand away. I feel the loss of his touch like the ripping of a bandage from my skin. I want to step closer. I want him to hold me again. But that would be crazy, right? I don't even know this guy. I'm just a chaotic double Pisces who gets his life saved by a beautiful man and immediately fights the toxic urge to ask, "Your place or mine?"

I look him over now that he's standing. He's taller than me, but I might be a little broader in the shoulders. He has a runner's build, long and lean. Except for his thighs. They're like tree trunks.

Fuck, stop looking at his legs.

And *say* something, Teddy.

Desperate not to scare him away, I opt for a very casual, "Hey, thanks, man."

He nods and turns to leave.

Oh god, I can't bear it. Someone crazy—totally not me—grabs his arm. "Wait."

He pauses.

"I—don't . . ." *Want you to leave,* I finish inside my head. *I don't want to be parted from you. Not yet. It's too soon. We've only just met.* Instead, I find the will to blurt out, "I don't even know your name."

He relaxes a little and smiles. I love how the smile touches his eyes more than his mouth. "It's Henrik." His voice is softer now, like he's talking to a friend.

Henrik.

He's looking at me, waiting. Oh fuck, I'm still holding on to him. "My name is Teddy," I manage to say.

"Teddy," he repeats. "Well . . . have a good day, Teddy."

I let Henrik go, watching as he walks away, lost to me forever.

I remember nothing of the rest of my walk to the Rays' practice center. I'm definitely late, but now I have an ironclad excuse. The intern coordinator's frown disappears the moment I regale her with the harrowing tale. I even earn enough sympathy from HR to be gifted a Rays T-shirt to replace my coffee-stained polo shirt.

Before I know it, I'm in the gym with Doctor Avery, head of

physical therapy. He introduces me to some of the players. There's Jean-Luc Gerard, a big, toothless Canadian everyone affectionately calls "J-Lo." Then there are several young guys. Paulie, maybe? Sam, who is also Flash. Westie. Patrick. Woody—no, Woodson, I think.

Fuck, do *all* these guys have three fucking names? Between learning all their names, nicknames, numbers, and positions, my head is already spinning.

"And this is Josh O'Sullivan," says Doctor Avery. "He's a forward and team captain. The guys all call him Sully."

O'Sullivan offers me his hand. "Great to meet you, bud. You a big fan of hockey?"

"Umm . . ." I don't want to lie to these guys, but the truth is that I don't know the first thing about hockey. We don't get a lot of hockey in Atlanta. I grew up watching football and basketball. In school, I swam and ran track. The only time I watch hockey is during the Winter Olympics.

O'Sullivan sees right through me. "That's okay. We'll make a fan out of you before the season ends."

"Thanks." I flash him a relieved smile. "I'm definitely ready to learn."

Before I can say another word, my breath catches in my chest. Oh my god . . .

"Hey, Karlsson!" O'Sullivan calls with a wave. "Get over here. Meet the new intern."

I can hardly believe it as my sidewalk savior locks eyes with me across the gym. He recognizes me immediately. His gaze dips past my face to my new T-shirt. He's wearing a different shirt too. He crosses the gym over to us.

"Karlsson, meet the new PT intern," says O'Sullivan. "This is—"

"Teddy," Henrik finishes for him. Then he holds out his hand. "We've met."

I take his hand like a greedy, lovestruck fool. Am I smiling? What is my face doing? Fuck, I don't even know. "Henrik," I say on a breath.

His smile flickers as those around us share confused glances. "Call me Karlsson. Everyone does." Dropping my hand, he breaks our cosmic connection . . . and my heart.

Out on the street, in his arms, he was Henrik to me. That was when we were strangers. *Henrik*. Such a beautiful name. But now, everything is different. We're off the street. We're in his gym, in front of his friends, his teammates. And we're no longer strangers. God help me, I think we're coworkers.

This can't happen. He's an international sports superstar. People wear his number and cheer his name. He can't be Henrik with me. I'm nothing to him, just a lowly college intern. But still, as I watch him walk away, an aching truth settles deep in my soul: I want this man, even as I know I can never have him.

This is going to be the longest fucking year of my life.

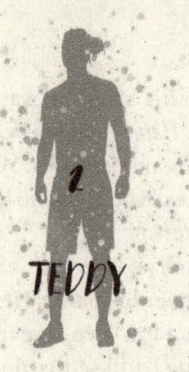

1

TEDDY

The Present

My phone buzzes as the coffee cart barista hands me my latte. "Thanks, Kelly."

"Good to see you again, Teddy," she chimes. "We sure missed you around here."

Smiling, I take a sip of my coffee and check my phone. It's my sister. *Again.* She's been pestering me all morning.

SHAE: Did you update your mailing address? You need to forward your mail.

I groan, quickly shooting her a message back.

TEDDY: You know I'm twenty-six, right? Also, I'm a literal doctor. I could kill you and make it look like an accident.

There's a long pause before she replies.

SHAE: Don't even play. I changed your diapers.

I sigh. Well, it was worth a shot. As the baby and only boy of the family, it's been difficult to shift the impression they all have of me as helpless and hopeless, constantly in need of saving. It's so frustrating. They have to let me grow up sometime.

She's right though. I *do* need to update my mail.

"Well, look what the cat dragged in!"

I spin away from the coffee cart to see Brad Brady crossing the atrium towards me. With his pale skin, square-framed glasses, and Clark Kent haircut, Brady looks like he belongs in a vintage comic bookstore. Instead, he earns a living making grown men cry on a PT table.

"Hey there, Doctor O'Connor." He wraps me in a hug. "It's so great to see you!"

I hold my coffee out to the side, returning his hug with one arm. "You too. It's been, what, four years? How's Dylan?"

"Retired, thank god. He sells motorcycles now."

His husband Dylan is a former MMA fighter. The last time I was in town was to attend their wedding. They're the cutest, odd couple. Brady is this sweet, unassuming comic book nerd. While Dylan is a 6'4" hairy bear, covered in tattoos. He's got a lip ring and gives off total leather daddy vibes. That he's now selling motorcycles feels almost *too* on brand.

Brady gives me a once-over. "Got your java? Ready to go sign some paperwork?"

"Yeah, let's do it."

He leads the way towards the admin wing of the practice center. "It was a stroke of luck you finished your DPT in time. They weren't going to let me hire you back without it."

"Totally," I reply.

I only just finished my doctorate of physical therapy degree in the spring. I always hoped to stay in the pro sports world, but the job market is tight. I snagged an hourly position assisting at a rehab hospital, where I worked with injured kids, and felt lucky to get even that. When Brady called me a week ago, asking if I could send him a reference letter, I literally cried into my lunch.

It turns out Rachel Price is going on maternity leave earlier than expected, and the team needs a few PTs to help fill in the gaps. They offered me a ten-month contract as an assistant rehabilitation therapist. I couldn't say "yes" fast enough. Now I'm here, walking through the hallowed halls of the Rays practice center.

Brady presses his thumb to the elevator button. "I'll take you up to see Vicki, but then I've gotta head back over to the gym. Come find me when you're done, yeah? I'm sure the guys will be excited to see you."

"Oh, I'm sure there are no guys who even remember me left."

God, I'm such a liar. As if I didn't pull up the team roster the second I got off the phone with him last week. I know exactly who's on the team. I know who I'm dying to see.

Brady leans against the silvery wall of the elevator. "You'd be surprised how many of the guys remember you. Novy's been bugging us to hire you since you left. I told him you needed to finish your degree first, but he didn't seem to care."

I laugh. "God, how is Novy still playing on those busted knees?"

Brady snorts, leading the way out of the elevator. "Are you kidding? They'll have to drag him off the ice and rip that stick from his hands. He's assistant captain now, did you know?"

"I bet the refs love hearing that mouth chirping at them from the bench."

"Eh, he keeps it in check for the most part. He reserves his chirping for the other team . . . and our rookies. Damn near made a kid cry last week."

We turn the corner to find Rachel Price standing in the hallway. Her back is turned away from us, her dark hair tied up in a messy bun. She's chatting with Vicki, the operations manager. I don't think I've ever seen Vicki without that single strand of pearls at her neck . . . or that unamused look on her face. She points down the hall at us, and Rachel turns, waving in welcome. "Teddy, hi!"

"Oh my god—" I bite back my words, but they've already left my mouth. I quickly school my expression, offering her a wide smile.

"Look at me, calling you Teddy," she calls down the hall. "You're Doctor O'Connor now."

"Hey, Doctor Price." My voice is falsely high as I lean in for a hug, trying to avoid squashing her giant belly. "It's great to see you again. You look amazing."

She huffs, patting my back. "Seriously? I practically have my own zip code."

Oh god, she said it, not me. But yes, this woman is massively pregnant.

"No, you look great," I assure her. "You're totally radiant."

I'm full of so much shit right now. I'm sure everyone in this hallway can smell it. Rachel just rolls her eyes as she steps back, brushing both hands over her bump. "That's sweet. But we all know I look like a python that swallowed an exercise ball. It's okay. You can be a little freaked out. It's a lot of belly."

Well, at least she can laugh about it, right?

"It might help to know there are actually two babies in here."

I gasp. "Shut up. Twins? That's so cool. I bet the guys are thrilled."

She smiles. "Yeah. These two are due after the New Year. So, your timing is perfect. With my first two pregnancies, I worked a little longer. Heck, with Jamie, I stayed on staff right up to my due date. But carrying two has been tougher on me, and my guys are being real jerks about me following doctor's orders. So . . ."

"We're thrilled to have you back," says Brady, patting my shoulder. "No one can replace Rachel. But I think, between the two of us, we can keep the place from burning down until she's ready to come back to work."

"Totally," I assure them. "I'm ready to work. And I've really missed you guys," I can't help but add. "There's something special about the Rays. It feels crazy to say it, because I was only an intern, but it sort of feels like coming home, you know?"

Rachel and Brady beam at me. "We do," she assures me. "We're glad you're here, Teddy."

"Once a Ray, always a Ray," Brady adds.

"Well, he's not a Ray until he signs my paperwork," says Vicki. "Come with me, honey. We'll see what we can do about getting you an access pass today."

"We'll see you over in the gym!" Rachel calls with a wave.

I wave back as the door shuts.

I t takes me over an hour to fill out all Vicki's paperwork, but I leave her office with a new ID card, a facility access pass, and a coupon for two free drinks from the coffee cart. I make my way over to the crowded gym. The first smiling face I see is Ryan Langley, jogging on a treadmill. He gives me a wave. "Teddy, hey!"

I wave back, unable to hide my smile.

In moments, there are calls of welcome as players abandon their workouts to come say hello. Woody and Paulie are defensemen who were rookies back when I was an intern. I think they're both married now. Paulie has at least one kid. His wife is a supermodel or something. I saw the news of their marriage in a tabloid.

"I'm a little sweaty," Langley warns, his arms spread wide as he swoops in for a hug.

"'Sfine," I grunt as he squeezes me.

"Great to see you," he adds, patting me roughly on the back.

"You too. How's the family?"

"Thriving, thanks. Emma is five. She starts kindergarten this year."

"Crazy."

He chuckles. "Right? We actually leave first thing in the morning for Aruba."

"Cool."

"Yeah, the girls are excited. Last little summer trip before the season starts, you know?"

I just smile and nod. I watched his whole whirlwind romance take place six years ago. I was there playing soccer on the beach the day he first met his wife, Tess. I watched them fall in love. Later, Tess and I bonded over an awkward lunch. I was the starving college kid, just there for the food, and she was Doctor Price's friend, secretly sleeping with a player. I caught her giving Langers "fuck me" eyes, and that was that. Instant friendship. We've sent the occasional texts to check in over the years.

"I can't wait to see Tess again—*oof*—" All the air leaves my chest as someone slams into me from behind. A pair of thick arms wrap around me, squeezing me tight. I look down to see they're covered in colorful tattoos. I grin. "Hey, Novy."

His voice is muffled, his sweaty face pressed in at my neck. "I'm so happy you're back."

I pat his forearm. "Good to see you too, Nov."

He lets me go and spins me around, one hand tight on my shoulder. "See this PT?" he shouts to the crowded gym. "This is my PT. You got that, assholes? I don't make the rules, but I *will* enforce them."

Some of the older guys laugh, while the rookies look ready to take his word as gospel. I pat his hand on my shoulder. "Sorry to sour this little reunion, but I'm actually gonna be working with the injured-list guys. If you're not injured, I can't promise any of my magic massages."

Novy drops his hand away. "The fuck you say?" He looks around the gym. "Who do we have to talk to? Brady? Don't even worry, bud. I'll have this settled in five minutes—"

"*No*—" I pull on his shirt to keep him from storming off. "Come on, man. Don't get me in trouble on day freaking one."

He settles down, still frowning.

"Who even is this guy?" one of the new faces asks.

Novy rounds on him. "This *guy*? How 'bout you watch your fucking tone, Bouch. This is Doctor Teddy O'Connor. We call him Teddy of the Golden Hands, because he's fucking magical. He gives the best damn leg massages I've ever had."

Langley and a few of the other older guys laugh. "I'm gonna tell Morrow you said that," Langley teases.

Novy shows no fear. "Go ahead. Hell, I'll tell him myself. I'll text him right now. That'll make my fucking night."

He pulls out his phone, and my eyes go wide. Fuck me, I am not getting in the middle of those two again. Back when Morrow was a player, he got a little territorial over how much Novy liked my massages. Ever seen a jaguar hunt a caiman while a helpless capybara watches? Yeah, I was the capybara. "Ohgod—don't," I hiss, slapping at his phone.

"It's fine." He body checks me with his shoulder as his thumbs type. "Besides, it's my ass, not yours."

I groan.

"Hey! Are you guys bothering the good doctor?"

We all turn to see Brady walking over between the row of treadmills. My heart fucking stops when I see who is walking at his side. Dressed in a Rays tech shirt and a pair of athletic shorts, Henrik

Karlsson looks every inch as beautiful as the first time I saw him. He's fucking magnetic, with those navy-blue eyes and the soft sweep of sandy-blond hair over his brow. His beard is shorter now, little more than stubble. God, he looks so fucking good.

I swallow, trying to stifle the annoying fluttering that's currently happening in my chest. This is so embarrassing. It's been six years. And it's not like we were ever . . . *anything*. That's the worst part about all this. We were literally nothing. For the whole year I interned for the Rays, I tried to give him as wide a berth as possible, content to torture myself with secret, longing glances from across gyms and hotel breakfast buffets.

I was too much of a coward to ever approach him casually. And when I was forced to work with him as part of my job, I was usually so tongue-tied, I couldn't even speak. I'd squeak out things like, "Pressure okay?" while I was massaging his calves. And once, while wrapping an ice pack on his shoulder, I swear to god, I said the words, "All set, chilly dog."

Seriously, somewhere inside this building, they're already digging a hole for me. When my shame builds high enough, I'll just lower myself down, and they can bury me. Henrik Karlsson is as untouchable to me now as he was then. Maybe even more so because now I have more to lose. I have it on good authority that Rachel may not be coming back to work after she has those babies. If I play my cards right, this position could become permanent. It's my literal dream job.

Whatever hand of fate dealt me these cards, I'm in the door. I have the job. And I mean to keep it. That can't happen if I'm too busy torturing myself, daydreaming over a man who has never looked twice at me. A man I'm not even sure is gay. A man who likely doesn't remember my goddamn name.

No, this is over. It's done. Henrik Karlsson is off limits. Frankly, I'm not interested. Do you hear me, Universe? There's absolutely nothing about him that would ever—

"Hey, Teddy." He smiles that smile that only reaches his eyes. God, I haven't seen that smile in six long years. "Good to see you again."

Well, fuck me. Apparently, the love of my life remembers my name.

3

TEDDY

"Oh, yeah . . . that's it. That's the fucking spot, right there. Don't stop."

I still my thumbs on the back of Novy's calf.

"Hey, I said don't stop—"

"What was our *one* rule?" I say over him.

He pushes up on his elbows to look at me. "Oh, come on. Those weren't sex sounds. I was just talking."

"Yeah, in a weird, growly sex voice."

Chuckling, he flops back onto his stomach. "My sex voice isn't weird."

"I beg to differ."

All around us, the other guys head to and from the showers. DeGraw, the starting goalie, is up on another table getting stretched out.

"I told you'd I'd give you a leg massage," I go on. "It's my first day back, and I'm willing to be a team player. What I won't do is go and get myself punched in the head by your jealous partner because *you* can't control your smart mouth. Now, am I finishing this leg in silence? Or are you limping your old ass to the showers on those rusty, crusty joints you call knees?"

Novy glares at me. "I think I liked you better as the intern."

I cross my arms. "Right. Well, I think we're done here—"

"No!" He grabs the hem of my T-shirt as I try to back away. "Come on, Doc, *please*. I'll be so good for you. I won't say another word, I swear."

I grimace. "See, it still feels like you're talking about sex—"

"Well, what can I do?" He sits up. "You wanna gag me so I can't talk? Would that make you more comfortable?"

I narrow my eyes. "You hear it, right? When you say the words, you're hearing it?"

"The seagulls on the beach can hear it," says DeGraw. He's a young Australian guy, new to the team this year. He's super handsome, with a tanned Mediterranean complexion, whiskey-brown eyes, and a mop of unruly, dark brown curls.

"No one asked you," Novy snaps at him.

I sigh. "Look, we'll try again another day, okay?"

"Nooo," he whines.

"That wasn't your last massage. But I do have to do my actual job. And I told you I'm working with the injured list this year. So, unless you want me to break that leg . . ." I leave the threat hanging in the air.

"Don't fucking tempt me," he mutters.

"I'll see you later, okay?" I turn to leave and nearly crash right into Karlsson. He's wearing nothing but a little white towel around his waist, his hair still dripping wet from the shower. His chest and arms glisten with droplets, showing off his cut muscles. As he steps around me, I get hit with a scent cloud of his body wash. Oh, fuck me, he smells so good. Like the beach on a winter morning, all windswept and fresh, with just a hint of sea salt.

"Excuse me," he says.

"Yep. All good. Not a problem," I ramble, backing away from him with my hands raised like he's walking poison ivy.

He ignores my antics, making his way over to his stall in the changing room. Most of the guys have already cleared out. A few linger, taking their time getting dressed or messing around on their phones. Rock music plays softly from the speakers, something classic with long guitar riffs.

I give Karlsson his privacy while he changes, only glancing over my shoulder when I'm sure he must be safely dressed. He sits on the bench in a fresh pair of shorts and no shirt. Unlike most of these hockey guys, he has no ink. Not even the Olympic rings. And he played for Sweden in the last Winter Olympics. They took home the silver medal.

I might have watched a few games.

Or every game.

"Hey, Teddy. Put these on the shelf for me, bud?"

Jolting, I turn to see the head equipment manager, Caleb Price, standing by a laundry cart. My god, six years and the man hasn't aged a day. He still looks like he's hiding a broody secret behind his dark eyes. I may have had a crush on him for a week or so back when I was an intern . . . before I clocked his unrequited yearning for Jake. He holds out a stack of white towels, nodding to the empty shelf behind me. "Can you reach?"

I blink. "What? Oh—yeah, of course." I take the towels and place them on the shelf.

"So, you're back then?"

"Yeah, assistant rehabilitation therapist. They gave me a ten-month contract. You know, while Rachel goes on maternity leave."

He raises a brow. "Maternity leave, huh? Already?"

Shit, did I just step in something here? "Yeah, uhh . . . you didn't know?"

He just shrugs, handing me another stack. "My wife knows her own limits. I'm done trying to get her to slow the fuck down."

Before I can respond, a bone-chilling cry nearly has me dropping the last stack of towels. I search for the source of the sound, and my gaze locks on Karlsson across the locker room. The other guys quickly take notice too. There's a flurry of confusion as someone mutes the rock music.

"Karlsson?"

"Fuck, what happened, bud?"

He lets out a wail that pierces my very soul. His expression crumbles as the phone drops from his hand, clattering to the floor. Then he falls forward off the bench, catching himself on the floor with his hands, shoulders wracked with sobs.

Fumbling the towels into the laundry cart, I cross the room to his side.

"Henrik, what happened?" Paulie asks again.

"You sick, man?"

"You hurt?"

"Everyone, get back," I shout, dropping to my knees.

The guys all step back, casting worried looks and shrugs at each other.

I place a hand on Karlsson's shoulder. "Hey, can you tell me what happened?"

He lets out a grief-stricken cry and a string of words in Swedish I can't understand. Then his arms are around me, face pressed to my shoulder. All I can do is hold him, my hands splayed across the warm skin of his back.

Caleb stands sentinel at my shoulder. "Does anyone know what the hell happened? Did he say anything?"

"Nah, man."

"I think he was on the phone," someone says.

Woody steps up next to Caleb. "You know Karlsson, Cay. He never says a word about anything."

The new forward—I think his name might be Tremblay—picks up Karlsson's phone. "Hey, he was listening to a voicemail," he announces to the room. He holds the phone up to his ear. After a moment, he frowns. "The guy's talking in Swedish. I can't understand him."

There's a flurry of talk before a tall blond steps up, holding out his hand. "Give it to me." I recognize him from the night I haunted the team roster. His name is Christian Lindberg. They just traded him in from the Golden Knights. Like Karlsson, he's a forward. And he's Swedish.

He puts the phone to his ear. As I watch, his expression changes, shifting from curiosity, to concern, to horror. Slowly, he lowers the phone, muttering something in Swedish that sounds like a curse.

"Well?" Caleb presses. "What happened?"

Lindberg locks eyes with me. I already know the news is bad. Feeling protective of Karlsson, I splay my hands wider across him as I try to cover him. But I can't keep him safe from this. The damage is already done. All we can do now is try to help him pick up the pieces.

"The voicemail is from a hospital in Stockholm," Lindberg announces.

Paulie steps in closer. "What happened?"

Lindberg's gaze is solemn as he looks down at Karlsson. "There was a car accident last night. His niece is in critical condition."

"Oh, shit," someone mutters.

"Fuck, man. I hope she's okay," says another.

But I'm still looking at Lindberg, studying the somber expression on his face. "There's more."

He looks from Karlsson to me. Then he nods.

"Just say it," I murmur.

Lindberg holds my gaze, tears rimming his eyes. "His sister is dead."

4

HENRIK

I feel numb. Nothing feels real. Not the chair I'm sitting in. Not the glass of water someone put in my hand. Not the man sitting across the desk from me. His mouth is moving. He's speaking words in a language I know, but I can't will myself to care.

Petra is dead. My only sister. My dearest friend.

I think I'm in shock. Medically, I believe this is shock. I've felt it once before. I was seven years old, ice skating on my family's lake in northern Sweden. The ice cracked, and I dropped straight through. The water was so cold, it stabbed the air from my chest. A stream of panicked bubbles spewed from my mouth as I sank.

My saving grace was my scarf, hand-knit by my mother. Petra managed to grab the end, tightening the knot our mother had tied at my neck like a noose. I thrashed in the dark water, my feet trapped in my heavy ice skates. From the surface, Petra stretched flat on her belly and pulled me up, testing the strength of the knot with everything she had.

A scarf saved my life that day. A scarf and my fearless sister.

Afterwards, I sat before the wood-burning stove in our old cabin, wrapped in quilts, body aching with cold. Our parents stood over me, quietly debating whether to take me to the hospital. I couldn't speak. I could hardly move. I was frozen with shock.

"Karlsson?" A gentle hand squeezes my shoulder.

I glance up, remembering where I am. I'm not seven years old, sitting before the wood-burning stove. Petra doesn't sit at my side.

No, inexplicably, it's Teddy O'Connor who sits next to me, his face full of concern.

I've always held a fondness for Teddy, ever since our curious meeting at the crosswalk all those years ago. It was a surprise when he showed up in our gym this morning, still so nervous and tongue-tied. He's tall and lean. His fair brown skin is dusted with freckles over his cheeks and nose. More than his kind smile, I've always noted his hair. He wears it in long, thin locs. At the moment, a spray of end pieces sticks out from the large knot, like the feathers of a bird's crown. His hair is bold and extravagant, so at odds with his generally meek demeanor. And yet, it fits him.

I get the feeling he only acts meek and tongue-tied around me. I've seen him with the others. He laughs and jokes. Few people can put Lukas Novikov in his place, but Teddy does. I'm not surprised he's different around me. I have that effect on people. They're made uneasy by my long silences and my general awkwardness. I'm certain I must make Teddy uncomfortable.

But in this moment, his hold on me is steady, tethering me to this room and this moment.

"We have to decide what we're doing here," says John Weiss from across the desk. As the new general manager of the Rays, he always wants a plan. "Karlsson, what do you need from us?"

"I have to go to Sweden."

Arjan Singh, the team's services manager, stands by the desk, brow furrowed with worry. "We can get you on a flight tomorrow."

"But we're less than two weeks out from the start of training camp," says Weiss. "Will you need a leave of absence to deal with this, Karlsson?"

I just stare at the glass of water in my hand.

"Karlsson?"

"I don't know, sir."

"Lindberg said his niece is still in critical condition," Teddy explains. He turns to me, those hazel eyes full of such worry. "How old is she?"

I swallow, feeling numb. "Five."

Every face in the room falls.

God, help me. Does Karolina know her mother is dead? Who told her? She's an ocean away, lying in a hospital in pain. The poor little lamb.

"Henrik, honey, I'm so sorry." Doctor Price stands behind my chair. Next to her is her husband, Jake, my team captain.

"Will anyone be there with her?" asks Teddy. "Her father, maybe? Can you meet him at the hospital? Or what about grandparents?"

"No father," I reply. "And my parents are elderly and in poor health. It's difficult for Mom to travel." I stand from my chair, setting the glass of water untouched on the desk. "It has to be me. There are arrangements to be made for my niece."

Jake searches my face. "Are you her guardian now? Will you bring her back with you?"

We're skating perilously close to me saying out loud that my sister is dead, and I'm not ready. I clear my throat. "I must contact the hospital first to better understand her injuries. If she can't travel, that will complicate matters. But, yes, I'm all she has left."

Tears in his eyes, he gives a curt nod. "Then she needs to be here. Go get her, Henrik."

Doctor Price takes my hand in both of hers. "Let me send you over on my family's plane. That way, even if she's injured, so long as she's stable enough to fly, you can bring her home."

Jake nods again. "That's a great idea, babe. Go call Hal."

"I couldn't ask that of you—"

"I'm offering," she says over me. "I'll go call my dad right now. We can have the plane here by tonight. You'll be in Stockholm by tomorrow morning."

"It's a good plan," says Singh. "And it's generous of you, Rachel."

"It's literally the least I can do," she replies, pulling her phone from her pocket. "We'll have you at Karolina's side in eighteen hours." She steps from the room, her phone already to her ear.

"What if you need help getting her loaded on and off the plane?" asks Weiss. "She could be confined to a hospital bed or be on crutches. Can you handle that on your own, Karlsson? Would you prefer we arrange a proper medical transport?" He's still thinking through all the contingencies. I'm glad someone is. I'm certainly in no fit state.

"Is there no one we can send along with him?" says Jake.

Weiss shakes his head. "Not ten days out from the start of training camp."

This upsets Jake and the three men argue, all talking over each other about schedules and priorities until a new voice enters the fray.

"Hey, send me."

We all turn to look at Teddy.

"What did you say?" asks Weiss.

Teddy shifts nervously in his chair. "Uhh . . . yeah. Well, I was just gonna say that I haven't *technically* started yet, right? I mean, I filled out my paperwork, and I gave Novy half a leg massage today. I'm covering for Rachel when she goes on leave." He turns to Jake. "Do you think she'd be cool staying on for one more week if I go help Karlsson?"

"She'd be totally cool with it," Jake replies, relief evident in his tone.

"I can't ask that of you," I say.

Teddy just shrugs. "I've got the qualifications. Injury rehabilitation is my jam. And I've worked with kids before. A lot, actually." His smile falls as he holds my gaze. "I can help, Karlsson . . . if you'll have me."

It would be easier to know I have support in this. I don't even know what I'm walking into. All I know is that Petra is dead and Karolina is injured. I tried calling the hospital back, but they said her doctor was in surgery. My phone sits heavy in my pocket as I wait for it to ring. Fighting the emotions threatening to tear me open, I just nod.

"Perfect," says Jake. "It's settled."

At that moment, Rachel steps back into the room. "What's settled?"

"Teddy is going with Henrik to Sweden. And you're covering for him until they get back."

She sighs. "Oh, that's perfect. I hated the thought of you going alone, Karlsson. Teddy, you're a treasure."

"It's nothing."

Standing, I turn and offer him my hand. "It's not nothing to me. I'll not forget this kindness, Teddy."

He stares down at my hand for a moment before he shakes it. "Anything for the team, right?" But then he drops it, eyes wide. "Oh, shit."

"What?"

"I gotta go make sure my passport isn't expired!"

5

TEDDY

What the hell am I doing? Oh god, I need to have my head examined. I signed a contract for my dream job today, and then *two* seconds later I threw myself at the world's most unobtainable man. Now, instead of getting ready for a busy week at my new job, I'm standing on the tarmac at the Jacksonville airport, staring up at Hal Price's private jet. I watch as Karlsson scales the steps ahead of me. After shaking hands with the flight attendant, he ducks inside the plane.

The U.S. customs official flashes his little light on my passport. "And what is the nature of your visit to Sweden?"

"Umm . . . business?"

His bushy mustache twitches as he frowns. "You're doing business in Sweden?"

"Well, it feels weird to say 'pleasure.' It's definitely not a vacation. We're going for family business, I guess. Karlsson's sister died. We have to get his niece from the hospital. I mean—are you—" I point at his flashlight and my passport. "You're not even writing any of this down, so does it really matter?"

"Why don't you let me ask the questions? Does that work for you?"

"Yep. All good." I stuff my hands in my pockets, rocking on the balls of my feet.

"When do you intend to return to the United States?"

"Honestly, I don't know. Like, a week from now, maybe? What was Karlsson's answer? I'm sort of just following his lead here."

"You're leaving the country, and you don't know when you'll return?"

Fuck, I'm going to prison.

"We're coming back in a week," I say again. "And I swear, I don't even have drugs or anything. And I won't get any drugs in Stockholm," I add, panic rising.

He just keeps staring at me. "Why would you even say that to me?"

I groan. "Look, I'm sorry—I'm just really nervous, I think."

"Do you have reason to be nervous?"

Jesus, I didn't know boarding this flight would require a mandatory therapy session. "Well, yeah, I mean, I guess I tend to make a lot of rash decisions. Classic Teddy, you know?"

"I don't—"

"Well, I can't just let a thing lie," I say over him. "I obsess, and I fixate, and I fantasize. I drive myself fucking crazy. And then I do something that's *too* big, you know? This is one of those big things. I just have this feeling that I'm about to get on this plane and my whole life is gonna change. Do you ever have those moments, Julio? Moments when you just *know* everything is going to be different?"

He casually flips through the blank pages of my passport. "No."

"Well, I'm having one of those moments right now. Because a week ago, I was eating a gas station chicken Caesar salad wrap on my lunch break. Now, I'm getting on rock-and-roll legend Hal Price's private jet to help negotiate the international medical transfer of a world-famous hockey player's injured niece. The fact that I'm head over heels in love with said hockey player is by the by, because his sister just died. Do you have any sisters, Julio?"

"No."

"Well, I have three sisters. And if I lost one, I'd be a total fucking train wreck. So no, this isn't about my insanely inappropriate crush, okay? This is about Karlsson and his sweet little niece. She's lying in a hospital, alone and scared. So, can you please just sign my passport, or stamp it, or do whatever the fuck it is that you do so I can get on Hal Price's freaking plane and—"

"Have a good flight." He hands me back my passport. "Don't bring back any drugs."

I stuff my passport into the front pocket of my backpack. "I won't. I swear to god, I'm so freaking clean."

"Good. Hope the little girl is okay. And good luck with the insanely inappropriate crush." With a chuckle, he steps aside, clearing the way for me to board the plane.

This fucking guy. He was winding me up on purpose. Not giving him a second to change his mind, I grab my duffel bag and launch up the stairs, taking them two at a time. I get to the top, where a flight attendant is waiting with a tray of drinks. "Good evening, Doctor O'Connor. Would you like an orange juice or a glass of champagne?"

Oh god, I can't be trusted to put alcohol in my body right now. And the sugar in orange juice might just send me through the emergency exit. "Can I just get a water?"

"Of course," she replies with a smile. "If you'd like to find your seat, we'll begin our departure."

I step onto the plane and walk through the galley. "Whoa."

The luxe interior is all creamy leather and faux wood paneling. Soft jazz music plays through the speakers. Karlsson is seated about a third of the way back in a club chair, phone in hand, hat pulled low, hiding his eyes.

I glance around, unsure of where to sit. There's another club chair directly across from him, but maybe he wants his space. I could sit up here at the front, but that feels a little awkward too. I don't want him staring at the back of my head for the whole flight. I guess I could keep going to the back. Maybe there's a bed or something. I could stretch out, get a little sleep.

The flight attendant makes the decision for me, stepping past with water on a tray. She sets the glass down on the little table next to the open club chair. "Would you like me to take your bag, Doctor O'Connor?"

"Sure." I hand my duffel bag to her, and she makes it disappear into a bin. I take my seat. Dropping my backpack at my feet, I glance over at Karlsson. "Did you hear back from the hospital?"

"I did."

"And Karolina?"

"They had to take her into surgery to set a bone in her leg."

"Shit. Well, did they say what happened yet?"

"From what the police have gathered, their car was hit from the side," he explains. "It was a young driver. Apparently, he walked away without a scratch. Meanwhile, Karolina has crush injuries to her left side. And my sister—" He bites back the words, tugging the bill of his hat lower. He doesn't want to say it, and I won't make him say it. When he's ready, maybe someday we can talk about her.

"But Karolina . . . they think she'll make a full recovery?"

He nods.

"Karlsson, that's good. Broken bones suck. There's no way around that. But broken bones heal. Just means she gets to spend a couple months being pampered with ice cream and movie marathons. I bet she'll be back on her feet in no time."

He nods again. After a moment, he sets his phone aside. "Teddy, before we go, I just . . . I want to thank you again."

"Hey, don't even worry about it—"

"No, I want to." His navy-blue eyes look so forlorn. "I'm not always good at expressing myself. And I know you haven't always been comfortable around me . . ."

Shit. Does he know? Has he known all this time? Oh god, this is so fucking embarrassing. My mind races as I try to think of what to say. "Karlsson, look—"

"You don't have to bother denying it," he goes on. "It's plain to see how uncomfortable I make you. I'm not the easiest person to talk to . . . or work with. But I will endeavor to do better. Just know this is a difficult time for me, so if I struggle to perform the niceties of social interactions—"

"Hey." I lean across the aisle, placing my hand on his arm. I see the pain in his eyes, the grief and fatigue. "You don't owe me an explanation. And you sure as hell don't owe me any kind of apology. There's nothing wrong with you, Karlsson. I'm weird because *I'm* weird, not because you're weird. You're perfect, okay? You just be you, and I'll be me, and we'll just be weird and awkward together. Sound good?"

He nods.

I smile, dropping my hand away. "So, tell me about Sweden. Do you think we'll see any polar bears?" He chuckles and my chest puffs with pride. I did that. I distracted him and put that smile on his face. See? I'm helping already.

"No, we won't see any polar bears in Stockholm."

I grin, leaning over in my seat. "But, I mean, never say never, right? There *are* polar bears in Sweden, right?"

"Not since the last ice age."

"That actually makes me kinda sad."

He's quiet for a moment, his lips pursed as he considers. "Yeah. Me too."

6

HENRIK

Our plane lands in Stockholm at ten in the morning. By eleven, Teddy and I are walking through the main doors of Saint Ingegerd Hospital. I suppose I must be grateful the ambulance brought Karolina here. They have a top-ranked trauma center. Reading the signs in Swedish, I lead the way towards the reception desk.

Teddy walks silently at my side. Since we landed, he's been quiet, which I appreciate. Not that I mind his conversation generally, but my thoughts are all scrambled, my emotions raw. I feel untethered, floating through the ether. Everything is darkness. A sea of grief with limitless shores stretches on inside me.

Surely some of this is just my fatigue. I should have slept on the plane. Teddy encouraged me to try, but my mind wouldn't shut off. Now, my heart is in my throat, my palms are sweating, and I'm trying not to think about it. But I can't help myself . . .

Somewhere in this hospital, my sister lies dead.

Suddenly, Teddy's hand is at my shoulder, his voice soft. "Hey, you okay? You need a minute?"

I blink, glancing around. I didn't even realize I'd stopped walking. We're standing in the middle of the hallway, still feet away from the reception desk.

"Good morning," the receptionist chimes in Swedish. "Welcome to Saint Ingegerd Hospital. How can I help direct you this morning?"

Shrugging away from Teddy, I step forward. "I'm here to see a patient. Karolina Karlsson. I was told she's in the pediatric trauma center."

The blonde nurse turns to her computer screen, clicking on the keyboard. After a moment, she looks up. "As a pediatric patient, she has a list of approved visitors. May I please see your identification?"

I pull my Swedish passport from my pocket and hand it to her. "I have a friend with me. Can you approve him as a visitor?"

"I'll need to see his identification too."

I glance over my shoulder at Teddy. "Give her your passport."

He jolts at my sudden use of English and pats down his pockets before pulling out his passport. "Yeah, here you go."

"Thank you," the nurse says in English. After a moment of typing, she gives it back. Then she says at me in Swedish, "Karolina Karlsson is on the third floor, room 312. Please check in at the nurse's station before entering her room."

Teddy stays at my side as I lead the way over to the elevator bank. We ride silently up to the third floor, and my heart begins to race faster. I still don't know if Karolina's been told that her mother is dead. I don't know the full extent of her injuries either. Fractured ulna, the doctor said. It was cracked but not misaligned. She'll need to wear a cast on her arm for four to six weeks. Three cracked ribs, hairline only. The most worrisome injury is the fractures to her leg. They required surgery yesterday. Oblique displacement, it's called. The surgery realigned the bones, and they secured it all with a metal plate and screws. She'll have to wear a cast on the leg for up to eight weeks and not bear weight on it as it heals.

A broken arm *and* a broken leg.

And no mother.

My poor, sweet little lamb.

The elevator slows, and the doors open with a soft *ping*. I just stare at the brightly colored flyers on the wall opposite.

"Come on," says Teddy, gently guiding me out. "You can do this."

Following the signs, we find the pediatric trauma center. A tall nurse wearing clear-framed glasses stands from the station desk as we approach. "Are you Mr. Karlsson?"

"I am."

He smiles. "The reception desk alerted us that you were on the way. Karolina will be so pleased to see you. She's been asking for you."

I breathe a sigh of relief. "She's awake?"

"Not at the moment. We gave her some medication for pain management about thirty minutes ago. It tends to make children drowsy. But you're welcome to go in and sit with her, even if she's asleep."

Teddy glances between us, trying to make sense of our Swedish.

"Thank you," I say in English.

"We alerted her doctor that you're here," he adds, switching to English. "She's with patients now, but she said she can stop by and speak to you in about an hour."

I thank the nurse again and lead the way down the hall. The walls here are so colorful. A muralist painted bright scenes of forest animals on parade. They wear party hats and carry balloons. The scene is so at odds with the somber feeling in the air. From behind closed doors, machines hum, providing life-saving support to other injured children.

The door to room 312 is open a crack. From within, I hear the beep and whir of more machines. Holding my breath, I push the door open wider. The only light comes from the large window. A TV mounted in the corner plays an old episode of *Bamse*, volume on mute.

I step fully inside the room. A large hospital bed takes up most of the space. Karolina lies asleep in the middle of the white sheets. With her eyes closed, her lips turned down in a pout, she looks like a sad little doll. Her blonde hair splays across the pillow.

Christ, she looks so small. I can see now the full extent of her injuries. The bruising around her left eye looks raised and purple. The side of her face is covered in scratches from the shattered glass. They still have her in a neck brace too. Her left arm is in a brace from hand to elbow. And her skinny leg sticks out from her blankets, freshly bandaged from knee to ankle. All around the bed, wires connect her to machines, the source of the soft beeping.

My eyes lock on the fuzzy pink sock on her foot. That's when I break. "Oh, Christ—" I catch the words, along with my sob.

Covering my mouth with my hand, I turn away, tears burning in my eyes. I try to push past Teddy, but he grabs me by the shoulders.

"Hey—no. Come on, man, you have to stay."

"I can't," I say on a gasping breath. "Can't see her like this—"

"You have to. Hey—Karlsson, she's alive."

I shake my head, overcome with grief and fear. I can't lose her too. I won't survive it. God help me, I can't—

"Look at me." He cups my face. "Karlsson, *look* at me."

I lift my gaze. Teddy's expression is so calm. Despite all the times I thought he was meek and nervous, in this moment, he's in control. His eyes flash as he holds fast to me. They're green only at the edges, shifting to an almost golden brown at the center.

"She's alive," he assures me. "Say it."

"She's alive."

He nods. "That's good. Just take a breath and slow down. Say it again."

I take a deep breath and let it out, both my hands holding tight to his shoulders. "She's alive."

He turns me around, one arm across my chest, and points at the monitor. "Look at her heart rate. She's so strong. Her pulse ox looks good too. God, look how strong she is. She's a fighter, Karlsson."

"A fighter," I echo, my eyes darting to take in all the machinery. I'm no doctor, but I can hear the slow, steady beat of the heart monitor.

"That's one tough little girl." His arm tightens across my chest. "But she needs her uncle now. So, you are gonna sit in that chair and hold her hand. Do you hear me?"

"I don't know what to say to her," I whisper, leaning against the support of his body. "If she doesn't know . . . If they haven't told her . . ."

Teddy's hold on me softens. "Then you tell her you love her. Tell her she'll always have a home with you, no matter what. As you loved your sister, you're going to love her daughter. It's as simple as that. She's yours now, Karlsson."

Resolve hardens in my chest as I look down at her fragile, sleeping form. "She's mine."

"Yeah, man. She's all yours."

I knew it was true in an abstract sense. With one missed phone call, my life changed forever. I became a parent. I'm beholden to someone other than myself now. God help me, I've wasted so much time already. There's so much to be done. For Petra, for Karolina. And I'm the only one who can do it. No more wallowing in grief. It's time for action.

I tap his arm, and Teddy lets me go. Turning away, I step past him towards the door.

"Whoa—*hey.*" He grabs my arm. "Where the hell are you going?"

"Stay with her. When she wakes, call me."

His eyes go wide. "What the hell are you gonna do?"

"I have to call my lawyer."

With a nod, he lets me go.

I've always been the backbone of my family. Petra may have been the older sibling, but whenever she needed something, she came to me. I paid for her apartment, her car, Karolina's school. I'm not leaving anything to chance now. Karolina is mine. I must make arrangements for us both to go home.

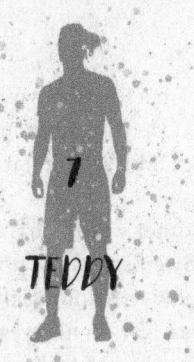

1

TEDDY

Karolina sleeps for another hour. The whole time, Karlsson doesn't come back. In the meantime, I stretch out in the uncomfortable chair by her bed, messing around on my phone. I text my sisters and my friend Colin. After our internship year, he was offered a full-time job with the Jacksonville Jaguars. We made plans to meet up for dinner this week to celebrate my return to the 904.

Well, I won't be making that reservation. There's now the slight inconvenience of an ocean in the way.

I'm just about to slip out in search of coffee or a donut when Karolina stirs on the bed. Oh shit, I didn't even ask if she speaks English. This could turn awkward quick. I glance desperately towards the open door. Then I shoot Karlsson a text.

She opens her eyes, whimpering a little as she shifts on the bed.

"Oh hey, try not to move, okay?"

Her eyes go wide as she looks at me.

"Do you understand English?"

Slowly, she nods. Poor thing, she looks miserable. She's got purple bruising around her eye and little cuts all over the left side of her face. But her eyes are the deepest shade of blue, just like Karlsson's. They're flecked with grains of grey, reminding me of faded denim.

"Are you Karolina?" I hope my expression looks sufficiently warm and welcoming.

She nods again, which looks difficult to do with her neck brace.

"My name's Teddy. I'm a friend of your uncle's." I glance towards the door again. "Uhh . . . Henrik. He should be here any minute."

At this, she perks up. "Morbror är här?"

"Umm . . ."

Before I can say another word, Karlsson comes rushing into the room, talking fast in Swedish on his phone. I don't have to know what he's saying to know he's ending the call. Then he drops the phone away from his ear, tears in his eyes. "Karro."

The moment she sees him, Karolina bursts into tears, reaching for her uncle with her unbandaged hand. "Morbror!"

He crosses the room to her bedside, both of them crying as he hugs her. His voice is soft and soothing. "Mitt lilla lamm, inga fler tårar. Jag är här nu."

She sobs, clinging to him.

"Jag är ledsen," he cries, brushing back her hair. "Lilla lamm, jag är så ledsen."

I don't understand his words, but I feel his grief, his resolve. He's going to take care of her. Nothing will part them now. I wipe away my own tears, letting the two of them have this moment together. They speak in fast Swedish as he pulls away, his hands everywhere as he inspects her. "She wants water," he says at me in English, before switching smoothly back to Swedish to speak to her as he adjusts her pillows and helps her sit up.

Making myself useful, I fill a cup with water from the little plastic pitcher on her bedside table. I offer it to her. "Here you go, honey."

She leans away, eyeing me warily.

Okay, ouch. Why is this hurting my feelings?

Karlsson says a few quick words in Swedish, gesturing to me, and her tension eases a bit.

"Does she speak English?"

"She understands it better than she speaks," he replies. "American shows and movies are quite popular here. But she's generally shy around strangers."

"Well, she comes by that honestly," I say with a smile. "I have a present for her. Do you think that might help break this ice?"

He raises a brow in surprise. "You have a present for her?"

"Duh." I hand him the little plastic cup of water and duck down for my backpack. "You don't visit a kid in the hospital without bringing them a present."

I spent the last six months working for a rehab hospital where the main clientele were kids with broken arms and legs. Gotta love summer sports and the carefree "my bones are rubber" attitude of overconfident teenage boys. My last patient broke all his arms and legs falling off his roof while trying to land on a trampoline. He showed me the video footage. Honestly, it was pretty epic until he went splat.

"When did you have time to shop for a present?"

"On my way to the airport. It's not god's gift to presents," I quickly add. "But I think it'll do as a first offering of peace and friendship." Wheeling the chair closer, I set my backpack on the edge of her bed with a flourish and make a show of unzipping it. "Can you tell me, Karolina, what's your favorite color?"

She chews her bottom lip, glancing from me to Karlsson.

He says something in Swedish.

"Lila," she says in her sweet little baby-doll voice.

I'm taking an educated guess here. "Is that like lilac? Purple?"

Karlsson nods.

Oh, thank god. "Well, am I a genius or what? I guessed you'd say purple. And look at this . . ." Slowly, I reach into my backpack and pull out a plush purple teddy bear.

Her curious look turns to one of excitement as she locks eyes with the silly purple bear.

"See? It's a teddy bear, like me. I'm Teddy." I glance at Karlsson. "How do you say 'teddy bear' in Swedish?"

"Nalle," they reply at the same time.

I grin. "Well, *this* is Nalle." I hand her the purple bear. "And I'm Teddy."

She takes the bear, inspecting it with eager eyes. She doesn't need to know I have three more in this backpack in three other colors. Thank god for capitalism, right? Why make one when you can make one in every color?

Karlsson says something to her, and she looks up at me, clutching to the little bear. "Thank you," she murmurs in English.

"Oh hey, no thank *you*." I scoot closer. "I was hoping I'd find a good home for him. You're gonna take good care of him for me, right?"

She nods, turning her attention back to the little stuffed bear.

I zip the backpack shut, hiding the other bears, and drop the bag at my feet. I'll make sure we leave them with the charge nurse to give to the other kids. Meanwhile, Karlsson says a few more words to her in Swedish. As they talk, he surprises the hell out of me by reaching across the bed and taking my hand.

What the hell is he doing?

Oh god, he's holding my hand. Henrik Karlsson is holding my hand. I can't breathe, can't think.

Never taking his eyes from his niece, he gives my hand a grateful squeeze, and I relax, all tension leaving my shoulders. In this moment, I think I'd be content to sit here and let Karlsson hold my hand for the rest of my life. He talks to his niece in Swedish for a while, and I just watch, listening to the rhythm of the words I can't understand. But the feelings are there: love, grief, safety.

"Karro has come up with a name for her bear," he announces in English.

I blink myself out of my stupor and sit forward. "Oh, yeah?"

"She doesn't want to call him Nalle."

"Well, what do you want to call him?"

Gazing across the bed at me, Karlsson smiles that smile that only touches his eyes. "She wants to call him Teddy."

TEDDY

After an epically long day of travel and sitting vigil at the hospital, I'm ready to brush my teeth and fall into bed. Any bed. Hell, I'll sleep in a dog bed on the floor. I'll sleep *on* the floor. Anywhere I can stretch my body out in a fully horizontal position.

My fatigue aside, it was a good day. Karlsson got to talk to Karolina's doctors and hear their rehab plan. She'll be in the hospital for a few more days, at least. She gets her arm casted tomorrow for the broken ulna, but they need the swelling in her leg to go down before they'll cast that too.

The hospital kicked us out a little after eight o'clock, declaring visiting hours over. Karlsson put up a fight, demanding he get to stay. Ultimately, I made a show of putting Teddy the Bear in charge of security for the room, which Karolina found funny. Teddy the Bear kicked Morbror Henrik out for being a noise nuisance, and I set him up as sentinel at the foot of her bed before I left too.

She's a tough little kid. Sweet and smart, if super shy. But with Karlsson as her uncle, that only makes sense. She knows her mother is dead. She knew without Karlsson having to say a word. I pray I'm wrong, but I think she might have been conscious when they pulled her from the car. Who knows what she saw that night? She's desperately sad about it all. They both cried on and off all day, holding each other and whispering soft words in Swedish. I gave them space to grieve as best I could.

Around lunchtime, I found my way down to the hospital

cafeteria. I bought Karlsson and me salmon salads and a couple bags of chips. I also found a coffee cart. Too nervous to try to order my fancy oat milk latte with a double shot of espresso, cold foam, and a drizzle of caramel, I just got us boring coffees. Karlsson usually drinks his black, but fuck that. I added two creams. We ate in silence, Karlsson not leaving his niece's side.

Now we're sitting in the back of a taxi, heading to what I hope is a hotel. I've just been on autopilot all day, following wherever Karlsson has led. Somewhere in all the chaos, I lost track of my duffel bag. Did it even make it off the plane? Am I going to be wearing this underwear for a week? Shit, my head scarf was in the duffel too.

The taxi pulls over, and Karlsson says a few words to the driver, flashing his phone on the card reader to pay for the ride. Slinging my backpack over my shoulder, I step around the taxi and up onto the curb. "This doesn't look like a hotel."

Karlsson is already headed for the double glass doors. "It's not," he calls over his shoulder.

"Well, then where are we?"

"My apartment."

Of course. Why wouldn't the multimillionaire professional hockey player own real estate in both the U.S. and Sweden? Here I am, ready to stay at a backpacker's hostel or a motel with a shared bathroom. But no, Karlsson keeps a pad in downtown Stockholm.

I follow him inside the lobby. It's sleek and modern, very Swedish. He leads the way over to the elevators, and we ride up together to the fifth floor. The doors open to reveal a narrow hallway. There are only four units. Karlsson leads me to the last door on the left, unit 5B. The door unlocks via an electronic keycard, then he's swinging it open. "I can't be sure what state I left it in," he warns, standing back to let me through first.

"I'm sure it's great."

He cuts on the light, and I do a slow half turn. Okay, this might be the coolest apartment I've ever seen. It has a massive, slanting glass wall that offers a great view of the city. The main floor is all open concept, with a kitchen, dining table, and living room all leading to a perched loft area. That must be the bedroom up there. There are no walls to close the area in, just sleek metal rails that frame the space. Under the bedroom platform is a room that looks like a mix of office and library, with bookshelves lining the back wall.

I turn to Karlsson with a wide grin. "You're a maximalist."

He raises a brow. "A what?"

I look around again. He's got stuff everywhere, but it's not messy. It all feels super curated. Stacks of books on every subject rest on more shelves and teeter in piles by the couch. Framed modern art prints are stacked along the wall, too many to hang. So much camera stuff. He has an impressive vinyl collection too. And don't get me started on the textures. It's a total mix of metals and woods, soft blankets in muted colors. A wide leather sectional looks plush enough to dive into.

I turn back to face him. "Does the IKEA Council know about you?"

"The what?"

"Karlsson, this apartment is awesome. I thought all Swedes had, like, four straight-backed chairs, exactly one pour-over coffee pot, and a MALM bed frame. This place looks like a thrift shop had sex with a library and made a baby. The vibe is so cool."

I can tell he doesn't know how to take the compliment. "There's no guest room."

I shrug. "The couch is fine with me."

"You might be more comfortable at a hotel."

"I'm comfortable here," I assure him, dropping my backpack to the floor. "I'd be even more comfortable if I had my duffel bag though. Did you get your bags off the plane?"

"I had a porter bring all the bags here." He points next to the stairs that lead up to his loft bedroom. There, on the floor, sits my blue duffel.

"Well, if it was a snake, it woulda bit me," I say on a laugh.

"What?"

"Nothing. Bathroom?"

He points to the open door tucked behind a bookshelf.

I weave through his living room over to my bag. "I'm so tired, I think my skeleton might just collapse. I'm gonna brush my teeth and crash if that's okay."

"Fine." He makes his way to the kitchen.

"But don't think I won't snoop around this place tomorrow," I call over my shoulder. "Your secret's out, Karlsson. You're a total magpie, and I love it."

"It awaits your snooping." His back is turned to me, but do I sense a hint of a smile in his tone?

Grabbing my bag, I head for the bathroom. This is totally fine. I'm in Henrik Karlsson's Stockholm studio apartment, and there's only one bed. I can already hear the screams from the family group chat—

No, I can't send this to the group chat. I mean, I told them I'm in Sweden, because that's the kind of thing you tell your sisters. What if my plane crashed? What if I end up in a Swedish jail? Oh god, I get anxious just thinking about it.

They were all supportive of my mission. If I know Shae, she's already put a care package in the mail for Karolina. But this? Exploring the secret mysteries of Karlsson's inner sanctum?

Yeah, I'm not sharing this with anyone.

I wake to the smell and sound of bacon frying in a pan. Sunlight blinds me as I blink my eyes open. Where the hell am I?

Oh, that's right. I'm stretched out half naked on Karlsson's cloud-like leather sofa, buried under a pile of blankets that smell like him. I'll make no comment about the state of arousal I might be in.

I sit up, gazing around at the majesty of this loft apartment. In full daylight, there's almost a sparkle to it. The studio feels like one part living space, one part library, and one part storage locker. There's a large book of nature photography on the coffee table. Under the table, I spy a bright pink box. I slide it out with my foot and find stuff for coloring and a mess of tangle-haired dolls. The box sends a clear message: Karro was here.

I smile.

"Teddy! Come!"

I jolt, eyes wide, as I take in Karlsson's shirtless form standing in the kitchen. He's got his phone up to his ear, spatula in his other hand. His expression is tense as he barks something in Swedish. Then he waves at me with the spatula.

"What—"

"Come," he says again. "Mind the bacon. I have to take this call." He sets the spatula down and hurries over towards what I now see is not a windowpane but a door set in the wall of glass. It leads out to a small terrace.

I scramble off the sofa, wearing nothing but my shorts. I trot over to the kitchen and grab the spatula. Eggs are frying in one pan, bacon sizzling in another, and I think there might be something in the oven.

Shit. I can't cook to save my life. I'm an okay baker, but skillets and I don't mix. I always burn everything. My mom and sisters usually won't let me touch anything but the salad spinner. But I suppose this looks easy enough. I flip the bacon as it crackles in its own grease. I don't know a damn thing about frying eggs though.

The oven dings, and I officially panic. I rattle open the drawers, searching for a pot holder, anything to avoid pulling a baking tray out with my bare hands.

"Aha!"

I strike gold in the drawer below the oven. Pulling the door open, I'm hit with heat and the salivating smell of fresh bread. It looks like cinnamon rolls. Karlsson did all this while I was sleeping?

"Oh—*shit*—" I drop the tray on the stove with a clatter, returning to the burning bacon. I only just manage to save it. The ends are black and crispy but still edible. I'll eat the burnt ends and give him the middles.

Someone must have delivered groceries while we were at the hospital yesterday, because the fridge has fresh milk and juice, assorted berries, and what looks suspiciously like cold brew coffee. I've literally never seen Karlsson drink his coffee cold (and I've been watching). Granted, it's been six years, but Henrik Karlsson is the kind of leopard who doesn't change his spots.

So . . . are these for me? How did he know I like cold brew?

I find a glass in the cupboard and make myself a coffee, mixing the cold brew and milk over ice. I even find a very Swedish-looking glass straw to stir it. I've just managed to set our breakfast plates, adding a garnish of fresh berries, when the terrace door swings open.

Karlsson comes charging back inside in a fury, his phone clutched tight in his hand. "Fuck!" He lets out a string of other words in Swedish that are most definitely curses.

"Whoa, what happened?"

The skin of his chest and arms is pink from the cold outside. It can't be more than forty degrees, but he stood out there for almost twenty minutes in nothing but a pair of athletic shorts. Oblivious to the cold, his eyes blaze with a fire like I've never seen. He paces in front of the kitchen island, still muttering in Swedish.

"Karlsson, what happened?"

His chest heaves as he turns, glaring at me. "That was my lawyer. She seems to think my case for guardianship of Karro is not strong."

It takes a second for his words to even register. "What? But that's absurd—"

"It's criminal!" he bellows, resuming his pacing.

"You're next of kin, right? You said your parents can't take her—"

He spins around. "My parents are seventy! They cannot care for a five-year-old child. My god!"

"Okay," I soothe, both hands raised. "So, it has to be you. What's the holdup?"

He groans, dropping his phone to the island. "Elin seems to think the Child Welfare Office will take issue with Karro leaving the country while she requires medical care. She says they will call it negligence."

Negligence? Seriously? I lower my hands to my sides. "Okay, I know I sound like a broken record here but . . . what?"

"She says the only way a court will agree to grant me custody is if I stay with her in Sweden, where she can get the proper medical care."

"But you work in America—"

"I know!"

I wince. Yeah, that was dumb, Teddy. "Well, they do know we have, like, doctors and hospitals and stuff, right? The United States can also manage to reset a tibia and cast a broken ulna."

"The American medical system is the laughingstock of the developed world, Teddy. And the child's welfare comes first, even at the expense of the wishes of the family."

My shock is only matched by my outrage. "That is complete bullshit. She belongs with you. There has to be a way."

His shoulders sag as he stops his pacing. "God help me." He drags a hand through his tousled hair. "I spent all this time worrying about *how* to get Karro back to Jacksonville. It never crossed my mind that they wouldn't let me take her."

My brain is processing in overdrive as I try to think of a fix. "I mean, sure, we don't have the world's *best* healthcare system, but you're also not some random accountant or retail worker selling shoes at the mall. You play for the freaking NHL. Did you tell them you play for the NHL? Because I really think that could help your case—"

"It's hurting my case!"

I flap my arms helplessly. "Well, that makes no fucking sense. You have access to some of the best medical care in the world. You've got doctors and physical therapists and athletic trainers on speed dial. Hell, you've got a literal doctor of physical therapy standing in your kitchen right now. What else could they want for her? Why is this a problem?"

He rubs the back of his neck with another pained groan. "I don't know . . . I *do* travel a lot. During the season, I'm away more than I'm home. Honestly, I see Elin's point. Maybe Karro deserves better than having me as a parent—"

"Whoa." I hold up a hand, my own anger rising now. "I'm gonna stop you right fucking there. My mom raised four kids on her own, often working two jobs, and we all turned out fucking amazing. Hell, your sister was a single parent. Don't you dare say single parents can't raise awesome kids. Not in front of me. Not if you want to keep all your damn teeth."

He has the good sense to look chastised. "I'm sorry, Teddy. I spoke in anger."

"Being a single parent isn't a crime," I go on, ignoring his apology. "And being a single parent who travels for work is totally manageable, especially for you. If you need help, it's not like you can't afford it. Hire some live-in help, even rehab specialists, for the season. That should more than satisfy some snooty child welfare board."

He nods, considering my words.

"Don't give up, Karlsson. We came here to bring Karolina home, and that's what we're gonna do. I'll be here to help however I can. The whole team will. Together, we'll have that girl doing cartwheels inside of six months."

His mouth twitches with the smile he can't bear to manifest. "Ballet is her current obsession."

"Even better. She'll be back at the barre, I promise." Stepping around the island, I dare to reach out and take him by the shoulders. His skin still carries a slight chill from the air outside.

He holds my gaze, wholly unashamed that we're both standing half naked in his kitchen.

"Call your lawyer back. Fight for Karro. I swear, you'll be glad you did."

His jaw tight, all the emotions he feels but won't express lie buried in his eyes. He just nods again. He raises a hand and squeezes my wrist. "Thank you, Teddy."

"No problem." Swallowing my own feelings, I drop my hands away from him and take a step back. "Now, about this breakfast . . . I may have burned the bacon a little. But I broke off the burnt ends and gave you only the middle pieces."

"All the bacon is for you."

"What? No. We're sharing it, right?"

He steps around me into the kitchen. "I ate two hours ago."

I glance at the clock. "You've been up since five?"

He just shrugs. "Couldn't sleep."

I gesture to the plates of eggs, bacon, and Swedish cinnamon rolls. "So, all this is . . ."

"For you." The words hit me like a coconut dropping on my head. Ignoring my awkward silence, he steals a few berries from one of the plates. Popping them in his mouth, he heads across the apartment towards the bathroom. "I'm going to take a shower. When you're ready, I'd like to return to the hospital."

"Yeah, sure," I call after him. "I'll be ready lickety-split."

For you.

That's what he just said, right? I didn't imagine it? The food currently cooling on the kitchen island seems like proof enough. Henrik Karlsson made me breakfast this morning.

In his apartment.

Shirtless.

Yeah, watch me ride the high of this moment until the next freaking ice age.

HENRIK

Elin Ågren sits across the table, her fingers cupping a mug of coffee. Her blue eyes are sharp as she holds my gaze. She's been my lawyer for eight years. Usually, she's navigating hockey contracts and endorsement deals. Family law is a first for us. We've been arguing on the phone for the last four days as she prepared my custody plan. It was finally time for us to meet in person.

The hospital cafeteria buzzes with early morning activity. Most of the tables are full, with more people coming through the doors in search of coffee or a pastry. Somewhere in this hospital, Karolina is finally getting her leg wrapped in a cast. It's the only reason I agreed to meet with Elin now.

I'm loath to leave Karro, even for a moment. I don't want her to be alone. In truth, I don't want to be alone either. Not today. Not now. At this very moment, my sister is being cremated.

As tired as I've been, I tossed and turned all night, my short moments of sleep plagued with dreams of screeching tires and crunching metal. I've been dreaming of car accidents since the day I received the phone call. With Karolina's screams echoing in my ears, I got out of bed, passed Teddy asleep on my couch, and went for a run early this morning.

He's been a godsend. These last four days, he's hardly left my side. While I'm busy caring for Karro, he cares for me, offering me food and encouraging me to stretch my legs. He stays with Karro when I have to take calls from my lawyers, my parents, my agent, the doctors, the team. He makes her laugh, using silly voices for her bear.

At night, we go back to my apartment and pass the time quietly. It feels strange to open my life to him in this way. No one has ever been in my apartment except for Petra and Karro. We order in food, and he explores my bookshelves or watches TV on a low volume. More often, we both just part ways and crash asleep, starting it all over in the morning.

Well, *he* sleeps. In fact, he snores. It's faint, but I can hear it. I lie awake on my back each night, staring up at the ceiling, mind racing, heart aching, and listen to the whisper-soft exhales of the man asleep on my couch.

Teddy sits next to me now, sipping his coffee. I can't help but glance over at him. He usually wears his hair pulled back at work. This is the first morning he left with it down. I've never really seen locs up close. Each strand falls well past his shoulders. They're darker at the root, lighter at the tips. Some look almost golden in this morning sunshine.

His knee bounces under the table, distracting me. Reaching down, I place my hand on his thigh. He jumps with surprise, but his knee stops shaking. I turn my attention back to Elin. "Please, continue."

"I've reviewed all similar cases from the past three years, and it comes down to this," she goes on. "In the eyes of the Swedish government, you are asking to remove an injured child from her home country, a country where she receives excellent healthcare. That's the immediate pressing concern. In the long term, you would also deny her a Swedish education, access to her Swedish culture and language. And with your demanding work schedule, you offer her no stability, no daily support. She'll spend more time in the care of strangers than she will with you. Can you deny any of this?"

"Perhaps while I'm in season," I admit. "But when the season is over, I always return to Sweden. For holidays too. And we'll speak Swedish together at home."

Elin considers for a moment. "I'm just not convinced it's a winning case to secure her immediate custody. There's still the issue of you being gone more than you're home. And do you have anything arranged for her yet? School? Medical care? Any kind of live-in support? Will they speak Swedish? Otherwise, how will she communicate with them?"

I fight the urge to groan. "I've told you. I can't arrange anything without first having proof of custody. I've been spinning my wheels needlessly for days, fighting with everyone from nursing companies to the Rays HR department. They all say they can't make a move without something signed proving I have custody of Karolina."

Teddy slides his coffee mug aside. "I'm sorry, I feel like I have to cut in here. It's Elin, right?"

She nods.

"Well, this all just seems crazy to me, Elin. I mean, Karlsson should get her." He jabs a thumb at me for emphasis. "He's the next of kin and he *wants* to take her. He has the means to provide an excellent life, either here or back in the States. Heck, her dolls will live better than me, and I'm a freaking doctor."

Dropping my hand from his thigh, I survey him. He's been so passionate about this. Am I really surprised? He worked with children in rehabilitation. And he mentioned he's a family man. He has three sisters, and they all have children. It makes sense why he's so good with Karro. He's had plenty of practice, certainly more than me. In this moment, I can only feel grateful. This has all felt so bleak, but his strength is giving me strength.

"What about what Karolina wants?" he goes on. "Do you think she'd rather go live with strangers in a foster situation or with her dear Morbror Henrik? Would staying in Sweden really make up for the trauma she'll experience being taken away from him now?"

Finding my voice, I sit forward. "I fail to see how anyone could care for my niece better than me. My financial disclosures alone should reassure the court that I'm capable of providing for her. More importantly, no one will love her more than me. She is my heart. She's *mine*, Elin."

With a patient sigh, Elin sets her coffee aside. "If you wish me to press your case, I will do everything in my power to see that you win."

I raise a brow. "But?"

"But I'm a pragmatist," she replies. "I want my clients to have all the facts so there are no surprises. Disappointments, yes. If you lose, it will be disappointing in the extreme. But it will not be a surprise."

"Total freaking bullshit," Teddy mutters.

I'm inclined to agree with him.

But Elin is the one who has all the research. She knows the legal precedent here. She wouldn't be pushing me like this if there weren't a real chance I could lose. She reaches into her bag and pulls out a folder. "We're ready with our plan. I can file today. But I urge you to first consider looking at these before you make any final decisions that may affect her life ... or your own."

A sinking feeling of doom settles in my chest. "What do you mean?"

She holds my gaze. "In this moment, two things are happening at once. You are grieving your sister, while making plans for your niece. One relies on emotion, but the other must be handled objectively."

Next to me, Teddy stiffens. "And what? You're worried he can't do two things at once?"

She's quiet for a moment. "I'm worried your grief may be clouding your objectivity, yes."

I cross my arms, glaring at her.

"Accepting a child into your life is no simple feat," she adds. "And you've always been something of a lone wolf, Henrik. Frankly, I question whether you're prepared for this."

I'm reeling with this truth. It's been on my mind, but Elin just gave it voice. Teddy's hand is quickly at my shoulder. "Jesus," he hisses at her. "Want me to hold his arms back so you can just punch him right in the fucking face?"

"You've been my client for nearly ten years," she goes on, looking only at me. "I'd like to think we're friends too. Will you hear these words from a friend?"

My heart is racing, stomach churning, but I nod.

"A child needs more than financial support to thrive. Especially an injured child, a grieving child, a child ripped from her country and her language, a child in need of building an entirely new support system while her sole caretaker is away more than he's home."

"But he loves her, and she loves him," Teddy challenges. "That has to count for something, right? I mean, the rest is just details. It's fucking geography."

"There are many forms of love," she replies. "Sometimes, truly loving someone requires knowing when to put their needs first and when to let them go." With that, she sets the folder on the table between us.

My gut clenches tight. "What's that?"

She splays her hand over the folder. "These are foster family applications—"

"Are you shitting me?" Teddy cries. "You brought those here? Now?"

"As I said, we are out of time. You may call me insensitive, but Henrik must know the full range of his options. Only then can he make the most informed decision." She turns back to me. "Sweden has a robust foster-to-adoption program. All these families have been thoroughly vetted. They're prepared for just this kind of situation."

"What situation?"

"A situation where a family member forgoes custody but wants to stay in contact. You could still see her," she assures me. "No one would ever question your right to a relationship with her. But you wouldn't carry the burden of care. You would be free to continue to live your life on your terms as her uncle, not her guardian. These families are ready to take in a child. Everything would be in place for her, Henrik. It would be seamless."

I sit back, Teddy's hand falling from my shoulder. Is this it then? Is this how I honor Petra and show Karolina my love, by letting her go? It will break my heart, but it's ultimately not about me. Her care must come first. She could stay here in Sweden. Better healthcare, better education. And they'll still let me see her, talk to her, visit her.

But just thinking it has my stomach twisting in painful knots again. I don't want to be free of the burden of care. If these last few days have shown me anything, it's that I *want* Karolina with me. If it means my life must change to care for her, then so be it. I've had enough of thinking and living only for myself.

Next to me, Teddy crosses his arms. "Well, let's get this over with then."

Elin raises a brow. "Pardon?"

He waves a hand at the offensive folder. "Tell us about these amazing foster families. You say Karlsson needs to know all his options, so let's hear 'em."

With a nod from me, she opens the folder and takes out the first file. Her eyes dart as she reads. "This is the application for Oliver and Britt Berglund. He's a grocery executive. And it looks like they have a dog." She shows us a picture of a kind-looking couple walking a labrador on a leash.

Teddy nudges me with his elbow. "Hear that, Karlsson? She could get a lifetime discount on apples. Never mind that you could buy her a whole freaking orchard. And Karro's afraid of dogs," he says at Elin. "I asked her yesterday. Next."

I stifle my smile as Elin flips to the next application.

"Hugo and Anna Ehrling," she reads out. "He's a florist, and she's a labor and delivery nurse."

Teddy scoffs. "Flowers attract bees, Elin. That doesn't sound very safe, does it? And Karolina is only five. She won't need the talents of a labor and delivery nurse for a good long while. Know what she *does* need? A physical therapist. Lucky for her, Morbror Henrik is friends with, like, fifty. One is sitting right next to him. Next application, please."

I don't bother hiding my smile now. Before this trip, Teddy always tiptoed around me like I was a sleeping giant. He was awkward and fumbling, dropping ice packs and saying odd things. But in this moment, he's the one standing ten feet tall, letting me collect myself in his shadow.

Elin flips to the next application with an irritated sniff. "Erik and Kerstin Fällman, and their daughter Maria—"

"You know, I'm sensing a bit of a pattern here," Teddy says over her.

She glances up. "Pattern?"

He leans forward, elbows on the table. "Yeah, it sounds like what the Swedish government wants is for Karolina to go to a nice little straight couple. Not very enlightened of them, is it? Families come in all shapes and sizes, you know, including single parents. I was raised by a working single mom, and I turned out great."

"Unfortunately, according to the Swedish government, there are many benefits to the two-parent household," Elin replies. "I make no commentary on whether their assumptions are correct," she adds before he can protest. "But I must work within the bounds of the system as they set it. That Henrik is unmarried does not help his case."

"Fucking medieval," Teddy mutters.

God help me, is this how I lose her? Because I'm unmarried?

I never thought to have a wife. I was always too busy building and maintaining my career. Professional hockey players start young. If you show any talent, you're quickly funneled into the elite junior league teams. From there, the top players all compete for spots on the European professional teams or the NHL. It's been my life's work to climb that ladder and stay at the top.

Outside of hockey, my teammates always made time for dating. Eventually, most of them settled down to start and raise families. It just never appealed to me. Perhaps because I'm as awkward with women as I am with my teammates. Women may find me attractive, but our conversations stall when I sit in prolonged silence or try to engage them with talk about my interests. I've learned through experience that discussing the comparative frames per second of different camera bodies is not exactly an aphrodisiac to ... well, any woman I've ever met.

And sex has never been a priority for me the way it is for some of my teammates. I don't crave it. The few times I had sex, I felt bored the whole time. I felt unattached, like my body was going through the motions while my mind was elsewhere. I tried it, didn't care for it, and haven't felt the need to try again.

Now, it seems my disinterest in sex, love, and marriage may cost me the one thing I *do* care about outside of hockey. Lost in my thoughts, I almost miss it when Teddy says, "So you're saying it would strengthen Karlsson's case if he were married?"

Elin glances between us. "Perhaps."

He shakes his head. "'Perhaps' isn't good enough, Elin. We're out of time here, remember?"

I grab his arm. "What are you doing?"

He shrugs me off. "If Karlsson were married to say, a doctor of physical therapy, trained to rehabilitate injuries exactly like the ones Karolina has, would that strengthen his custody case?"

My heart stops. "Teddy . . ."

Across the table, Elin raises a brow. "I assume this partner would live at home with the child while Henrik travels?"

"He would," Teddy replies. "Oh, and would that matter? That he's a he? I don't know what the gay scene is like here in Sweden."

She fully frowns now. He doesn't know she's married to a woman. "Despite the limited selection of foster applications I sampled for you, Sweden is accepting of gay couples adopting children, yes."

"Cool, because I keep totally normal workday hours. And I won't be traveling with the team. I could pick her up from school, take her to physical therapy, ballet, whatever she needs."

I grab his arm again. "Teddy, I can't ask that of you."

He ignores me. "Karlsson will be there every moment he can, and I'll fill in the gaps. Naturally, she'll have school, too, and her hobbies. And I wouldn't be some stranger or in-home medical aid. I'd be her uncle's legal partner. A two-person household, two incomes. The millionaire hockey superstar and the board-certified doctor of physical therapy who specializes in injury rehabilitation. Would that help him win custody of Karolina?"

Elin glances between us again. "It would certainly help, yes." Her gaze settles on me. "But if the government suspects that you're committing fraud to gain custody of a child, the consequences could be quite severe. You would have to follow through with this and live as partners. They would do a set of in-person wellness visits."

"We can make that work," Teddy assures her.

"And this is for temporary custody only," she clarifies. "We're deciding whether Karolina goes with you now or goes into foster care while her case is fully processed. I warn you that the adoption process can be arduous. There will be interviews with your friends and family, your coworkers, financial audits, a home study."

Christ, what is happening? I feel like several important steps were skipped here, like Teddy asking my permission first. Call me old-fashioned, but getting married ought to come with a conversation at minimum, right? Even a fake marriage to a colleague.

Squeezing tight to his arm, I rise and pull him off his chair. "I need to speak with you," I growl in his ear. Elin has the good sense to turn her attention back to her coffee as I drag him over to the corner. I don't care that other people in this cafeteria are watching us.

He grunts as I all but shove him against the wall. "Ouch—"

"What the hell are you doing?"

He dares to look confused. "What does it look like I'm doing? I'm helping you get custody of Karro—"

"By marrying me! Are you mad?"

He grins. "If by 'mad,' you mean brilliant, then yes."

I groan. This has been the week from hell. Too much is changing. Too much grief. Too many decisions I don't want to make. It's all just too much. "I can't—Teddy—" I claw at my chest, trying to free the words locked deep. But I can't speak, can't express this fear, this loss, this creeping anger that chokes the air from my lungs.

Sensing my distress, Teddy steps closer. Grabbing my wrists, he lowers his voice. "Hey, just breathe."

I shake my head, fighting his hold.

"Breathe, Karlsson. I know this all feels huge. So, let's just break it down. One thing at a time, yeah? Right now, you need to compete with Bergdorf the grocer and the couple with the bees, right?"

I nod.

"You need stability and a two-person household—which I still maintain is bullshit," he adds with a pointed glare. "But you heard Elin the Mirthless over there. You're out of time. Karro will be discharged from the hospital any day. The court's not waiting, and apparently there's a line of happy little Swedish families just itching to get their hands on a doll like her. They want to take her and make her theirs. Is that what you want?"

"No," I growl, twisting in his hold until I'm gripping tight to his forearms.

"Well, this is your best option to get immediate custody. I'm here, and I'm saying yes."

I search his face. "Why?"

His eyes go wide with shocked indignation as he pulls away. "Why should you fight for Karro? Are you fucking kidding me—"

"No, why would you marry me? Why help me in this way?"

His expression immediately shutters. He does this a lot, I've noticed. He changes his mood so quickly. One moment he's confident and commanding, the next he's nervous and retreating. Now, he's folded himself inward, shut up tight like a clam. How I'd love to climb inside his head and know exactly what he's thinking in this moment.

"It's the right thing to do," he says with a shrug. "You know, for Karro . . . and for the team."

But I shake my head, still frowning. "This goes so far above and beyond anything a team would ever require, Teddy. This is your life. And you heard Elin, we'd have to make this legal immediately."

"I know."

"That means we would have to get married."

"Yeah, I know."

"We'd have to tell people."

He shrugs. "That's kind of the point, right?"

"Everyone would know. The team, the media, our governments, our families."

At this, he falters slightly, swallowing his nerves. "Yeah, I mean, that's cool with me, if it's cool with you. And there's no skeletons in my closet or anything. I'm totally clean and—well—I don't mean like that. Not, like, with sex, obviously."

My shoulders stiffen.

"No!" He waves his hands. "I said *not* with sex. You're not even gay, right? So that would be crazy. This would be a totally fake marriage. I'm clean with, like, my record. I'm just a normal guy who likes sports and anime and helping people. And I wanna help Karro . . . and you." His nerves settle a little as he holds my gaze. "I can help, Karlsson. Please, let me help you."

This is more like the Teddy I remember from all those years ago, the distracted young man who walked into traffic and prattled nervously as he wrapped my shoulder with ice. He's older now, more commanding and self-assured. But he's also still the same Teddy.

Taking a deep breath, I give him one last chance. "You would really marry me?"

He considers for a moment. "I would, yeah." Then his eyes shoot wide. "Oh god." He looks around. "Is this a proposal? Are you proposing to me in this hospital cafeteria right now?"

I can't help but chuckle. "I suppose I am." Squaring my shoulders, I offer out my hand. "Teddy O'Connor, will you marry me?"

I can see the anxiety flashing across his face, and I don't blame him. This is reckless, and wild, and completely out of character for me too. But I can't be parted from Karolina. I won't. Not now, and never again. And I may hardly know him, but I trust Teddy. He's a good person. Noble, kind, loyal. If Teddy is saying yes to this mad plan, then so am I.

After a moment, he takes my hand. "Yeah, Karlsson. I'll marry you."

I give his hand a grateful squeeze, relief flooding me. "In that case, it's probably best you start calling me Henrik."

10

TEDDY

Oh my god, I've officially gone crazy. That's what you call it when you agree to fake marry your colleague just so he can win temporary custody of his injured niece and drag her from her home country, thereby forcing her to experience the horror that is the rectangle pizza in an American public school cafeteria . . . right? We call that crazy?

Okay, Karolina is *not* eating that pizza. I know I'm not technically her fake gay uncle yet, but my first order of business will be researching the top nonreligious private schools in Jacksonville. Our girl is getting the best education that money can buy. I'm sure the WAGs have a list. And Morbror Henrik can definitely afford it.

And fuck me. Henrik? "Start calling me Henrik"? That happened, right? I thought I was going to pass out right there on the damn floor of the cafeteria. Now I'm sitting on a stiff bench in the lobby of an administrative building in downtown Stockholm, staring at the back of Henrik's head while he applies for our marriage license.

Because we're getting married.

Me and Henrik.

Teddy O'Connor, hopelessly romantic double Pisces with boundary issues and a near-pathological need to please. And Henrik Karlsson, strong and silent Swedish hockey star who never says three words if none will do.

We're getting married.

Today.

Now.

Oh, I am so fucking fucked! And not in the fun way. What am I doing? I have to stop this. It's not fair to him. And it's really not fair to me. In fact, I think the scientific term for it is torture. To be married to someone and not be able to *be* with them? Touch them, hold them, love them out loud? I won't be able to take it. I'll crack. I'll fucking shatter. I'll say the wrong thing or do the wrong thing and ruin Henrik's chance at securing full custody of his niece.

At this last thought, I swallow a groan, shifting in my seat.

God, I'm such a self-centered ass. This isn't about me. It's not even about Henrik. This is about that sad little girl, lying in a hospital, grieving her mom. Henrik asked me why I'm doing this, and my answer is simple: Karolina. I saw her face the moment he first entered that hospital room. I saw the relief there, the love, the marrow-deep trust and affection. I've watched her with him all week. Karolina loves her uncle. To lose him now would be devastating. At her young age, she'd think he didn't want her. She'd blame herself. You don't recover from that kind of soul-piercing abandonment.

Trust me, I know.

My dad was in the navy, always in and out of our lives on deployments. One time he went out and just never came back. Like most kids, I blamed myself at first, but some people just aren't meant for staying. Mom did the most to hold it all together. My sisters helped. A lot of the burden got placed on Shae as the oldest, and then I got to feel guilty about that. While her friends went out to the mall and the movies, she drove me to track practices and swim meets.

I know what leaving looks like, and I know what it means to the ones left behind. So, I'm here, ready to put my own happiness on the line to help keep a family together.

Next to me on the bench, Henrik's stony gargoyle of a lawyer furiously taps on the keys of her laptop, updating the case file. "You said you could get me the names and contact information for the team support staff. Including familial support?"

I jolt, tearing my eyes away from the back of Henrik's head. "Yeah." I pull out my phone and shoot off a quick text to Doctor Price. Her response is almost instant. My phone pings as she sends me copies of the team contact list, including medical staff, athletic trainers, physical therapists, and more. Not that any of them would treat Karolina in a professional capacity, but I know any one of them would drop everything to come over and help if Henrik needed it.

Rachel also sends me the WAG contact list. It has the names and numbers of every partner associated with the players. Kids' names and ages are listed too, convenient for setting up playdates. The last thing she sends is a WAG-certified babysitter list. On it are the names and numbers of every person in the Jacksonville area deemed reliable enough to provide childcare. I air-drop them all to Elin as my phone pings with another text.

RACHEL: What's Karolina's favorite color? Favorite Disney princess? Animal? Food?

Smiling, I quickly text back. Now that the ice has thawed, Karro talks to me in her accented English, with Henrik filling in the gaps. I've learned a lot over the last couple days.

TEDDY: Purple. Rapunzel. Unicorns. Chocolate milk.

RACHEL: Chocolate milk isn't a food.

TEDDY: I said what I said.

A few moments pass before she responds.

RACHEL: Fair enough. How's Karlsson holding up? Everything going okay?

I glance over to where he stands with his back still turned. We haven't told anyone back home what we're doing yet. We're not going to implode our lives until we know temporary custody of Karolina is secured. Elin assured us that the super invasive family history portion of the adoption process will come later.

TEDDY: All good here. She'll get discharged in a day or two.

My phone pings with her response as Karlsson turns and says, "I need your passport."

Fumbling, I put my pinging phone back into my pocket as I try to extract my passport at the same time. "Sure. Here it is. Need me to fill out my own form? I can help."

He raises a brow. "Do you read Swedish?"

"Shoot, not on Tuesdays," I reply lamely.

He takes my passport and turns his attention back to the electronic form. "Nearly finished," he mutters with his back to me.

I feel completely useless. He's working, Elin is working, and I'm just standing here.

Wait . . .

It hits me all over again that this is technically my wedding day. What am I even wearing? I glance down. Oh, fuck me. Seriously? I'm wearing sneakers, athletic pants, and a white Nike Swoosh T-shirt. Sighing with frustration, I search my pocket for a band to pull back my locs.

I don't want to come across as one of those stereotypical gays who has already planned his dream wedding down to the table favors and DJ set list . . . but if the shoe fits, right? And this is not how I imagined my big day. First, we wouldn't be getting married at city hall. We'd get married on the edge of a forest at twilight. Second, I wouldn't be wearing scuffed sneakers and a branded T-shirt. I have a whole Pinterest board saved of wedding looks. And I'll tell you right now, not one Pin features polyester pants with zippers at the ankles.

And my family would be here with me to celebrate. That they're not here hurts more than I can say. Keeping this from them has been the hardest part. I want them to know . . . but I'm also afraid of what they'll say. I'm afraid they'll talk me out of it. And my mind is made up. This is the right thing to do.

Henrik exchanges a few words with the man behind the desk as he passes the tablet over to him. Then he half turns, holding out my passport. "Finished."

"Cool." I slip it back in my pocket. "So, are we doing it right here then?" I glance around the sterile atrium.

"They have a chapel down the hall. We'll do it in there once they call our names."

Hearing the word *chapel* has my blood freezing to ice. Oh shit. I'm gonna have to lie in front of Jesus? I stuff my hands in my pockets. "Chapel, huh? Are you religious then?"

He just shrugs. "Not particularly. My family has always celebrated Christmas and Easter."

"Yeah, same."

"But we also observe Midsummer with bonfires, schnapps, and a naked swim in the lake at midnight," he adds.

Aaaaand now I'm picturing him naked.

Just fucking perfect.

He must sense the anxiety in my tone. "Are you religious? I believe we can request a prayer or blessing." He starts to turn away, but I grab his arm.

"No, it's fine. I mean, if this was a real wedding, maybe I'd want more."

Yeah, *more*. That about sums up what I'd want if this was real.

But it's not.

"Really, it's fine, Henrik." Saying his name is the one indulgence I'm allowing myself. "Let's just get this over with. It's just on paper anyway, right?"

He nods and I drop my hand away. "They should call us back soon. Excuse me." Stepping around me, he heads for the restroom.

The moment he's gone, Elin slaps her laptop shut and stands. "I have to get back to the office. Tell Henrik I'll need a copy of the signed marriage certificate as soon as possible."

"Okay."

"I've incorporated all your information into the application."

"Cool."

At her insistence, we've included my résumé and copies of my degrees and licenses. She wants my background of working with kids in rehab settings to strengthen Henrik's case.

Slipping the strap of her leather bag onto her shoulder, she pauses to look at me, her pale blue eyes searching my face. I blink, trying to hold still. What is she looking for? What is she seeing? I straighten my shoulders, waiting. She takes a step closer and grabs my hand, giving it a gentle squeeze. "It's a noble thing you're doing, Teddy. Just be sure you're doing it for the right reasons."

"Right reasons?"

I get the feeling those Swedish laser eyes are looking straight through me. "He can never love you the way you want him to. It's just not how he's wired." With that, she drops my hand and walks away.

Before I can take a breath, the secretary behind the desk clears his throat. He's a young white guy with reddish hair and dimpled cheeks. "Doctor O'Connor?"

"Yes?"

"They're ready for you."

I glance around, looking for Henrik. "Uhh, he's still in the bathroom."

"When he returns, you may both make your way down to the chapel."

Fuck me, nothing about this moment is how I imagined it would be. I don't even have my somethings old, new, borrowed, or blue. I know this is a fake wedding and a fake marriage, but I want something about this to feel, I don't know . . . reverent? It feels like too much of a jinx on the whole institution to not observe anything sacred.

Eyes narrowed, I scope out my options. There's a cup of pens on the corner of the desk. I spy a blue one. Inching closer, I pluck it from the bunch and slip it in my pocket. I nearly jump out of my skin when the secretary speaks again.

"Would you like a pen, sir?"

I smile sheepishly, taking the pen from my pocket. "Sorry. I thought I might need it. I'll just . . . I'll go ahead and put this back." I awkwardly return it to the cup as the secretary smiles.

"I only meant I can give you a new one." He pulls out a box of brand-new blue pens and offers me one. New and blue.

I take it. "Thanks." Spying the watch on his wrist, I get an idea. "Hey, is that old?"

11

TEDDY

*H*enrik and I walk down the hall towards the chapel, following the lead of the officiant. He's an older man, very European looking, with silver hair. Instead of a tie with his blue suit, he wears a yellow silk ascot tucked into his open shirt collar.

I wonder if he'd swap fits with me, something else I can borrow. I'm already wearing the secretary's watch on my wrist. Felix was cool about it, immediately offering it to me when I asked. Apparently, it was his dad's, so it's old too.

The officiant pulls open the chapel door and—

"Whoa."

All thoughts of what I'm wearing leave my head, and my mouth drops open. I assumed a chapel tucked inside an administrative building would look a bit like a hospital chapel—a few bench seats, a spray of fake flowers in a vase, maybe a crucifix perched on a table. But no, this is a proper freaking chapel.

I half turn as I follow Henrik inside. It looks like they dismantled a medieval chapel and reconstructed it inside this long, narrow room. The walls are wood paneled, draped with what looks like real tapestries. There's an altar set before a floor-to-ceiling stained-glass window. It even smells old in here. Now I feel even more self-conscious about my stupid Nike Swoosh tee and my sneakers. At least Henrik isn't dressed any sharper.

The officiant says something in Swedish and Henrik responds. As I watch, the officiant steps behind an ornately carved lectern, opening a blue folder placed on top. He says something else and Henrik nods, handing him our printed marriage license.

"The ceremony will be in Swedish," Henrik says under his breath. "I hope that's alright."

"Yeah, that's cool." I mean, what the hell else am I gonna say? Of course a wedding in Sweden is done in Swedish. They'll just have to let me know when it's time to say, "I do."

Henrik takes his place in front of the lectern, hands folded. I mirror his pose, trying to keep my eyes from darting around to the carved details of the crown molding.

As soon as we're staged, the officiant begins. His voice is low and pleasant. I don't understand a word until I hear my name. I jolt, tearing my gaze away from the wall tapestry. "What? Oh, yeah, that's me. Am I saying 'I do' now or . . ."

Henrik smiles. "We're not quite there yet."

The officiant reads a few more sentences. When I hear him say Henrik's full name, I freeze. Oh fuck, this is real. I'm getting married to Henrik Johan Björn Karlsson.

"Wait." Backing away, I raise a hand. "I just . . . can we . . . I think I need a minute."

Henrik looks concerned. "Are you unwell?"

"Well, that really remains to be seen, doesn't it?" I press a hand over the heart now racing in my chest.

The officiant says something in Swedish and Henrik shakes his head. Oh god, I have to tell him. I can't trap him in a lie. Not one this huge. I'm terrible at keeping secrets. I'm even worse at keeping my feelings buried. He has to know. Henrik takes a step closer. "Teddy—"

"I need to talk to you," I say over him, my hand still pressed to my chest.

"Now?"

"Yeah, this really can't fucking wait." I tug at the collar of my tee. "Fuck, is it hot in here?"

"You can tell me anything."

My gaze darts to where the officiant stands, watching us. Do I really have to do this in front of a live audience? I jab my thumb at him. "Does he speak English?"

"Of course," Henrik replies.

At the same time, the perturbed officiant frowns. "I'm fluent in seven languages, sir, including English."

"Perfect. Then I need to talk to you over there." Spinning around, I march to the far end of the chapel.

Henrik says something to the officiant that sounds like an apology. Then he follows me to the corner and lowers his voice. "What's wrong?"

I brace my hands above my knees, half folded over as I suck in air. "Oh, you know, just casually defrauding the government with Henrik fucking Karlsson."

His hand settles on my shoulder and I wanna scream. "If this is too much for you—"

"No, it's cool." I stand up straight, breaking our connection. "I'm not backing out. I said I'd do this, and I will. But I just . . ." I groan, fighting to find the right words. "Look, I know everything about this will be a lie, okay? But I can't marry you in a lie. Does that make sense?"

His brain is clearly churning as he tries to follow my point. "I don't understand."

I can't help but laugh. "Yeah, I don't either. I just know . . . Okay, so there are things about me you don't know. And I feel like I can't marry you unless you know them. They're just sitting on my chest, like a weight pressing me down. Our marriage will be a lie, but I can't marry you without you knowing this truth. Does that make sense?"

"What truth do you need me to hear?"

Taking a deep breath, I hold his gaze. This is it. This is my moment. "I'm . . ." My brain races as I try to think of what to say to finish the sentence.

In love with you.

Dying inside.

Constantly overcompensating for my anxiety with humor.

Afraid you'll never see me as anything more than the intern who once walked into traffic.

But I just think all those things as the only word that comes out is, "Gay."

Henrik blinks. "What?"

Yep, we're rolling with this. "Henrik, I'm gay. I've never said that to you, and you deserve to know before you marry me. People are gonna say a lot of things about us when this all leaks, but that at least will be true. I'm very much gay."

His shoulders relax as he offers me a weak smile. "I know."

I lean away, eyes wide. "What? How do you know?" It's not like I hide it, but I also don't walk around carrying a rainbow flag and ringing a bell.

"When you were an intern, I caught you kissing a rookie at Shelby O'Sullivan's birthday party. Do you not remember?"

Fuck. Was that him? "In the garage?"

His smile falls. "No, in the bathroom."

Double fuck, because now he looks annoyed.

"You don't remember?"

"Uhh . . ."

Yeah, that party really hurt my cred. I dressed up as Merlin from *The Sword in the Stone*, got sloppy drunk, and woke up the next morning in Sully's backyard dressed as an astronaut with his damn dog licking my face. I remember dancing. I for sure remember drinking. And I remember getting handsy with someone in the garage. But I have literally no memory of kissing anyone in a bathroom. I definitely have no memory of getting caught by Henrik! Oh my god, the thought of it is going to haunt me till I die.

Time to pivot back to my point . . . if I ever had one. "So, you really don't care? That I'm gay, I mean?"

His annoyed expression disappears as he takes a step closer. "Of course not. Teddy, you are your own person. I would never judge you for how you live your life. And this marriage will change nothing for you, I swear it."

I huff, crossing my arms. "Seriously? Fake or not, we're still getting married right now. We're not buying lemons at the store."

"I know—"

"Well, you can't just say shit like that. You heard Elin. This has to look real. We have to tell people. Everyone's gonna know. And they're gonna say you're gay too, whether or not it's true. Are you ready for that? Because coming out as gay as a professional athlete isn't easy."

"I know," he says again.

"You were there when the Prices came out, when Novy and Morrow came out—"

"I know," he says over me, his frustration clearly rising. Good. Anything is better than this cool, calm complacency.

"Teddy, I—" His words fall short with a shake of his head.

I step closer. "You what?"

His navy-blue eyes look steely in this light. "I will not trap you. On paper, we will be married, yes. But in private, you will be free to live your life on your terms. And as soon as I can set you free, I will. I swear it."

Set me free.

Because, to him, this marriage will be a cage. That's how he sees this, how he sees me. My heart sinks further, if that's even fucking possible. But this isn't about me and it never was. I square my shoulders at him. "We're not doing this for ourselves, remember? We're doing it for the little girl waiting for you at the hospital. She needs us. We're just gonna take this one step at a time, yeah?"

Slowly he nods. "Any other truths you need to share?"

My mouth goes dry as I search his beautiful face. "Nope. I think that was the big one."

Liar.

He gestures towards the altar. "Then, shall we?"

I let him lead the way, and we resume our positions. Henrik folds his hands, so I fold mine. Henrik looks at the corner of the lectern, so I do too. But the moment the officiant opens his mouth to resume the ceremony, my panic has me spiraling out all over again. I throw up my hands. "I'm sorry, but we've gotta hit the big red pause button again. Henrik, that's not the only thing I needed to tell you."

The officiant may be annoyed, but only concern lines Henrik's face. "Teddy, please, you can tell me anything."

I look from him to the officiant, my heart racing. "Fuck, seriously? You want me to just say it right here in front of Swedish C-3PO?"

The officiant's frown deepens.

Henrik sighs. "Teddy . . ."

"Fine." I raise my hands again. "Fine, I'll say it. It's really no big deal, but I feel like I can't *not* say it, so I'm just gonna say it. I had a crush on you, okay? I'm gay, and when I first started interning with the Rays, I had a big gay-boy crush on you. But, you know, it's your own fucking fault because you saved my life. So, that's it. That's the big secret." I wave my hand at the officiant. "Okay, C-3PO, you go. What's the Swedish for 'I now pronounce you man and man,' because Karolina has to be out of her scans by now. And Felix really needs this watch back—"

"Hold on."

I wrap my hand around the borrowed watch on my wrist, suddenly feeling about ten inches tall. I'm such a fucking coward. I only told him half the truth. I just can't bear the thought of his dismissal. Not when I'm standing at this altar, literally marrying him. He already sees this as a trap we can't escape. I can't tell him that part of me *wants* to walk into this cage. My heart couldn't take the rejection.

"Teddy, look at me."

Oh fuck, anything but that.

Taking a deep breath, I look Henrik in the eyes. There's so much pain there, hidden under his river of outward calm. He's so tired. I know he's not sleeping, not with the nightmares. He woke me last night with his shouting. He thinks I don't know. He thinks I don't watch him leave the apartment every morning before the sun rises, determined to run his grief away.

A muscle twitches in his jaw as his gaze drops to where I'm gripping my wrist. "Where did you get that watch?"

Seriously? I just admitted to my crush and his only question is about the watch? "It was something old. And borrowed."

"What?"

"Something old, new, borrowed, and blue," I recite. "It's just a silly wedding ritual. It's nothing. Forget it. Are we doing this?" I look to the officiant.

"Teddy . . ." Henrik reaches for me but then drops his hand.

I bite the inside of my cheek, fighting the urge to cry.

"Look at me," he says again, softer this time.

Blinking my eyes clear, I glance up, meeting his quiet gaze.

"Tell me the truth. Why are you marrying me?"

"For Karolina," I reply, praying this earnest feeling in my heart is reflected in my eyes. "Henrik, I swear it."

"She means everything to me," he presses.

"I know."

"She is my only reason for standing here."

"I know," I say again. "She's my reason too."

He holds my gaze. "Is she your only reason?"

I won't lie to him again. Swallowing my nerves, I square my shoulders. "She's the only reason that matters. Trust me, Henrik. I'll not fail you. Or her."

Silence stretches between us as the seconds tick by. Finally, he nods. "Then shall we do this?"

"Yeah. I'm good."

The officiant raises a brow at Henrik, waiting. Henrik nods, and the officiant continues the ceremony. I measure this moment by the rapid beating of my heart as Henrik doesn't take his eyes from me. He's so calm, so steady. The officiant pauses and Henrik says, "I do." He says it in English, no doubt for my benefit.

A few more words are spoken, and then they're both looking to me. I know what's expected. I'm ready to play my part in this charade. Heart pounding, I look only at Henrik. He nods in reassurance. "I do," I declare.

And then it's over. The officiant says a few quick words before he closes the book. Henrik visibly relaxes. Reaching over the lectern, he shakes the older man's hand.

Wait . . .

The officiant pulls a pen from his pocket, still talking to Henrik. He hands him the pen, pointing with his finger to the signature line on our marriage license.

"Wait," I hear myself say.

Henrik glances up, pen poised over the license. "What?"

"Well . . . is that it? We're married? Just like that?"

"Once we both sign this, we are." He scratches his name on the signature line. Then he's holding out the pen to me.

"But—" I press a hand to my chest, leaning away.

"What?" he says again.

"But we didn't even kiss." I glance between them. "Is it even legal if we don't kiss? That seals the deal, right?"

"This makes it legal," Henrik replies, gesturing to the license with the pen.

"Sign with your full name, if you please," says the officiant.

I feel empty, hollowed out. This was my wedding day, and there was no jumping the broom. No teary-eyed family, clapping and cheering for me. No pictures. No champagne. Nothing to mark this moment except two names hastily scratched on a page.

Stuffing all my emotions in a box, I take two steps over to Henrik's side and pluck the pen from his hand. I look down at the marriage license. It's in Swedish, of course. I could be agreeing to donate all my organs right now. Or transferring all my worldly goods into his name. I wouldn't know. This is an exercise in blind faith.

"Just here," says the officiant, tapping the blank line next to Henrik's signature.

Heart in my throat, I sign my full name, Theodore Malik O'Connor. My slanting cursive glimmers up at me in shiny blue ink. I hand the pen back to my husband. "There. We're married."

Married to Henrik Karlsson, and I didn't even get a kiss.

This was a big fucking mistake.

11

HENRIK

"So, what did you tell them about me?"

I glance to the side as I drive. Teddy sits next to me, his eyes hidden behind his sunglasses. We picked up a rental car this morning. Normally, I would have taken the car I keep in the city, but that's the car Petra was driving in the accident. Even if they could repair it, I don't want it now. In fact, I would pay dearly to crush what remains into a dense metal cube and sink it to the bottom of a lake.

"I told them what they need to know," I reply, flicking my blinker before coasting around a slow-moving truck.

My parents still live in the same home from my childhood. It's in a sleepy little town about two hours south of the city along the coast. I wouldn't have left Karro alone at the hospital today, but this was a task I could entrust to no one else. My stomach feels hollow as my gaze darts to the rearview mirror for the hundredth time. My sister's urn watches me from the back seat. Today, I'm taking Petra home.

"Do they know we're married?" Teddy presses.

"They know."

"And they know why we did it? Like, they know it's not real? And they're not mad?"

I sigh, hands gripping tight to the wheel. I've spoken to my parents a few times since Petra's death. Dad wanted to come to the hospital, but it's too hard with Mom. She likes her routines. And he couldn't come alone. She gets too anxious when he's away, even if a neighbor comes over to stay with her.

The news of Petra's death devastated them, causing Mom to be even more confused. She keeps taking the phone from him and demanding that I put Petra on the line. Then we have to tell her all over again that she's dead. Her grief cuts like a knife every time.

I waited to call Dad last night until I was sure she'd be asleep. Then I told him about Teddy, about our plan to take Karolina with us back to Jacksonville. "He knows this is what's best for Karro."

Teddy doesn't press any further. I glance his way, catching the reflection of the road in his dark sunglasses. He's been acting strange since we left the municipal building last night. He's been quiet, almost taciturn. It's so unlike him. He feels far away. His body may be strapped in the front seat of this car, but his mind is elsewhere.

No, it's more than his mind. It's his *everything*. His light, his color, his energy that hums like a fluorescent bulb day and night. Always shining. Always on. But since we walked out of that chapel, he's been off. And I want to know why. For the foreseeable future, my fate is bound to this man. Breaking my cardinal rule of minding my own business, I reach for the volume dial and turn down the radio. "What are you thinking about?"

Teddy stays quiet, one long finger tapping the side of his thigh. He doesn't look my way. "Nothing," he finally says.

I bristle, hands gripping tighter to the wheel. "Look, I'll not ask for much in this . . ." What do I even call us? Husbands? Partners? Skipping over the language, I plunge ahead. "There are many things I can tolerate, but lying isn't one."

He shifts in his seat, still not looking at me.

"For as long as you are in Karro's life, I have to know I can trust you. I have to know you'll be open with me. When I ask you a question, I expect an answer. This won't work any other way."

My words act like a switch, and suddenly he's on again, his body humming with life. He turns slowly to look at me, my own face reflected in his sunglasses. "You really wanna know what I'm thinking about?"

"You can't shut me out now. Our situation is too precarious."

He huffs, crossing his arms. "Our *situation* is totally fucked! That's what I've been thinking. I think we made a terrible mistake.

Huge. Colossal. God, like, what were we even thinking? We got married!" He turns in his seat, gesturing between us. "You and me. We're married."

"I know."

"We're husbands. And it's legal, like, everywhere! Except a few countries in Africa and Asia. I don't know, we'll have to check. But in a hundred and fifty-something countries, I am now your legal partner."

"I know," I say again.

"Well, then pardon my fucking French, but why are you not more freaked out right now? Why are you so fucking calm? You're like Frosty the fucking Snowman over there. Meanwhile, I'm Elsa, totally out of control, just turning everything to ice with my chaos fingers!"

He wiggles his fingers like he's doing magic, and my brow furrows in confusion. "None of that was French—"

"It's an expression! You see? This is what I mean! I'm married to a man who doesn't know the expression 'pardon my French.' And now I'm on my way to meet his parents—two people who, until last night, didn't know I fucking existed. And when we get back to Jacksonville, I'm gonna have to tell *my* family. I have to tell them what I did, Henrik. My mom, my sisters—ohmygod." He jerks his sunglasses off and rattles them down to the cupholder, dragging a hand over his face.

I hate that this is distressing him so much. The last thing I want is for this to strain any relations he has with friends or family. "Will they be upset?"

He groans into his hand, making a sound somewhere between a laugh and a snort. "Are you kidding? They're gonna murder me. And they'd be right. This is just like me. Classic Teddy, always trying to solve other people's problems." He twists around to face me again. "I told Julio this would happen. I fucking called it. I should've bet money on it."

My head is spinning. "Who's Julio?"

"The TSA guy," he says with a distracted wave of his hand.

"Who?"

"Julio," he cries. "Julio, with the flashlight and the mustache and the 'How long are you traveling to Sweden?' bullshit."

"Wait, you're talking about the immigration officer who checked our passports?"

"*Yes*. God, will you keep up?"

His voice carries a tinge of panic as he spills forth everything that's been boiling inside him overnight. Forget Elsa, he's like some kind of mythical volcano, all quiet and serene, until you feel the ground start to rumble. Now he's spouting hot lava all over the inside of this rental car, and I'm powerless to stop it.

I may also be the one who set him off.

"I need to know what the fuck we're doing here," he goes on. "This was so fucking irresponsible. Of both of us. I need rules, Henrik. I need a plan. We got married with *no* fucking plan. I mean, who does that?"

"Teddy—"

"No, I know me, obviously. But you? You don't do this. You don't make life-altering changes at the drop of a hat. My god, you wear the same brand of socks under your skates for every practice and game. You eat the same fucking breakfast every day. You're a robot. You drink your coffee black, Henrik. No milk. No sugar. Who drinks their coffee black?"

I shrug, changing lanes to move around a truck. "I like my coffee black." Though it hasn't escaped my notice that when he makes me coffee, he adds a little cream. His way tastes good too.

He huffs, his left knee bouncing like he's tapping out a distress signal in Morse code. "You're not getting it. I know all these things about you, but you don't know me. I mean, do you know anything about me besides my fucking name? I'm your husband now—"

"I *know*," I say for what feels like the hundredth time.

"Well, if we're gonna pretend for the sake of some Swedish child welfare review board, you should maybe know, like, one real thing about me. But you never ask. About anyone. Ever! You make no effort, Henrik. You don't know me. You don't know *any* of us. And now we're stuck together, and I don't know how the hell we're gonna fake this."

His harsh words cut almost as deep as his clear lack of faith in me. "I know you, Teddy. I'll admit, not well. But I *do* know you."

"Prove it."

I keep my eyes on the winding road. "How?"

His knee stops shaking as he considers for a moment. "Give me three things."

"What?"

"Three things you know about me. Prove that I'm not crazy. Prove there's something here, something we can build a foundation on. It won't be a real marriage, and I know that. I'm not asking for that. I'll *never* ask you for that. But I need to know you can at least be my friend. I can't do this if you're not even my friend. I can't pretend. It'll kill me, Henrik."

I'm quiet for a moment, considering.

In my silence, he curses under his breath. "Seriously? God, just pull over."

"Teddy—"

"Pull the fucking car over!"

Slowing down, I pull over onto the wide shoulder, leaving plenty of space for cars to pass around. "There. Better? Now, let's just take a moment and—"

Flinging off his seat belt, Teddy throws open his car door and exits the vehicle.

My anger surges as I unbuckle. "What the hell are you doing? Get back in the car!"

"Just go," he shouts over his shoulder. "I'll find my own way back to Stockholm."

I launch from the car and chase after him. "Teddy, wait!"

"Go away!"

"Don't you think this is a bit dramatic?"

"*Yes!*" He spins around, eyes blazing. In this moment, he's the personification of a volcano as he stares me down, hands fisted at his sides. "Of course this is dramatic. Because *I'm* dramatic!" He splays a hand over his chest. "Which you would know, if you knew me at all!"

"You drink oat milk lattes!"

His breath leaves him in a huff as he stares me down. "What?"

I don't know where that came from either. But it's said now, and he's no longer running away from me. Cars whip past as I jog along the guardrail, closing the distance between us. A fine mist hangs in the air, remnants of this morning's rainstorm. "From the coffee cart," I say on a breath. "At the practice arena. You order iced oat milk lattes with a double shot of espresso. And you prefer window seats to aisle seats on airplanes."

His eyes narrow at me. "Is that all you know about me? My coffee order and my seat preference?"

My feet crunch on the fine gravel as I stop in front of him, mind racing to come up with more. "Your favorite Disney princess is Moana." I listened to him compare all the princesses with Karro a few days ago. "And you snore."

"Fuck you, I don't snore."

My mouth twitches with a smile. "You do. That's something only a friend would know, right? Not just a colleague or a passing acquaintance." I hold his gaze, daring him to look away. "That's four things, not three. And I could keep going. I'm your friend, Teddy. I *want* to be your friend. And I need you to stay. I need you in this with me. So, tell me what you need. What do we do to make this work for you? You want rules? Set them. I'll do anything you ask."

A muscle ticks in his jaw as he levels his stare at me, the fire cooling in his eyes. "You can't call me your husband."

I lean away, surprised at this first request. "But in the car, you just said—"

"*Ever*," he says over me. "You can't call me your husband ever. Swear it."

"I swear," I assure him. "What am I to call you then?"

He thinks for a moment. "You can call me your partner."

I nod again. "It's done."

"Am I moving in with you?"

Christ. I've made so many choices this week. Impossible choices. Before this exact moment, the logistics of them all were merely hypothetical. For days now, I've felt like that scared seven-year-old boy who fell through a crack in the ice. I was treading dark water in heavy skates, kicking for the surface. I saw Teddy's hand as a lifeline, a way out, so I grabbed on.

But he's not pulling me out. I'm pulling him under. It's been one day, and we're already standing on the side of the road shouting at each other. And I deserve all his anger, all his confusion, because *I* did this. I grabbed his hand and pulled him under, and now we'll sink or swim together.

I'm so frustrated. And ashamed. Shoving my hands in my pockets, I rock on my heels, feeling too guilty to look at him. "I suppose you'll have to, won't you? I'll need you in the home to help me with Karro."

He crosses his arms. "Then I need my own room."

"Done. My apartment has three bedrooms. We'll each have our own room. You'll take mine for the duration of your stay. It's larger."

"I'm not taking your room—"

"You will," I say over him. "I insist. We'll call that one my rule. Just as I insist that you continue to live your life. I will do whatever is needed for this to have as little of an impact on you as possible."

His eyes narrow again. "Live my life? What, like you want me to go out and date other men? Want me to fuck them too? Maybe bring them back to the apartment? What size bed am I working with in your room?"

As I picture him leading a strange man through my house, my chest suddenly feels tight. I'm a private person by nature, and I don't like sharing my spaces with anyone. I grimace, hands fisted in my pockets. "No men in the apartment. I won't have that upsetting Karro or her routines. But you're free to do whatever you want outside of my home with friends or family or . . . whomever. But keep it private. We must maintain a public image of . . ."

"Fidelity?"

I sigh, knowing he's trying to bait me again. "No romantic partners in the apartment. For either of us."

"Done."

My frustration settles a little. "Anything else?"

He considers. "I want to pay you rent."

"Out of the question."

He steps forward, his eyes flashing with anger. "It's *not* out of the question."

"You're already sacrificing too much for me. I can't allow it—"

"Henrik, I need walls! Barriers that help reinforce what this is between us. My salary is shit, but I can contribute my fair share. And I will. Please, give me this."

It will cost me my pride to accept money from this man. But what is my pride worth if it gets me Karro safe and living in my home? "Fine. Anything else?"

Teddy holds my gaze. The wind whips at his loose locs, tugging a few in front of his face. He flicks them back with a curl of his finger, tucking them behind his ear. "Don't kiss me."

As he speaks, a large lorry whooshes past. I'm unsure I heard him right. "What?"

"I said, don't kiss me," he repeats.

I groan, dragging a hand through my hair. Does he really feel like such a rule is necessary? What must he think of me? What must he expect? "Trust me, I won't," I assure him.

His face falls, and I know I misspoke.

"That is to say, I don't," I add, knowing it's not enough of an explanation. He admitted to once having romantic feelings for me. I certainly don't want to embarrass him or hurt his feelings. But how do I make him understand the nature of what I am, when I don't rightly know myself? "Look, Teddy. I'm not . . ."

"Gay?"

"Looking for a relationship. With anyone. It's just not how I am. I'm focused on my career. And now Karro. With your new job duties, I doubt you'll find much time for romance either."

He shrugs. "Oh, there's always time for a little romance. Life is short, Henrik. I intend to live mine to the fullest."

At his words, flashes of a memory come unbidden to my mind— Teddy with his arms wrapped around a blond rookie. The rookie's hands on Teddy's ass, pressing him up against the sink. Their gasps of surprise at being interrupted. The glass soap dispenser shattering as it slips to the floor, knocked askew by the rookie's roving hands.

Pushing the memory away, I fight a scowl. I'm all too familiar with Teddy's willingness to live his life to the fullest. I can only pray he heeds my wishes and keeps those activities private. I'm not one to judge another's actions, but I have Karro to think about now. Her safety and comfort must come first. Always.

"We can't stay out here," I call over the noise of another passing truck. "It's dangerous. Are you finished making your demands?"

Teddy leans away, surprised by my sudden change in tone. I've surprised myself. Why do I feel so frustrated? So angry? He's only trying to help me. "Yeah, I'm good."

"Good. Then let's go. I want to be back in the city before dark." Turning on my heel, I lead the way back over to the rental car. Teddy follows.

As we get in the car, he shuts his door and looks my way. "I thought of one more thing."

"What?"

Our elbows brush as we buckle our seat belts. Then he grabs his sunglasses and slips them back on his face, hiding his eyes away from me. "Seeing as you're the international hockey superstar and I'm just a lowly PT, *you* get to tell Poppy St. James what we did."

I stare out the windshield, hands gripped tight to the wheel. "Fuck."

He snorts a laugh. "Right?"

We really did *not* think this through.

13

HENRIK

Dad is waiting on the front porch of the house when Teddy and I pull up. He rises from his rocking chair, waving to us in welcome. Gripping tight to the porch railing, he makes his way down the front steps, clearly favoring his good knee.

My parents were in their forties by the time they had my sister and me, meaning they're now in their seventies. I've tried to move them out of this house for years, but they won't hear of it. As Dad's mobility declines and Mom's health worsens, I worry we may reach a point where the decision is no longer theirs.

For now, I have helpers from town who deliver groceries, manage the lawn, and shovel the snow in winter. Mom still keeps a garden, and Dad tinkers with his boat. It's a small life, but they need nothing else.

"It looks nice," Teddy says, peering through the windshield at the house.

It sits perched at the top of a hill, which slopes down to a small lake. The ocean is only a short bike ride away. In the summertime, Petra and I discovered every path between here and the beach, often racing to find out which was the fastest.

I take in the house's red-sided walls and the steep, shingled roof. A few years ago, Petra converted the little boat shed down by the lake into an apartment. That's usually where I stay when I come to visit in the offseason. I would stay tonight, but I don't want to make Teddy uncomfortable. At least in the city, he can have his own bed, even if it's just my couch.

Dad waves again, making his way down the gravel drive. "Hej hej! Welcome home, son!"

Teddy glances my way, slipping his sunglasses off. "Are we getting out?"

With a curt nod, I exit the car.

Tears fill Dad's eyes as he crosses to my side. "My boy. My Henrik."

We embrace, and I can't help but inhale, breathing deep the smell of him. There's a lifetime of memories in the scent of his shaving cream, the wool of his favorite sweater, the hint of coffee on his breath. He's as tall as me, though thinner, his body growing frail with age. But his hands are still strong. They grip me like iron.

"Come inside," he says. "There's coffee waiting on the stove."

I lean away, blinking back my tears. "Dad, I brought Petra home."

He nods, holding tight to my forearms. "Good. Family belongs together."

"Mom?"

"She waits inside."

Before either of us can turn, Mom calls out, "Gunnar, where is he? Let me see him."

I smile, glancing over Dad's shoulder. Mom stands in the open front door. She's dressed in a cream sweater and a long knit skirt. Her grey hair is tied up in a bun at her nape. As her memory goes, she sometimes struggles to recall faces. Each time she remembers me is a blessing.

Stepping around Dad, I walk her way. "Mom, I'm here. I'm home."

Making her way down the porch steps, she *tsk*s, brushing me aside. "I know you're here, Henrik. Such a good boy, you always come home. I was talking about *him*."

I follow the direction of her point. Teddy stands by the side of the car. He glances from my mother to me, brows raised in confusion.

Shit. I sometimes forget he doesn't speak Swedish. "My mother wants to meet you," I say in English.

"Of course I want to meet him," she says, switching to English too. "It's not every day your only son brings his new husband home to meet the family."

I wince at her use of the word *husband*, shooting Teddy a quick look of apology.

Next to me, Dad chuckles, still speaking in Swedish. "You gave us quite the surprise last night. Your mother hasn't stopped talking of it since. She's been cooking all morning. I hope you're both hungry," he adds to Teddy in English.

Remembering my manners, I step forward. "Teddy, these are my parents, Gunnar and Maria Karlsson. Mom, Dad, this is Teddy O'Connor, my . . . partner." It feels strange to say it out loud.

"Nice to meet you," Teddy says with a nervous smile, tucking a stray loc behind his ear. "Sorry, I don't know any Swedish."

"Quite alright," says Dad. "You're welcome here, Teddy."

I hurry around the car, trying to intercept Mom, but she's too fast. She reaches out with both hands, pulling Teddy into a tight hug. With a soft grunt, he accepts her welcome, patting her on the back. "You have a lovely home, Mrs. Karlsson."

She pulls away, cupping his face with a weathered hand. "We're family now. You may call me 'Mom' too." She narrows her eyes at him. "Are you afraid of me, Theodore?"

Teddy smiles again. "No, ma'am. Should I be?"

She just chuckles. "Theodore. That's your name, ja?"

"Yes, ma'am. But most people call me Teddy."

She brushes her thumb over his lips before feathering her fingers over the locs on his shoulder. "You're a good person, aren't you?"

"I think so. My own mother might disagree sometimes."

She *tsk*s again, running a hand over his stomach. "But you're so skinny. They don't feed you enough. Make sure Henrik eats too."

"I will," he assures her.

She steps back, hands on her hips. "Well then, I suppose you'll have your reasons for rushing into this marriage. But you'll be good to him, won't you?"

"I'll certainly try."

She nods. "Yes, I can see it. You're an old soul, like my Gunnar. Henrik picked well."

Teddy's brown skin is so fair, I can see that he's blushing. I step in behind Mom, placing a hand on her shoulder. Once she starts in on someone, it can be difficult to pry her away. But I will if it means Teddy is spared any embarrassment.

She pats my hand, her gaze still locked on Teddy. "Karlssons only marry once, you know."

Teddy stiffens, glancing over her head at me. "Is that right?"

"Why do you think my Petra never married that wastrel of a boy who was always sniffing around the garden shed? A Karlsson may be picky, but we always pick well. You'll be happy together."

I clear my throat. "Shall we go have some coffee?"

She brushes my hand away, reaching for Teddy instead. "Get the coffee yourself. Theodore and I have work to do." Weaving her fingers in with his, she leads him towards the house. "Have you ever made kanelbulle?"

"Kanen—what?" He glances over his shoulder at me.

"It's Henrik's favorite," she goes on. "His husband has to know how to make kanelbulle the Karlsson way. Come, I'll teach you."

"Mom, we can't stay long," I call out in Swedish.

I go to follow them, but Dad stops me. "Let them go," he says softly, his hand on my arm.

"If she gets him in the kitchen, I'll never get him out—"

"Please."

At his tone, I pause, glancing over my shoulder.

His pale blue eyes are somber as he watches them walk away together. "Let her have this."

"Have what?"

"A child was taken from her. Now a new child is given. Let her bond with him awhile. You and I will go lay your sister to rest."

A few hours later, I return to the house to the smell of freshly baked cinnamon rolls. Mom and Teddy sit at the kitchen table, laughing and talking together like old friends. Her hands work mechanically, cutting up chunks of potato, dropping them into a pot. Teddy moves a little slower, peeling a carrot with careful strokes.

"Hey," he calls out, pointing to the plate of spiced cinnamon rolls sprinkled with pärlsocker. "Look, we made kanenbulla."

"Kanelbulle," Mom corrects. "Your Theodore is a quick student," she adds at me.

"Well, I had a good teacher," he says, charming her with a smile.

I move around the table to kiss the top of her head. "Mom, Teddy is our guest. We can't have him peeling the vegetables."

She huffs. "I suppose you think dinner will just make itself then."

Teddy grins. "Really, I don't mind, Mrs. Karlsson. In my family's kitchen, this is all I'm usually allowed to do. I've gotten pretty good at it. Look." He points to the bowl of peeled and chopped carrots.

"Theodore said you're not staying for dinner," she calls in Swedish as I cross over to the sink to wash my hands.

I sigh, turning on the tap. "We have to return to the city, remember? We have to get back to Karolina."

She just huffs again. "Petra can watch her own daughter for one night, Henrik. Your place is here with us. I've already made the lamb meatballs. They're in the oven."

I grimace, keeping my hands under the hot water. I can't do it again. I can't remind her that Petra's dead. Not when Dad and I just laid Petra's ashes to rest at the root of her favorite oak tree. I told him we should wait for Mom, but he just smiled and said, "Today is a good day. Let it be good."

He stayed outside, wanting a moment alone with my sister.

"My son only comes home twice a year," Mom goes on, switching back to English. "It's only right that he has dinner with his family before he goes away again."

As she talks, Teddy gets up from the table and walks over to where I'm standing at the sink. "I really don't mind," he says under his breath. "I brought a bag just in case. I mean, if you wanna stay . . ."

I turn off the water and reach around him for the hand towel. "There's not a lot of room here is the problem. They don't even have a couch anymore. And my old bedroom in the attic is hardly big enough for Karolina."

"Where do you usually sleep when you stay here?"

"The boat shed."

He shrugs. "I'm sure I've stayed in worse places."

I raise a brow, fighting a smile. "You haven't seen the boat shed."

His own smile falls as he leans in closer and whispers, "I don't think she knows your sister is dead."

Christ, I didn't tell him. I had the whole car ride down from Stockholm to tell him about her memory issues, but I was too busy worrying about what *he* was thinking. And I'm protective of my mother. I don't want others judging her or pitying her. But each time I visit, I'm confronted with the bitter truth: she's only getting worse. Piece by piece, she's slipping away.

As if he can read my thoughts, Teddy's fingers brush lightly down my arm. "Let's give her this. We can do one meal, right? Karolina's safe at the hospital. And I mean . . . how many good days does your mom have left?"

Covering his hand with my own, I nod, relieved that he's making the decision for us.

"Good news," he calls out. "I worked my magic on old cranky pants, and we're gonna stay for dinner."

Mom glances between us. "What are crank pants?"

Teddy laughs as he retakes his seat, and I step in behind him. "That's just my fond little nickname for Henrik," he teases. "Hey, do you have any photo albums, Mrs. K? I'd love to see a picture of Henrik in lederhosen."

I lean over him, stealing a cube of carrot from the bowl. "Lederhosen are German."

Mom turns in her chair. "Oh, but we have that fine picture of you and your sister from Midsummer, Henrik. Fetch it for me. He's wearing the jolliest little hat with blue and yellow ribbons."

Teddy laughs. "God, is there anything better than a jolly hat?"

I step away, taking a moment to watch them. He's so good with her. After watching him with Karolina this week, did I really have any doubt? His chair is turned towards her, and he's listening with his whole body. His face is expressive, laughing as she tells jokes, always nodding along. He's giving her his full attention, something she's been starved of for so long.

"The picture, Henrik," she directs over her shoulder in Swedish.

I smile, a soft warmth glowing in my chest. "I'll get it. I just have to make a call first."

Leaving them in the kitchen, I walk through the front room and out onto the porch.

So much about the last week has felt impossible. There was even a dark moment when I thought my grief at losing Petra might overtake me. As I drove to the airport that first night, the idea entered my mind to jerk the wheel into the wall and end it all. There's no pain when you're dead. No grief.

But then I thought of Karolina alone in a hospital, needing me. I thought of my parents, mourning the loss of both their children. And I thought of Teddy, waiting for me on the tarmac. He thinks this can work. He's stressed and worried, but he's *here*. He's fighting for Karolina. He's fighting for me. Even now, he's inside, comforting my mother as her fragile mind fights to protect her from the truth that her daughter is gone.

I'm going to fight for *him*. I'm going to protect him from any backlash this might bring. In a few short days, we have to return to Jacksonville. God willing, we'll return with Karolina at our side. And then the truth will come out. Teddy's right—we need a plan.

There's only one person I trust to help me keep Karolina and Teddy safe. Slipping my phone from my pocket, I pull up my contacts and scroll until I reach her name. Taking a deep breath, I sink down onto my Dad's favorite rocking chair and tap the little green circle. It takes a few calls before she picks up. But the moment she does, I hear her voice, and I know everything will be okay.

"This is Poppy St. James."

Letting out my held breath, I rock back in the chair. "Hello, Poppy. This is Henrik Karlsson, calling from Sweden."

14

HENRIK

Teddy disappears shortly after dinner while I help Dad clear the dishes away. Once everything is set to dry, I leave my parents to their nightly ritual. Mom always makes them each a cup of chamomile tea, then they play a game of skitgubbe at the kitchen table before bed.

It was a good day, but she's tired. Every day, her memories pour like sand through her fingers. What she easily recalls in the morning, she forgets by evening. During dinner, she asked me three times to pass the salt when it was right by her hand. By the end of the meal, she was asking Teddy his name. I could tell having to keep repeating it for her was starting to upset him.

I step outside on the front porch and look around. Both the rocking chairs are empty. Where the hell did Teddy go? I grab my bag from the car and make my way down the narrow, winding steps that lead to the lakeshore. The boat shed sits at the end of our dock. Flickering light glows from the shed's two little windows. I'm sure Dad set a fire in the wood stove to take the bite out of this sudden chill.

I look up as I walk, knowing this path by heart. The stars twinkle over the lake, partially covered by clouds. Crickets chirp, and the last of the summer frogs hum in the mud. This autumn will be a short one. Soon, the lakeshore will turn quiet with winter's waking.

I'm about to open the door to the shed when I spy movement. I relax when I see who it is. Teddy is sitting in Petra's favorite cushioned deck chair. He has a sweatshirt on with the hood pulled up against the cold. In the glow of the dock light, I see the glint of something in his palm.

"Hej," I call out.

He jumps, closing his fist tight.

"I didn't mean to startle you."

He makes no reply.

Dropping my bag by the door, I sink into the empty chair. "And I'm sorry I didn't warn you."

"Warn me about what?"

"About my mother. About her dementia. I should have told you."

He's quiet for a moment. "Yeah . . . why didn't you?"

I decide to give him the simplest version of the truth. "It's hard for me to talk about it. Hard for me to admit how bad it's getting, even to myself." I turn to look at him. "But I want to thank you."

He raises a dark brow. "Thank me?"

"You were kind to her today. You gave her a good day. And, like you said, she has few left."

He shrugs. "It was no problem. She's really nice." Opening his fist again, he looks at the object in his hand.

"What's that?"

"It's your mother's wedding ring."

I take in the shape of the thin gold ring. "Why do you have it?"

His frown deepens. "She gave it to me. Called it a wedding present. She said it's been worn by a Karlsson for over a hundred years."

He offers it to me, and I lean away. "What are you doing?"

"Take it."

"I can't take it."

"Henrik, *take* it."

I shake my head. "She gave it to you. It was a gift."

He scoffs. "Yeah, for your loving husband, your heart's fire, mate of your fucking soul. She practically recited an epic poem as she worked it off her finger. This ring sounds magical, Henrik. And our marriage is totally fake. I put this on, and your ancestors will know. They'll smite me. They'll drown me in the lake. No fucking thanks."

"Teddy . . ."

"No, I'm not putting it on. I am not inviting the bad karma of a magical wedding ring into my life. Find another husband to wear it because it won't be me." Leaning over further, he taps my elbow with the ring, silently urging me to relieve him of it.

I relent, plucking it from his fingers. Once it's in my hand, I mirror his action and place it in my palm. "What am I supposed to do with it?"

He shrugs. "Wear it on a chain? Wait and give it to Karolina? Or just save it for a partner you actually love, cherish, and adore."

I wince, his words rubbing me like sandpaper. It's less about the words. It's their delivery. He's hurt. Somehow, I've hurt him again. I didn't even give him this damn ring, but still I hurt him. "Teddy, I'm sorry—"

"It's fine." He rises from the deck chair, unfolding his long legs. "I'm tired. Wanna show me this boat shed?"

I slip my mother's wedding band on the smallest finger of my right hand and stand. "Fine, but you've been warned. It will be a tight fit."

"Clearly, you've never shared a room with three sisters. Consider my expectations managed."

I lead the way down the side of the dock and back over to the shed. The handle takes some rattling, and the bottom of the door requires a little nudge with my toe, but I get it open. I step in first, crossing the small room to set my bag on the bed.

Teddy follows me in but stops in the doorway. He blinks in the brighter light, taking in the wood paneling, the two simple chairs wedged by the door, and the black wood stove. The kitchenette is little more than a sink and a small refrigerator. But there's a coffee maker on the counter, and Mom left us some fresh bread and apples.

Teddy's gaze locks on the far wall of the shed. "Are you fucking kidding me?"

I glance around, looking for the source of his displeasure. "What's wrong?"

He points. "There's only one bed."

I shrug. "I told you it was a tight fit."

Groaning, he rubs two fingers at his temple. "Okay, you're gonna have to stop saying the words 'tight fit' to me, like, yesterday."

"What?"

"There's only one bed, Henrik. A very small, practically twin-sized bed. If I'm on the bed, where are you gonna sleep? I don't see a couch in here." He does a half pivot, as if certain he must have missed part of the shed. He points to the door in the corner. "Where does that lead?"

I fight a smile. "That's the toilet. Would you prefer one of us sleep in there? Perhaps we could flip for it."

He glares at me. "Is this a joke to you?"

I drop into one of the chairs and start taking off my boots. "It's just for one night. Have you never shared a bed before?"

He crosses his arms. "Yeah, of course. With my *sisters*. Not my—"

I glance up, boot in hand. "Your what?"

He holds my gaze, his eyes reflecting the bright flames of the fire. "Not with you."

I tug my other boot off, dropping both by the door. "If it's really a problem for you, I'll just sleep on the floor."

He huffs, tugging his sweatshirt off. "Seriously? You're an NHL superstar who's a week out from the start of a new season. We're not messing up your joints or your alignment by making you sleep on a wooden fucking floor. You take the bed. I'll just take a blanket and go sleep in the chair out on the dock."

My own sweater muffles my groan as I strip it off. Freeing my arms, I toss the sweater onto the chair. "You're not sleeping on the dock."

He slips past me, heading for the bed. "Why not? I like nature."

Taking my chance, I move to the door and lock it.

"Hey—"

I turn around, pressing my back against the locked door.

Teddy stands across the shed, the bed's quilt bundled in his arms. "You can't keep me trapped in here, you psycho."

"I can, and I will."

"Henrik—"

"You're not sleeping on a goddamn deck chair, exposed to the elements. Not when we have a perfectly good bed, and a fire, and a door that locks."

He blusters, trying to find a new excuse to flee. "The elements? What, are you expecting a hurricane tonight?"

I cross my arms. "No, but we have bears in Sweden."

He gasps. "You said there are no polar bears in Sweden. Was that a fucking lie?"

"Brown bears. Not polar bears. And we have wolves. And many large birds of prey. And you're on the edge of a lake, which means mosquitos. They'll eat you alive. Shall I keep going? Do you need more reasons for staying indoors tonight?"

I watch as his expression falls. He knows he's defeated.

Good.

Christ, how can a man who is so kind and gentle be so obstinate? So maddening?

I gesture towards the toilet. "Would you like to go first, or shall I?"

He glances over his shoulder at the closed door. Then he drops down to the edge of the bed, still clutching the quilt. "Knock yourself out."

When I finish, I step out to find Teddy stretched out on the bed. One knee is bent, and he has an arm thrown back over his head as he scrolls on his phone. He's stripped down to his T-shirt and a pair of formfitting boxers. His pants, his sweatshirt, and even his socks are all neatly stacked with his shoes over by the door. His blue head wrap is in place, covering his locs. He wears it every night, sometimes putting it on as soon as he gets back to the apartment.

I can feel the tension weaving itself through the long lines of his body. He doesn't like being alone with me. Hoping to set him at ease, I clear my throat. "I spoke with Poppy St. James earlier."

He sits up. "What? When?"

"This afternoon."

"Why didn't you say anything?"

I shrug. "You were busy looking at pictures of me dancing around a maypole." Mom kept him laughing for two hours, telling him stories of our misadventures on holidays. She confused most of the details, but she was still all too eager to tell Teddy about the time I tried to steal a penguin from the Stockholm zoo.

His phone sits ignored as he follows my movement. "Well, what did she say? Was she mad? Oh god, am I gonna lose my job?"

Once again, I'm hit with a wave of regret. Teddy is risking everything by helping me. Not just his family's ire or his personal reputation. As Poppy not-so-gently reminded me today, this could impact his job security. Fraternization between PTs and players is deeply frowned upon. The team had to move mountains to keep Doctor Price on staff when it came out that she was in an undisclosed relationship with our goalie. The Rays are disinclined to go through that again.

But Teddy and I have done nothing wrong. He was signed with the team for all of three hours before he dropped everything to join me here in Sweden. He never once treated me in any medical or professional capacity. If they dare try to punish him for this, I will fight. I won't let his helping me stand in the way of his career.

"She's going to help us," I assure him.

"What does that mean? Help us how?"

"It means she knows what we've done and why, and she intends to help." Undoing the buckle of my belt, I drop my jeans to the floor and step out of them. I fold and place them next to his neat pile of clothes. "Do you mind if I take off my shirt?"

His eyes go wide. "What?"

"I prefer fewer layers when I sleep."

He blinks, then looks quickly away. "I . . . no. That's . . . nope. Do your thing."

Turning my back to him, I pull my T-shirt off, adding it to my pile of clothes. If I were being completely honest, I'd tell him I prefer to sleep fully nude. Since I'm an athlete, my metabolism is always working in overdrive, so my body runs hot. With the fire lit in here, and with sharing a bed, I'll likely sweat through the damn sheets all night.

Maybe *I'm* the one who should be sleeping out on a deck chair . . .

I cross over to the bed. Teddy scoots as far over as he can, wedging himself up against the wall to make room for me. I think by American measurement standards, you'd call this bed full-sized, not twin. But I'm a 6'o" professional hockey player, and Teddy also has an athlete's long, toned body. We're going to be stacked together like sardines in a tin.

He grunts, shifting his weight to adjust his pillow. "There's really no extra bedroom up at the main house?"

I sink down next to him, resting with my back against the wall, legs stretched out atop the quilt. "They converted Petra's old room into a sewing room when she moved to the city for university. And my room was in the attic. It's mostly storage now. They keep a child-sized bed in there for Karro."

Our shoulders brush as we both bend our elbows, holding up our phones to scroll the internet. Tension buzzes around Teddy like a hive of bees. Meanwhile, I'm only pretending to read the stats on this Swedish hockey site. I hate that he's still so uncomfortable around me. He didn't seem this anxious when we were in my apartment in Stockholm. We were alone then too. We sat on the couch together, just like this. We watched TV and ate takeout curry. He stole my egg rolls. It was comfortable . . . or so I thought.

What's changed?

He stills his thumb from scrolling. "So, did Poppy say anything else?"

"She told us not to worry. Our focus now is Karro and bringing her safely home. She said when we return, she'll be ready with a plan."

He glances my way, one dark brow raised. "A plan to what?"

I just shrug. "A plan to get us safely out of this mess."

15

TEDDY

"Henrik—*hey*—wake up, man." I shake his shoulder, trying to wake him. Fuck, he's drenched in sweat. He thrashes again, groaning in his sleep. I was actually having a good dream until he kneed me in the hip, jolting me awake. Now I'm pressed against the wall while he cries out, flailing like he's drowning on dry land.

"Henrik, come on," I say, louder this time, grabbing him by the shoulders and pinning him down. "*Wake up.*"

I know the moment he finally wakes, because all the fight goes out of him like a robot powering down. He groans, his naked chest heaving for breath. But the second he feels me hovering over him, he gasps and tries to sit up. Cursing in Swedish, he frantically pulls away.

"Whoa, whoa—hey, it's just me. It's Teddy."

"Teddy?" He's clearly still confused. "I—what happened?"

"You're awake," I soothe, letting him go. "It's okay, man. You're okay."

He presses a hand to his chest. "I couldn't breathe."

"It was just a dream."

Still panting, he looks my way. "Did I hurt you?"

"No," I assure him, even though my hip is throbbing. The man has iron kneecaps.

He groans again, stretching an arm over his head to better catch his breath. "It always feels so real." His voice sounds haunted. Is this just about his sister? What other demons does he carry?

I lie back down on my side, tucking my arm under my pillow. "Do you wanna talk about it? Sometimes that helps."

He goes still as he considers. "No."

It's hard not to take that as rejection. "You've been having nightmares all week. Is that common for you?"

He sighs, cracking the knuckles in his fingers with a practiced flex of his hands. "No."

"You've been dreaming of the car accident with your sister."

"Yes."

It wasn't really a question. We both know it's true. Reaching out, I rest my hand on his forearm. He flinches at the contact but doesn't pull away. "Henrik, it wasn't your fault. You're not to blame for what happened to Petra."

His breath catches as he turns to look at me. "You've never said her name before."

I shrug. "I didn't feel I had the right."

"And now you do?"

I search his face in the weak moonlight. I can make out little more than the bridge of his nose and his brows. He's not mad. He's genuinely asking. "A lot has changed in a week," I reply.

He flops back to stare up at the ceiling. "Bit of an understatement."

"I know I never met her, but I'm here with you now. I've met Karolina and your parents. I saw Petra's pictures and heard her stories. She's not just a name to me anymore. She's a person. She's *your* person. It's my honor to say her name for you, to remember her with you."

He's quiet for a long moment. "This was a mistake."

I prop up on my elbow. "What, getting married? Yeah, I've been saying that since we left the freaking chapel."

His breath leaves him on a tired sigh. "No, it was a mistake to come here. To stay here."

"What do you mean?"

He looks around the dark room. "Petra liked doing renovation projects. This shed was one. She turned this into an apartment for whenever we visited my parents."

I smile, picturing Karro running up and down the dock, playing while her mom ripped out old boards and installed cabinets. From the smiles in her photos, I bet Petra had a great laugh. "The shed is perfect."

He's quiet again, but I can feel his mind humming. "She was the last one to stay here."

"How do you know?"

Surprising me, he sucks in a sharp breath that catches in his throat like a sob. "Gud, hjälpe mig."

"Henrik?"

"The bed linens still smell like her."

Oh god. How can one sentence hold so much power? Tears fill my eyes as I take in the faintly floral scent of the sheets. I thought it was just laundry soap. It's soft, like lavender. Warm, like sunshine. It's Petra.

My hands reach for Henrik on instinct as he rolls to his side, his body going tense as he finally breaks. In the week since Petra's death, he's been holding it all together. He had that one moment of raw emotion in the locker room, but since then he's been bottled up tight.

At first, I thought it was just a stoic Swedish thing, or maybe the macho, straight man, no-crying thing. But I think Henrik is actually just a master at compartmentalization. He hasn't let himself feel his sister's loss because there have been too many other things to do. He had to get here and take care of Karolina. He had to deal with the lawyers, comfort his parents, marry me.

Fuck, it hurts that I'm on the list of distractions keeping him from grieving. But I won't be a distraction now. He needs to feel this. He needs to feel *her*. I pull him to me, wrapping my arms around him as he cries. "It's okay. You just feel it all."

His arm bands around my waist as he buries his face against my chest. I feel the heat of his breath as he pants for air, his fingers fisted tight into the back of my shirt. Shifting my weight, I roll us until I can unpin his left arm. Our legs snake together, and he's practically on top of me.

"She's dead," he groans against my collarbone, his tears wetting my shirt.

I brush my fingers through his soft hair, sweeping the honey-nut strands back from his face. "I know."

His arms tighten around me as his hands grip my back. "I'll never see her again."

That's always the kicker, right? First, there's the sadness that someone is gone. Then comes the resentment that you didn't know the last time would be the last time. I stare up at the beams on the ceiling, blinking back my own tears. "I know."

He shifts until just the side of his face is pressed against my chest. Then he sniffs, trying to choke back his tears. "God, I'm so *angry*."

My fingers stroke lightly down the vertebra of his neck. "I know." He groans again, clinging to me hard enough to crack my ribs. "Be angry all you want. I've got you."

But after those three confessions, he's silent except for the sound of his muted crying. I don't know how long we stay like that, limbs twisted together. I stroke his hair, his back, humming under my breath as he grieves. Even once he's calm, he doesn't pull away. He lets me hold him, lets me comfort him.

It must be nearing morning when he finally pulls away, only shifting far enough to lift his head from my shoulder. I give him whatever space he wants. Our legs are still entangled, and my arm is pinned under him. It fell asleep ages ago.

"I wasn't dreaming about the car," he says, breaking the sacred silence of his grief.

If he's opening this door, I'm walking through it. "What were you dreaming about?"

He rolls onto his back, freeing me from his heavy weight. How is it possible that I already miss it? "When I was seven, Petra and I went ice skating on the lake. The surface cracked, and I fell through."

"This lake? The one outside?"

"No, a different lake."

I settle back against my pillow, flexing feeling back into my fingers. "What happened?"

"I almost drowned," he whispers. "It was awful."

"How did you get out?"

He's quiet for a moment, staring up at the ceiling. "Petra saved me. She threw herself flat on the ice and grabbed the end of my scarf as I went under. She risked her life to pull me to the surface just before I drowned."

As he shares his haunting tale, my mind fills with images of my own sisters, fearless women all. I know they would brave any danger to come to my aid. "She sounds amazing."

"She was."

Reaching over, I take his hand. "I'm sorry I never got the chance to meet her."

He squeezes my hand. "She would have liked you."

His words send my nerves buzzing in my chest. "Why do you say that?"

"Because she would have seen in you the same thing I see."

"And what do you see?"

Even in the dark, I know he's looking at me. I feel the weight of his full attention, the deep anchoring of his soul behind his eyes. "Ett rent hjärta," he whispers in Swedish.

If I ever knew how to breathe, I've long forgotten. "What does that mean?"

The knuckles of his right hand brush over the point where my heart thrums in my chest. "It means you have a pure heart."

16

TEDDY

"Wait—no, you have to use the straw! Only the straw, remember? You gotta pop 'em quick." I laugh, blowing another stream of bubbles over Karolina's hospital bed.

She giggles, her casted arm holding tight to Teddy the Bear as she waves her free arm through the air, swatting at the bubbles. She's looking much better today. Her left arm and leg are both casted in bright purple. The bruising around her eye is fading to a mottled yellow brown. The thin cuts along her cheek and brow are healing well too.

"No, like a sword. You gotta jab," I tease, miming the movement with the bubble wand.

"Morbror, watch," she squeals.

On the other side of the bed, Henrik smiles and hums, sipping his coffee. Fuck, he looks good enough to spread on toast. He's wearing a charcoal cable-knit sweater. He hasn't bothered to shave this week, which works out well for me. His cheeks that were stubbly now look bearded. And his wavy hair is sort of flopped forward, a day's worth of product making it stylishly messy.

I usually only ever see him in his hockey uniform or in shorts and a T-shirt. Well, and game-day fits. You haven't lived until you've seen Henrik Karlsson walk off a plane wearing a tailored three-piece suit. Fuck me, that's what I want: Swedish Henrik and game-day fit Henrik. I'll spread one on toast and down the other like a shot.

Okay, these thoughts are completely inappropriate to have while I'm playing bubble tag with his niece. *Get it together, Teddy.*

Henrik gets distracted from our silly game when his phone starts to buzz. Shooting me a tense look, he answers the phone and stands. Speaking in quick Swedish, he heads for the door. Fuck, what was that look? Is it the doctor? His lawyer? In this moment, I have never regretted more than I can't understand a word of Swedish. Looking for any distraction, I blow more bubbles for Karolina.

Things have been tense since we got back to the city this morning. We made a quick stop at the apartment to change our clothes (cue the cable-knit sweater moment). Then, almost as soon as we walked through the hospital doors, Henrik was alerted that Karolina is getting discharged today.

We should be celebrating. It means all her surgeries are done. All she needs now is time to rest and heal, and she can do that from home. The trouble is that we still don't know *which* home they'll send her to. If Henrik would just stay in Sweden, they'd approve the emergency custody order. But a new hockey season is about to start. Henrik has to get back to Jacksonville.

I know the Rays have been in touch this week, asking for updates. It sucks, but I also get it. The NHL is a multi-billion-dollar-a-year industry. They're all for supporting family emergencies, but Henrik has a contract with the Rays. The team can't wait for him forever. Not when so many talented guys stand waiting in the wings. Henrik's game clock is officially ticking down the last few seconds.

I'm about to blow more bubbles for Karolina when he pokes his head in the room. "Teddy, come."

Heart in my throat, I leave the bubbles on the bedside table.

"No," Karolina cries.

"We'll be just outside the door, honey." Ducking into the hallway, I stop, eyes wide. Elin Ågren is standing next to Henrik. She looks as severe as ever. Square-framed black glasses, no makeup. Her long blonde hair is slicked back in a straight ponytail. She's wearing a black pantsuit with a cream pussybow blouse. God, she's like the anti-Poppy. Where Poppy St. James is all color and life, Henrik's lawyer exists only in humorless shades of grey.

I glance between them. "What's going on?"

Henrik glares at her. "She wouldn't tell me until I called for you."

"As your legal partner, this news concerns him as well," she replies coolly.

My heart skips a beat as I grab Henrik's hand. "Oh god, did the judge decide already?"

Elin nods. "Given the unconventional circumstances of your case, we managed to get the decision expedited. The welfare court ruled this morning."

I squeeze Henrik's hand tight, sending up every good thought and prayer to the high heavens. "Just tell us."

She spares us the torture of more waiting. "You were both awarded temporary custody of Karolina Karlsson."

All the air leaves my chest on a sharp exhale. "Oh, thank god." I grab his arm, even as I keep squeezing his hand. "Hen, you did it. You *won*."

Henrik presses his free hand to his chest, eyes shut tight as he mutters what sounds like a prayer. Then he looks to me, tears in his eyes. "I really thought I was going to lose her."

I wrap my arm around his waist, keeping him from sinking to the floor. "She's yours," I assure him. "She's coming home with you."

"I've emailed you the judge's ruling," Elin goes on. "And I have a copy here that you both must sign."

I go still. "Wait, I have to sign something?"

Elin levels her icy-blue stare at me. "Of course. Henrik's temporary custody is conditional. You are now part of those conditions."

My heart freaking stops. "What?"

"I told you to consider carefully what you were doing," she replies. "The judge only approved this because of you, Teddy. She appreciated your expertise in injury rehabilitation and your record of working with children."

Henrik stiffens. "I don't understand. Is the court awarding custody of Karolina to me or to Teddy?"

Elin purses her lips. "They're awarding custody to *both* of you. As legal partners, you will share the duties of raising this child, will you not? You will both be her surrogate fathers. And this is only temporary. You'll have to complete the adoption process before the court will consider making it permanent."

I sink back, my shoulders hitting the wall as I drop Henrik's hand. For the thousandth time in the last three days, the thought flashes like a bright neon sign inside my mind: We did *not* think this through.

Now I'm Karolina's father? I was doing this just as a friend thing. Henrik will be the one to love her and care for her, not me. I was just gonna help out. You know, teach her some PT exercises, pick her up from school, watch movies together, make mac and cheese, maybe braid her hair . . .

Which are all things a parent would do.

Oh god, I think I'm gonna be sick. Why are they looking at me?

Henrik's brows are knit with concern as he reaches for me. "Teddy . . ."

I pull away from him. "Don't."

Elin's frown deepens. "You see now the seriousness of your situation. This isn't a game. There is no winning. There is only Karolina and what's best for her. The two of you now hold the fate of a young girl in your hands. Henrik, so long as you're playing professional hockey, traveling as much as you do, the court's opinion is clear: If Teddy walks away, they'll likely reconsider your custody. For now, as her next of kin, you are approved as her temporary guardian, contingent on Teddy living in the home to assist with her rehabilitation."

Oh, fucking fuck. This cannot be happening. I'm now the glue of this whole operation?

"The court has further ordered that your offseasons be spent here in Sweden," she goes on. "This is to ensure that there is no detrimental loss of culture or language for Karolina. Will you agree to this term?"

Henrik nods. "Of course. I always come home for the summers anyway. Christmas too, if I can manage it."

Where the hell does that leave me? Am I now committing to spending all *my* summers in Sweden until Karolina turns eighteen? I have a job. I have sisters and niblets and friends. I have my own travel I want to do. I want to hike across Southeast Asia. I want to go to Burning Man. My god, can you imagine Henrik at Burning Man, wearing nothing but leather chaps and a cropped lace top?

Elin pulls out the folder containing the court's custody settlement, completely oblivious to my freak-out. "So long as you provide the court with proof of her medical insurance and enrollment in an American school, she is cleared to travel with you back to America. As we've already discussed, there will be a series of in-home placement reviews as the adoption process moves forward. I'll send you both a schedule for the visits when I have them."

Henrik takes the paperwork and a pen from her. "Teddy, turn around."

I feel like I'm having one of those cartoon out-of-body experiences. Like, I'm here, but also I'm floating somewhere near the ceiling. I turn, and Henrik uses my back to sign the paperwork. The *custody* paperwork. For a child. Because apparently, we're both becoming fathers today. Surrogate fathers, but still, the word *father* is definitely in there.

He taps my shoulder, and I turn. Then he hands me the papers and the pen.

"Sign where you see your name," Elin directs, pointing to the form.

And there it is. In the jumble of Swedish, I see a thin black line. Under that line is my name: Theodore Malik O'Connor. For the second time in as many days, I'm about to sign my life away. I press the papers flat between Henrik's shoulders, the pen poised over the signature line. If I sign this now, I'm accepting shared temporary custody of a child. And not, like, a cat child, or a plant, or a bearded dragon. A *human* child. A person.

Karolina.

I've only known her for a less than a week, and now I'm gonna be her father? "What if she doesn't like me?" I whisper, my fingers pinching tight to the pen.

Henrik glances over his shoulder. "What?"

"Karolina. What if she doesn't even like me? I don't know the first thing about being someone's dad. What if I do the wrong thing or say the wrong thing? What if I hurt her feelings? What if I get it all wrong?"

Elin's eyes narrow. "All questions that should have been asked *before* I filed."

Ignoring the papers, I round on her. "You know what, fuck you, Glacier Ice Barbie. We know we rushed into this, okay? This was a rash decision. And you've made your opinion on it crystal fucking clear. But Henrik was out of options."

Henrik's arm bands across my chest, pinning me to the wall. "Don't."

"She fucking started it," I growl, pointing at her with the pen.

"Not here."

"Well, my god, Henrik. If not here, then *where*?" I gesture around the hallway of this Swedish children's hospital ward. "Where am I allowed to completely lose my shit? Point me in that direction, because I am officially losing it."

"Hey," he says again, his free hand cupping my face. "Look at me."

"Your lawyer is a jerk—"

"Don't look at her. Look at me."

My chest heaves as I let myself look at him. Fuck, I could lose myself in the blue of his eyes.

"She doesn't matter." He turns us so my back is to her. "Nothing else matters. Not the lawyers or the coaches, the agents, the doctors. Let them all fade away. At the end of the day, this is about you, me, and Karolina. Together, we *will* find a way to make this work. I swear it to you, Teddy. I will not fail you in this. One step at a time, right? Those were your words."

Leaning against the wall, I search his face. "How can you put so much faith in me? You hardly know me."

Without hesitation, he splays his hand over my heart. "Rent hjärta, remember? I trust this."

With his free hand, he grabs my wrist, the pen dropping to the floor, and presses my palm to his chest. I flex my fingers, feeling the beating of his heart. "Do you trust me, Teddy? Do you trust my heart as I trust yours?"

He's asking the wrong question. This isn't about whether I trust the strength of *his* heart. The question is whether I can trust him not to crush *my* heart. Because he has it in his hands in more ways than one. As surely as it now pulses under his palm, I know it beats only for him. Can I really trust him not to break it?

God help me, I know the answer is no.

But I pick up the pen anyway.

And I sign the form.

17

HENRIK

It's been a whirlwind three days. Karolina was discharged from the hospital, and we finalized our travel back to the States. I also had to arrange the packing and storage of Petra's apartment. Teddy helped me collect items for Karro, including some toys and clothes. Everything else that wasn't perishables went into boxes. When the season ends, I'll go through it all properly. For now, it's just too painful. And we're out of time.

Karro is sad to be leaving Sweden, but she perked up when Teddy told her I live less than three hours away from Disney World. She sits with him now on the private jet's long sofa, her casted leg stretched out. She slept for most of the flight. They've been watching movies together for the last two hours. Teddy laughs when she confuses the words in the songs, singing in a silly mix of English and Swedish.

Before we began our descent into Jacksonville, he had the flight attendant make us all smoothies with a mix of fruit and veggies. I think he had her add a shot of vodka to mine. I don't mind. In fact, I think it's relaxing me. I take another sip.

The wheels rattle down in a rough landing, and the pilot announces our arrival. Tension builds in my chest as I peer out the window. Over at the private hangar, a small crowd waits for us. I curse under my breath. "What are all those people doing here?"

Teddy peers out the window and smiles. "Looks like we've got a welcoming committee."

"A what?" I look closer, and some of my tension eases. My mind immediately went to this being some kind of media scrum. We get those on game days, especially during the playoffs. I wasn't about to bring Karolina down in a wheelchair to the flash of a bunch of sports reporters' cameras.

But the people aren't reporters; it's my team. I see the Prices standing on the end, all four of them with their children. Mars holds the little blond child on his hip. Caleb squats next to them, helping their older boy hold up a sign that says "Welcome Home, Karolina" in bright colors. Langley is here too with his wife and daughter. Poppy St. James waits front and center. Like Rachel, she's pregnant. She and her daughter hold hands, waving at us.

"Look, honey." Teddy points out the window, helping Karolina sit up. We have to be careful with her cracked ribs. None of them are misplaced, but she's still not meant to do any twisting or bending for a few more weeks. "See all the signs they made for you? Look at all that glitter. It's like a parade for a princess, right?"

She smiles even as I sense her flash of nerves. Teddy talks quietly, pointing to the kids in the crowd, telling her their names. His words from the other day still sting. He told me I don't know any of my teammates, and he was right. I play with these men day in and day out. I attend their weddings and their baby showers. But the details of their lives feel so far away. It's not my life, not my routine, so I don't really pay attention.

In contrast, Teddy pays attention to everyone and everything. He was only an intern for the Rays, and that was six years ago. I couldn't tell you who was on the team six years ago. I bet he can. He knows their families too. He watches. He listens. He's instinctively attentive to those around him at all times.

Feeling my gaze, he glances across the aisle. "What's wrong?"

"Nothing."

"I bet you're ready to get back on the ice, huh? Back to the routine?"

I nod. My whole life is run by my sport. My diet and exercise, my sleep and travel schedules, my holidays. I operate with the consistency of a well-crafted watch. Or I did. Now, I look across the aisle of this private jet, and I see two lives suddenly tied to mine. Two *people*. Two personalities with different wants and needs, different pulls on my attention. In the span of two short weeks, I went from being alone, a perfectly coordinated timepiece, to being . . . what am I now? A father? A guardian? Christ help me, a husband?

No, we're not using that word.

Partner. Teddy O'Connor is my legal partner . . . at least until I can find a way to free him. Then I'll pursue finalizing Karolina's adoption on my own. Once the welfare court sees how happy she is with me, surely they must grant me full permanent custody.

But that's a problem for another day. Any moment now, the plane's side door will open, and I'll walk down the airstairs with the man I just legally married. Teddy O'Connor is my partner, which makes me gay. It's a lie, of course. When it comes to sexual attraction, I don't think I'm . . . well, anything, really. Is that even possible? To be attracted to no one? I've always just assumed there's something broken in me, some software update that never got properly installed.

"The stairs have a hydraulic lift," says Teddy, distracting me from my thoughts. "And Rachel arranged a medical transport to get her home. She'll be more comfortable than trying to get her into your sports car."

Shit. Why didn't I think of that? I drive a blue Porsche 718 Cayman. Ostentatious, I know. It was the one indulgence I allowed myself when I signed my first Rays contract. But it only has two doors. There's no way to get Karolina in and out safely. I suppose I need a more versatile vehicle now. I'll have my agent trade in the Porsche as soon as possible.

The flight attendant helps us get Karro's wheelchair ready at the top of the lift. Teddy makes the transfer, helping her get situated with her casted leg propped up. She holds tight to Teddy the Bear, looking so nervous as she tries to find a smile. I brush my hand over her hair. "Hey," I murmur in Swedish. "You know, you make me very happy."

She nods, giving her bear a tighter squeeze.

"I'm glad you're here with me, mitt lilla lamm. This is a new adventure for us both. Hold my hand?" I hold out my hand, and she takes it. I give hers a squeeze. "Don't let go." I nod at Teddy, and he smiles.

"Alright, Princess. Time to go greet your new loyal subjects. You ready with a royal wave? Hen, you gotta wave too."

"Why do I have to wave?"

"Because you're Princess Karolina's court jester." This makes Karro giggle.

"And what does that make you?"

"I'm her official food taster and popcorn maker," Teddy teases.

Below us, the crowd of Rays all smile and wave, calling out in greeting.

"Welcome home, Karlsson!"

"Hey, Karolina!"

"Välkommen hem," Lindberg shouts.

The flight attendant operates the lift, and we slowly begin our descent.

Teddy does a silly gesture with his hand that makes Karro laugh again. They're both all smiles, treating the lift like a rollercoaster as we glide slowly downward. I can't help but smile too. Shaking my head, I wave. A few people in the crowd laugh.

We get down to the bottom, and another attendant is ready to help us off the lift. Poppy's daughter rushes forward, her blonde ringlets bouncing as she holds out a sparkly pink crown. "This is for you, Lina."

"Oh, wow." Teddy drops to one knee. "So pretty. Want me to help you put it on, honey?" Karolina nods and he takes the crown from her, fixing it to the top of her head. "This is Grace," he adds, ruffling the little girl's curls. "And see her mommy right there? That's Miss Poppy. Doesn't she look just like a pretty Barbie?"

Poppy St. James looks as glamorous as ever in a bright purple dress and lilac high heels. With her curled blonde hair and bright pink lips, she really does look like a Barbie. "Oh, aren't you just a doll baby?" she coos, bending down with a smile. "I heard your favorite color is purple. Do you like my dress?" She does a little sway as Karolina smiles and nods, eyes wide.

Feeling protective, I give Karro's hand a squeeze. "She's a little shy."

Poppy laughs. "Well, my Grace'll fix that. Won't you, baby cakes?"

Langley's daughter isn't shy either. She charges forward with another gift, talking in fast English. I'm sure Karro can't fully understand. I would know Langley's girl anywhere by her bright red hair. Her mother's hair is just the same. Tess stands a few feet away, laughing and hugging Teddy.

As the little girls entertain Karro, the adults press forward. My teammates all welcome me home. Many of them shake my hand, offering their condolences. It doesn't escape my notice how warm everyone is with Teddy. He gets hugs, while I only get handshakes. And it's not just the players who welcome him. He knows their partners too. I hear him exclaim about how much some of the kids have grown since he last saw them, and I feel all over again the sting of his admonishment. I don't know these men, and they don't know me. They don't even know what to say to me other than "welcome back" and "sorry for your loss."

While I stand guard like a stone sentinel, gripping the back of Karolina's chair, Teddy is surrounded, playfully shoving Novy's arm off his shoulder and saying something that makes my teammates howl with laughter. How does he make it look so easy, so effortless?

While her men are busy laughing and teasing Teddy, Poppy steps in at my left.

"I'm sorry." The words blurt from my mouth. "I know this was reckless. I know I've made work for you."

She shakes her head. "Henrik, honey—"

"I had no other options." Lowering my voice, I turn slightly away from Karro. "They were pushing me to put her into the foster care system."

"I know." She pats my arm. "Honey, I'm not mad. You did what you had to do. Now we spin it in the most positive way we can. But all that can wait a day or two, okay? I just wanted to wish you a welcome home. You need anything, day or night, the team is here for you, Henrik."

"Thank you, Poppy."

She smiles. "Well, I think we've bothered these fine airport people long enough, don't you? Let's get you two home."

"Three," I correct.

Behind her oversized sunglasses, I can see the raise of her brows. "Three?"

"Teddy is coming home with me. He'll be living with us for now, until we figure out a plan of what to do."

She pats my arm again. "Well, that knocks the first thing off my to-do list for our PR crisis meeting. Which is scheduled for Monday morning, by the way. I'll expect you and your new husband in my office at nine o'clock. Don't be late." With that, she walks off to thank the ground crew.

By the time we get Karolina loaded into the medical transport, she's been showered with more gifts. She now has a sparkly necklace to match the tiara, a row of colorful beaded bracelets up her cast, a pink Minnie Mouse purse, and her first official Pelly the Pelican stuffed animal, the popular Rays mascot.

Rachel Price steps in behind me as I'm handing Teddy the bags. "Hey, if you give Ilmari your keys, he'll get your car back to the apartment so you can ride in the transport with Karolina."

I glance over my shoulder to see Ilmari Price towering behind his wife. Making eye contact, we both nod. He retired from the League a few years ago. He was one of the few men on the team who ever understood me. I think it must come from us both being Northern European. He never minded my silences. And he speaks excellent Swedish. It was such a relief to know there was always someone I could speak to without constantly doing the labor of active translation in my head.

"I don't want to inconvenience you," I say to him in Swedish.

"It's no inconvenience," he replies in English, surely for his wife's benefit. I've been doing the same thing with Teddy.

Rachel smiles, one hand on her pregnant belly. "He really doesn't mind. We're all headed that way anyway. Let us save you the trip back."

I glance between them. "You're headed which way?"

"To your apartment." At the look on my face, her smile falls. "Wait . . . did Tess not clear it with you first?"

Tension coils in my chest. "Clear what with me?"

Heaving a sigh, she calls out. "Tess!"

Langley's wife saunters over. "Hey, what's up?"

Rachel levels her with a stare. "Tess, why do I get the feeling that Karlsson here has no idea there's a potluck dinner happening at his house tonight?"

Tess schools her expression. "What, did Teddy not clear it with you?"

Teddy turns. "Did Teddy what? I just heard my name."

Rachel turns to him. "Teddy, did you not tell Karlsson about the plans for the potluck dinner?"

Catching my glare, Teddy's smile drops. "I—*you* said you cleared it with him," he cries, pointing a finger at Tess. "Henrik, I swear to god, it was all her idea. I said you'd just want a quiet night in, but she insisted. They *all* did."

"All?" I glance between them. "Exactly who is coming to my apartment tonight?"

There's a positive twinkle in Tess's eyes as she smiles. But it's Ilmari who answers my question in Swedish. "Everyone."

Everyone?

Fuck.

18

HENRIK

The first thing I notice when I arrive at my apartment? Someone—or many someones—have been inside it while I was away. My perfect, quiet apartment. My sanctuary. I own a top-floor corner unit with great views of the St. Johns River and the downtown Jacksonville skyline. The door opens into a spacious living room, walled on one side by glass that leads out to a private balcony. The other two walls are a crisp white.

Unlike my apartment in Stockholm, everything in this space is utilitarian—clean lines, minimal furniture, no decorations. Past the living room is the open-concept kitchen, also walled in on one side by glass.

Being on the top floor, my view is constantly changing, from morning golden light over the river to the colorful evening glow of the downtown skyline. Now, my walls of glass are covered in balloon arches—purple, white, and silver, with pops of bright yellow. There's a medieval feast's worth of food in my kitchen emitting a thousand new smells. And a horde of dirty shoes wait by the front door. Kids I don't know sit in my living room, watching my TV. How the hell did they all get in here? Who gave them a damn key?

"Breathe," Teddy murmurs, squeezing my hand as he passes. He leaves me by the front door, making his way deeper into the apartment, pushing Karolina in her wheelchair. There's a bit of commotion in the kitchen as those who weren't at the airport rush to greet them.

"What can I get you to drink, Karlsson?" one of the wives calls from behind the island.

The door behind me hits my shoulder as Paulie enters without knocking. "Hey, Karlsson. Welcome home, man." He pats my back as he passes, his Brazilian wife following with their baby asleep on her shoulder. Two more people come in after them.

"Oh *wow*," I hear Teddy call from down the hallway. "Henrik, you gotta come see this!"

"It's perfect," Karolina squeals in Swedish.

The excitement in her voice is the only thing that gets my feet moving. I cut across the living room and duck down the hall, stopping at the first open doorway. "What the . . ."

What was my plain-white home office has been transformed into a colorful princess room. The far wall has been painted to look like a mural from the movie with the girl with the long hair. It's actually quite impressive. There's a stone tower in one corner and fluffy clouds in the sky. A stream flows across the wall through a field of wildflowers, disappearing behind the bed.

That's new too. There was no bed in here before. It's canopied with frilly white curtains, framed by twinkle lights. The bedding is a bright purple, with delicate little flowers on her sheets.

Where the hell is my desk? And the computer? And my exercise bike?

"Look! Pascal!" I glance down to see Karolina clutching a new stuffed animal shaped like the chameleon from the movie. She hugs him tight, holding him like he's the most precious of treasures. Then she looks up at me, her smile blinding as she says in Swedish, "Thanks, Morbror. I love it."

She looks so happy, I can't help but smile. Reaching down, I brush my knuckles gently over her cheek. "You're welcome, mitt lilla lamm."

Oblivious to our Swedish, Tess's daughter throws open the doors of the closet to reveal a trove of new clothes, princess gowns, and more toys. "Look over here, Lina. You've got a Barbie playhouse! I picked it out!" She roots around inside the walk-in closet, dragging out a large pink-and-yellow Barbie house, much to the delight of Karolina.

Tess and Rachel stand in the corner of the room with Teddy. A few more wives squeeze in the doorway behind me, and then Tess walks us all through the features of the room. I'm most interested in the new corner-mounted nanny camera and the fully automated bed that will fold up and let Karolina sleep in a seated position that won't strain her ribs.

Feeling deeply moved by this consideration, I cross over to Tess. "You will send me the bill."

She just waves her hand. "No way. It was too much fun. We were all happy to chip in."

"I would appreciate being able to pay you back."

But Tess is firm. "Save your money for when her ballet lessons start again. Trust me, all your paychecks will go to tutus and pointe shoes. Then you'll be dreaming of the day you got a free room makeover." Her cheery confidence falters as she takes in my harried expression. "Seriously, it's okay, Karlsson. I was happy to help."

"Well . . . thank you," I mutter, unable to say more. I offer out my hand, and she shakes it.

"You're welcome. But really, you should thank Teddy. This was all his idea."

I stiffen, swallowing the nerves humming in my chest. "I'll want my apartment key back," I say before she can move away. The corner of her mouth tips with a smirk. We both know I've never given a copy of my key to anyone in this city. "How did you get it?"

She laughs. "Turns out your doorman was easy to bribe. All it took was some of Poppy's famous salted-caramel chocolate-chunk pretzel cookies and one of Ryan's old jerseys signed by the team." She pats my shoulder and walks away, eager to show the other wives the en suite bathroom makeover.

I turn my attention to Teddy. He stands in the corner with a soft smile on his lips, watching the little girls put Barbies in Karro's lap. They all talk at once, showing her the different dolls and their accessories. She holds Teddy the Bear and Pascal, delighted by all the attention, the little jeweled crown perched crooked on her head.

I step closer to Teddy, lowering my voice. "You did all this."

He winces, bracing for my anger. Am I really so much of a bear?

"I mean, if we wanna get technical, Tess did it. Or she hired the people who did it."

I cross my arms, mirroring his stance. "But it was your idea, wasn't it? You told her what to do. You knew what Karro would like best."

He shrugs. "I just wanted her to come home to a place ready for some good memories. She's had enough of the bad ones for a while. Don't you think?"

When I say nothing, too overcome to speak, he steps in closer. "Hey, are you really mad? I can have them put everything back the way it was. I'll even paint it back myself. I'll—"

I silence him with a hug, surprising us both with the action.

He sucks in a breath, leaning away.

"Thank you," I say against his shoulder. "Thank you, Teddy."

His arm wraps around me. "Wait, so you're not mad at me?"

"I was," I admit. "But I'm not anymore."

With a nervous laugh, he relaxes further, properly hugging me back with both arms. "Well, good. 'Cause that would have been a major dick move. This room is fucking awesome. I might just sleep in here too."

I chuckle, feeling the rumble of his laugh against my chest. It's odd to smell my cologne on him. Odd, but not unpleasant. He's actually wearing one of my sweaters too. He ran out of clean clothes yesterday, but we were both too tired to do any laundry, not with our early flight planned for this morning. I told him to take whatever he wanted from my closet instead. He took my favorite cable-knit sweater. I run my hand down his back, feeling the ridges of the knit design.

One of the women dramatically coughs, and Teddy and I break apart with a jolt.

"Do you two need a minute?" Paulie's wife teases.

Her friend laughs. Behind her, Tess's smile falls. She glances between us, her gaze settling on me. All of a sudden, it feels like she's looking at me like I'm a wolf loose in the room. Next to her, Rachel looks at Teddy like he's the sheep I intend to eat.

Feeling self-conscious under their weighted stares, I step away from him.

19

HENRIK

$\mathcal{S}$omehow, I survive the evening. Practically everyone from the team filters through my apartment, including some of the support staff friendly with Teddy. They all leave gifts for Karolina and food in the fridge. The food is good, I'll admit. And I now have enough alcohol to last me through the rest of my NHL career.

When it's clear Karolina has reached the limit of her endurance, falling asleep on the couch with one hand still in the popcorn bowl, the adults begin cleanup. I keep offering to help, but I'm endlessly rebuffed.

By eight o'clock, my fridge is stocked fit to burst, my kitchen is spotless, my living room is vacuumed, the balloons have disappeared, and every pair of shoes by the door is claimed and removed by its owner. Teddy puts Karolina to bed while I see the last of the guests to the door with many repeated words of "thanks" and "no really" and "too kind."

Shutting the door as the last of them leave, I hardly have the energy to turn around and lean against it for support. I think I might be a little drunk. Wives kept putting beers and plates of food in my hand all night. I ate my weight in taco dip and drank so much, my fingertips feel numb.

Teddy appears at the end of the hall. He's shuffling too, fatigue making his shoulders heavy. He catches my eye and stops. Crossing his arms, he leans against the corner and looks around the now-spotless living room. "Long day."

"Exceptionally long."

"But a good one, right?"

I purse my lips, saying nothing.

He sighs. "They just want to be there for you, Hen. For Karolina. They're all trying, and you have to give them that. Besides, you want her to have family here, right? Friends? You saw Emma Langley tonight. She cried when they dragged her away. Unless I'm mistaken, Karro just made a friend for life."

"You know all their names."

He shrugs. "Well, I mean, not *all* of them. I met a bunch of the new wives and girlfriends tonight. Like, I'd never met Paulie's wife before."

"But you know them now. And you know their kids. You know all their names and ages."

"Yeah, I guess. There aren't that many, so it's not like it's hard."

Pushing off the door, I cross over to the couch and sit down. "Will you teach me?"

"Teach you?"

"Teach me their names. I want to know."

"What, now? Like, right now?"

I lean back against the cushions with a groan. "No. I've had too many beers to try to remember anyone's name besides my own tonight."

He joins me on the couch. "Good. Because I think I forgot them all anyway. Man, jet lag is a bitch, huh? Can you believe we started this day in Sweden?" He glances around the apartment. "Hey, can I ask you something?"

I hum my assent.

"Where's all your stuff?"

"What do you mean?"

He sits forward, gesturing around at the simple furnishings of the living room. "I mean, if I hadn't seen your secret loft in Stockholm, I wouldn't know this apartment belonged to the same person. There's nothing here, Henrik. No books, no camera stuff, no art. Where's all your stuff?"

I just shrug. "I don't live here."

He laughs.

"What?"

"Hen, that makes no fucking sense. You spend more time living here than you do in Sweden."

"I *work* here," I correct. "My life is in Sweden. It will always be in Sweden."

"Wow."

"What?"

"Oh, nothing."

I sit forward with another tired groan. "A noise from you is always something. What does the 'wow' mean?"

He dares to roll his eyes at me. "Okay, it means, 'Wow, I had no idea you were a fourth-degree black belt in compartmentalization.' I suspected it, obviously. But this is off the freaking charts, even for you."

"What?"

"Henrik, you've put literal *living* in a box. And apparently that box stays in Sweden. So, this place is . . . what? Where you just power down like a robot? Rest and refuel between games?"

"Pretty much."

He snorts another laugh. "Let me guess, you're a Virgo. No wait—" He holds up a hand. "Oh god, don't tell me you're a Capricorn."

"I have no idea what you're talking about." I've lost track of how many times I've said that to him over the last two weeks.

"When's your birthday, Henrik?"

"January ninth. Why?"

"Yep." He slaps both his thighs as he slowly bends forward and stands. "That explains it."

"Explains what?"

"I'm fake married to a Capricorn. It's my own fault, really. I made this bed of thorns, and now I'm gonna lie in it."

Virgos and Capricorns? I understand now. In my tired state, it took me a moment to translate it in my head. "You believe in the zodiac?"

"And you don't, right? Typical Cappy." With that, he wanders off towards the kitchen.

"What makes you think I resemble a Capricorn?" I call after him.

He turns around, both hands raised. "Look, I don't think either of us is sober enough to open this particular can of worms tonight, okay?"

I rise to my feet, wobbling only slighting. "Go on, tell me."

"Fine. Where to start?" He ticks each point off on his fingers. "How about being a super serious workaholic who is inflexible, stubborn, a total pessimist—oh, and totally repressive towards feeling his own emotions?"

I cross my arms, glaring at him. "A damning list of faults, to be sure. Have I any virtues in your eyes, *partner*?"

He blinks, swaying a little too. I sense the exact moment he doubles the defenses on his high walls. Damn, how does he do that so fast? "I can't remember."

My irritation rises. "You're lying to me. What did I say about lying?"

He groans, turning away. "Look, it's late. And I've still gotta call an Uber."

My annoyance pops like a balloon. "Wait—you're leaving?"

"Well, yeah."

I follow him, my heart suddenly racing. "Teddy, it's late. We've been traveling all day. Where are you going?"

"My hotel." He ducks behind the side of the couch, grabbing his blue duffel and backpack off the floor.

Alcohol and fatigue are making my brain feel foggy. "Why would you go to a hotel?"

Teddy turns, searching my face as if I'm now the one with acute memory problems. "Because I *live* there. Or at least I was living there, remember? Vicki set me up in hotel until my unit at the team apartments was ready. But now I don't need it because I'm moving here."

"So then why are you leaving?"

"Because look around." He waves with his free hand. "Do you see any of my stuff here? It's all over at the hotel. I gotta go get it and bring it here."

"I still don't see why you need to do that tonight. You're tired, Teddy. We both are. Surely it can wait until morning."

He shifts his weight, not looking at me.

I step in closer. "What's wrong?"

"I'm out of clean clothes, remember? We couldn't do laundry because we were traveling, so I've got nothing to wear. Come on, it's no big deal," he adds, stepping around me. "I'll only be gone for one night. I'll do laundry, get my shit, and be back tomorrow. Besides, you're a natural with Karro. You don't need me here to do a wheel-chair transfer, right?"

"No," I admit. Because he's right. I don't *need* him here. Not so long as my schedule allows me to stay with Karro.

"Anyway, I'm sure you're dying to get me out of your hair, right? Don't think I didn't see you climbing the walls all night having strangers in your crib. I'd take it back if I could but . . . well, it's too late now," he finishes under his breath.

I don't even realize that I've followed him to the door. "Teddy . . ."

"Really, it's okay. You're a private person, and that's totally cool. If I felt more sober, I'd just drive myself over there. But an Uber works too. Why don't you shoot me a text in the morning, or whenever, and we'll make a plan from there? I'll only come back when you're ready. That cool?"

He goes to open the door. He gets as far as turning the knob and pulling it in an inch. Then I'm right behind him. Reaching over his shoulder, I push the door shut. "Stay."

He stiffens, hand still on the knob. I practically have him pinned between me and the door. "What are you doing?"

"Stay," I say again. "You're tired, and I think you're a little drunk. I'd feel better if you stayed."

"I need my stuff. Henrik, I gotta change my clothes."

"I have everything you need here. Please. What's mine is yours, you know that." He should know it. He's standing here now in my sweater and jeans, a spritz of my cologne at his neck.

He groans, pressing his forehead to the door. "Will you stop being so damn polite? I know you want me out, okay?"

Christ, is that what this is about? I drop my left hand down from the door and place it on his right shoulder. "Look at me, Teddy."

He lets himself be turned, back pressed against the door. "What do you want from me, huh?" His green eyes are narrowed, jaw tight. His stance is almost defiant. I know what he's doing. He gave it away with his little speech. This isn't about needing clean clothes. He had no problem hunting through my "fly as fuck" closet back in Stockholm. He's running from me because I made him think I don't want him here.

I hold his gaze, my hand still on his shoulder. "I'm not mad at you."

"Man, whatever." He tries to turn away. "I'll just see you in the morning—"

I press in as he turns, pinning him to the door.

He drops his bags, both hands going to the door as he pushes back with his hips. "Henrik—*fuck*—"

"I want you here."

He groans. "Come on, man, don't."

"Fuck the others. Having them all here was admittedly very difficult for me. Because you're right—I'm a private person. I don't like sharing my spaces with anyone."

"So then let me leave," he says, his tone almost pleading.

I drop both hands down to his shoulders. "Not until you understand the difference."

"What difference?"

"You are not anyone to me," I pant. "Not anymore."

The fight goes out of him as he presses himself to the door. "Then what am I?"

Christ, what a loaded question. Do I even know the nature of what Teddy is? Of what he's becoming? Six years ago, Teddy was the silly intern who walked into traffic. Two weeks ago, he was the kind soul who tethered me to reality when I received the worst news of my life. Last week, he was the friend who helped me grieve for my sister and my mother. This morning, he revealed himself to be a valuable partner, someone who thinks through the things I overlook, like decorating Karro's room to make it feel like home.

"What am I, Henrik?" he asks again.

I give him the only answer I have. "You're someone. You're *my* someone. And I want to take care of you. Please, Teddy—you've been taking care of me so well for weeks now. Let me return the favor. Don't drive off in the dark to go sit alone in an empty hotel room. *Stay.* Stay here with me and let me take care of you for a change."

He sighs, shoulders sagging with resignation.

I sigh too, but in relief. Pushing off the door, I give him the space to fully turn. He eyes me warily, clearly unsure what to do next. I offer out my hand. "Come."

"What are you gonna do?"

"Just come with me."

He places his hand in mine, and I lead him down the length of the apartment, back towards the kitchen. Cutting left, we take the second hall that splits between the laundry and hall bathroom on one side and my bedroom suite on the other.

Teddy's feet shuffle as he walks behind me. "Henrik, seriously, what are you doing?"

"Showing you my favorite room in the house."

"I swear to god, if you have a red room back here . . ."

"What's a red room?"

He snorts. That's all I get for an answer as I lead him first into my bedroom. Like the rest of the apartment, the walls are white, not red. The furnishings are simple, just a pair of long and tall dressers and a king-sized bed on a platform frame. One wall is full glass that I can fog over with the touch of a button. It offers the best view of the sunset over the river.

Teddy looks around, his gaze landing on the bed. "Henrik . . ."

"Come," I say again, leading him through into the bathroom.

"Whoa." He stops in the doorway and looks around. The bathroom is almost as large as the bedroom. The short wall by the door features a natural wood vanity with a deep-sided basin sink. A lighted mirror hangs over the sink, reflecting the colorful lights of the city skyline. The longest wall is glass from floor to ceiling.

"It's one-way," I assure him. "No one can see in."

He steps into the room and half turns. "It's impressive."

I walk over to the deep, soaking tub, leaning my hip against the side. There's a stone-walled shower with double shower heads too. And in the far corner, near the door to the large walk-in closet, there's a therapeutic home spa with steam and dry-heat functions. "This is my favorite room in the apartment. I designed it."

He nods, still looking around. "Yep, I can see that."

"What do you mean?"

"I mean, it's so . . . you." He points to the corner. "Is that a personal freaking sauna?"

"Yes. And the tub is deep enough to fully submerge your body. You can do ice treatments, hot baths. Perfect for rehabilitation, muscle relaxation, and improved circulation."

He smiles. "It's a very nice bathroom, Henrik."

"It's yours now. As is the room just outside. And anything in this closet." I walk over and tap the button that opens the sliding mirrored door, revealing my deep and wide walk-in closet. The feature lights come on automatically, glowing golden over the sleek back row of designer suits, all arranged by color. The right wall is a menagerie of shirts and folded sweaters, shoes, and stacks of slacks and denim. The left, shortest side is almost exclusively athletic wear.

"Fuck me," Teddy mutters, unable to hide his look of glee. We discovered back in Stockholm that we wear the same size in everything but pants, even down to shoes.

"If you can't find something to your liking in this closet, then there's a bathrobe hanging on the back of the door." I point it out for him. "Give me an hour, and I'll have all your clothes washed and ready for you. I'll fold them and place them on the bed."

"Henrik . . ."

I walk back over to the tub and turn on the hot water tap.

His eyes go wide. "What are you doing?"

Reaching under the sink, I pull out a fluffy white towel. "I'm drawing you a bath."

"What?"

"I'm drawing you a bath," I repeat.

"Why?"

"Because you're exhausted. You've pushed yourself to the limit these last two weeks. You deserve to take a rest. Please, allow me this."

He glances around again, hands fisted in his pockets. "Lemme get this straight . . . You want me to sit in your tub and wear your designer pajamas while you do my damn laundry?"

"Yes."

He just blinks.

"Would you like a beer while you relax? Some wine maybe? Music?"

The sound of the filling tub breaks the silence stretching between us as I wait, giving Teddy time to decide what he wants.

"I . . . A beer would be nice," he finally says.

"What kind? I think we have enough to open our own pub at the moment."

His mouth tips with a smile. "Maybe an IPA? Something pale and hoppy. Novy has good taste. I'll have one of whatever he brought."

"And music?"

He shrugs. "I can just play something on my phone."

"This room has Bluetooth speakers. Feel free to connect." Stepping past him, I head back to the kitchen. I spy his blue duffel by the front door, grab it, and do as I promised, starting a load of his laundry. Then I go hunt down some toiletries from the guest bathroom, making sure he has everything he needs.

By the time I return with his frothy beer in a cold glass, the water is off, Teddy is in the tub, and music is softly playing over the speakers. I recognize the artist. It's Norah Jones. I think I have one of her records back at my loft.

Teddy has his locs pulled up, piled high on his head in a messy bun. As I watch from the doorway, he sits forward in the tub with a tired groan, rolling both his shoulders until they crack. Then he sinks back, water sloshing. I knock on the half-open door, making him jolt.

"Uhh . . . come in," he calls over his shoulder. "I thought you must have fallen asleep out on the couch or something."

"I was just giving you some privacy."

One of his dark brows arches. "Privacy in your room? In your tub?"

"It's your room now," I remind him.

"Henrik, come on. You have to let up on your stupid rule. This bathroom is great but let me stay in the guest room. Honestly, I'll be fine in there."

I just stare him down. He's the one who called me stubborn, right? Inflexible? "Are you going to lift any of *your* rules?"

At this challenge, he stiffens, not daring to look at me. "No," he says in a soft voice.

"Then the room is yours. And here." I offer him the glass of beer.

Reaching an arm out over the deep side of the tub, he takes it. The tub blocks all but his head and shoulders from my view. "Thanks."

"How's the tub?"

He groans again, sinking back into the steaming hot water. "So fucking good. I can't remember the last time I got neck deep in a tub that wasn't a gross hotel hot tub. I like knowing no kid in shark float-ies has peed in here recently."

I chuckle. "No kids have touched this tub. Just me. And now you."

He stills, his lips touching the rim of his beer glass. Slowly, he takes a sip of the frothy golden pale ale. "You have to stop feeling so bad about all this."

"What?"

"You have to stop," he says again. "Stop feeling so sad and guilty, and like you've trapped me here against my will. It makes me feel like we're doing something wrong. And this isn't wrong . . . right?" He looks up at me. His cheeks and brow sheened from the steam of the bath.

"No," I reply. "This isn't wrong."

He offers me a smile, nodding at the glass in his hand. "The beer is really good."

"I'll be sure to tell Novikov."

"Tell him in front of Morrow, and you may just get a show."

"What?"

"Nothing."

We're both quiet for a moment.

"Hey, Henrik?"

I perk up. "Yeah?"

"You gonna stand there all night and watch me sit here naked in your tub?"

Warmth rises in my cheeks as I quickly turn away. "No, of course not. I—good night, Teddy."

"I mean, you can," he teases. "It's still your house, right?"

"I said no."

"Pull up a chair. Hey, do you have any shark floaties I can borrow?"

"Good night, Teddy," I say more forcefully, shutting the door as I leave.

20

TEDDY

"**M**orbror?" The baby monitor on my bedside table crackles, waking me up. A soft voice echoes around my room. "Morbror? Jag behöver hjälp."

I sit up, rubbing my face.

Oh fuck.

Realizing where I am and why, I lunge for the monitor. Karro's awake. Poor thing is probably as jet-lagged as we are. I don't know what she's saying in Swedish, but I imagine it likely has something to do with using the bathroom.

Ignoring my own call of nature, I shrug on a T-shirt and hurry from my room, leaving the monitor on the dresser. I trot through the kitchen and weave around the sofas in the living room. Ducking down the hall, I stop in her doorway to see Henrik already in her room. He's crouching down beside her bed. They talk softly in Swedish. He pets her messy blonde hair as he helps her sit up.

"Hey," I say, stepping into the room. "Need any help?"

"I think we're fine." Henrik shifts her to the side of the bed. He uses the technique I taught him in Sweden to keep her ribs from twisting. Then he's helping her shimmy up her nightdress and positioning the bed pan for her.

"I can help you get her to the bathroom," I offer. "Less chance of a mess."

"I have this," he replies. "Thank you, Teddy."

Feeling dismissed, I step out of the room and make my way back to the kitchen. Determined to do something helpful, I start on breakfast.

I've chopped up fruit and veggies for smoothies and I'm in the middle of frying a couple eggs when Henrik comes into the kitchen.

"What are you doing?" he asks, heading for the coffee maker.

"Making us breakfast. You want two eggs or three?"

"I already ate."

I peer around at the spotless kitchen. "When?"

"I've been up since five," he replies. "In truth, I never really slept."

I wiggle the eggs a little with the spatula, unsticking them from the bottom of the pan. "More nightmares?"

He just shrugs, clicking on the coffee maker.

"How's our girl doing?"

He rustles around in the cabinet above the coffee maker. "She says her leg is hurting her more today than yesterday. Is that normal?"

I flip the eggs, trying my best not to overcook them. "Pain is normal. Some days it may feel achy, like a deep throbbing. Other days it might feel sharp and sort of piercing. The good thing is that these are all healing pains. We can up her meds a little today if you want, just as she's still transitioning and getting on a new sleep schedule. But it's important we start to wean her off the hard stuff. How many eggs will she eat?"

"None."

"What?"

"She doesn't like eggs."

I look down at the eggs frying in the pan. "Well, I guess these are all for me then."

"Sorry, I should have told you."

"It's no problem." Using the spatula, I scrape the fried eggs onto a plate. "Maybe we should make a list of foods she does like to eat, just so I know for the future."

He nods. His shoulders are so tense, and he looks so tired as he makes a note in his phone.

"I really *can* help, you know. That's why I'm here, remember? You don't have to do this all alone."

He smiles, but it doesn't touch his eyes. "Karro is my responsibility, Teddy."

"And I totally respect that. You get final say in all matters Karro.

I'm just saying you're not alone in caring for her. I'm here. So, you know, put me in, Coach."

His smile has a little more warmth now. "I appreciate that."

I cross my arms, leaving the eggs to cool on the counter as I lean against it. "So, what's on the agenda for today?"

The coffee maker hums as a fresh brew pours into the waiting mug. "Hanna Nilsson comes this morning," he replies. "She should be here in thirty minutes."

"Hanna Nilsson?"

"She's a registered nurse, licensed for in-home care. She's coming to interview for the position of Karolina's temporary caretaker."

I blink. "Oh. Well, did you need me to look over her résumé or anything? I can vet her qualifications for you."

"Already done. She came highly recommended by my agent. I had Laura run a search and collect names and résumés. Same for Karolina's in-home tutor. I'll meet with her on Tuesday."

Laura Miller is Henrik's sports agent. She's sort of his American Elin. She helps him with his NHL contracts and all his North American endorsement deals. He told me a bit about it on the plane ride back over from Sweden. "Well, it looks like you've got it all under control. If we've got company coming over, I'm gonna eat this breakfast and go get cleaned up. Does Karro still need some breakfast?"

"I'll take care of it."

Right.

Smiling through this awkward tension, I turn away. Nothing about this transition was ever going to be easy. Henrik is so used to having his own way. I get the impression that everything has been on his shoulders for a long time. Even when Petra was alive, he was the life raft that kept them all from sinking. I guess when you're used to treading water, even a lifesaver feels like nothing but a rope trying to drag you down.

I'm deep in Henrik's closet, ogling his impressive watch collection, when the doorbell rings. The in-home nurse candidate is here. Checking my fit in the floor-length mirror, I nod at my reflection. Until I get over to the hotel to grab the rest of my stuff, all I have are the clothes I packed for Sweden. At least Henrik washed them for me.

I enter the living room in my jeans, T-shirt, and bare feet. I stop at the edge of the sofa, eyes wide, as I take in the smiling face of the prettiest woman I've ever seen shaking Henrik's hand. She's young and blonde, with perfect white skin, straight teeth, and sparkly blue eyes. Her smile lights up the whole dang apartment. In her matching pink scrub set, she looks like a literal Disney princess: healthcare edition.

It takes a moment for my brain to process what's happening. Wait . . . is she Swedish? They're definitely not speaking English right now. And why is Henrik still shaking her hand?

Actually, it looks like she's the one holding *his* hand. Their right hands are clasped, and her left hand is folded over his, giving it an emphatic squeeze as she says . . . well, god knows what. He's nodding along, talking with his voice low. The Swedish flows out of him like a song.

Meanwhile, I stand here feeling like a totally useless asshole. I almost miss it when she turns her attention on me. "And you must be Doctor O'Connor. Mr. Karlsson here has spoken very highly of you," she adds, batting her lashes at him.

Apparently, Nurse Hanna knows about me. But I know literally nothing about her. Except that her English is flawless. Her accent is completely American. "Are you Swedish?"

Her smile brightens. "I am. Or I should say my mother is. I have dual citizenship, but I was born here."

"Please," says Henrik, gesturing for her to sit.

She floats into the room, dropping onto the edge of the sofa. She sticks to English for my benefit, but her attention is all on Henrik. "So, you said you're looking for someone with a flexible schedule. Someone who can cover day or night, including the possible overnight?"

"Yes, exactly," says Henrik. "My schedule is quite variable, so I need someone with a high degree of flexibility. I will give you as much notice as I can, but things do tend to be added last minute."

"That's totally fine," she replies. "I believe I mentioned on the phone that I'm between jobs at the moment, so I have the flexibility to make Karolina my top priority."

"Between jobs?" I say. "What does that mean?"

She turns to me. "I've decided to pursue my doctorate in nursing. My program won't start until the spring, and the contract I was on with my last job was set to either renew or expire. I chose to let it expire." She turns back to Henrik. "Which means I can make myself fully available to you, if you still want me."

Her suggestion sinks like an arrow into my chest. I know she didn't mean it to sound like an advance, but it's been a hell of a two weeks. I'm jet-lagged, real married to a fake husband, and now he's looking at her like she's the answer to all his problems. "How old are you?"

Both she and Henrik turn my way. "I'm thirty-two," she replies, still smiling.

Meanwhile, Henrik is looking at me like I've just grown two heads.

"Are you married? Do you have any kids?" Yep, I'm still talking, apparently.

"I don't see how that's relevant to her employment," says Henrik. "So long as she performs her tasks, her private life is her own."

Hanna just laughs, flicking her blonde braid off her shoulder in a very Poppy-like way. "I don't mind." She turns to me. "No, Doctor O'Connor, I'm not married. And I don't have kids. But I have a lot of experience working in pediatric nursing."

Of course she does. And I bet birds help her wrap bandages while squirrels administer medications.

"Any hobbies?" I say, determined to dig my hole just a little deeper.

Henrik gives me the universal glare for "shut the fuck up."

I just look to Hanna, hands folded primly in my lap.

"I'm a runner," she replies. "Does that count? I try to run five to ten miles every day. And I love Disney World. I have an annual pass, and I run all their marathons. Well, as many as I can manage. Did you know some of them sell out in seconds? It's very competitive."

Of fucking course she loves Disney World. They probably just let her in without paying.

"Would you like to meet Karolina?" says Henrik, clearly trying to get his interview back on track.

Her eyes brighten. "Oh, I'd love to."

I stay seated on the couch as Henrik leads her away. The second they cross into the hallway, they switch back to Swedish. Once Hanna enters Karro's room and I hear the way Hanna exclaims with delight, I know it's all over for me. The world's most perfect Swedish nanny is about to swoop in and steal my fake family right out from under me.

Within the hour, Henrik is escorting Hanna back to the front door, shaking her hand for the fifth time, as he assures her that she does indeed have the job and he does, in fact, expect her to start tomorrow. She waves goodbye at me, still all smiles, and leaves.

Henrik stays at the door, his hand pressed flat above the lock. I consider making a run for it, but then he turns, eyes blazing. "What the hell was that?"

"What?" I feign ignorance as I rise off the couch.

"You had no right to question her like that, Teddy. She was here as *my* guest. And why were you so rude?"

Dropping all pretense, I flap my arms. "I'm sorry, I guess I just find it hard to believe that you would trust your sports agent to vet an in-home nursing candidate more than me, the literal doctor of physical therapy."

"Laura has been with me for seven years!"

"Yeah, and loyalty to the Karlsson brand means fucking *nothing* when it comes to providing medical care to an injured child!"

He reels back. "You don't trust Hanna to care for Karolina?"

"I don't know! I haven't seen her résumé. All I know is that she speaks Swedish and runs in circles around EPCOT."

He groans, leaning against the door. "Teddy, I'm doing the best I can."

"I'm sorry, but in this particular instance, I have to beg to differ."

"What do you mean?"

He wants me to say it? Okay, I'm gonna fucking say it. "Henrik, doing your best doesn't always mean doing it all on your own. When it comes to caring for another person, if you're out of your depth, doing your best means relying on the reasoned opinions of experts. I mean, do you trust your sports agent to do your taxes?"

He sighs. "No."

"Do you trust your sports agent to examine your prostate?"

"No, Teddy."

"Then *why* would you trust your sports agent to select Karro's caretaker over me?"

I let my question hang in the air between us.

Softening my tone, I close the distance between us. "Look, maybe this is all gonna be great. Maybe Hanna really is as perfect as she seems. God, I hope so. Karro deserves someone with her sweetness to float in here and make every day feel like the best day."

"Well, if you liked Hanna, then what's the problem?" he all but shouts.

"My problem is you pushing me aside! You did it this morning with Karro's toileting care. You did it at breakfast. You did it again by not including me in Hanna's selection, not even asking my opinion. I mean, we've been together every hour of every day for the last two weeks. When did you even get résumés? When did you review them? On the plane? When I was sitting right next to you?"

He dares to shrug, tucking his hands in his pockets. "I didn't want to bother you."

"Well, fuck, Henrik. Next time, bother me! All I was doing was watching reruns of *Charmed* on my iPad. Karolina's care is a little more important than finding out if Cole and Phoebe will ever find their way back to each other!"

He sighs. "I've never been any good at this, okay?"

"Good at what?"

"Letting people in. Letting them help me. I'm always the one others rely on."

"Oh, yeah, that's crystal fucking clear. That's why we're talking about it now. Because I'm *here*, Henrik," I say for what feels like the hundredth time. "It's my name on those custody papers too. Yours and mine. I'll defer to you when it comes to Karro's care, but

I'm also gonna demand that I at least get to be part of the process. For as long as I'm here, I'm the first thought. Not the afterthought. Agreed?"

After a moment of deliberation, he nods. "I accept those terms. And I'm sorry, Teddy. Truly."

"Well . . . good. Then I accept your apology."

The last of the tension between us fizzles away.

Looking for any way to salvage the rest of the day, I perk up. "Hey, wanna get dressed and take Karro out for lunch? Then we can swing by the hotel and pick up the rest of my stuff. We'll all fit in my Subaru."

His gaze darts down the dark hallway. We both know Karro is sitting safe in bed watching a movie. "I'm not sure I want to move her."

"Oh, Mr. Karlsson, please?" I bat my lashes like pretty Nurse Hanna. He just rolls his eyes and I laugh. "Come on, man. She's not made of glass. And this is her first official day in Florida, remember? Worry can wait a few more hours. Let's go get hot dogs at the beach and show her the pelicans."

I know he's weighing my idea against the million and one things he has ricocheting around in his head. He has urgent calls to make. Hot dogs aren't in his diet. Karro can't be moved. There are sharks in the ocean. He doesn't trust my beat-up old Subaru. Suffice it to say, I fully expect him to say no.

Surprising the heck out of me, he nods. "Yeah, okay. Hot dogs at the beach sounds nice."

11

TEDDY

"**H**ere." Henrik turns away from the coffee cart to hand me my orgasm in a cup. It's my first proper coffee in weeks. I immediately take a sip, savoring the sweet, nutty taste.

"Fuck, that's good." My eyes close as I enjoy a second sip.

It's Monday morning, and the practice center is hopping. Figure skaters fill the lobby, tying their laces and talking excitedly with friends. The little girls look so cute in their '80s leg warmers and scoop-necked sweatshirts. Over at the bigger rink, the hockey boys are already out on the ice doing drills. The bite of a shrill whistle echoes in the rafters.

Henrik leads the way over to the Rays admin wing and flashes his badge on the access panel. We walk down the long hallway, angling for the elevators. He checks his smartwatch. He's been doing it every four minutes since we left the apartment.

"Relax," I say, pressing the elevator Up button. "I'm sure she's fine."

Today is the first day Karolina is being left alone with Nurse Hanna, who is still so pretty and perfect, it's actually a little annoying. Like, she doesn't have to be *that* pretty, right? She could tone it down.

"What's wrong?" Henrik asks, as we both step into the elevator.

"Nothing."

I'm jealous of our nanny.

"Something's wrong," he mutters, sipping his coffee.

I fake rotating my shoulder. "Just a little tight. I think I slept funny."

Another lie. They come so easily now. Henrik's bed is like sleeping on a literal fucking cloud. I'm getting the best sleep of my life.

The elevator doors open, and we make our way down the hall to the PR office suite. A young, Chad-looking kid sits at the front desk. "Hey, can I help you?"

"Henrik Karlsson and Teddy O'Connor to see Poppy St. James," Henrik replies.

Chad does a double take. "Whoa. You're, like, a player."

Snorting into my coffee, I roll my eyes. "Dude, where do you think you are right now? Of course he's a fucking player."

Henrik raises a brow at me. And yeah, whatever, I'm on edge. Our perfect nanny made my fake husband oatmeal this morning with freshly cut peaches and a swirl of cinnamon. He doesn't want my eggs, but he definitely wants her oatmeal.

I mean, sure, she made me some too. And it was fucking delicious. But she served Henrik his bowl in Swedish. For all I know, she was complimenting his dick.

I take another sip of my coffee as Chad presses the intercom button on his office phone. "Hey, Poppy. Some guys are here to see you."

The phone beeps. "Trevor, honey, what did we say about using guests' names?"

"Uhh . . ." Poor fucking Trevor. He glances over the desk at us, pushing the button again. "It's Karlsson and . . ."

"Teddy O'Connor," Henrik repeats, pronouncing each syllable of my name.

Poppy appears in the doorway. "Well, if it isn't my two favorite newlyweds!" Then she's ushering us into her fancy corner office. "I'd ask if I can have Trevor get you anything, but I see you already stopped by the coffee cart. Please, have a seat."

I follow Henrik's lead and sit next to him on the couch.

Poppy takes the nearest chair, sinking onto it with a sigh, both hands bracing her pregnant belly. "How's Karolina settling in so far?"

"Well," Henrik replies. "Her nurse started today. I think she'll be a good fit."

"That's wonderful. She's such a sweet little girl. Grace hasn't stopped asking when they can play together again."

When Henrik doesn't respond, I give him a nudge.

Catching my hint, he sits forward. "Yes, we should set that up. Your daughter is welcome to my home anytime."

"Oh, she'll be so glad," she replies with smile.

And because I'm in that much of a mood, I smirk, taking another sip of my coffee. "Trevor seems nice."

Her smile falls. "Don't get me started."

I snort. "Come on, spill the beans, Pop. How did you get stuck with him? Don't tell me his last name is Talbot."

She crosses her arms over her belly. "A nephew, or so I'm told. And I'm giving him exactly *one* more day to learn how phones work before I march him up to Mark's office by his stupid, floppy surfer-boy hair." She takes a deep breath, then lets it out. "But we're not here to talk about my seemingly endless staffing problems. We're here to talk about you, about your delicate situation."

I force a laugh. "Delicate situation? Jeez, you make it sound like we're made of glass over here."

"The analogy isn't far off," she replies. "Announcing a player's coming-out can be tricky enough. Add in a surprise adoption and a quickie marriage, and this is a recipe for chaos. If even one of our cards is out of alignment, this whole house collapses. And I'm not just talking about the two of you."

Henrik and I exchange a glance. "What *are* you talking about?" I ask for both of us.

"I'm talking about the dangerous precedent you've set. I'm talking about the potential ramifications that could spiral outward, engulfing us all. This is so much bigger than you now. You understand that, right?"

I watch the way her hands guard her baby bump, and a bolt of shame zaps me in the chest. I set my coffee aside. "Poppy, this won't blow back on anyone else, I swear."

Her blue eyes are cold as ice as she glances between us. "But of course it will. Do you not realize that your actions constitute *everything* the close-minded jerks in this country have come to fear about people like us?"

Next to me, Henrik sets his coffee aside. "I don't understand."

Poppy sighs. "Gentlemen, the homophobia in this country is a river that runs deep. What do you think the fans will do if they find out your marriage is a sham? That the only reason you got married was to trick two governments into giving two men custody of a young child? Worse still, a young female child? In short, you are their worst nightmare. You are everything they've been told to fear."

My stomach twists in uncomfortable knots. I've worked so hard to convince myself this was the right thing to do. But is Poppy right? Have I really done wrong? Have my actions put others in danger?

Ignoring my squirming, Poppy goes on. "What impact do you think that kind of negative press might have on the rest of the team? You have queer teammates, Henrik. We have children too. Families." Her hands splay wide over her bump, protecting the baby she shares with her two partners. "Try as we might, we are not safe from their hate. Our lives are made of invisible nets of legal protections—adoptions and powers of attorney, civil unions, joint bank accounts, shared assets. But it's not enough. It will never be enough. We are, at every moment, just *one* cruel law away from being torn apart. I'd call that pretty darn fragile, wouldn't you?"

Fuck, I think I'm gonna be sick. "Poppy, I'm sorry."

"Don't." She raises a hand. "Put in your position, I probably would have done the same thing. As I told Henrik at the airport, now we just have to focus on minimizing any potential damage."

Henrik finally speaks. "You have a plan, yes? You know how to see us through this?"

She looks to him. "I do."

He nods once, wholly resolved. "I'll do anything you say. I will protect Karolina and Teddy with my life. My career means nothing to me. Not if it costs them peace or happiness."

She smiles. "Well, I'm certainly relieved to hear you say that." Then it's like she flipped a switch, and all her gloom and doom is gone. "Right then, let's do this." She swipes a little remote off the coffee table and clicks it over her shoulder. A projector in the ceiling hums to life, flashing onto the blank white wall behind her. "Welcome to your crisis management orientation session."

I lean back. "You made a PowerPoint?"

"I did." She clicks the remote again and the slideshow starts. "I'm calling my PR plan 'Operation Mighty Oak.'" The slide shows a corporate-looking logo featuring an oak tree. Jesus, she had to take her time to design this. I very much doubt it was Trevor.

Next to me, Henrik stifles a groan.

She glances over her shoulder. "Something wrong, hun?"

I can't hide my grimace either.

"No," Henrik mutters.

She glances between us. "Well, don't be shy now. This is a group project. I want everyone's input here."

I dare to say what we're both thinking. "It's just . . . Well, I mean, does it have to sound so . . ."

Her brows arch. "So what, honey?"

"Gay," Henrik finishes for me.

Oh god, he said it, not me. "Yeah. I'm sorry, Pop. But it does sound *really* gay. And I'm gay," I add.

Poppy huffs. "Gracious, will you two get your heads out of the gutter? The mighty oak is not a reference to your penises. This is about your marriage. Your loving, committed—if admittedly spontaneous—marriage. Now, what are the essential parts of an oak tree?"

Henrik and I share another glance. "Seriously?" I say. "Like, you want us to just start naming the parts of a tree?" At the same time, Henrik says, "Acorns."

Poppy beams at him. "Oooh, you're getting a bit ahead of me there, honey. I was looking for *roots*." She clicks the remote, and a new slide pops up featuring the root system of a tree. All around the roots, she's added in little words and phrases like "friends to lovers" and "inevitable."

"Now, all good relationships, like strong trees, require roots buried deep. In your case, we need to build the case that you have these roots. So, here's the spin: yours is a love kindled from nearly a decade of friendship. Henrik, your niece's unfortunate situation merely sped up the timeline you were both already on. Do you understand what I'm saying?"

I nod up at the words on the screen. "We're inevitable."

Now I earn a smile. "Yes, exactly, Teddy."

"Friends to lovers," I add, still reading the screen.

"Yes. That's the story of your roots. You met six years ago when Teddy was an intern. You didn't pursue anything then, because you were keeping things professional. Also, Henrik, maybe add in something about Teddy being a little too young for you. Maybe a bit too immature."

Okay, ouch.

Also, accurate.

"But you stayed in touch over the years, and the romance blossomed. Are we tracking with this story? Because you'll both need to memorize it. And *don't* deviate," she adds, pointing a finger at us. "There's nothing worse than having Teddy say your first kiss was on a plane when Henrik tells the press scrum it happened on the beach."

Henrik's eyes are wide now. "They'll ask us about that?"

Poppy shrugs. "Probably. But when in doubt, deflect. There's nothing wrong with saying you want to keep parts of the story private. Now, I'm taking care of things on my end to create a convincing narrative of your shared past. I want the two of you more focused on the present, which is selling the lie."

"Which lie?" Henrik asks.

"The lie that you're a happily married gay couple." She clicks to the next slide, which features a very phallic-looking tree trunk. "Like our friend, the mighty oak, you two must now share one strong, united front. You are married, and you must appear so to the public—" She pauses when there's a sharp knock on the door.

"Hey-o," Novy calls out, opening the door. "Special delivery for my queen. Rush order, as requested." He holds up a little black bag stuffed with white paper. The name of a jewelry store flashes on the side in shiny silver letters, and my heart fucking stops. I know exactly what's in that bag.

Poppy's eyes light up. "Oh, thank you, honey."

"Anything for my love." He sets the little bag down on the table.

"Your timing is literally perfect," she coos, looking up at him like he invented attraction.

Novy bends over her chair, giving her a very PG-13 kiss that leaves her breathless. Then he's brandishing a coffee with a flourish. "I also brought you a decaf pecan latte with extra whip."

"Oh, you're an angel." She takes the coffee and another kiss.

"Oh god." The words escape me as I swipe my own coffee off the table.

Next to me, Henrik grunts his agreement.

Novy is still leaning over Poppy as he turns to me. "You got a problem there, bud?"

"I think it's just seeing you being so sweet to another person. It sorta feels like watching an alligator play the clarinet."

"It's unsettling," Henrik mutters.

"Right?" I jab my thumb at him. "What he said. Unsettling is a good word."

Novy just straightens with a smirk. "Well, get used to it, assholes. So long as my girl is pregnant, she gets whatever she wants from me. She could tell me to dance naked on this table, and I'd fucking do it."

Poppy pats his arm.. "That won't be necessary, honey."

"What's that?" Henrik nods to the little black bag. It's like we both already know, and he clearly wants to get it over with. Which makes me feel fan-fucking-tastic.

"Oh—" Poppy takes a sip of her iced latte before setting it aside. "I'm so glad you asked." Reaching for the bag, she pulls out the tissue with a flourish. "Now, we can get these resized if needed, but I hope they'll do the trick." She pulls out two black ring boxes. "One for you," she sings at Henrik. "And one for you, Teddy, honey."

I feel like a robot as I mechanically reach out my hand and take the box from her.

Henrik opens his box and pulls out a shiny gold wedding band. "Is this really necessary?"

"It's customary for married couples to wear rings as proof of their status," Poppy replies. "Even in Sweden—and yes, I checked. In your case, it really is a PR necessity." Then she glances between us, smiling brightly. "Well? Try them on. Let's see."

With a sigh, I open my box. A shiny gold wedding band sits tucked in a bed of black velvet. At least this one doesn't carry over a hundred years of Karlsson family history.

Henrik turns to me, ring lying flat in his palm. "Is this acceptable to you? I don't want to break any rules ..."

He's right. We have a lot of rules in this fake marriage. There's the "no saying husband" rule. And the "no kissing" rule. Then there's the "I pay him rent" rule. We haven't actually discussed the terms of that one yet. His "I sleep in his room" rule is working out great for me so far. But we don't have a "no wedding rings" rule. Not technically. I just told him I wouldn't wear his mother's cursed ring.

"No, it's fine," I say. But then I hesitate, glancing his way. "Are *you* fine?"

With a nod, he slips the ring on his left hand, closing his fist around the glint of gold. He's still wearing the cursed ring on his right pinkie.

"Well?" Poppy says with a smile.

"It fits," Henrik replies.

She turns to me. "Teddy? Your turn, hun."

I slip on the ring, feeling the coolness of the metal as it glides down my finger. Fuck, it's a perfect fit.

Don't read anything into this!

I glance up at Novy, always the prankster. "These won't turn our fingers green, will they?"

He crosses his tatted arms. "Fuck you. Those are twenty-four-carat gold. You're welcome."

Henrik glances up sharply. "Send me the bill."

"I'll pay for mine," I say in a quiet voice. Though I don't know with what money.

"Out of the question."

"Henrik—"

"I said no," he growls. "Call it my third rule," he adds more gently.

Right. So his rules for me in this fake marriage are that I have to sleep in his bed (even without him in it), I can't have other men over to the apartment, and I can't pay for my own wedding ring. It appears Henrik is something of a traditionalist.

"Well, you both look dynamite," Novy says. "If I didn't know any better, I'd think you were married."

"They *are* married," says Poppy, waving to him as he leaves.

"Anything else?" Henrik asks as the door shuts.

She laughs. "Well, obviously. We only have to talk about the most important part of the whole PR plan." She sets her coffee aside again. "Now, when you think of a tree, what's the most important—"

"I'm sorry, but can you spare us any more of the protracted tree metaphors?" I say over her. "Please, just tell us what you want us to do."

Henrik smirks, clutching his coffee with his newly ringed hand. I know he's thinking the same thing as me.

Poppy presses the clicker, changing the PowerPoint slide to an image of the top of a tree. "I was going to say *leaves*. They're the flashiest part of the tree. And the final prong of this PR campaign will mirror their 'hey, look at me' approach when it comes to the media."

"I don't understand," Henrik says for both of us.

"We need the world to look at you," she explains. "We want to shove it in their faces that you two are a happily married gay couple and that one of you just happens to play in the NHL."

Henrik sits forward, a worried look on his face. "I thought this was about minimizing attention. It's about keeping Teddy and Karolina away from the media, not shoving them under a spotlight."

"Yes, but the best way to minimize attention in this case is to seek it out. We all know that the easiest way to hide something is to show the world you have nothing to hide."

It clicks in my head. "Oh, that's clever."

She smiles. "I know."

"Well, so what do you propose?" I ask.

Her smile widens. "I propose we go *big*. Total shock and awe. We'll show them so many pictures and video clips of you both being happy and well-adjusted, that pretty soon they'll just move on. There's nothing the media finds more boring than two people living their happy, unbothered lives."

"And then what happens?" asks Henrik.

"And then we win."

He considers for a moment. "Okay. How do we do it?"

She clicks the remote, and a new slide appears with three

columns. Bullet-pointed items are listed in each column. "Over the next few weeks, I've arranged a set of PR activities for you both, starting with an interview with my friend Janine over at ESPN."

Why does that name sound so familiar? With a gasp, I sit forward. "Wait, Janine Marsh? Didn't she do the interview with the Prices when they first came out?"

"Yep. And she owes me a favor. We'll sit you both down for an interview. And don't worry," she adds, looking to Henrik. "It'll be scripted. Janine will know what to ask."

"And then what?" I say.

She uses a laser pointer to circle each column on the slide. "From there, you'll go on a few public dates. We'll have you photographed on each one. You know, nice candlelit dinner, maybe a walk on the beach holding hands. It's gonna be so stinkin' cute. Date one will be just the two of you. And I'm sorry, but we'll need some PDA for that one. That'll be your big 'look at us, we're gay' moment. The second date will be a group date. Doesn't that sound fun?"

It takes everything I have to stifle my pained groan. Not only did I marry my dream man and move into his house to awkwardly co-parent his injured niece. Now we're both wearing shiny, matching wedding rings. Oh, and I have to confess my not-so-fake love for him on ESPN. And Poppy's making us go on romantic fake dates together. Publicly.

This is just fucking perfect.

Henrik looks to me, waiting. Because, apparently, I'm calling all the shots now.

"Fine," I say.

Henrik turns to Poppy and nods. "We'll do it."

She claps her hands together. "Excellent. And it should go without saying that Karolina will be protected in all this. I'm not the type of media director to use a child to score cheap PR points."

"We appreciate that," Henrik replies.

"I'm just glad to have so much enthusiastic cooperation. Pick an evening for next week when you'd like to go on your first date. Meanwhile, I'll set up the ESPN interview with Janine. Sound good?"

Henrik nods.

I do nothing.

"Oh, and Teddy—" Poppy turns to me. "We're gonna have you attend the opening night home game. That way we can get some shots of you with Henrik out on the ice. You know, the whole 'cheering for your man' angle."

I'm on autopilot as I stand. "Well, it sounds like you've got it all figured out. Just tell me where to stand and smile for the cameras."

Henrik rises next to me, still looking at me warily.

"Don't worry." Poppy walks us to the door. "I have everything under control. Give me a couple weeks to work my magic, and we'll make this all go away. Then we can all get back to hockey as usual."

Henrik looks relieved as he shakes her hand. Meanwhile, I feel even smaller than I did on the day we got married. How is that possible?

We'll make this all go away.

She means me. I'm what will go away. Henrik getting clear of this mess means getting clear of me. And apparently, he can't fucking wait.

22

HENRIK

"Look, Henrik, I don't know what else to say. You made a commitment. They set the campaign filming schedule around the preapproved dates *you* sent to them back in July—"

"But my situation has changed," I snap into the phone, juggling three bags of groceries one-handed as I reach in my pocket for my apartment keys. "Did you tell them my situation has changed?"

"I did—"

"I can't fly to New York right now to shoot an ad campaign. My niece needs me here. The season is about to start, so I'll already be traveling. Christ, I haven't even secured her a teacher yet. I just—I *need* you to ask them for an extension. Four months. Surely, they can extend my contract and film within four months?"

My agent is quiet for a moment. In her silence, I make my way out of the elevator and down the hall to my apartment door. "Henrik, trust me, I understand your situation. But I'm telling you that they can't offer you that kind of extension. If you can't make the dates work now, dates *you* picked, then it's looking like you're gonna have to let this campaign go—"

I hang up the phone. It's the height of rudeness, and I'll apologize profusely later, but in this moment, I just need it all to stop. This is the third piece of bad news I've received this morning.

It all began when my parents' neighbor, Petter Friberg, woke me at four in the morning to tell me my father sprained his ankle falling off a stepladder. Apparently, he was trying to change a burned-out light bulb in the kitchen. Mom was in distress, and Dad was saying he wouldn't go to the doctor. I managed to calm her down enough to convince her to let Petter's wife stay for coffee while Petter took Dad into town.

Shortly after I got the update from Petter that it was only a sprain, Karolina's new at-home tutor messaged to say she was taking a different teaching job. Now my agent is saying my latest endorsement deal is gone because I can't drop everything and fly to New York to shoot the ads. That campaign was going to earn me over a million dollars. But I just can't do it. Not now. Not with the season opener and Karro and—god, what am I going to do about her teacher? She can't attend school, injured as she is. Not until January at the earliest. That's what Teddy and I agreed.

But she *must* have a teacher. The conditions of the custody agreement are strict. Elin is already breathing down my neck every day, asking me for the documents I can send to the court as proof of her enrollment.

I just don't know what to do. Everything feels so impossible. I couldn't keep Petra from getting hit by a drunk driver. I can't mend Karro's broken bones. I can't keep my father from climbing ladders. Can't hire a teacher. Can't fulfill my contractual commitments to my sponsors. I can barely get my damn key in the door!

After fumbling with the lock, I push the door open, all the while juggling the heavy bags of groceries.

Teddy sits up. "Hey, Morbror's home. Wanna see what we did today?"

"Morbror, look," Karolina calls.

Hanging my keys on the hook by the door, I take in their smiling faces. Karolina is sitting on the sofa, surrounded by art supplies. Scraps of paper and every color of crayon and pencil lie scattered all over the coffee table. Her cheeks are rosy with laughter, all evidence of her black eye nearly gone.

Teddy's smile falls. He gets up from the floor, the paper in his hand fluttering away. "Henrik..."

"Look," Karolina says again, pointing with her crayon at the wall. Taking a deep breath, I turn. The narrow stretch of white wall next to the doorway is now a five-year-old's personal art studio. It's a riot of color—rainbows and princesses, unicorns, flowers. There's even what looks like a portrait of me playing hockey and Teddy holding Teddy the Bear.

"Teddy calls it 'Princess Karolina's Magical Wall of Fun,'" Karro says in Swedish. "I wanted to draw your friend Elin, but Teddy said lawyers aren't fun."

"What are you saying about me?" Teddy teases in English.

Karro goes stiff, eyes wide, looking like she's just been caught sneaking cookies from the jar.

"I'm hearing my name. What did we say about speaking Swedish when Uncle Teddy is in the room?"

She giggles. "I won't say it!"

"What's the rule?" he challenges. "If you speak Swedish and Uncle Teddy hears his name, you have to say it."

"No," she squeals, trying to hide under her blanket.

"Say it!"

"No," she says through a muffled laugh.

"Say it, or I'm eating all the ice cream!"

Slowly, she peels down the corner of her blanket, still giggling. Her face is bright pink, eyes alight, as she glances from me back to Teddy. Finally, she opens her mouth and gasps out in English, "I'm a Swedish meatball!"

Once the words are said, she disappears back under her blanket, laughing hysterically. Teddy uses the distraction to cross to my side. His voice is low and tense. "What's wrong?"

Glancing her way, I just shake my head. I can't do this here, not in front of Karolina. Or Teddy. I have to stay strong for them. I have to stay focused.

Teddy grabs my arm, takes the grocery bags, and guides me around the back of the sofa. "Karro, honey, Morbror and I will be right back. Don't move, okay? Make like a meatball and just sit."

She laughs harder at this. The joyous sound should bring me comfort. Instead, it only makes me feel worse. I'm failing her. I'm failing them all. God, my parents. Mom sounded so panicked on the phone this morning.

"Come on." Teddy pulls me through the apartment, tossing the grocery bags on the counter in the kitchen. He doesn't stop until he's dragged me all the way through my bathroom and into the closet. Dropping my hand, he turns, blocking the doorway, hands on his hips. "Okay, now tell me. What the hell happened?"

I just shake my head. I feel like a dam, holding back the worries of the world. God, and if I break?

He sighs. "Henrik, I can't help if you won't tell me."

"I'm failing," I say on a breath. "Teddy, I can't—can't do this. It's too much."

"What's too much?" He steps closer. "Talk to me. Let me help you."

I close my eyes tight. "I'm trying. Christ, Teddy, I don't know what else to do."

"Well maybe I *do* know what to do. Tell me what's wrong. Let me try to help."

I take a deep breath, and let it out. Then I open my eyes, letting the kindness in his expression anchor me. "My dad fell off a ladder today."

His eyes go wide. "Oh shit. Well, is he okay? And your mom?"

"She was shaken up, but she's okay. And it was just a sprain. Their neighbor called and woke me at four in the morning to tell me."

"Jesus," he mutters. "Why didn't you tell me this morning?"

"Teddy, I don't know what else to do. They won't go to a care home, and they won't let me hire in help." Groaning, I step away from him, sinking back until I drop down onto the bench seat. Elbows on my knees, I hang my head, gaze locked on the carpet. "I thought Petter was calling to say one of them was dead. Or maybe Mom left the stove on and burned down the house. Whenever I get a call now, I'm always expecting the worst."

"Hen . . ." Teddy drops to his knees in front of me and places his hands on my forearms, giving them a gentle squeeze. "I'm so sorry. That has to be so scary."

I just nod. What else can I do?

He rocks back on his heels, searching my face. "Is that all that's bothering you? I mean, that's plenty. But . . . is that all?"

I take another breath and let it out. "Karolina's teacher canceled her contract."

"What? Why?"

"Apparently, she got a more lucrative job teaching English in Portugal. She moves there in two weeks."

"Well, shit. Did you have any other names you can call? Any leads?"

It pains me to admit the truth, but I have no pride left. "None. Honestly, I don't even know where to look. And just now, my agent called to tell me I lost a brand endorsement deal. It was worth over a million dollars."

"Fuck. Did she say why?"

Sighing, I lean back against the wall. "It was a timing issue. I can't shoot the ads now, and they won't renew or extend the contract."

He's quiet for a moment, considering the options. "Okay, well, I won't pretend I know anything about endorsements or brand sponsorships, so Laura's gonna have to handle that for you."

I nod. I know I owe her an apology. She's been nothing but good to me. I'll just add it to my growing list of things to do.

"As for your parents . . . you know, these things often have a way of working themselves out," he says gently. "It could be that this fall helps them see their own mortality. Maybe it will scare your dad into being more willing to accept help. I say give him a couple days to recover, then call and broach the subject again."

It's a sensible suggestion, even if I feel certain Dad won't see reason.

"And as to the problem of Karro's teacher, leave that with me."

"Teddy, I can't—"

"Can't what?" he says over me, rising to his feet. "Can't trust me?"

"No, of course I trust you."

His hands go to his hips as he glares down at me. "Oh, so you just can't rely on me. I've let you down one too many times?"

"You know you haven't."

"So, then you just can't bother me. Is that where we're at again? Karolina's schooling is too far beneath my notice?"

I sigh, utterly defeated. "Teddy . . ."

"Leave it with me," he says again. "You tried it your way. Now it's my turn." He slips his phone from his pocket, typing away with his thumbs.

"I already tried calling the local schools. They won't release the names or numbers of any certified substitute instructors."

He just scoffs, turning away. "Yeah, as if I'd waste my time doing that. I said trust me, Henrik. I'm gonna have this settled within the hour."

"What are you doing?" I follow him out of the closet and back into the bathroom. "Who are you talking to?"

"The people *you* should have been talking to the moment we signed the papers back in Sweden," he says over his shoulder, still walking away. "The people who know the most about starting over in a new city with a young family."

"Who?"

He stops in the hallway, and I nearly bump into him. His phone is already pinging with alerts. Turning around, he flashes me his phone screen. He has three new messages. "Who else? Your teammates' wives."

13

TEDDY

"Thank you so much," Henrik says for the third time, holding open the door. "We truly appreciate your time."

"Hey, it's no problem. Just happy it all worked out. Give me a few days to get myself in order, and we'll get started first thing Monday morning. Sound good?"

"Perfect," says Henrik. "And thanks again."

Karolina's new tutor slips on his shoes and gives Henrik's hand one more shake. Then he's out the door, headed for the elevator.

Henrik closes the door and turns, leaning against it. His whole body relaxes as he closes his eyes and takes a deep breath. Meanwhile, my chest fills with warmth. I did this. We had a problem, and I fixed it. I helped. Henrik *let* me help.

Well, technically the WAGs helped. It only took about thirty minutes of texting the other day before I had a list of four potential candidates for a state-approved private tutor. I let Henrik vet the résumés on his own, and he picked the same guy I would have picked.

Sam Torres is so fucking cool. I want him to be *my* tutor. He has a BA in biology and a master's in early childhood education. He was in the Peace Corps in Sri Lanka. He's scuba certified. He forages for edible plants on the weekend. *And* he's a licensed yoga instructor. To top it all off, his family owns a farm up in Yulee, with cows, and chickens, and a beehive. We're going to take Karro up there for nature classes.

"Well?" I say, crossing my arms.

Henrik smiles. "He's perfect."

"Right?" I hurry forward, my excitement bubbling. "Isn't he *so* cool? I could listen to him talk about mushroom hunting for hours. Karro's gonna love him."

"I agree. Thank you, Teddy."

My body feels aglow with his praise. "It was my pleasure. Anything for Karro, you know that."

He checks the time on his phone and groans. "I have to go. Practice."

I stuff my hands in my pockets and step back. "Yeah, sure. Go. I've got everything covered here."

"I'm sorry about this. It was Hanna's only scheduled time conflict when she took the job."

I just laugh. "Her sister's baby shower is a legitimate excuse to not come in for work for *one* day. Besides, I'm already here. Remember?"

He nods, but he still looks guilty.

"You don't have to try to get childcare coverage every time you need to leave the house. If I'm available, I'm happy to be here with her. That's the point of this whole arrangement. And I love kids, remember?"

Worry is still etched on every line of his face. "She said she was in pain again this morning."

"Which I'll monitor. Seriously, Henrik. You can go. I promise, she's in the best of hands. I'm gonna keep things totally chill until you get back. Just a casual schedule of jet-skiing, followed by his-and-hers back tattoos. And if we're feeling really chill, we'll go rob a jewelry store. You like opals, right?"

He just rolls his eyes, fishing his keys off the hook. "I'm more of an emeralds man."

I grin. "Good to know. And hey—" I place a hand on his shoulder before he steps out the door.

He glances back at me.

"You're doing everything right, and everything is fine. You got this, Henrik."

His smile almost reaches his eyes this time. "Thank you, Teddy."

The door closes and I let out a heavy breath, glancing around this sad, empty apartment. We're making slow progress. Karolina's art wall adds some much-needed color. And I may have sneaked in a couple new blankets for the couch. Isn't Henrik supposed to be Swedish? His Stockholm pad was so effortlessly cool. Why am I the one responsible for hygge-fying this place to match?

He gave me his credit card last night, which was an epic mistake on his part. I instantly bought three hundred dollars' worth of art supplies, electric candles, and throw pillows. When he complains about it later, I'll just whip out our new heated neck massager . . . which should arrive in two business days.

Slow and steady, Teddy. You got this.

"Okay," I call down the hallway. "Who's ready to rewatch *The Swan Princess*?"

"Me," comes Karro's sweet voice.

I grin. "I'll get the popcorn. But I'm warning you now, *I* get to sing Odette's parts this time. You have to play Lieutenant Puffin!"

"**W**hat are these?" Curled up next to me on the bed, Karro brushes her fingers over my hair.

I smile down at her. "They're called locs. You do it by rolling and twisting the hair. See? Like this." I pick one up and gently roll it with my palms.

"Why?"

"Because it protects my hair and helps me keep it long. Plus, it looks cool. Right?"

She nods.

I brush my hand over her blonde hair. It's so thin and fine, like gossamer. "If you want, I can teach you ways to do braids that will work for your hair. Would you like that?"

"You can braid?"

I laugh. "Girl, I grew up as the only boy in a house with four Black women. I can do every braid you can imagine, and some you can't."

"Morbror can't braid."

"Well, we'll fix that immediately. Hey, wanna play beauty parlor with me? I can wash and condition your hair, dry it, and put it in French braids. Sound fun? My little nieces *love* playing beauty parlor."

Her eyes are alight, but her smile falls a little.

I sit up, cutting off the end credits of *The Swan Princess* with a click of the remote. "Honey, what's wrong?"

Her lower lip trembles. "Mamma did my hair."

Her words pierce right through my heart. I brush my hand over her messy hair again. "Oh, honey, I bet it was so pretty. I bet she was really good at it too. Wasn't she?"

Karro nods.

I clear my throat, setting the remote aside. "Well, I know I'm no replacement for your mamma, but I'm good at hair too. My sisters and nieces can provide strong references. If you'll let me, I'd like to do yours. Would that be okay?"

Her bottom lip keeps trembling as her blue eyes fill with tears. "Jag saknar Mamma."

I lean down, kissing the top of her head. "Can you translate for me?"

She sniffles, pulling Teddy the Bear onto her lap with her casted hand. "I miss Mamma."

I let my own tears fall as I hold her, wrapping an arm around her thin, little shoulders. "Oh, honey, I know."

There's no shame in our tears. I may have never met Petra Karlsson, but I feel her absence too. I stand now in the gaping hole she left behind, arms outstretched, just trying to keep this cosmic wound from growing larger for the two people who remain. "Your mamma was so pretty," I whisper against her hair.

She looks up at me. "You knew Mamma?"

I brush her tears away with my thumbs. "Your grandma showed me pictures of her when I was in Sweden. She was funny, wasn't she? And strong. I know you're so funny and so strong because your mamma taught you how."

"I don't have a picture of Mamma."

Fuck, this girl is breaking me. "Don't you even worry. I'm gonna fix that first thing in the morning. Morbror Henrik's gonna get us a picture, and I'm gonna put it in a pretty frame that we can set right on your bedside table. Would that be okay? I think we should put one in the living room too."

She nods.

"And I think there should be pictures of you with Morbror. Wouldn't that be nice?"

"And with you."

The realness of this moment rocks me to my fucking core. In Sweden, Elin warned us what accepting custody of Karro would mean. But until now, I hadn't fully considered the ramifications of inserting myself into her life. She doesn't know this is all supposed to be temporary. All she knows is that her mother died. Then suddenly I appeared at her uncle's side, ready to help them both pick up the pieces. Her trust in me is already steadfast, because her trust in Henrik is steadfast.

Holding her in this moment, crying with her, I know that no matter what happens between me and Henrik, I want to stay in Karro's life. I *need* to stay. Rejection is too cruel. Kids don't recover. Could I do that to Karolina? Could I swoop in on a rock star's airplane, rip her from her life, promise her my love and attention, and then just walk away?

Fuck, I feel sick even thinking it.

Recalling her question, I kiss the top of her head again. "Of course we'll get pictures of me and you. Don't be silly. There's gonna be more pictures of me on these walls than smelly Morbror. He's not even that handsome."

She giggles. "He is."

"No, he's not. I'm the handsome prince. Morbror Henrik looks like a shoe."

That has her laughing harder. "No, he *is* handsome!"

"He looks like a penguin in a wig."

"No! He's like Hercules!"

Okay, fuck me. I'm not gonna picture Henrik as a stoic, bearded Swedish Hercules. My imagination doesn't need that kind of kindling. Slipping off the side of the bed, I turn and reach for her. "You know what? I think he looks like Pegasus."

She considers for a moment, clearly deliberating. It's adorable. "Pegasus is pretty," she accepts with a nod.

"Yeah . . . Pegasus's *butt!*"

This sends her into peals of laughter that echo as I bring her into the bathroom. The laughter continues while we play beauty salon, all the while comparing Morbror Henrik to animals' hind ends.

24

HENRIK

With hockey back in my life, I feel grounded again. It's a relief to have at least a few things under my control—my food intake, my workout routines, my sleep schedule. Sure, I may be sleeping in the guest room now, but the bed is comfortable.

At Teddy's insistence, we moved the exercise bike out of my bedroom and into the living room. Honestly, I prefer it this way. Now I start each morning watching the sun rise over the river as I bike, stretching out my calves and regulating my circulatory system.

He thinks I haven't noticed the other changes he's making, but I do. How am I supposed to ignore new bookshelves? Just last night, I signed for a trio of boxes that arrived from a home goods store. Do I know why we needed a fruit bowl or a decorative wooden tray? No. And I'm not going to ask. If it makes him happy, Teddy can buy whatever he wants.

I can't think about home decorations. With Karolina's healthcare and education set, I can only think about hockey. We're officially one day out from our first game of the season. It'll be a home game against the New York Islanders.

Despite my time in Sweden, I haven't lost my starting position. I'm still holding the line with Langley and Lindberg. We skate well together. Langley is fast, and Lindberg makes a great center. He's quick and decisive, always willing to pass the puck. He has one of the highest assist rankings in the NHL. I was glad when the Rays traded him in from the Golden Knights.

"Are you ready, Mr. Karlsson?" The ESPN producer leans in, smiling in my face.

All thoughts of this morning's drills flash from my mind as I look up. "Yes."

They've been rearranging the lights for the last ten minutes. All the while, Teddy and I have sat side by side on this leather sofa, silently waiting. He's wearing my favorite cable-knit sweater again. His hair is down, framing his face. They put a powder on his cheeks that dulls some of his freckles. I don't like it.

I feel like I'm all elbows, sitting here in my favorite navy-blue suit. Poppy made me take off the tie. She said no tie made me look more approachable. Any second now, the reporter will start asking us questions. Teddy has been quizzing me on our answers whenever we've gotten a spare moment. Just last night, he charged into the bathroom while I was neck deep in the tub, shouting, "What if they ask if we kissed at the wedding? Do I lie? Oh, this is so fucking fucked!"

The story is that I pursued him. I invited him to Sweden, where we rekindled our friendship (and started our romance). We decided to leave in the part about me proposing in the hospital cafeteria. Poppy says it's more believable if we weave in as many real aspects as possible.

"Okay, if you're both ready, we'll get started," says Janine. She's nice enough. Pretty and polished, she sits in the chair across from us, one camera angled on her.

Poppy set this all up in one of the corner offices at the practice arena. Behind us, there's a great view of downtown. It's golden hour, and the lighting is perfect. We need to do this quickly, before the light changes.

I glance over at Teddy. He keeps tugging at the neck of my sweater. And his new nervous tic is spinning the ring on his finger. I glance down at my own ring. It's a simple band of yellow gold. Since I put it on, I've hardly noticed it. I have to take it off during practice, but slipping it back on before I shower already feels like a habit.

For Teddy, it's apparently a distraction, an itch he can't help but scratch.

"Quiet on set," someone calls out, which makes Teddy stiffen.

Reaching over, I take his hand, weaving our fingers together. He relaxes a little, scooting closer to me. Behind the row of cameras, Poppy stands watch, giving us both a nod of encouragement. If Janine tries to do anything fishy, Poppy will go full Godzilla and knock over the cameras to help us save face.

At the signal from her cameraman, Janine begins, her focus straight down the main camera's lens. "Good evening, I'm Janine Marsh with ESPN. Tonight, I'm sitting down for an exclusive interview with one of the most elusive players in the National Hockey League. Hailing from a little seaside town outside of Stockholm, he's a five-time member of the NHL All-Stars and an Olympic silver medalist for Team Sweden. A founding player of the Jacksonville Rays, now their starting forward, please join me in welcoming Henrik Karlsson." She turns to me. "Henrik, hello. It's so great to finally meet you."

My years of media training click on as I smile too. "And you, Janine. Thanks for having me."

"Oh, it's my pleasure. I'd like to add that we're actually not alone for this interview, are we?" She smiles warmly at Teddy.

If he were ever going to run, now would be the moment. He didn't ask for any of this. But he sits still, hand clasped in mine, waiting for me to speak. Clearing my throat, I squeeze his hand. "Yes, this is Doctor Teddy O'Connor. He's the assistant rehabilitation therapist for the Jacksonville Rays . . . and he's my partner."

"Oh my goodness." Janine feigns surprise. "When you say he's your partner, do you mean he's your husband? Are you two married?"

"Yes, we're married."

"Well, congratulations. Wow, that's so exciting!"

Teddy flashes a nervous smile and lifts his left hand, wiggling his ring finger for the camera. "He's officially off the market."

Janine laughs. "Is that why you wanted to sit down with me tonight? To tell the sports world that you're an out and proud gay athlete?"

My gaze darts to Poppy. She told me Janine wouldn't ask the

question quite so bluntly. I'm about to speak before Teddy leans forward. "Oh, come on, Janine. Do we really need to put labels on everything? Let's just say he's married to me and let the fans draw their own conclusions."

"Fair enough," she replies. "Well, how did you two first meet? Because—now, correct me if I'm wrong, Doctor O'Connor—but you were once an intern with the Rays, right?"

He rests our joined hands on his knee. "I was, yeah. But that was six years ago. Another life, really. I joined the team as a PT intern while I was still in undergrad."

"That must have been so exciting for you."

He laughs. "If by 'exciting,' you mean wrapping this guy's shoulder in ice after every game? Sure, very exciting. Oh, and don't forget about the Mario Kart. It turns out being an intern on a pro hockey team means playing hours and hours of Mario Kart."

"So, how did it go? Did your eyes connect over an exercise bike? Was it love at first sight?"

"Hardly," Teddy replies. He's so good at this. The nerves have clearly worn off. Now he's just talking, charming her like he does everyone. "I had to make him work for it a little."

Finding my voice, I nudge him with my shoulder. "Actually, I swept him off his feet. Remember, babe?"

That's the other piece of advice Poppy gave us: Use pet names. Couples in love don't use each other's first names. We decided he would call me "baby" and I'd call him "babe." Though it sounds strange now in the moment, like trying to wear a shoe that doesn't fit.

Janine glances between us. "Oh, is that so?"

Next to me, Teddy stiffens. I know we rehearsed the gym meeting story, but Poppy also said to layer in as much truth as possible. "The moment I first met Teddy is the moment I saved his life."

She gasps. "Wait, do you mean literally? You saved his life?"

"I mean, I tackled him to the ground before I ever knew his name."

"Goodness, why?"

"I had to. A truck was about to squash him into jelly. That's how we met. One moment, I was Henrik, walking to work on a Monday morning. The next, I was on the ground, with this stranger in my arms, his cold coffee leaking all over my shirt. We both fell. And we've been falling for each other ever since. Right, babe?"

Teddy nods, his smile tight.

"Well, that sounds just like a fairy tale."

"I guess when you know, you know." I look to Teddy, squeezing his hand. "Right?"

"Yeah. I'd say from that first moment, I just knew."

"What did you know, Doctor O'Connor?"

He holds her gaze, unwavering in his answer. "I knew that Henrik was the only man for me."

We make it through the rest of the interview without incident. Janine asks some carefully worded, Poppy-approved questions about my sister and Karolina. We share some of the lighter moments from our time in Sweden. Teddy mentions trying to order a coffee in Swedish, and I make a joke that he snores. Before I know it, the sound team is taking off our mics.

"Oh my goodness." Poppy rushes forward. "Boys, that was fantastic. You both did so well. I seriously couldn't have done it any better myself. You came off so natural and approachable. You were both a little nervous, which will play great. Oh, I could just kiss you!"

Teddy chuckles. "Easy there, Pop. We're married men, remember?"

"Ugh, and that story about your first meeting? You sweeping him off his feet to save his life? *So* romantic," she cries with a slap to my arm. "The fans are just gonna swoon. And it all felt so real!"

We get untangled from the mic wires, but the photographer holds us back for more pictures. He poses us like we're a couple on a cruise ship, with Teddy seated in a chair and me standing behind, one hand on his shoulder. Then they take a few pictures of us up against the windows. Teddy is in front. The photographer poses us with my arms around him.

"Just do it," Teddy says, holding still while the photographer angles my face until I'm all but breathing down his neck. He snaps a few pictures of us like this. With each click, I fight the urge to look up and inspect which camera body and lens he's using.

Once they free us, Teddy darts away. Swiping his backpack off a chair, he heads for the door.

Janine steps in just as I go to follow. "Oh, Henrik, I wondered if I could get just a few more pull quotes for the article—"

"No." I step around her. "Please, excuse me." Something's wrong. I can feel it. I follow after Teddy. "Hey," I call out just before he ducks into the stairwell. "Teddy, wait."

He pauses, back turned, one hand holding open the stairwell door.

"Where are you going? We drove here together, remember?" He turns as I approach, and I stop in my tracks. There are tears in his eyes. "Teddy, what . . ." I reach for him, but he jerks away, backing into the stairwell.

"What the fuck was that?"

I'm reeling, trying to pinpoint what upset him. "Did someone say something to you? Or do something? Who was it? Tell me—"

"*You* did!"

I blink. "What?"

"You told those assholes about the sidewalk!"

"And that's . . . bad?"

He huffs, crossing his arms. "We agreed that our first meeting story would be in the gym when you walked up with Sully. Remember, *baby*?"

"Teddy, I—but you heard Poppy. She said to tell the truth as much as we were able. That's all I did."

"The sidewalk story was private. It was ours. It—*fuck*—" He spins away, daring to flee.

I grab him before he can leap down the stairs. "Teddy, wait. Please, just tell me what I did wrong. Make me understand. I can't apologize if I don't know why I'm apologizing."

"Sure you can. You just say, 'Teddy, I'm sorry for being such an insensitive ass.' And then you let me fucking go."

But I don't let him go. I band an arm around his chest, holding him to me as he tries to elbow me. Losing my patience, I curse in Swedish. "Du gör mig galen—just use your words, huh? Teddy, I'm sorry for being such an insensitive ass. There. Now tell me *why* I'm an ass, and I'll apologize again."

The fight leaves him on a groan. I feel the rise of his chest against my arm. "I just wanted the sidewalk to stay ours, okay? It was the only thing that—" He sinks into silence on a muttered curse.

I soften my hold on him. "Go on. It was the only thing that what?"

He pulls away enough to turn in my arms. I relax a little, letting my hand drift down to grip his forearm. He's still in my hold, but we both know it's a choice now. He could easily escape. Instead, he dares to hold my gaze. "Sometimes it feels like our moment on the sidewalk is the only thing between us that's real."

I search his face. "What do you mean?"

"I—" He blinks, then looks down, breaking our connection. "I don't know what I mean."

"Don't." I tip his chin back up. "Don't pull away from me. Don't hide, and don't deflect. We're in this together, remember? Now, tell me what you mean."

He's quiet for a moment, considering his words. "In that moment, we were just two creatures of instinct. There were no jobs or responsibilities, no egos, no names. Just raw human connection. In the end, I think that's all anyone wants, you know? To connect?"

It's a beautiful sentiment, poetic in its simplicity. "I know."

"Well, say what you want, but we connected on that sidewalk, Henrik. I *know* you felt it too. Not in a gay way maybe," he adds quickly. "More like . . . as humans, you know?"

"I do."

"Yeah, well, the moment ego entered the picture, the moment we had jobs, and names, and responsibilities, we let that bond snap. For you, it was a momentary pain. You moved on. Look at you, you're fucking fine. But me?" He twists his other arm free and presses his hand to his chest, fingers splayed over my sweater. "Henrik, I'm not fine. I don't recover as fast as you. Wounds to the body are one thing. I know how to heal those. But wounds to the soul?" He just shakes his head, sinking into silence again.

"Teddy . . ."

"Look, I'll be fine eventually," he says over me, always ready for deflection and self-preservation. "It just took me by surprise in there, okay? We had a plan, and I would have preferred it if you stuck to the plan. If you want to apologize to me, apologize for that."

"Teddy, I *am* sorry."

He lowers his hand. "It's fine. Apology accepted. But from now on, the sidewalk story is just for us, okay?"

"Fine. I'll never mention it again . . . except to you."

He nods, still inching away from me. This time, I let him go. His eyes flash as he rebuilds his walls, shutting me out. "If it's okay with you, I think I'm gonna head out tonight."

My gut clenches tight. "Out?"

"Yeah, my friend Colin invited me out for beers. We were supposed to do it before, but I was in Sweden. You good to go home and relieve Hanna alone?"

He's still mad at me. Now he's leaving, and I can't stop him. I haven't the right. I promised him freedom, and he'll have it. Even if it burns like a fire in my chest to say the words. "Of course. Go have fun. Tomorrow is a game day, so it'll be an early night for me."

"Cool." He takes another step away, and I fight the urge to follow. "Well, then maybe I'll just stay out. I can crash at Colin's—"

"No." The word slips out before I can stop it.

He raises a dark brow in a mix of defiance and open question.

"You don't have to stay out all night," I quickly amend. "Come home at any hour."

"I don't wanna wake you up or upset any of your game-day rituals. Besides, Hanna comes again in the morning, right? So, you don't even need me there."

I want to tell him it's not a matter of needing him. But that feels like manipulation. He wants to go, so I'll let him go. I feel hollow as I offer him what I hope is a reassuring smile. "My home is yours. Come and go as you please."

He takes another step back. "If I don't see you before the game, you know I'll see you there, right? Gotta give Poppy a few more media moments."

"I'll be the one in teal," I joke.

Neither of us laugh.

"Yeah. Well . . . night, Henrik."

"Good night, Teddy."

He turns away from me and hurries down the stairs, taking them two at a time.

Make this make sense. One moment, he's sitting at my side, squeezing my hand, laughing at my jokes, and telling Janine Marsh he likes my eyes. The next, he's yelling at me in a stairwell and telling me he plans to spend the night with a man named Colin.

As I stand here, heart racing, the truth settles over me: I don't want Teddy out with another man tonight. I want him home, laughing with Karro on the couch, making banana splits, and teaching me to braid her hair.

I want him home with me.

25

TEDDY

I flee down the steps, taking them two at a time. I have to get out of here. I can't fucking breathe in this goddamn sweater. It feels like him and smells like him, and I feel like I'm fucking suffocating. I all but trip on the last step as I tug the sweater off, stripping down to just my T-shirt and jeans.

Fine, his jeans. Whatever. Semantics.

Pulling my phone from my pocket, I'm about to order an Uber when I see fifteen missed calls and messages. *Shit.* My phone has been on silent for, like, two hours because of all the interview stuff. Two of my three sisters tried to call. Twice. Each. Then they left voicemails. I'm sure they're both over five minutes long.

Look, it may be juvenile, but I've been taking a "what they don't know can't hurt me" approach to this whole "I married a famous Swedish hockey player and have joint custody of his niece" thing. By not telling them I married Henrik, I get to spare myself the pain and humiliation of all the women in my life telling me I've made a terrible mistake.

I *know* I made a mistake. I don't need them to fucking tell me. It's all I can fucking think about.

On paper, my life is perfect right now. Karro is awesome, the apartment is getting better, and I think I might be more in love with Henrik than ever. He's thoughtful and attentive. He genuinely cares about my comfort. I fall asleep on the couch, and he covers me with a blanket. I skip a meal because I'm too busy playing with Karro, and he brings us both sliced apples and cheese. He doesn't know I'm strictly a peanut-butter-with-apples guy. But still, it's a really nice gesture.

This professional athlete, who smashes men into boards for a living, is as gentle as a lamb. He draws me baths and rolls up my clean socks. He's quiet, and noble, and loyal, and I fucking love him. Sounds perfect, right?

Wrong.

Because while I'm falling more in love with him and his adorable niece every day, I'm ultimately just part of a problem he's trying to fix. Sure, he put on a good show for the interview. He was looking at me adoringly, brushing my locs off my shoulder, laughing at my jokes. But that's all it fucking was: a show. Henrik was acting. The man's had years of media training. They started rolling those cameras, and it's like he became a different person.

Well, I wasn't fucking acting. I don't know how to pretend to *not* be in love with my fake husband. I don't know how to keep myself from brushing Karro's hair and singing silly songs to make her laugh. But it's like I told Henrik the other day, I made this bed, and now I'm gonna lie in it.

Or cry in it.

Both.

One thing's for certain. My window for not telling my family is closing fast. Until now, Poppy's been enforcing a total press gag about us. Not a crumb has leaked out to the media about Sweden, his sister, the marriage, any of it. It was easy to do because the season hadn't even started yet. All spotlights were off.

But Janine said the ESPN interview will go live in three days. Then the whole sports world will know. And tomorrow night, Poppy's gonna prop me up right on the plexiglass and make me take pictures with Henrik. Those will be the first photos she intends to leak, along with an official Rays press release announcing our marriage.

She showed us the article tonight, the written one they already finished. It's got a bunch of well wishes from the team and some pics of all of them cheering for us at the airport. Henrik's quote has been rattling around in my head for the last two hours: "Teddy is kind and generous to a fault. I'm honored he chose me as his partner."

Generous to a fault.

In Henrik's eyes, my generosity is a fault. I know it's true. I'm too kind, too obliging, too willing to help. It leads people to take advantage of me. Friends, coworkers. My god, don't even get me started on my past romantic partners. When you're generous, people take from you. They fucking drain you dry. And you're too goddamn nice to stop them. You would let the life drain from your own eyes if it meant you were seen by others as a good person.

It's why I've been dodging all my family's calls and ghosting them in the group chat. I don't want my sisters to hold a mirror up to me and show me my own lifeless eyes. I just wanted more time to pretend this wasn't happening, pretend I was satisfied. Pretend I wasn't putting three lives at risk with my reckless choices.

But I'm out of time. I have to tell them what I did. If they find out from the media, shit's gonna get a thousand times worse. So, I unlock my phone and go to tap Natalie's name. Of all my sisters, she'll be the least likely to make me cry. She'll just listen to me. She'll leave it to our mom to bring down the hammer.

Before I can tap her name, a new text pops up in my notifications. It's from Tess Langley:

TESS: Are you coming?

What? Coming where? I tap our text thread and see the message she sent two hours ago:

TESS: Rip's. Tonight. 7pm. Be there or be square.

I check the time. It's only a little after seven o'clock. And Rip's is less than twenty minutes away. I could be fashionably late. And I was lying to Henrik. I don't have plans with Colin. I just needed any excuse to fucking leave. I'm sure if I called Colin now, he'd be up for a drink. But the texts from Tess have me intrigued . . .

Just as I've made up my mind to call Colin, a new text pings from an unknown number.

UNKNOWN: Attendance at Rip's is nonnegotiable. Get your ass here.

Before I can suck in a righteously indignant breath, there's another ping.

UNKNOWN: This is Caleb Price, btw

Oh, what the actual fuck? Why is Caleb Price texting me? And apparently, he's with Tess? Is there some kind of team dinner? Henrik didn't mention anything earlier. Dinner out with the team is definitely something he would have mentioned. Unless he just intends to go without me ...

No, he was going home to relieve Hanna. He wanted me to go home too.

But what if he gets home and decides he wants a night out? I swear to god, if I take an Uber over to Rip's and find him there? If perfect, pretty Hanna is feeding him French fries dipped in mayo, I'm gonna fucking lose it. Our big coming-out won't be him blowing me kisses through the plexiglass at tomorrow night's game. It's gonna be grainy cell phone footage of me throwing a barstool at the wall.

I may be generous to a fault, but no one fucking cheats on me. Especially not my fake husband.

Decision made, I order my Uber. Destination? Riptide's Bar and fucking Grill.

26

TEDDY

The Uber pulls up in front of the beachside bar. Even before I get out, I hear rock music. It's not karaoke night, but there's definitely a party in full swing. I've been with the guys in the gym all week, and no one mentioned anything . . .

Entering the busy restaurant, I look around for anyone I know. Tess's flaming red curls are hard to miss. Man, it's packed in here. People are clustered by the bar, waiting for tables to open. I don't see any Rays. Definitely no sign of Henrik.

The hostess perks up as I approach. She's a pretty Chinese girl with a septum piercing and pink hair in tight space buns. "Hi! Did you have a reservation?"

"Uhh, actually, I'm looking for the hockey team."

"Yeah, sure. Everyone's already outside. Are you one of the guests of honor?"

"Guests of what? No, I don't think so."

Her smile falls a little. "Oh, well, everyone's outside. Do you know the way?"

"Yep, all good." I duck around her stand and head for the double doors. Through the wall of glass, I can see out to the crowded beach bar area. Yeah, it's definitely the Rays. But I don't see any actual players. There's Maribel, Paulie's Brazilian supermodel wife. Erica Woodson is laughing with DJ Perry's girlfriend, Jessica. And they're all wearing matching bedazzled jackets.

Wait, did Tess invite me to a WAG party?

I step outside, and someone instantly yells, "He's here!"

All the women turn as one, cheering and screaming my name. I swear to god, I jump a foot in the air. "What the fuck—"

"Teddy!"

"You made it!"

"Welcome to the WAGs, Doctor O'Connor!"

My backpack is left at the door as the crowd of women surround me. Very much against my will, I'm led over to the corner booth, where Tess is waiting with Caleb and Mars Price. They stand as I'm hauled forward like some kind of sacrificial tribute. The Price guys are wearing the same jackets as the women. I know exactly what they are, and hell is gonna freeze over before—

"Glad you finally decided to show up," says a deep voice. I glance over my shoulder to see Colton Morrow standing behind me. Like the others, he's wearing a sparkly WAG jacket.

"Oh god." Without hesitation, I wrap my arms around him in a tight hug.

"*Oof*—" He laughs, patting my back. "Good to see ya, Doc."

It's no secret that Colton Morrow is one of my NHL idols. Like me, he was a Black kid just trying to make it in a sport that's been notoriously hostile towards any efforts at diversity. I may be fighting behind the bench, but our struggles are the same. I got to watch him play with the Rays during my intern year. I watched him come out to the world too, declaring his love for Poppy and Novy. Black and queer in hockey? Just consider us a couple of trailblazers.

"I'm so glad you're here," I mutter against his chest.

He pulls away first. "Come on, it'll be more fun than you think. I promise."

I take in his flashy jacket. "Not possible."

"Alright, that's enough." Poppy leads me away. Man, she must have left the interview quick. And she changed out of her little business suit. Now she's in jeans and a white T-shirt, stretched tight over her baby bump. She's also sporting a WAG jacket. Morrow's jacket has Novy's number twenty-two on the arms, but Poppy has the number one on the arms and back. And across her shoulders it just reads, "POPPY."

"What, you didn't wanna rep Novy at the games?" I tease.

"Oh, I think I rep him just fine," she says, patting her pregnant belly. "But at the games, I'm usually on the clock too. And there's only *one* Poppy St. James."

"Point taken." I glance around at all the chaos. "You couldn't have warned me about this earlier?"

"What, and miss seeing the look on your face? I recorded it, by the way."

Of course she did.

She leads me to the front of the pack, not stopping until I'm standing before Tess, Caleb, and Mars. A giant Finnish ex-goalie, Mars stands in the middle with his arms crossed in his bedazzled WAG jacket. "Ilmari" is embroidered in a script font over his left chest, with Jake's number forty-two on both arms. Under his name is what looks like a motorcycle club patch that reads, "PRESIDENT."

Oh, you have got to be fucking kidding me.

My gaze darts to Tess's jacket. Her patch says, "VICE PRESIDENT." Caleb's says, "SGT. AT ARMS."

"Of course," I mutter. Caleb Price *would* be an enforcer. Even though the guy played forward for his whole hockey career, he gives off fierce d-man energy. Probably why he ended up married to Jake and Mars.

All the other wives and girlfriends press in behind us, laughing and sipping their fruity cocktails. Someone turns the music down, as all eyes focus on Mars. It feels like the scene in *The Lion King* where all the animals are waiting for Simba to roar.

"Are we supposed to bow?" I whisper at Poppy.

"Shh. Just wait."

With a huff, Tess finally elbows him. "Come on, Mars. You know you have to say it."

A muscle ticks in his jaw. His eyes narrow, then he declares, "As president of the Jacksonville Rays' Wives and Guys Club, I now call this meeting to order."

A cheer ripples across the group. Behind me, Maribel raises her martini and shouts in her thickly accented English, "I second the motion!"

"I third it," chimes Courtney Fields.

I glance down at Poppy with a raised brow. "Wives and Guys?"

She sips her pink mocktail, swirling the cherries with her straw. "Well, we couldn't very well stay the 'wives and girlfriends,' could we? Not with so many handsome men about." Glancing over her shoulder, she winks at Morrow.

I'm distracted when Tess steps forward, hands on her hips. Her WAG jacket shimmers with the number twenty on each arm. "A new season of the Rays means we have some new members to induct," she calls to the group. "New members, please step forward."

Everyone cheers again as two women weave through the crowd. One I recognize as Christian Lindberg's wife. She's a white European woman. The other woman, I haven't met. She's cute and young, with light brown skin and long black hair. Her perky boobs fill out her top, and she's paired her WAG jacket with a miniskirt and boots.

Poppy gives me a push. "While we're young, Teddy, honey."

With a groan, I step up and take my place next to Lindberg's wife. Her jacket has the number thirty-eight bedazzled on the back in teal and diamond gemstones. The nickname "LINDY" crosses her shoulders.

"We were thrilled when we found out we'd be inducting, not two, but *three* new WAGs this season," Tess calls out to the group. "Astrid and Kelsey, you received your jackets last week." There's a smattering of more cheers for them. Then Tess turns her smile on me. "Tonight, we also welcome Doctor Teddy O'Connor. Teddy, as Karlsson's husband, you are officially the newest member of the Jacksonville Rays Wives and Guys!"

I'm sure I must turn as red as a tomato as the other WAGs go wild for me.

"Yeah, Teddy!"

"Lock him down, Ted!"

Just when I think the worst might be over, Mars steps forward, offering me a large gift bag. Oh god, this is too fucking much. I don't deserve to be a WAG. I *definitely* don't deserve a jacket. Not when this is all a fucking lie. "Please," I hear myself say. But there's a lot of commotion. Someone turned the music back up, so I lean in closer to Mars. "Hey, you can stop this, right?"

He raises a brow. "Why would I stop it?"

"Surely there's, like, a trial period or something, right? Shouldn't we have to make it past some kind of annulment deadline before I qualify for a jacket?"

"Are you married to a Ray?"

I huff, flapping my arm. "I mean, *technically* yes."

"Then technically, this is your jacket." He tries to hand it off again.

Tess pops up next to Mars, glancing between us. "Something wrong over here, Prez?"

"No. Teddy was just conveying his gratitude." He holds out the bag for a third time.

Seeing no other choice, I take it.

"Open it," a wife calls out.

"Yeah, let's see it, Teddy!"

Tucking the gift bag awkwardly under one arm, I pull out the tissue paper, dropping it to the ground. My fingers brush over the soft plush of the WAG jacket, and it sends a literal chill up my arm. Of all the things I've already done in this fake marriage—signing the temporary custody papers, meeting his parents, wearing the damn ring—now *this* is a bridge too fucking far?

"Try. It. On! Try. It. On!" The ladies all start to chant as I slowly pull the WAG jacket free of the last of the tissue paper.

Poppy takes the gift bag, letting me hold the jacket with both hands. It's a black, plush bomber-style jacket. They used actual jersey numbers, I think, sewing them onto the black material, then bedazzling them with matching rhinestones. Henrik's number seventeen flashes on both arms. The front left chest is embroidered with "Dr. O'Connor." The collar and cuffs are striped and fitted, like something on an old high school letterman jacket.

Honestly, this jacket is fucking awesome. I flip it around, and my breath catches. Henrik's huge number seventeen covers the back too. And across the shoulders in sparkly block letters it reads, "TEDRIK."

"Don't you just love it?" says Poppy, brushing her fingers over the jewels.

God fucking damn it. I *do* love it.

"What's Tedrik?" I ask, feeling breathless.

"It's your ship name," she explains. "Some of the names work better for it than others. Like Cake and Calilmari over there," she adds, pointing at Caleb and Mars.

I raise a brow. "Cake?"

"Caleb and Jake," Caleb replies, hands tucked in the pockets of his sparkly WAG jacket.

Calilmari explains itself. Though, as Mars turned, I saw that the back of his jacket reads, "NO EXIT" above Jake's number forty-two.

"Put it on," someone shouts again.

"Fashion show!"

"Show it off, Doctor O'Connor!"

I know this won't stop until I put the damn jacket on. Whatever, I'm already wearing a wedding ring. I slip my arm into the sleeve, tugging on the jacket. I snake in my other arm and shrug it up my shoulders. It's a perfect fit.

"Let's see it, WAGs!"

"Yeah, Kelsey!"

"Lookin' good, Astrid!"

Camera flashes make me blink as several of the women hold up their phones, taking pictures of us. Astrid puts an arm around me, and all I can do is plaster on a smile. The music is cranked louder, and the crowd starts to disperse over to the bar.

"Come on," says Astrid, linking her arm in with mine.

I let her lead me over to the bar, where some drink that is teal and garnished with a fruit skewer gets placed in my hand. Everyone is talking all at once. People hug me, offering congratulations. One tipsy girl asks me what it took to turn Henrik gay. She's quickly pulled away by a friend. Then Heather Walsh is behind me, sipping a margarita. "Did you pick Karlsson's goal song yet?"

"What?"

"His goal song. It's a Rays tradition."

"I'm not familiar." I take a sip of what I think is a blue hurricane. Fuck, it's way too sweet.

Bobby Tremblay's wife, Janna, steps in behind her. "For the first home game of the season, the WAGs get to pick the goal song for their player," she explains. "If your guy scores and your song plays, you earn a thousand bucks too."

Well, shit. Doctor O'Connor could use a thousand dollars. I glance between them, taking another sip of my shitty cocktail. "Isn't there kind of an unfair advantage for the forwards? Don't they have a better chance at scoring?"

Janna laughs. Like Henrik, her guy, Tremors, is a forward. "That's kind of the point. If girls like Heather wanted to win, they should have picked a player who knows how to score. Right, Teddy?" She winks at me.

Oh god.

Heather just rolls her eyes. "Yeah, yeah. Remind me, Jan. Is Tremors a first-line guy?"

"Eat me," Janna replies, popping a fried pickle chip into her mouth.

Both women laugh.

Heather makes some response, but I'm distracted by the form sitting on the bar. Most of the WAGs have already filled it out. Apparently, comedy is the name of this game. Janna and Heather both picked Madonna songs for their guys. If Langley scores tomorrow night, the whole arena is gonna cheer to the chorus of "Who Let the Dogs Out."

Smiling, I set my hurricane down on the bar. I slip my phone from my pocket and pull up my workout playlist, scrolling with my thumb. This shouldn't make me so giddy, right? But teasing Henrik with Karro has quickly become one of my new favorite hobbies. Spotting a strong contender, I smile and pick up the pen.

This is one fake husband task I'm more than happy to do.

11

TEDDY

It's after one in the morning by the time I get back to the apartment. It's so dark and quiet. After the chaos of the karaoke bar, there's almost a fuzzy humming in my ears. The doors to Karro's and Henrik's rooms are both open, so I tiptoe on socked feet through the living room and into the kitchen, trying not to rustle the damn paper in my massive gift bag.

Man, those WAGs sure can hold their liquor. I tapped out after two hurricanes. Switching to root beer, I scarfed down a cheeseburger, half a basket of fried pickle chips, and an order of mozzarella sticks, and I *still* feel like I have springs for legs.

Leaving my backpack and the gift bag on the island, I slink around to the fridge. Henrik's hyper organization is most clearly manifested in his food preparation. I see now what an anomaly it was for us to eat takeout curry on his couch in Stockholm. Now that we're back, the man is meticulous with his diet.

Twice a week, a private chef name Alex comes over and preps a bunch of stuff for Henrik to eat—grilled chicken and rice, creamy vegetable soups, salmon avocado poke bowls, a dozen hard-boiled eggs, overnight oats. There's always fresh fruit and veggies and some kind of prepared starch. I'm still learning what food I'm allowed to take that won't mess with his mojo.

Reaching for a glass container of leftover mashed potatoes, I pause, glancing over my shoulder. Did he just call my name?

I wait, listening to hear the sound again. But there's nothing.

The fridge door starts beeping at me, and I curse under my breath, pulling out the container of potatoes. I shut the door as quickly and quietly as I can. Skipping right past the reheating phase of my midnight munchies, I open the cutlery drawer and pluck out a spoon. I'm digging into the cold potatoes when I hear the sound again. I set the spoon down, leaving the potatoes on the counter, and tiptoe towards the living room. Is Henrik up?

A distressed groaning filters down the hallway from his room.

Shit. I thought he was starting to move past this? I don't want to wake him if I don't have to. He's mentioned before it can be hard for him to get back to sleep. Restless sleep is better than no sleep the night before a game. I turn to go back to my potatoes when his cry sends a chill down my damn spine.

Then I hear Karro's voice. "Morbror?"

Oh fuck, he woke her up.

His shouting gets louder, and I'm on the move, jogging across the living room.

"Morbror?" Poor Karro sounds so scared. She knows she's not supposed to get up without help because of her ribs. "Teddy!" Her panicked cry twists my heart.

"I'm coming, baby!" Ducking into her room, I click on the twinkle lights strung to the frame of her bed. They flicker, casting a halo of golden light over her. Karolina's lying in the middle of her pink flower sheets, surrounded by her stuffed animals. There's a haunted look on her face.

"Morbror's hurt," she cries, tears in her eyes.

"He's not hurt. He's just having a bad dream. I have to go help him, okay? You stay right here—"

"No, don't go!"

From the room next door, Henrik howls like a dog with a broken leg.

Karro reaches for me with both hands, and I hurry forward, taking them in mine. I kiss each one, my lips brushing over her purple cast. "Baby, I have to help Morbror. You take Teddy and you squeeze him tight, tight, tight. Hold him till I get back." I hand her the bear and kiss her forehead, ignoring her cries as I dash from the room.

Stumbling into Henrik's room, I cut on the light. He thrashes on the bed with the sheet twisted up around his naked hips. His legs are tangled too, adding to his panic. His chest is slicked with sweat.

Shutting out the sound of Karro's weak cries, I charge forward. "Come on, man. Wake up."

He groans as I touch him, rolling away.

I shake his shoulder. "Henrik, *wake up.*"

Mistaking me for some kind of life raft, he latches on, practically pulling me down onto the bed as he tries to climb my body. Cursing, I roll with him. "Henrik, it's me. It's Teddy. You need to wake up."

He pants, his sweaty, heavy body wrapping itself around me like a giant squid.

"Henrik, *please* wake up." Fighting fire with fire, I wrap my arms and legs right back around him, doing everything I can to trap down his flailing arms. "I'm not hurting you. Just wake up."

I feel it the moment he does. The pained groaning stops, and his muscles spasm as he fights my hold. I instantly let up, relaxing all my muscles so I'm just holding him, not holding him down. "Shh. You're okay. Henrik, it's me. It's Teddy. You were just having a bad dream again."

He grunts, trying to shift out from under me. "I'm awake," he says on a breath.

"Are you sure?"

He taps my shoulder. "Let me up."

From beyond the wall, Karro cries out again. "Teddy, come back!"

He curses in Swedish. "Karro—"

"No." I push myself off him. "I'll go to her."

He grabs my wrist. "I should go—"

"No," I say again. Glancing down, I take in his sweat-slicked, naked form. His chest is heaving. His pupils are dilated. He looks panicked and scared. "She doesn't need to see you like this."

With a groan and a nod, he lets go of my wrist. I slip off the bed, hurrying back into Karro's room. She's sitting up now, clutching tight to Teddy the Bear. "Morbror's hurt?"

I find her a smile and cross over to her bed. "No, honey. He's not hurt. He was just having a bad dream. Do you ever have bad dreams?"

"Yeah."

I sit down on the edge of the bed and place a hand on her knee. "So, then you know. It's not very fun, is it?"

She shakes her head, her lower lip trembling.

"Oh honey, he didn't mean to scare you. Your morbror loves you so much. You're the most important thing in the world to him." I help her get settled back against her pile of pillows, resetting her stuffed animals in order of emotional importance.

"And you?"

I shift her stuffed giraffe to the end of the line. With a name like Mister Sparkles, it's no wonder he's practically in exile. "Me what, honey?"

"I'm important to you?"

I sit up, blinking back my sudden tears. Reaching over, I cup her face, brushing the velvet softness of her cheek. "You're so important to me. And I'm so glad I met you. We're best friends now, right?"

She nods.

"You're my little warrior princess. You're so strong, honey. I wanna go on all your adventures with you. Like Puffin and Jean-Bob and Odette. Can I do that?"

She nods again as I hand her the rainbow unicorn to wedge in next to Teddy the Bear.

"You know, as soon as these casts come off, we're gonna go ride horses on the beach and learn to surf. Won't that be fun?"

She snuggles into the blanket as I tuck her in. "Yeah."

"And you're gonna do ballet again, and you'll teach me all the steps. We'll make Morbror do it too."

She smiles weakly, her fatigue taking over now that the rush of her adrenaline is leaving her. "In a tutu?"

I smile back, brushing a hand over her braided hair. "And ice skates."

Her smile falters as she squeezes Teddy the Bear. "He was yelling."

"Not at you. Never at you, honey bun. Henrik would pull down the sky for you. You're his most favorite person in the world."

Right on cue, Henrik appears in the doorway. He's cleaned himself up and put on some shorts and a T-shirt. "Karro?"

She takes him in, looking for any sign of injury. Then she breaks down crying. "Morbror."

He hurries over to the bed, dropping down next to me. Folding himself over her, he hugs her, talking in fast Swedish, offering soothing words and touches that calm them both. I scoot down to the end of the bed, giving them room. Henrik says something that involves my name. That part, at least, I understand.

Karolina peeks under the crook of his arm at me and I see her smile. Then she starts to giggle.

Henrik sits up. "Vad är fel?"

"You have to say it," she says in English.

"Say what?"

She peeks around him at me. "He has to say it, ja?"

I can't help but smile, warmth blooming in my chest to know she's okay. This didn't scar her for life. "That *is* the rule, yes."

Henrik glances between us. "What rule?"

"If you talk about me in Swedish, you have to say, 'I'm a Swedish meatball' in English," I explain.

This causes Karro to squeak with laughter, hiding her face behind her unicorn.

Henrik feigns a glare. "Absolutely not."

"No, you do," she cries. "It's the rule."

Henrik raises a brow. "The rule, you say?"

She nods.

He considers for a moment. "Well, I suppose in that case . . ."

We both wait. I flash her a wink and she stifles her giggles as Henrik sighs dramatically. "Very well, then. I'm a Swedish meatball."

Karro laughs, falling back against her pillows.

Heavy moment over, we both tuck her in, giving her and Teddy the Bear kisses.

"God natt, mitt lilla lamm," he says. "Sov så gott."

"God natt," she murmurs, relaxing in the comfort of knowing she's loved and protected. "God natt, Teddy."

I glance to Henrik. "What do I say? Teach me something."

He smiles. "Say, 'Dröm underbara drömmar.'"

"What does it mean?"

"Dream wonderful dreams."

Leaning over Karro, I give her one last kiss. "Dröm underbara drömmar, honey bun."

She nods, her eyes already closed as she holds tight to her bear.

Henrik and I sit there and wait, watching her under the glow of her twinkle lights. Then he turns, and he's looking at me. What is he trying to see? Feeling awkward, I break first, rising from her bed. Henrik follows me from her room. I wonder if he'll go right back to his room, but he doesn't. He follows me through the living room and into the kitchen.

Desperate to put distance between us, I slink around the island and reach for my forgotten potatoes.

"What the hell was that?" he says, breaking the silence. "What are you even doing here?"

"What?" I glance around, confused. "I *live* here, remember?"

"You said you were staying out tonight."

"Well, I didn't. And it seems like I came home pretty much right on time."

He crosses his arms, and I try to ignore the way they bulge so beautifully in his too-tight T-shirt. "I had everything under control."

I snort, snapping the lid back on the mashed potatoes. "Yeah. Clearly."

"Hey, I was taking care of myself long before you ever entered my life, Teddy. Karolina too. We are not your responsibility."

His words hit me like a slap. "How the fuck do you figure that? I fucking married you, Henrik. I signed her custody papers. Or did you forget that too?" I point towards her room. "That little girl is half mine. And I am *all* hers. I'm not gonna just stand by and watch while she cries, panicking, because *you* can't sleep through the night."

His nostrils flare as he glares at me. "I vowed this would impact you as little as possible. I vowed you'd be free to live your life. And so you are. You should be out now, living that life. Not trapped here with me."

"Oh god, don't be such a fucking martyr. You're not the first person to live with night terrors. They suck, but they're treatable. And preventable. But you have to want to help yourself. You have to actually *seek* treatment. If not for you, do it for Karro. She doesn't deserve to be woken up, scared in her bed, thinking you're in the next room fucking dying. She's experienced enough parental death for one lifetime, don't you think?"

Now he's the one reeling back.

Fuck, how did we even get here? Why are we arguing at two in the morning in the fucking kitchen? He has a game tomorrow. And we're both exhausted. No good can come of this.

"I don't wanna fight," I say, releasing all the wind in my sails. "If you want me to go that fucking bad, I'll go—"

"Don't." He closes his eyes as if my words pained him. "Don't go." He opens his eyes, looking right at me. Fuck, what is he looking for so intently? "I want you to stay. I want you here, Teddy. I didn't want—that is to say, I don't . . ."

I tilt my head, trying to make sense of his gibberish. "Did your internal translator just break?"

"I don't own you," he blurts. "Even with that ring on your finger, even with the contract signed, you are not mine. But I'm possessive, Teddy. I'm precious about my things and about the people close to me. I like control, and I like to feel . . . ordered. But I don't get to do that with you. I haven't the right. I—tonight was difficult for me," he adds, all but stuttering over the words. "But that's my problem. I had no right, Teddy. And I'm sorry. With better sleep, I think I'll be more articulate."

The words are a jumble, but he's said enough. More than fucking enough. And now my heart is racing. Is this . . . is Henrik admitting to feeling *jealous*? That's a big emotion for him. Was he jealous tonight, thinking I was out with Colin? Is that what set him off? Restless and anxious, he came back here alone, and his out-of-control feelings led him to have a night terror?

I should feel mortified, right? In his inability to process his own emotions, I caused a man to have a night terror. That's mortifying.

So why am I also flattered?

Henrik feels possessive over *me*. Precious, he said. He wants me, wants to keep me close. Inside, I'm crowing like a damn rooster. He gave me his truth, so I give him mine. "I wasn't out with Colin tonight."

He blinks, registering my words. "What?"

"I didn't go out with Colin tonight. That's not where I was."

A dozen fresh emotions flash across his face before he squashes them down. "Where did you go?"

"Rip's."

His head tips to the side. "The karaoke bar?"

"Yeah."

"Why?"

"Check the bag."

He glances around. "What?"

I sigh, pointing across the island. "The massive gift bag right in front of you. Open it."

His curiosity gets the better of him, so he rustles through the tissue paper, pulls out the puffy WAG jacket, and holds it up. "What is this?"

"Another manifestation of your ownership of me."

He glances around the jacket. "What?"

I huff, crossing my arms. "It's a WAG jacket, Henrik. I was forced to attend a WAG induction party tonight on pain of Caleb Price's foot up my ass. I showed up, they shoved me in that jacket, then Colton fucking Morrow, my literal hockey hero, hugged me and told me how proud he was that there was another queer Black man in the Rays' Wives and Guys Club."

"Wives and Guys?"

"Well, they can't still call us the 'wives and girlfriends,' can they? Not when four of us have big, swinging dicks."

He turns the jacket around, reading the back. "What's Tedrik?"

I lean against the counter with my hip. "It's our ship name. You know, Teddy plus Henrik equals Tedrik. It's just a silly nickname. Most of the WAGs have something like that on their jackets. Caleb's says "CAKE" for Caleb and Jake."

He lowers the jacket to the island, his thumbs brushing over the rhinestone-covered number seventeens on the shoulders. "You think this jacket represents ownership?"

I just shrug. "It's a pretty big freaking deal in your world, Hen. There's only one way to get a jacket like this: a player has to claim you. And the WAGs expect me to wear this. Maybe not all the time. But for game one, they want us in them. And for the playoffs and stuff like that."

He drops his hands away from the jacket. "You don't have to wear it. If anyone has anything to say about it, you send them to me. Agreed?"

I consider for a moment, arms still crossed. "And if I want to wear it? If I *choose* to wear my 'if found, please return to Henrik Karlsson' jacket?"

A ghost of a smile flits across his lips, and I have my answer. He wants me to wear it. Fuck me, in that case, I'll never take it off. "I would respect your wishes," he says, his tone measured. "Whatever you want, Teddy. You can have whatever you want from me."

Someday I'm gonna replay those exact words on a loop in my mind while I jerk myself off in the shower. Not tonight, obviously. But soon.

For now, we've had enough of an emotional roller coaster. Any more thrills, and I'll be performing CPR on this overwrought Swede. This level of emotionality is still so new for him, so raw and unfiltered. Heck, for me it's a boring Thursday night. Banal, even. But for Henrik, I get the feeling this has been the equivalent of pulling some hard G's. He needs a cooldown. And a reset.

"Come on." I slip the container of potatoes off the counter and return them to the fridge.

"What?"

"Come with me."

Curious, he leaves the jacket on the island and follows me down the hallway and into my bedroom. "What's wrong?"

"Get in the bed."

He stiffens, glancing from the bed back to me. "Teddy, we have rules. You require your own room, remember?"

"Yeah, well, I'm breaking my rule."

"Teddy . . ."

"Hey, it's mine to break. And I get whatever I want from you, remember? Your words, not mine."

He crosses his arms. "What exactly do you want?"

"I want you close in case I have to wake you from another nightmare. And I want you further away from Karro so you don't wake her up and scare her again."

He groans, dragging a hand through his already-mussed hair. "I'll go see Doctor Tyler this week. I'll get a prescription for a sleep aid."

"Sounds good. But that can't help us tonight. Get in the bed, Henrik."

Too tired to fight me, he shuffles around to the far side of the bed and crawls under the covers. I excuse myself to the bathroom and get ready for bed, not coming out until my teeth are brushed, face is washed, locs are moisturized, and head scarf is wrapped snugly around my head. As I come out, I strip off my T-shirt, dropping it to the floor.

Henrik is stretched out on the bed, quiet and deadly as a fucking mountain lion. His eyes are open, those denim blue irises swallowed up by the black of his pupils as he tracks my every movement. Even this man's casual attention sets my every nerve on fire. Now, feeling his possessive stare? Let's just say I'm about to release a breath I didn't know I was holding.

I slip under the covers on my side of the bed and roll away from him, pretending he's not even there as I get my phone charging and take my nightly vitamins. Then I click off the lamp and nestle into the pillows. I wait a beat, listening for the sound of Henrik's slow, even breathing. I know he's still awake. Reaching behind me, my fingers brush over the sheets until they feather lightly up his arm.

"What are you doing?" he whispers.

Wrapping my hand around his wrist, I tug him closer.

He lets himself be reeled in, closing the distance until he's pressed as close as we were in that tiny bed in the boat hut.

"Teddy, I can't," he rasps, a slight catch in his voice. "I don't want to hurt you."

"Shhh." I drape his arm around my middle, luxuriating in the feel of his bare skin pressed against mine.

He scoots in close, all but resting his head on my pillow.

"There," I soothe, taking a deep breath and letting it out. "You can't drown if you're holding onto the dock. Now go to sleep. You have a game tomorrow." I feel him relax behind me, his breath warm as it fans across the back of my neck. "God natt, Henrik."

He shifts his hold on me, curling his arm up until it's banded against my chest. "God natt, mitt hjärta."

Within minutes, he's asleep.

28

HENRIK

"**K**arlsson!"

I glance over my shoulder to see Coach Johnson standing in the doorway to his office, hands on his hips. All around me, my teammates are going through their pregame rituals, preparing for our first game of the season. Rock music plays through the speakers, adding to the noise.

"Yes, Coach?"

"Get in here." Without waiting for a response, he disappears into his office.

I toss my moisture-wicking undershirt into my stall and stand. My skates are already on, shin pads secured, socks taped. My hockey pants sit loose around my waist as I cross the dressing room.

Is he about to tell me I'm not starting? I know I've been off these past few weeks, but I actually skated better this morning. I finally slept, thank Christ. Never mind that I woke to find myself wrapped around Teddy, our arms and legs entangled. There was no way to extract myself without waking him, but my alarm was going off. He groaned, rolling with me as I turned, reaching for my buzzing phone.

"Whattimeizit?" he mumbled.

"Early," I replied, slipping from the bed.

He let me leave, his body stretched out like a starfish across the sheets as he chased more sleep.

I stumbled into the bathroom and stood at the sink, early-morning light glowing pink in the mirror. I stood there and stared at my own reflection, wondering how I could go three decades feeling like sharing my bed with another person was an unwelcome invasion of privacy. Now, in the span of less than three weeks, I've come to feel like I can't sleep without Teddy next to me.

What is happening to me?

"Guys, squash in," says Coach. "Make room for Karlsson. I'll make this quick."

Pausing in Coach's doorway, I glance around. The small office is cramped with my teammates, all in a similar state of partial dress. Jake, my team captain; Langley and Novy, the assistant captains. Fuck, this can't be good. He really is going to take my starting spot away.

Even Caleb is in here, standing in the corner with his hands in his pockets.

Wait . . . why would our equipment manager be here to discuss a line change?

I slip inside the door. "What's wrong?"

Coach leans forward in his tailored grey suit, hands splayed on his desk. "It's been brought to my attention that you're making a little announcement tonight."

I go still. "Sir?"

"Otherwise, why would Poppy St. James deliver this to my office?" He picks up a folder, flipping it open. "It's a press release announcing that you went off to Sweden and married our new PT. Is that correct?"

I sigh, leaning against the doorway. "Yes, sir. Teddy and I are married. It's been cleared with HR. Everything is legal and, you know . . . ethical." I try not to look Jake's and Caleb's way. Their own coming-out was marred by the sticky situation of Doctor Price being Ilmari's treating physician. "Poppy's team is handling the press release."

"Oh, she's handling it alright. I've got the release right here, along with strict instructions that I'm supposed to throw you to the wolves tonight after the game, win or lose."

Shit. Poppy didn't inform me I'd be doing press tonight. I knew the release would go live during the game. It will likely be all over the internet by the end of the first period.

Just perfect. As if I wasn't already distracted enough.

Reading my mind, Coach shakes his head, dropping the folder to the desk. "You men, I swear. Never in my thirty years in the League have I dealt with so many personal revelations on one team. I mean, how does this even happen? How are you *all* gay?"

Next to me, Novy snorts. But Jake sits forward in his chair. "Well, not to be too pedantic here, sir, but Caleb is actually queer, and I'm bi. I'm pretty sure Novy is straight, plus Morrow. And Mars is just . . . well, Mars," he finishes with a shrug.

"And retired," Caleb adds.

"And I've been told I have major bi-wife energy," says Langley, sitting in the only other chair. "Also, my wife is bi . . . if that becomes relevant."

Novy nudges Jake's arm. "Hey, great use of 'pedantic' there, bud."

Jake smiles, glancing up at his husband. "Did I use it right?"

Caleb nods.

"Yeah, man, I think that was right," says Langley.

"Sounded right to me," says Novy with a shrug.

"Enough," Coach shouts. "I won't have this distracting us all from going out there and playing our best game tonight. Karlsson, you've already been on the back foot since your return from Sweden. I need to know if your head is in this. And what are these?" He pulls out a stack of papers from the folder.

Novy crosses his tatted arms over his barrel chest. "How can we possibly know that without looking at them first?"

Coach glares at him. "Well, I'll just tell you then, shall I? These are letters written in support of Karlsson and O'Connor, detailing their years-long, slow-burning, secret gay romance. Does this sound familiar?" He slips on his cheaters and reads from the first letter. "'Henrik Karlsson is as gay as the day is long. I always knew he and Teddy would get together.'"

"Oh, hey." Novy perks up, raising his hand. "Coach, that's mine. I wrote that one."

From the corner of the room, Caleb smirks. "Gay as the day is long? Seriously?"

Novy chuckles. "What did you write, asshole? Some emo song lyrics?"

Coach holds up more papers. "Langley, yours is five pages long. Front and back."

Langley shrugs, going a little pink at the ears. "I felt passionately about it."

"It's in legalese, Langley! It cites three federal statutes and a ruling from the Supreme Court of Florida."

"All good arguments should be backed up with facts, right?"

Coach shakes the papers at him. "There are footnotes!"

"Dude, just admit Tess helped you," Novy mutters.

Langley rolls his eyes. Everyone on the team knows he has severe dyslexia. "Fine. Yeah, obviously she helped. But I support every word of it."

"Read mine next," says Jake.

"I'm not gonna stand here and read all these out! Sweet Mother Mary, the picture Novikov paints would make a damn sailor blush." Coach drops the pile of papers to his desk. "Will someone just fill me in so I know what the hell is going on? Why are we doing this now? Why do you think we need this distraction right at the start of the damn season? Why do you *all* have to make such a public deal out of your damn private lives?"

My teammates all go still, glaring at Coach.

"It's for Operation Mighty Oak," Novy explains.

Coach narrows his eyes at him. "Operation what?"

"Operation Mighty Oak," he repeats.

"Mighty what?"

"Please don't say it again," I mutter.

Novy sinks into silence.

"Look, just ask Poppy," says Caleb.

"I'm asking my damn players! You know, the men I pay to play hockey?"

"It's no big deal," Jake assures him. "She asked us to write the letters so Karlsson and Teddy can show the Swedish and American governments proof of a prior relationship. You know, for their custody case. It's for Karlsson's niece, Coach."

"We're all ready to swear before any court that the stuff in those letters is true," Langley adds.

"Trust us," Jake goes on. "We're not hurting the team, Coach. We're *helping* it. Team means family, and family sticks together. Karlsson just needs to get through press tonight, okay? You know the vultures; give them a little taste of blood, and they'll back off. But the rest of us are focused. We're taking home the W, and the Islanders will go back to New York in tears."

Coach levels his gaze at me. "And you, Karlsson? Six years with you on this team, and I've never once had to question whether you were fit to play. But now?" He lets out a heavy sigh. "Well, son, I'm asking. Are you here? Are you in this?"

My embarrassment feels ready to boil me from the inside out. I don't do this. I don't make public statements about my personal life. I don't give interviews and write press releases. And I don't lie.

And this is all a lie. Every word in those letters is a fabrication designed to deceive. I'm so grateful to every man in this room who is coming to my defense. They're protecting me, protecting Karolina and Teddy. But if their defense comes at the expense of their integrity? How do I live with that? How do I look them in the eye?

"Hey." From behind me, Novy squeezes my shoulder.

I glance his way.

As if he can read my every thought, the corner of his mouth tips with a reassuring smile. "It's okay, bud. We've got you. You're a Ray, Karlsson. And Rays flock together . . . or, you know, whatever shit rays do out in the wild."

"School, maybe?" Langley offers.

"Swim?" says Jake with a shrug. He turns to Caleb. "Hey babe, what's the group noun for stingrays?"

We all turn as Caleb stands there, hands in his pockets. "I . . ."

The tension in the room breaks as Jake gasps, tugging on Langley's arm. "Oh my god, take a picture."

Novy pushes off from the wall, eyes alight. "He doesn't know."

Langley fumbles in his pocket as Jake shakes his shoulder. "Take the fucking picture!"

Laughing, Langley holds up his phone. "Did we finally do it, Cay? Did we find the limits of your dazzling intellect?"

Jake looks like a kid on Christmas as he points at his husband. "You don't even know, do you? Admit it."

"Fuck you," Caleb mutters, throwing up a hand to try to stop Langley from taking his picture. "None of you knows either, assholes."

"Send it to Mars!" Jake directs as Caleb lunges over him. "Tell him Cay needs to ask him a very important question—*ouch*—" He and Langley cackle as Caleb folds himself over Jake's chair, trying to wrestle the phone away.

"Give it to me."

"*Ow*—babe—hey, not so feisty in front of Coach!"

"Here—catch!" Langley tosses the phone to Novikov.

"Fuckers—"

"Sent," says Novy with a smug grin.

Meanwhile, Coach looks as red as a tomato as he slams his fist down on the desk. "Enough!"

The guys all jolt as Caleb quickly tries to unfold himself from Jake's lap. But Jake wraps an arm around his hips, keeping Caleb pinned.

Coach looks around at all of us with a disappointed shake of his head. "Why I haven't retired already, I swear I'll never know. Now, all of you, get your heads out of your asses, get out of my damn office, and go get ready for the goddamn game!"

Before any of us can move, there's a knock on the door.

"What?" Coach shouts.

Brad Brady pops his head inside the door. "Hey, is Karlsson in here?"

Coach sighs. "He's right here, Brady. What do you need?"

Brady turns to me. "Uhh . . . it's Teddy. You better come quick."

"Christ have mercy," Coach mutters.

My heart drops. "What happened?"

Brady just shakes his head. "I don't know, man. He's sorta freaking out though."

I move for the door, my mind already imagining the worst. "What happened?" I say again.

Brady swings the door open, letting me exit. "He says his mom is here."

I stop. "What?"

"Yeah. He says she wants to meet you."

19

TEDDY

Twenty Minutes Earlier

"And down that hallway is where they keep the Zamboni," I say, holding up my phone as I walk. Hanna and Karolina watch through the video chat. Karro wanted to see the arena where Morbror Henrik plays. So far, she's only been allowed to visit the practice arena. We're waiting until we get the all clear about her cracked ribs before we even consider bringing her to the chaos and bustle of a live game day.

"Through there is where we do PT with the players," I go on, pointing out the double doors of the PT suite. "Morbror Henrik likes to get a leg massage before and after each game."

"Do you give him massages?" asks Karro in her cute little button accent.

I chuckle. "No, honey. I'm Morbror Henrik's partner, remember? I'm not allowed to treat him while we're at work."

Off work is a different story. But I imagine hell will freeze over before Henrik asks me for a sexy oil massage. His loss. I really am magic.

"Hey, you wanna watch Mr. Caleb sharpen some skate blades?" I walk down the hall, following the telltale sound of the blade sharpener.

I don't know if I'm technically supposed to be back here right now. But I never come to games unless I'm working them. It feels too weird to just wander around up on the concourse with all the normal fans. What am I gonna do, buy a foam finger?

Fine, maybe I'm hiding out. The moment I go up to my seat, the cameras will be on me. That's what we're here for, right? This isn't fun. It's work. I'm walking around in this damn WAG jacket, my hair is done, my jeans are pressed, the shoes are fly, and I'm wearing one of Henrik's gorgeous European watches . . . and his cologne.

This is all armor. Because any minute now, Poppy is going to text me to meet her at section 102, and then I'll be on stage. Lights, camera, action. Until that moment, I'm gonna stay down in these tunnels like a groundhog and pretend I'm not afraid of my own shadow.

"Can I see Morbror?"

"Not right now, honey. He's getting ready for the game, remember? But I'll take so many pictures and videos for you once he's on the ice, okay?"

"Will you bring me candy?"

I laugh. "Girl, I will bring home *so* much candy. When this game is over, we're gonna sit on that couch together and rot our teeth eating Milk Duds and Swedish Fish and German roasted pecans. Morbror Henrik is gonna have to fire Nurse Hanna and hire a live-in dentist."

Hanna rolls her eyes with a patient smile. I swear, I *do* like her. The jealous diva in me just aches to think of her as competition. Me and pretty, perfect Hanna? Yeah, that's a contest Teddy wouldn't win.

Before I can turn the corner to show Karro the blade sharpener, I hear a shout of "Teddy!"

Poppy marches my way in her sky-high heels. She's sporting a navy-blue pantsuit, her silky blouse stretched tight over her basketball of a baby bump.

"Hey, Pop, what's up?"

She huffs, her Barbie-blonde curls bouncing around her shoulders. "Well, I see you have your phone, so that's clearly not the reason you haven't answered a single one of my calls. Good. I'll mark that off the list and circle 'he's just ignoring me.' Mystery solved!"

"Pop, what—"

"I've been trying to reach you for two freaking hours! And, apparently, mine aren't the only calls you dodge. Your own mother, Teddy? Unless she's anything like *my* mother, she doesn't deserve this cold shoulder!"

"Whoa, whoa." I hold up my free hand, still holding up the

phone with Hanna and Karro on video chat with my other. "Poppy, what the heck are you talking about? I haven't missed any calls—"

She holds out her own phone, showing me the call log screen, including four outgoing call attempts to me.

I check my phone and groan, ignoring the confused looks of Karro and Hanna. "Sorry, Pop. I guess I don't have any service down here. I used Wi-Fi to do this video call."

"Well, have you been using Wi-Fi all dang week? 'Cause that's how long your mom has been trying to get ahold of you. Your sisters too."

"My—" I gasp, all the pieces clicking together in my head. "Ohmygod, Poppy, you didn't!"

Her cheeks bloom pink. "Don't you *dare* blame this on me. You said you were close with your family. You talk about your sisters and your little niblets all the time! And you tell *me* when you get indigestion. How was I supposed to know you wouldn't tell your own family that you got married?!"

Oh my fucking fuck. There's a reason my sisters each tried to call me *five* times last night! I turn to Hanna and Karro in the phone. "Girls, I gotta go." I don't wait for their response before I hang up. Then I stare down Poppy, who's standing with her hands on hips. "You invited my family to the game tonight."

"Yes."

I close my eyes tight, stifling a groan. Oh, this is bad. I open my eyes. "Who came?"

"Teddy, I didn't think—"

"Who came!"

She crosses her arms over her belly. "All of them, okay? I asked them all, and they all said yes. I flew them out first class and put them up in a hotel last night. I reserved *you* a room in their block too. They asked to be the ones to surprise you, but you never answered their many, many calls. So, well . . . surprise," she finishes, doing jazz hands.

"My mom is here? Now?"

Poppy nods. "She's waiting for you. They all are."

I sigh, tucking my phone in my pocket. "Well, the media loves a good dramatic moment, right? I hope they've got their cameras ready because I'm about to go cry on national freaking television."

30

TEDDY

I follow Poppy as she leads the way up out of the tunnels and over to the lower-level VIP area. "Wait . . . we're not going up to the seats?"

"I thought you might want a moment of privacy to greet your family. I had my staff bring them over to the press area. You'll get a bit more privacy there."

"Privacy in the *press* room?"

She waves her hand dismissively. "Oh, no one will be in there before the game except maybe a few interns taping down cords." She flashes the guards her badge, escorting me through. Then she stops, placing a hand on my arm. "Do you want me to stay with you? You just say the word, and I will."

I shake my head. "No," I finally croak out. "I think I need to do this alone."

With a nod, she drops her hand from my arm. "Well, then . . . good luck, honey. And hey—" She stops me again. "I know I don't know them like you do, but they sure do seem to love you. Honor that. But honor yourself too." With that, she really does let me go.

Taking a deep breath, I turn the corner and enter the press corral. Through the jungle of camera stands and sound equipment, I see my family huddled together on the other side. My sisters and their partners, my mom. Natalie bounces baby Gianna on her hip, while my nephew Baz chases his sister Camila around the press table. Jayla calls their names, warning them to act right. To a person, they're all wearing Henrik's jersey, a big number seventeen on their backs.

They're *here*. They came. Even mad at me, they came. And they're wearing my partner's jersey. I all but trip over the bundled camera cords as I call out, "Mama!"

They all turn.

"Mom, Teddy's here!"

"Hey, Uncle Teddy!"

The youngest niblets rush to greet me first, but I have eyes only for my mom. After everything I've been going through with Karro, helping her grieve her mom, I feel the tears stinging hot and heavy. My sisters step back, making room for me.

"Mama, I'm sorry." They're the only words I get out before I'm hugging her, pressing my face to her shoulder. My senses fill with the familiar scent of her rosewater perfume. Awash with shame, I cling to her. "I'm *so* sorry. I should have told you. I've been so messed up. I never meant to lie."

Her arms go around me. Returning my hug, she pats my back. "It's okay, Teddy baby. Mama's here. You can tell me now."

I hold tighter to her, not ready to let go.

"We deserve an explanation," Shae says at my shoulder to mutters of agreement from my other sisters.

I finally pull away, sniffing back my tears.

My mom has worn the same style of bobbed wig for almost twenty years. The tight black curls frame her round face as she smiles up at me. "Boy, look at you. You're a mess." She pulls a tissue from her pocket and hands it to me.

I dab at my eyes and wipe my nose, trying to catch my breath.

"We need to know what's going on," says Jayla.

"It's not like you committed a crime, right?" Nat says at the same time.

"Except the crime of fashion," Jayla mutters. "Teddy, what is this jacket?" She plucks at it with a manicured hand.

I swat her hand away. "It's a WAG jacket. And no, I haven't committed any crimes."

"Well, so . . . you're married?" Shae crosses her arms, one brow raised, waiting for me to deny it. "That's the big secret?"

Jay pushes in, arms crossed too. "Last thing we knew, you were in Sweden with that hunky hockey player."

"Yeah, then you went radio silent," Nat adds with a glare. "Darius had to take my passport away to stop me from flying to Sweden to come find you!"

"I told you I was back," I mutter with a shrug.

"And you *adopted* that little girl?" Jayla says over me.

"What, you're so famous now?" Shae adds. "You can't talk to your own sisters? We need to go through a publicist to get to you?"

"What happened to you, Ted?"

"You better say something."

"We deserve more—"

They all press in, talking over each other until I shout, "I'm sorry, okay? What else can I say?"

"Sorry means nothing right now," says Shae. "We want answers."

Nat steps in, still bouncing baby Gianna on her hip. "You gotta fill in the blanks. Who even is this guy?"

"Raf looked him up," says Jay. "Beyond his hockey stats, there really wasn't much to find."

Reeling from all their questions, I glance over Jayla's shoulder at my brother-in-law. Rafael and Jayla both work in banking IT, handling stuff like theft and fraud, so I'm not surprised their solution was to try to dig up dirt on my fake husband.

"'Sup, Ted," he says. "You sure know how to make an entrance."

"For the record, I like the jacket," Shae's husband, Marcus, teases.

Shae just waves him back, eyes only for me. "Tell us what's going on, Teddy."

"And tell us why the team flew us out here—"

"Do we get to keep these jerseys?"

"Can we get some popcorn?"

My niece, Camila, steps in, tugging on Jayla's sleeve. "Mom, I have to go to the bathroom—"

"Alright!" I throw up both my hands. "Everyone, can you just *stop*? I feel like I can't fucking breathe!"

Mom *tsk*s, finally breaking her silence. "Language, Teddy. Come on now, I know I raised you right." Placing a hand on my shoulder, she looks in my eyes, rooting me to the spot. "Just take a breath. Then start at the beginning."

I wrap my hand around hers, giving it a squeeze. Then I take that deep breath and let it out. Then I start at the beginning.

Well, I start at *a* beginning.

They don't need to know that Henrik is the player who swept me off my feet six years ago. Like I told him after the ESPN interview, that story is just for us.

And they don't *really* need to know about my deep and abiding, totally one-sided crush. Again, what does it really add to the narrative? They want to know why I married him, and that reason hasn't changed. Slipping my phone from my pocket, I hold it up and press the little green camera button under Hanna's name.

"What are you doing?" asks Jayla.

"You all want to know why I married Henrik? I'm showing you."

Before they can respond, Hanna picks up the call. She's in the kitchen. I can see flour dusted on her chin. "Hey, Teddy. Everything alright? We were worried before—"

"Hey, Hanna," I say, cutting her off before she can recount for my entire family how freaked I was at finding out they were here. "Can you pass the phone to Karolina? I want her to meet my mom."

"Of course." The phone jostles as she moves over to Karolina's side.

"Hej, Teddy." Karro waves with her good arm. She's propped up on a bar stool, sticky whisk in hand. "We're making hallongrottor!"

"Yum. Save me some?" I have no idea what a hallongrottor is, but Hanna is an amazing baker. And it's great therapy for Karro. Just seeing her sweet little face makes me feel so much better. Henrik may want *us* to be temporary, but me and this little girl? In a few short weeks, she's become the ketchup to my freaking mustard. "Hey, honey bun. Would you like to pause your baking for a sec and meet a real queen? She's the most beautiful queen in all the lands."

She practically flings the whisk aside. "Yes!"

Laughing, I wrap an arm around my mom's shoulders and angle

the phone down, fitting us both in the frame. "Princess Karolina, fairest in all of Swedenhamshire, may I present my mother, Queen Keziah of . . . Atlantia."

Mom nudges my ribs, lips pursed in annoyance, as the rest of the family chuckles. But her expression softens as soon as she takes in the little girl with the casted arm and the sad, faraway look in her eyes. "Well, look at you," she coos, reaching up to wrap a hand around mine on the phone. "Hello, Karolina. I'm Teddy's mama. But you can call me Miss Ziah."

Hanna translates everything, even though I know Karro can understand just fine. Unsure of what to do, Karro holds up her stuffed purple bear, showing it to the camera.

"Isn't that a pretty bear?" says Mom. "Does she have a name, honey?"

Letting her nerves get the best of her, Karro says something in Swedish. She's always nervous around strangers. So different from the fireball who giggles with me on the couch.

Mom glances to me, clearly worried she's upset her.

I just smile. "The bear is a boy, Mama. And his name is Teddy, just like me."

31

HENRIK

Dressed in my full hockey kit, I make my way down the hallway, protective covers on my blades. Nothing about this day has conformed to *any* of my typical pregame rituals. If I were a more superstitious player, I'd probably be breathing into a bag by now. Instead, I'm skipping my final equipment check to meet my new mother-in-law.

"He's just through there," says Brady, pointing down the hall to where an open door waits. Patting me on the padded shoulder, he disappears.

As soon as I enter the room, Teddy hurries forward. "I'm sorry. Henrik, god, I'm *so* fucking sorry to bother you. But I was freaking out because I didn't want you to feel ambushed or, like, throw you off your game or—"

"Where's your mother?"

He blinks, dropping his hand away from my arm. "What?"

I glance around again. "I was told I was meeting your mother here."

"Oh, no. Not here." He waves a hand up towards the ceiling. "They're all up in the stands already."

"They?"

He groans. "Yeah. Okay, so, I know this isn't technically your problem. Fake marriage, and all that. But my entire fucking family is here to watch this game. Like, everyone."

I blink. "Everyone?"

"Down to the last niblet. She's two. Her name's Gianna. Actually, she's pretty cool. She's got this adorable little—"

"Teddy, *focus*." I grab him by the shoulders. "I only have two minutes. Look at me, focus, and tell me only what I need to know."

He takes a deep breath and lets it out, nodding. "Yeah, okay."

When I'm sure he's not going to keep spiraling, I let him go. "Well?"

"Poppy invited my whole family to this game. You're about to skate out there and see my mom, my sisters, their partners, and all my niblets. The whole Wilson-O'Connor-Fulton-Osman clan. They're here, and after the game, they want to meet you."

I absorb this information, filing it away under "No immediate action needed." Then I say, "And what do they know about us?"

"I mean, pretty much everything. They just met Karro. I did a video chat with her and Hanna and—oh god—" He presses a hand to his chest. "I hope that's okay. I didn't even think to ask you first. I swore I'd defer to you with all things Karro. I know how protective you are. And this was sort of huge, letting her meet my family. I'm sorry—"

"It's fine. You've got sixty seconds. Anything else?"

He shakes his head. "Nope. I just really didn't want you to skate out there and be surprised."

I nod, already conducting the mental calibrations needed to shift myself back into pregame mode. "Thank you for telling me. But I really have to go."

"Yeah, totally." He backs away. "Go play hockey. Win pucks, or whatever."

I let my gaze trail away from his panicked expression to take in the rest of him. He's wearing the WAG jacket with a white T-shirt, jeans, what looks like a pair of my shoes, and my favorite Swiss watch. "Looks like you had fun in my closet today."

He shrugs, grinning. "Our closet now, remember?"

On his first night at the apartment, I told him he could take anything he wanted. He looks good in my clothes. And he smells good in my cologne.

He looks me up and down too, eyes narrowed. "You look better today. More well rested. You feel ready?"

We both know the only reason I'm rested is that he let me sleep in his arms last night. Like a child, I clung to him, using the rhythms of his body to reset my own. "Thanks to you," I say, offering him a weak smile.

His gaze heats as he steps back, crossing his arms in the jacket bearing my number. "I should be careful with that, huh? You hockey players and your superstitions. If we set a pregame precedent and it proves lucky for you out on the ice, we may just have to repeat it . . . right?"

I swallow, unsure how to compute this conversation with my brain's current efforts at recalibration. Is he offering what I think he's offering? I should say no. He wanted these barriers in place for a reason. We're letting our emotions get the better of us. On no account should I go crawling back to his bed tonight, desperate to feel the warmth of his skin against mine.

I *should* say no. Instead, I step forward in my skates, our heights more pronouncedly mismatched. He sucks in a breath, leaning away, as I wrap my arm around his shoulders. Lowering my face, I drop my forehead to his and close my eyes, content to just breathe him in.

His hands flutter at his sides, finally resting on the thick pads at my hips. We stand there, breathing in sync, as he lets me hold him. He gives me too much. Like a glutton, I take. I can't help myself. Outside that door, chaos swirls. But in here? In Teddy's arms? There is only peace. I want to chase this feeling. I want to take and take until I'm full up of him.

"You're gonna be late," he whispers. "And then you won't have to worry about telling the press about us because I'll be shark bait."

Groaning, I lean away.

He clears his throat, shoulders stiffening. "Good luck out there, yeah?"

"Thank you, Teddy."

He just huffs, backing away with his hands in his pockets. "Oh, don't thank me yet."

"Why?"

"You haven't met my family."

32

TEDDY

The arena hums with the energy of a hive as 18,000 people watch the Jacksonville Rays take to the ice for the season opener game. When Henrik is announced, my sisters jump and scream, grabbing at my arms. I'm jostled as I watch him skate in a graceful arc around the defensive zone and glide behind the net, where DeGraw is busy scuffing up the ice.

Fuck me, my fake husband looks so fucking good. When he came charging into the AV room, I swear, my brain short-circuited. His sandy blond hair was swept across his brow, already wet with sweat. And he's still doing his whole no-shaving thing, which is really fucking working for me. I never thought I was into the hairy-bear type, but my Swedish, sweater-wearing hockey man can grow that beard out as long as he wants.

"That's his husband," Jayla screams, pointing over my head for all the fans around us to see.

"Will you *stop*?" I cry, trying to pull myself free of her grasp.

"Hey, you said you're going public tonight anyway, right?" She spins around, cupping her mouth like the crazy woman she is. "Number seventeen is my brother-in-law! They just got married!"

A few fans behind us cheer and return her offer of high fives.

"Oh my god." I don't dare turn around.

In the row right behind us, my niblets are all busy devouring buckets of popcorn. Poppy spared no expense, having food and drinks delivered to our seats that included hot dogs, nachos, beer for my brothers-in-law, and wine coolers for my sisters. She even brought my mom a root beer.

My own beer sits ignored under my seat. I'm too nervous to drink tonight. Henrik is focused on the game, but I'm focused on what comes after. Poppy said the story about us will go live during the first period. The moment this game is over, Henrik has to face the press. And after the press conference, he has to meet my mother.

Honestly, I don't know which will be worse.

Don't get me wrong, I love my mom to the moon and back. But she's a tough nut. And she always knows exactly how things ought to be. As a high school administrator for almost thirty years, she's used to running things her way. Everything is about logic and orders of operation.

I smile, clapping along to the music, as Henrik skates by in a flash. They actually have a lot in common. They're both used to managing things on their own and leading as the head of a family that relies on them for financial and emotional support. She's the heartbeat of our family for sure, the calm center, the final opinion.

And, boy, does she have opinions about me and Henrik. She held back earlier in the press room, but I could see it on her face. Mama was calculating. My sisters didn't get to ask too many questions because we were interrupted by a volunteer docent leading twenty VIPs in for a behind-the-scenes tour of the arena.

Whatever Mama thinks about me marrying Henrik, she's keeping it to herself for now. Which is why Teddy won't be touching a drop of alcohol tonight. Not until this is all over.

The lights come up as the Islanders and the Rays skate around their respective ends of the ice. Henrik skates with Lindberg, each of them taking a few shots on the empty goal while DeGraw stretches in the corner. Henrik does a few puck handling drills, bouncing the puck on his blade, before whacking it into the back of the net. Then he's skating past us again and Shae tries waving him down.

"Henrik! Hey, Henrik!"

"Guys, stop," I beg. "Don't distract him—"

"Hey, KARLSSON!" Behind me, Marcus bellows so loud, it rattles my damn rib cage. "Sweden SUCKS!"

Both Henrik and Lindberg look our way.

Spinning around, I punch Marcus in the arm. "Can you not?"

He just laughs, rubbing his arm. "Hey, it got his attention, didn't it?"

"Oh, he's coming over," says Jayla.

"It worked!" My niece, Winnie, squeals, jumping up and down.

"Daddy, you did it!" says her sister Desiree.

Our fan section cheers as Henrik and Lindberg skate over to the plexiglass, sliding to a stop right in front of us. Lindberg holds back a little, calling out in Swedish.

Henrik answers before turning to me.

Natalie pushes me forward. "Blow him a kiss!"

Shae jostles her, holding up her phone. "Smile for the camera, Teddy!"

Wishing I could sink right through the floor, I do the lamest possible thing and press my left hand flat to the glass. My wedding ring glints under the arena lights, making my stomach flip.

Henrik only waits a beat before he slips his glove off and presses his hand to mine. There's no ring on his finger. It shouldn't bother me, right? The guys all have to take their jewelry off when they play. I know he'll put it back on the moment the game is over. When he's with us off the ice, he's always wearing both rings. I shift my hand, lining it up with his.

"I don't have a lot of time."

"It's fine," I say, feeling breathless.

He glances over my shoulder. "This is your family?"

I groan. "Yes, but—"

"We're his sisters."

"And his nieces!"

They push in behind me, all trying to talk at once.

"I'm Jayla, and this is my husband, Rafael."

"Hey, man."

"And I'm Natalie, but you can call me Nat—"

"My name's Winnie!"

"Will you all cool it?" I try to wave them back. "He has, like, *two* seconds. He'll meet y'all later."

"Doctor O'Connor, look this way please!"

I turn to see one of the media guys over on the stairs, holding up a big camera.

Oh, shit.

"Karlsson, up here! Big smiles!"

Before I can even blink, he's flashing his camera at us, snapping pics. Then a whistle blows, and Henrik drops his hand away from the glass. "I have to go."

"Okay." I don't know what else I'm supposed to say in front of a crowd of hockey fans who are actively piecing it together that the player they've been watching for over a decade is currently outing himself as gay and married to a Black man. Mentally, I'm prepared for them to start booing. I mean, this *is* still the NHL.

Henrik is about to skate off when I shout, "Hey!"

He glances over his shoulder.

"I need you to score a goal tonight."

He chuckles. "I'll do my best, babe."

Ignoring my sisters' obnoxious cooing sounds, I press my hand back to the glass. "No, like, I *really* need you to score a goal. It's a WAG thing. You wouldn't understand."

He skates closer until he's right on the glass again. Up and down the plexiglass, fans pound their fists, trying to get his attention. But he looks only at me. "What did you do?"

I just shrug, flashing him a smile.

His eyes narrow on the glint of silver at my wrist. "I'll want that watch back."

I laugh, wrapping my hand around it. "Score a goal, and we'll see."

Then, because I'm completely crazy, and because cameras are on me—and fuck all the haters, this is my special moment—I give into my sisters' demands and blow Henrik a kiss as he skates away.

33

HENRIK

The puck drops for the third time in the first period, and Lindberg claims it, passing it across to Langley. I try to get myself in position, but there's a lot of traffic as we move down the ice. The Islanders are fresh off their summer too, and just as hungry for their first win of the season.

Each time I get the puck, I send it back to Jake or Novy. I just can't catch my breath with the way these guys keep swarming me, and I can't seem to move the puck forward.

Coach calls for a line change, and I race to the bench, hopping the side as Westie takes my place out on the line. As soon as I drop down to the bench, Assistant Coach Denison steps in behind me. He places a hand on mine and Lindberg's shoulder pads. "We gotta be moving the puck faster out there, boys. Read each play and find those openings. Karlsson, you're playing it too safe. That new guy Ramsay is all over you. But he's a lightweight, first year in the League. Probably still thinks Santa brings him his hockey sticks for Christmas."

Around me, the other guys laugh.

Denison slaps my shoulder pad. "Let's rush these forward lines and get some real two-on-one action going, eh? Let's make some real plays out there! Come on, let's go!"

We all grunt our assent as our brief, fifty-second respite ends. The line changes, and Langley, Lindberg, and I take to the ice again. I shoot across the rink, instantly picking up my new shadow. Coach is right—my usual gameplay isn't working with this guy. He's all over me, reading me like a book. Time to get creative. Rather than stay in my lane and wait for Lindberg or Langley to get a clean shot to pass, I rush the goal, cutting in towards the center line. Both Islander defensemen scramble, bracing for Lindberg to pass the puck to me.

But Lindberg uses my sudden surge to slip the puck behind Ramsay and out of the middle. Langley just barely snags the puck with the tip of his blade. In one stride, he's recovered it. In two, he takes his first shot on goal. It shoots like a bullet across the ice, cutting right past the goalie's toe and into the back of the net. The siren lights up, the horn blasts, and the arena erupts with cheers.

A textbook line rush. I didn't get the goal. I didn't even get the assist. But the play would have been impossible without me. And now the score is 1-0. Lindberg and I skate in to Langley, congratulating him for getting the first goal of the season. "Well done," I tell him, slapping his back and tapping our helmets together.

Jake skates in behind me, wrapping an arm around Langley. "Seriously, Langers? The Baha Men?"

I glance around, only just noticing the commotion. Half the fans are barking like dogs and dancing to the song "Who Let the Dogs Out."

Langley groans. "Oh, fuck me. The WAGs picked our goal music for tonight, remember?"

I glance between them. "What do you mean?"

Jake laughs, patting me on the back. "Score a goal, and you'll find out."

From my spot on the ice, I can see Teddy standing right on the plexiglass, surrounded by his family. They're all laughing and smiling, leaning in to touch him, saying things in his ear that make him laugh. And they're all wearing my jersey, even the littlest children. By showing up and supporting me, I know they're actually supporting him.

Good. He deserves good people in his corner, ready to fight for him and give him everything he wants. Is this what he wants from me? He wants me to score a goal so he can embarrass me with whatever song he picked?

Done.

Lord knows he's done enough for me already. Whatever my husband wants, he gets.

The ref holds up the puck, and we all get into position. Just before he drops it down, Ramsay gives me a nudge. "Say, you must be nearing retirement age there. Eh, bud?"

With a growl, I check him with my hip and race off after the action. Lindberg didn't claim possession, and the Islanders sink the puck deep into their zone. A defenseman glides around the back of the net with the puck, waiting for his front line to try a play.

When you've played hockey as long as I have, there are moments of clarity on the ice when you just *know* what's going to happen next. I feel the moment the energy shifts in Ramsay. He's going to break away from me and shoot down the ice, looking for a deep pass.

I give him the half second he needs to think he's breaking away before I follow. He's fast, but I'm faster, with a longer wingspan. The Islander defenseman sees the breakaway and makes the pass. The puck zips down the ice towards us. I extend out my stick and hook the puck away from Ramsay. I hardly register the hum of the crowd as I slide to a stop, spraying ice, and change directions. The other Islander forwards were ready to follow Ramsay. They scramble, chasing after me, but I have the two-second lead I need.

Their left-side defender is a giant of a man. I've played against him plenty of times before. His hits rattle my damn bones. But he's slow. I dart his way. His partner falls back to guard the net. This is a three-on-one between the Islander defensive line and me. I have no chance.

Time to dangle.

It all happens in seconds. I weave and dart, making quick movements with my stick and quicker work of my feet. I slip the puck right between the giant's legs, recovering it on the other side. I cross the slot, luring the other defenseman to follow. He charges at me, ready to block. With him between me and the goalie, I have no choice but to extend the puck out with my stick, trying to clear him for the shot.

At the last moment, I tuck in tight, lift the puck, and flip it right into the corner of the net. As the siren blasts and the cherry lights up, I let the defenseman's momentum take us both into the boards. He crushes me to the plexiglass and we both grunt. With a muttered curse, he skates off, just as Lindberg and Langley skate in.

"Dude, that was fucking awesome!" Langley slaps my back.

"Very impressive," Lindberg says in Swedish.

They both skate with me towards the bench. The music is blasting as the stadium keeps cheering. I've been in enough clubs in my career to know the song Teddy picked for me. It's "Money Maker" by Ludacris. I can't help but smile. A song about paying women to shake their butts for money? It's utterly ridiculous.

But I must admit, the crowd seems to enjoy it. The jumbotron shows a replay of my goal, and the cheering intensifies. The Rays bench is celebrating too, laughing at the song choice. They hold out their gloved hands for me to tap as I skate past.

Gliding down the wall, I stop in front of Teddy. On the other side of the glass, he's grinning from ear to ear. All around him, the crowd dances and cheers. Fans pound the plexiglass with their fists.

"That's his husband," one of Teddy's sisters shouts again, jostling his shoulders.

Cameras flash as I slip off my glove and raise a finger, eyes now only for him. "That was one. Second goal wins me back the watch."

Teddy laughs, flashing me the expensive Swiss timepiece. "You know I got it. So come and get it."

The game ends with a score of 3-1. We won, but I didn't score our third point. That honor went to Lindberg. I suppose that means Teddy will be keeping my watch for now.

"Good game," says Denison, patting my back as I make my way down the tunnel to the dressing room.

It was a good game. Not my best, but I haven't been at my best for weeks now. It still felt good to be fully back in my element and doing what I love. My performance tonight gives me hope. It's a feeling I haven't felt in the longest time. It tells me everything may just be okay.

"Hey, Karlsson! Hurry up. They need you and Jake for press!"

How could I forget?

I strip off my kit as quickly as possible. The assistant equipment manager, Cody, takes all the pieces that will go to laundry. After the quickest shower of my life, I tug on my Rays tech shirt and shorts and a pair of athletic slides. The last things I grab is the pair of gold rings tucked in the inside pocket of my suit coat. I slip the smaller ring on the pinkie of my right hand, my mother's wedding ring. The larger ring goes on my left hand, proof of my marriage to Teddy.

Jake is ready almost as fast. Then we make our way down the hallway towards the press corral. He nudges my shoulder as we walk. "Hey, you good?"

"I'm fine." I know by the look on his face that he doesn't believe me.

"K . . . well, I'll be right there. Say the word, and I'll strip my shirt off and bawk like a chicken. That'll give them something to talk about."

Smiling, I gesture with my hand, letting him lead the way out to the corral. Denison is waiting there to take the stage with us. Poppy appears as I turn the corner, dropping her phone from her ear the moment she catches my eye.

"Oh—hold on, Dale." She hurries over to me, squeezes my hand, and lowers her voice. "The release is live. The press was already buzzing with it because Janine over at ESPN dropped a 'sneak preview' of your interview. The little minx. I know she's just trying to steal my thunder by stealing my headline. But if she thinks she'll get another favor out of me this century, she's got another thing coming—"

"It's okay. This all had to come out eventually."

She releases a sharp breath. "Really? You're not mad? I know Janine was my idea."

"You've been wonderful," I assure her. "But this is my problem. Trust me to handle it?"

She chews her bottom lip, her eyes darting as she searches my face. I know why she's hesitating. Trust is as hard for her as it is for me. She's used to being the one who takes care of everything. Whether she wanted the control is beside the point. She has it.

I find myself in the same position—caring for my parents from an ocean away, paying all their bills, and arranging the services that ease their life. I was paying for Karolina's schooling even while Petra lived. I paid for the apartment they lived in too. Anything to make their lives easier. Now Karolina lives in my home, and with her came Teddy. Even Hanna feels like my responsibility.

I didn't ask for this position of authority. But it's mine now, and I will do what I must to protect those who rely on me. Squaring my shoulders, I drop Poppy's hand and follow Jake and Denison out onto the press stage. The media scrambles as cameras flash. They're already shouting for me as we take our seats.

"Karlsson, we hear congratulations are in order!"

"Hey, Karlsson, when did you first know you were gay?"

"Hey, Coach, what's with these guys all marrying your PTs?"

Denison leans into his microphone. "If anyone has any questions about the game or this franchise, we'd be happy to answer." He looks around, eyes narrowed against the lights, and points. "Yeah, Gill?"

Off to the left, a beefy-looking white guy lowers his hand. "Great game there, Coach. This question is for Karlsson. How did it feel to score your first goal of the season in the first game of the season?"

All eyes and all lenses focus on me.

Clearing my throat, I lean in towards my microphone, elbows folded on the table. "It felt good. Just before the puck dropped, Ramsay told me I should consider retiring. I'm not sure if he even made it to the neutral zone before I scored with the puck they passed to him."

The press laughs. Leaning over in his chair, Jake shakes my shoulder. "Come on, man. Don't leave me now. We've got a pact, remember? We're both gonna play till we're ninety."

Before he loses his chance, Gill catches my eye again. "And hey, Karlsson—big news announced tonight. You got married this summer?"

Denison leans forward. "Let's try to get at least *one* more hockey question asked and answered before we turn to personal stuff."

Gill just shrugs, looking every inch the New York reporter. "Nicky, come on. Your own PR team broke the news. You want us to run with this or not?"

"It's fine," I say into the mic. Standing near the doorway, Poppy offers me a double thumbs-up. I turn my attention back to Gill. "Ask your question."

He perks up. "The Rays announced during the first period that you got married this summer to your team's new physical therapist."

Holding my smile in place, I shrug. "I didn't hear a question."

A few people chuckle. "Fair enough," says Gill. "So, is it true? Did you marry Teddy O'Connor?"

"Of course it's true. That's why we reported it."

There's more laughter at this.

"Teddy O'Connor started here as an intern six years ago," Gill goes on. "Is that when you two met and started . . . you know?"

Sighing, I cross my arms and lean back from the table. "If you're asking me whether I first met Teddy when he was an intern, the answer is obviously yes. Of course I met him then. He was as valuable to the team as an intern as he is now." I lean forward, eyes locked on the reporter. "But if you're asking if I somehow used my position as a player to take advantage of him or otherwise act inappropriately, then the answer is no."

"But that *is* when you met," shouts another reporter. It takes me a moment to find him in the crowd. He's a pale, lanky guy with a patchy beard.

"That is when we met, yes," I repeat.

"And after his intern year, he left the team," the lanky reporter goes on. "And you didn't see him again for five years. Then, exactly one week into his new job with the Rays, he flies off to Sweden to marry you?"

I bristle, arms still crossed. "There was no question asked."

"Everything about the situation is a big question mark," the reporter challenges. "It feels like you're trying to announce that you're gay as some kind of cover, hoping we won't ask any questions about the circumstances of this marriage."

At this, Denison leans forward. "Okay, look, if we can't focus on hockey, then this press conference is over—"

"No," I say over him. "It wasn't a question, but I'll answer." I let my gaze drift across the crowd of curious press. "This will be the first and last statement I make regarding my marriage to Doctor Teddy O'Connor."

They all wait. Even Jake and Denison have their eyes locked on me.

"In my ten years playing in this League, I have never once stolen a headline for any reason other than my exemplary performance on the ice. This has been by design. You see my reluctance to speak on this issue now as me somehow keeping secrets, but you're wrong. I just firmly believe in keeping private lives private. The only reason we chose to make this marriage a headline is because we knew you would do it anyway. And we prayed to have some small ounce of control over the narrative that was spun about us."

I shift my gaze from the lanky reporter to an Asian man holding a small video camera in the front row. "Because here's the truth I know you won't accurately report: If Teddy were a pretty young blonde woman who I rushed to the altar this summer, the news of our marriage would have warranted no more than a flurry of well-wishing comments left on an Instagram photo. But Teddy is a man. And Teddy is Black. And that makes our marriage worthy of spectacle and intrigue and unfounded conspiracy."

I lean forward, staring them all down. "Because, regardless of whether any of you wish to acknowledge it, racism and homophobia still run rampant in this League. It swirls and festers like a plague. You think I haven't seen it?" I search the crowd, eyes narrowed under the bright lights. "I've had the privilege of skating alongside Jake Price for six years. You think I don't know the heinous things you've said about him and his family?"

Reaching over, Jake squeezes my hand.

I shift away from him, turning my gaze back to Gill. "I was there when you all made the jokes about Novikov and Morrow too. I saw the awful headlines you wrote. I comforted them and stood by them when the toxicity *you* unleashed emboldened other players to bring their racism and homophobia out onto the ice. I heard the slurs they muttered. I've slammed more than one man into the boards for it, and I've happily taken the penalty."

Pressing my hands flat to the table, my eye catches the glint of gold encircling my finger. Feeling bold, I stare right down the lens of

Gill's camera. "Teddy O'Connor is my partner, and that's all you get to know. That's all any of you *deserve*. He's mine, and I will fight as fiercely for him as I have for every other man on my team. More so, because at the end of the day, my teammates go home to their partners. I go home to Teddy. The only question you get to ask me about him for the rest of my time in this League is how happy he makes me. And my answer will never change: He makes me very happy. Now, someone ask a question that's actually about hockey."

34

TEDDY

In the silence that follows Henrik's speech, we could hear a freaking pin drop. My family is crowded around the TV in the WAG room, eyes locked on the screen. Poppy let me bring them all back here while we waited for Henrik to finish the press conference. We're the only ones left except for a pair of caterers cleaning up the sandwich trays.

The kids hang out in the corner, eating popsicles and playing with their balloon animals. I'm wedged on the sofa between Marcus and Raf. Across from us on the other couch, all three sisters are staring at me.

Natalie clears her throat. "Well, that was . . ."

"Surprising," Jayla finishes for her.

Shae crosses her arms, glaring at me. "I thought you said this was a fake marriage."

"It is," I reply.

They all just keep staring at me.

Okay, yeah, so I'm very aware that I'm currently sitting in the WAG room in a bedazzled jacket, smelling like Henrik's cologne because I used some while I was getting dressed in his closet. Because I live in his house.

And married him

Oh, and we slept together last night.

I tip up my chin, defiant in the face of their stares. "You all just have to trust me. I know what I'm doing."

From the pub chair on my left, Mama sighs. "Oh, Teddy."

"What?" I glare around at my family. "If y'all got something to say, just go ahead and say it. Don't hold back now. Spit it out, before Henrik gets in here and you switch to nice mode."

Marcus huffs. "Nice mode, huh? I didn't know my wife came with a nice mode. Is that only available on one of them newer models?"

"Oh, I'll show you nice mode," Shae snaps at him. "Right after Teddy tells us what he's doin' marrying a man he's not in love with. A man who's *clearly* in love with him!"

"I told you—" My breath catches in my chest. "Wait, what?"

"This isn't you," she reasons.

"Are we sure he's in love with Teddy?" Natalie asks at the same time.

"Yeah, you're always the one getting lost in love," Jayla adds.

Shae sits forward. "Do you even know how many times we've had to hold you while you cried because some boy who ain't shit did you wrong?"

I hold up a hand, glancing around at all of them. "Hold up . . . You're all worried that I'm *not* falling for my fake husband?"

"You said this was just a friend thing," says Natalie. "You said Henrik needed the help."

"Yeah, that it was about keeping a family together," Darius adds.

"And we got that part," says Shae.

"We would have done the same," Jayla says over her.

"Family sticks together," Rafael adds with a sage nod.

"It was wrong to take that little girl away from her uncle who wanted her," says Shae.

Next to me, Marcus pats my knee. "You did good, Ted."

"But you need to be careful is all we're saying," says Natalie.

My head is spinning. "Careful why?"

Shae points to the TV, where Henrik is still visibly suffering through the end of the press conference. "Because if that man is in love with you, you're in trouble, honey. You need to watch out."

"Watch out?" I'm fucking reeling right now. "Like, for what? Falling pianos?"

"She's just saying you need to protect yourself," says Marcus, patting my knee again. "Protect your heart, Ted."

"Yeah, we all know how sensitive you are," says Natalie. "He may want you."

"Oh, trust me, he does," says Shae.

"To me he seems like a cold fish," Nat says over her.

"We just want you safe," says Jayla. "And we want more for you than a fake marriage to someone who can't love you the right way."

"Does he love you right, Ted?" Shae presses.

I glance over at the TV again. Henrik is silent now, leaning away from the table, arms crossed, as Assistant Coach Denison answers some question about draft prospects. I lick my lips, trying to suck moisture back into my mouth. How did my own family so wildly misread this entire situation? Henrik Karlsson want me? *Love* me? I think fucking not.

"You guys, you've got it all wrong," I finally say. "He doesn't love me. He's just acting up there. That's just his media training. He's a professional and he's done it before."

Shae raises a brow. "Before when?"

"We were interviewed for ESPN," I admit. "The interview will go live in a couple days. Guys, he's just a really good actor. Like, Olympic level. Literally. But I swear, he doesn't think about me that way."

Natalie's eyes narrow like a fox on a chicken. "I knew it."

But next to me, Marcus leans in, draping an arm around my shoulders. "You know, Ted, you're right. When I'm not interested in someone, I make sure to stare at them every chance I get too."

"He wasn't staring," I say on a breath, heart racing.

"Oh, please," cries Shae. "Don't listen to Nat. He couldn't keep his eyes off you! Why else do you think he kept skating by, batting those handsome lashes?"

"Hey now," warns Darius, perched on the arm of the couch by her side.

I shrug out from under Marcus's arm. "He's a hockey player. He was skating by because he was playing hockey!"

"Is that what he was doing between quarters too?" says Jayla. "When he came over to flirt with you? Pressing his hand to the glass and running those fingers through his hair all, 'Oh, hey, Teddy, look at me lookin' so fine out on this ice. Think we could melt it?'"

"They're called periods, Jay," Raf mutters.

She waves him off. "Whatever! My point is that Henrik had more than hockey on his mind."

Raf shrugs. "Well, if you're gonna talk about it, get it right."

Ignoring their bickering, Shae leans forward. "Do you really not see it?"

I think my brain is fucking exploding right now.

She huffs, leaning back. "I swear, Teddy, you spend more time dreaming up the men *not* interested in you. Now you got one with a ring on his finger, standing up for you like that in front of the whole world, but you're over here telling us he's just a friend? He's just acting? Pretending to love you for a bunch of cameras?"

"Ted, that ain't right," Marcus says with a shake of his head. "You deserve better than to be some man's fake trophy husband."

"I'm not convinced it's fake," Jayla adds. "The way he was looking at you all night?" She pretends to fan herself. "Hoo, he looked like he wanted to eat you with a spoon."

"I think it was the jacket," Raf teases.

"Enough!" I launch from the couch and march over to the TV, cutting it off. "Can we stop plotting a romance novel, please? Henrik and I are married, yes. But for purely technical reasons. There is nothing between us. Henrik's made it clear he doesn't want that from me. Ever. We've never even kissed, okay? It's not a real marriage, so, everyone, just stop. There are no lingering touches. No prolonged eye contact, or whispered words, or-or flirty banter . . ."

I fall silent, waiting as my world tilts on its freaking axis. Because oh my fucking god, we've done *all* those things. Well, not the kissing. But even with no cameras rolling, Henrik and I are touching literally all the time. He never hesitates to take my hand or brush against me, sit right next to me on a sofa or chair.

And eye contact? Are you kidding me? We're constantly catching each other's gaze and holding it until I feel my insides heat with longing. Whispered words? Check. Flirty banter? Uhh, pretty sure I challenged him to sleep with me again tonight. And if his body language was any indicator, he plans to accept. Sure, we're just sleeping. But it's still pretty intimate to hold a half-naked man all night.

And what the hell was that in the AV room earlier? He pulled me to him. Not the other way around. He came to me, and he held me. He held me like ... god, like I'm the only thing in his life that makes the world stop spinning—

Stop.

I close my eyes, stifling a groan. I can't do this. I can't go here. No, because they're right. This is what I do. Teddy O'Connor loves to be in love. I love reading between the lines and looking for the romantic subtext in every interaction. I love throwing myself heart-first into another man's arms, just praying that he, or god, or a strong wind will catch me.

But I knew what this was going in. I'm helping him get and keep temporary custody of Karolina. Once the court sees how good they are together, he can file for full adoption on his own. That's when he'll kick me to the curb, and not a moment before.

He won't keep me from Karolina once we've split. I know he'd never do that. But knowing Henrik and I are only temporary, I've de-liberately tried to do things differently. I've been trying to be more like him, more rational and even-tempered, leading with my head over my heart.

I mean, I'm still me. Hello, I've still been chaotic and emotional. I didn't get a personality transplant in Sweden. No, what I got was a family. Or, more accurately, a family got me. They picked me up and placed me in their lives, desperate to replace their missing piece.

Everyone here is so focused on whether Henrik wants me in his life. But what about Karro? She didn't even get a choice. She just woke up in a hospital one morning, and there I was, smiling and speaking English, pulling magic bears out of my backpack. My wildly inappropriate crush on her uncle has taken something of a back seat, as we've both just focused on making sure she's happy and healthy and moving through her grief.

"Teddy?"

I turn to my mother, blinking back my tears. "Yeah, Mama?"

She's wearing her glasses with the red frames, hands folded over her middle. Slowly, she stands. Then she holds out her hand. Heart in my throat, I step forward. Crossing to her side, I place my hand in hers, gazing down at her. With her free hand, she cups my cheek. I fight the urge to pull away. Tears fill my eyes, and I close them quick.

"Look at me, baby."

Letting out a shaky breath, I open my eyes.

Her hand drops down to my shoulder, brushing my locs back. "Do your sisters have the way of it? Are you indifferent to the man you married?"

Groaning, I try to pull away. "I can't do this—"

Her hand tightens on my shoulder. "Don't pull away from me. You are my Teddy. I knit you from scratch." Shifting her hand lower, she presses it to my chest. "I made this heart, baby. Are you hiding from me now? Are you hiding from yourself?"

"Mama . . ."

"Does your heart beat for that man and that little girl?"

After a moment, I nod. Then all my breath leaves my chest on a sob. God, I can't keep stifling this truth. I can't keep playing pretend. "I don't know what happened," I admit. "I can't make it stop, Mama. I can't walk away. She needs me. I don't wanna walk away. Not when I know he needs me too."

She nods. "You've always loved to feel needed, baby. And you're so good at helping others. You give and give. Lord knows you'd give until there's nothing left for yourself."

"I know," I murmur.

Reaching up again, she tucks my locs behind my ear. "Your sisters are right to caution you, baby."

"Why?"

She offers a faint smile, dropping her hand from my cheek. "There's always gonna be someone who needs what you have to offer. But some day, you're gonna realize that being needed isn't where true happiness lies. Not for someone like you who loves with his whole heart and soul."

I sigh, searching her face. "What do I do, Mama?"

"True happiness for you is only gonna come when you're *wanted*, baby. So, you need to ask yourself: Does this family just need you . . . or do they really want you?"

Before I can answer, Henrik comes walking through the door.

35

HENRIK

"Hey, there he is!" A tall Black man rises from the couch the moment he sees me enter the WAG room. "Great game. Really fun to watch."

He nudges the Latino man next to him, who also rises. "Uhh . . . yeah. Hey, yours was the best goal of the night."

"Thank you," I say on reflex.

Something's off. Tension hangs heavy in the air. Have I interrupted some private moment? Their pinched smiles give them away. Ah, I see. They were all just talking about me. I look to Teddy, but he has his back turned, nodding as his mother says something low.

In an instant, all three sisters rise from the nearest sofa and turn as one. There's a flurry of introductions as I shake the hands of Shae and her husband, Marcus. He's the taller man. Then there's Jayla and her husband, Rafael. Jayla is the one who was screaming at the game, telling everyone in their section that Teddy is my husband. Her hair is long and braided, with a few colorful strands woven in to make a rainbow effect. Her complexion is fair, like Teddy's, while the other sisters have darker skin, like their mother.

The willowy athletic-looking sister is Natalie. She doesn't shake my hand because she's holding a sleeping baby. Her boyfriend Darius shakes my hand. He's short and lean, with a wide smile.

Why do I get the distinct impression that they're keeping me cornered, buying Teddy time to speak to his mother alone? I can feel the tension flowing off him, even from here. Did they upset him?

"And those are my kids," says Jayla, pointing across the room. "We have Bastian, the only boy cousin in the family. We all call him Baz. And see the one with the pink beads in her braids? That's Camila. She's eight—"

"Wonderful," I say, extracting myself from her hold. "Please excuse me." I duck around her, weaving past the other children until I'm free to approach Teddy.

"Mama, meet Henrik," calls Shae.

Teddy's mother gives his shoulders one last squeeze before she steps around him, her hand outstretched towards me. "Mr. Karlsson? I'm Keziah Wilson, Teddy's mother."

"Please, call me Henrik," I say, shaking her hand. I don't miss the way Teddy wipes under his eyes, his shoulders stiff, as he lets his family expertly handle me, buying him the time he needs to rebuild his walls and box me out. Goddamn it, what did they say to him?

"You two really know how to make a statement," she says, dropping my hand. "Is all this attention really necessary?"

"My team's PR director seems to think it is," I reply.

She purses her lips. "Hmm. And you trust this woman? This Poppy?"

"I do," I say. "Implicitly."

Teddy finally turns. "Poppy's the best in the business, Mama. I told you that." He stays by her side, just out of arm's reach of me.

Fuck.

"We all thought we'd go out to dinner to celebrate your big win," says Jayla, stepping in at my left.

"And your big news," says Shae. "Our baby brother is married. Can you believe it?"

Their mother just crosses her arms. "I can't believe we had to hear about it from a stranger before we ever heard it from him. My only son, married, and I wasn't invited to attend. According to him, y'all don't even have a picture."

Teddy groans. "Mama, I said I was sorry—"

"I'm afraid that blame lies with me," I say over him.

All eyes look to me.

"Henrik, don't," Teddy whispers, shaking his head.

His mother's frown only deepens. "You, Mr. Karlsson?"

"Yes, I'm afraid I asked Teddy not to tell anyone what we'd done, including friends and family. Not until we returned to Florida and sought the counsel of my PR director. I trust you watched the press conference just now?"

She holds my gaze, her eyes framed by red, thick-rimmed glasses. "We sure did."

"Then you see how sensitive situations like this can be, given the public nature of my job. It was unfair of me to ask it of him. But I wanted us to have a plan in place first. Especially since I also have my niece's safety to consider."

Her lips purse. "Of course. Your niece must be a serious consideration for you."

"She is my only consideration," I assure her with a nod.

A smile flashes on her face as she slowly turns to Teddy, patting his arm. "Hear that, baby? What a loved and truly wanted little girl. We should all be so lucky."

Teddy looks stricken as he turns away with a muttered, "'Scuse me." Then he slips away, disappearing into the bathroom.

I don't know what happened, but I feel confident I just made an error. I only meant to protect him. He doesn't deserve to shoulder the ire of his family alone. If his mother needs someone to be mad at, she can be mad at me. "If it's any consolation, my parents weren't at the wedding either," I offer.

"It's not, Mr. Karlsson," she replies flatly. "But thank you."

"It was a quick affair," I add. "Little more than a quarter of an hour spent at a Stockholm administrative building. And I believe there *is* a picture in the official public record."

Jayla pats my arm. "Honey, stop. Keep digging and you'll be in China."

"What?"

"I said, do you like Chinese food?"

I'm so tired, I feel like my brain can't translate her English fast enough. What is she saying?

"Don't tease the man, Jay," says Marcus.

Rafael steps in behind him. "Okay, I made us all a reservation at someplace called Poe's Tavern. They have burgers and stuff."

"It's Edgar Allen Poe themed," says Natalie. "How cool is that?"

"And it's over by the hotel," Darius adds. "Henrik, you in?"

I glance in the direction of the shut bathroom door. "I'm afraid I can't join you tonight. I have to go home and relieve the nurse who cares for my niece."

Rafael shrugs. "Well, go home and get her. The more, the merrier."

"That's not an option," I reply. "Not at this time. Besides, I fear I'd make poor company tonight. Game nights are difficult for me. There are routines I must attend to."

"Hey, you don't need to explain to us," says Marcus with his hand on my shoulder. "I played football at Georgia Tech for two years. The body is a temple, right? You gotta take care of it."

"Exactly." I offer a weak smile, happy to be understood.

The bathroom door opens, and Teddy reemerges in just his T-shirt, his WAG jacket slung over his arm.

"Hey, Ted, we're all going to get some food," calls Darius. "Henrik's out. You in?"

Teddy looks at me, but it's like he's not even there. Who is that looking back at me? Where did Teddy go? My gut twists as I fight the urge to rush to his side, grab him by the shoulders, and ask him exactly that question. The last I saw him, he stood behind the plexiglass with the biggest smile on his face, nodding at me as the buzzer sounded. Game over. Rays win. Now he looks like he was just told he has to attend his own funeral.

I can't bear it. I cross the room and reach for his hand, but he shrugs me away. "What happened?"

"Nothing."

Lie.

My frustration rises. He's not going to tell me anything so long as his family is here. "Come home with me."

He blinks, glancing up at me. "Henrik, I can't. My family is here to see me. To see *us*. They came all this way. I have to go with them."

"No, you don't." I take his hand, holding it tight. "You can come home with me now, and we can talk. I—we should talk, yes?" His hand feels limp in mine, like a dead fish. "Teddy—"

"Hey, Ted, you coming?" Rafael calls again.

"One second," Teddy calls back. Then he's slipping his hand from mine. "I'll see you later, okay?"

"Don't do this."

He feigns confusion. "Do what?"

Before I can respond, his mother is stepping in at my side. "Mr. Karlsson, we really do need to get going. Teddy baby, come on. You can ride with us." She holds out her hand, willing him to choose her over me.

I don't know what happened, but I know she's to blame. She said something. She poisoned him against me. Worse, I think she might have poisoned him against himself. Teddy looks stricken as he steps around me, letting himself be lured away.

But this isn't what he wants. I can feel it. I *know*. So, I reach out on instinct, wrapping a hand around his wrist. "No."

His mother narrows her eyes at me. "No? You don't get to tell Teddy where he goes or who he sees. According to him, this isn't even a real marriage. You're playing a part to my son, pretending to love him while the cameras roll. This is nothing but a pretty handful of lies."

I let go of his wrist. Is that how he characterized us to his own family? A handful of lies? Is that how he sees all the time spent laughing and baking with Karro? Is that how he felt when he held me last night?

I look to him, but he won't look at me.

"Oh, come on, Mama," says Jayla. "Don't stir the pot."

"I'm stirring nothing," their mother replies. "I'm just looking out for Teddy's best interests. Someone has to. Don't they, Mr. Karlsson? It surely won't be you."

My hackles rise as I try to breathe around the rock now sitting in my chest. "And what do you mean by that?"

She squares off against me, all 5'4" of her glaring up at me. "By your own admission, your hands are already full. Your niece is your only concern, right? Well, perhaps that's as it should be. But you don't get to keep my Teddy underfoot, fetching and carrying for you—"

"He doesn't fetch and carry—"

"If you needed help keeping your house in order, you should have hired a maid or a laundry service," she says over me. "You don't marry my son, then refuse him all the rights of being your husband."

"Mama, stop," Teddy begs, clutching her arm.

I glare at her. "My house is his—he knows that. My cars, my clothes, my credit cards. Teddy wants for nothing, Ms. Wilson. I take care of him. I take care of everything."

She just scoffs. "Things, things, wonderful things. And in the end? All *worthless*."

I blink, leaning away.

"You know, Mr. Karlsson, *this* is why you're such a bad match for my Teddy. And if he'd told me what he was gonna do before he did it, I could have warned him off you."

"Go on then," I say. "Tell me how I've already failed him."

She holds my gaze, her dark eyes almost obsidian. "Teddy doesn't want a thing from you, Mr. Karlsson. And if you knew him at all, you'd know that. He just wants *you*." She looks me up and down. "But that's the one thing you'll never offer. You can play whatever games you want with the press, but I see you now. I see behind that handsome face with all those practiced smiles. You're an empty glass with no bottom. Teddy's gonna keep pouring into you, and all his light is gonna rush right out. Because you don't know how to hold on to the things that really matter."

Her words pierce me with the power of prophecy. I want to hate her. I want her to take back every syllable uttered. I want to rage and storm away. Instead, I stand here, breathless, hands empty, heart hollow.

"My Teddy is gonna see you're no good," she says, hammering her prophecy home. "I don't need to take him with me now. He'll leave on his own. And I'll be there to comfort him when he does. I always am."

"Come on, Mama." Jayla pulls at her arm.

With one last look at me, Mama lets herself be led away.

Shae stays at Teddy's side, tears in her eyes, as she looks at her little brother. "Don't be mad at Mama. She just wants more for you. You deserve better than this."

Better than me. That's what they all mean. Because I'm a drain. I'll drag him down with me, drown him in my depths. It's not something I haven't thought before. I can't be his husband, but I knew that going in. Now, it turns out, I can't even be his friend.

His sister holds out a hand. "Come on, Ted."

"Shae, Ted, let's go," calls Rafael from the door.

Teddy stares down at his sister's hand, chest rising and falling with each deep breath. "Y'all are unbelievable, you know that?"

Natalie and Darius stop at the door, Mrs. Wilson between them.

Shae drops her hand. "Teddy, we're only trying to help."

He glares at them all. "You're supposed to be on my side here, remember?"

His other sisters dare to look a little guilty. But his mother just stands defiantly.

"I've never asked any of you to understand my choices, but you *do* have to respect them," he goes on. "Because if you're right, if this marriage turns out to be a huge mistake, then I'm gonna need you. *All* of you. So don't ruin things now by crowing over me before this even has a chance to turn bad."

Stepping forward, he puts himself between me and his family. "And Mama, you know I love you. I respect you. And I'm truly sorry for all the hurt I caused." Hands on his hips, he stares her down. "But if you *ever* talk to my husband like that again, it'll be the last time you ever talk to me."

Shae gasps, stepping back, as the other sisters look stricken. His mother just stares daggers at me, as if this is all my fault. I'm the reason her son dares to challenge her in this way. I've ruined him. I've made him like me.

Speech over, Teddy turns to me. Heat blazes in his eyes as he takes my hand, weaving our fingers together. "Well? I said you had to meet my family. You've met them. Now take me home."

36

TEDDY

Henrik makes no attempt to drop my hand as he leads the way past my startled family, out of the WAG room, down the empty corridor, up a flight of stairs, and through an emergency door out onto the sidewalk. I cling to my WAG jacket with my free hand, following him.

It's a balmy Florida night, jarring compared to the chill of the arena. The crowds of fans have cleared out enough that no one tries to stop us from circling the side of the building, cutting back around towards the team entrance to the parking garage. Cops are still out, directing the last of the traffic. The blue lights of their patrol cars flash. A man stands on the corner, busking with a saxophone, filling the night air with smooth jazz. It's calm. Idyllic, even.

But my heart is in my throat. I'm alternating from feeling breathless and feeling buried.

What the fuck was that? Why did Mama have to go and fucking do that? Why did she have to plant those seeds of doubt in me? And what she said to Henrik? Distracted, I stumble on a crack in the sidewalk, squeezing tighter to Henrik's hand. "Hey, do we need to walk so fast? I promise they're not chasing us."

But he doesn't slacken his pace. He doesn't even look at me. Doesn't speak. He just weaves around the "PRIVATE PARKING" signs, scaring the shit out of the attendant who was half asleep in a folding chair.

"Mr. Karlsson?" The older white lady gasps, sitting up and

adjusting the radio clipped to her parking vest. "Are you—" She glances at me, then peers around. "Honey, where's your car? And shouldn't you be coming at me from the other direction?"

"Have a good night, Pearl," is his only reply as he slips around the arm of the parking gate. He pulls me along behind him.

"We can drive separate," I offer. "My car is just over in Lot D. Really, I don't mind—"

"No."

I all but trot to keep up with him as we round the corner of the near-empty garage. His gorgeous Porsche 718 Cayman sits alone under the humming lights, waiting for us. It's the perfect shade of ocean blue. He was going to get rid of it when we first got back from Sweden, which felt like a crime against god, and nature, and the car itself. In the end, I convinced him to open his damn purse strings and invest in a more sensible SUV. A man like Henrik can certainly afford two cars.

Now he's striding forward in his custom grey Prada suit, thin black tie, and Italian leather loafers. The headlights of the car flash in welcome as he approaches. Fuck me, this is what fantasies are made of. Fighting a groan, I try to pull away again. "Seriously, you can just drop me off at my car—"

"Stop!" he shouts, his voice echoing around the empty garage.

I blink back tears of surprise. "Don't yell at me."

He drops my hand like it burned him. His chest rises and falls as he takes a step away from me. He looks confused, almost concussed.

I reach out on instinct. "Henrik . . ."

"Just go."

Now I'm the one who feels burned. "What?"

"Go back to them."

"No." I step in closer, shrugging back into my WAG jacket. "Henrik, I wanna go with you." With a flick of both wrists, I free my locs from the collar of the jacket.

But Henrik turns away, striding over to his car. "I can't do this. I'll not be the thorn that festers your relationship with your family. Teddy, please just go back. Do what you can to make it right. Before it's too late."

I'm reeling. What the fuck is happening? "Too late?" He tries to open his door, and I lunge forward, blocking it with my hand. "Hey, *stop*. Henrik, what the fuck? You stand up for us all night, defending me to the press and holding your own against my sisters and my scary-ass mother. And now you're just rolling over?"

He shakes his head, unable to even look at me. "Your family is waiting for you. They came all this way. Please, go be with them. I can't—" He presses the back of his hand to his forehead, looking around like he's lost. "Teddy—"

I try to reach for him again. "Henrik . . ."

He tugs at his tie, loosening it. "I can't do this," he says again.

Shit, he's spiraling out, and I don't know how to stop it. Taking a deep breath, I ghost my hands over his arms, afraid to touch him, afraid he'll break. "Henrik, look . . . What my mom said back there . . . I'm the baby of the family, okay? She was always gonna take my getting married too much to heart, no matter how it happened. She was just upset—"

"She was prophetic!"

I search his face, seeing the hurt there, the confusion and pain. She wounded him. Each of her carefully sharpened arrows clearly found their target. Reaching out, I press my hand to the middle of his chest, my fingertips brushing over his mussed tie. "Take me home," I whisper. "Henrik, please, just take me with you."

He shakes his head, and I wanna die. Wrapping a hand around my wrist, he removes my touch from his chest. "Your mother is right. I took advantage of you to serve my own ends. I trespassed on your kindness, your goodness."

"Stop," I plead, twisting free of his grip. "I offered, remember? You have to trust me to know the limits of what I can handle. She never has, and that's her problem. They're always trying to protect me, and then they take things too far, like what just happened in there."

"Someone has to look out for you. I'm glad you have such fierce defenders." He offers me a wan smile that doesn't reach his eyes. "Now I know where your loyalty to Karro comes from."

"And my loyalty to *you*." I grab both his arms. "Henrik, I did this for Karro, but I did it for you too."

"What do you mean?"

I drop his arms and step back, heart racing. "What I mean is . . . well, where's your defender, huh? I watched you out on that ice to-night. Your shining moment? Your big score of the game? You did it alone. Not one person from your team was there for you, Henrik. They were all scrambling just to catch up. You were on your own. You are always all on your own. You take care of everyone and everything. Karro has you, and now she has me. But where's *your* defender?"

Silence stretches between us before he finally just shakes his head. "I don't know."

With a growl of frustration, I step in, cupping his bearded face with my hands. "I'm standing right in front of you, asshole. Do you even see me? *Look* at me, Henrik."

His sad blue eyes lock on me, and I feel it, this magnetic thing we have. My mother was right. I was a fool to try to deny it. There's no holding this back. It's like part of me has been lost and looking for this man my whole life. With Henrik, I am found.

I hold his gaze, determination burning through me. To be seen by him. To finally be heard. God, to be wanted. "You seem to have fundamentally misunderstood the nature of our arrangement. So let me enlighten you. Your job is to take care of everyone else. And my mama's right. You're drowning, Henrik. So many people are making demands of you, dragging you down—your parents, Karro, her doctors, the team, your agent, your sponsors. The list just keeps getting longer. I see how hard you work for them. I see how they pull at you, how they need you."

I step in closer, daring him to look away. "But I am not on that fucking list. Do you hear me? Six years ago, yes, you pulled me away from that speeding truck. But that's the only time you get to save me. Because you're on my list now. You're *mine*, Henrik. And I'll be damned if I let anyone, my own mother included, make you think you're not worth saving—"

I'm gasping out a breath as Henrik pushes me back against the side of the Porsche. His hands are on my hips, possessive and firm. My hands still cup his face, thumbs brushing over the soft hair of his beard. Our faces are inches apart. I can feel his breath warm against my lips.

Oh god, he's gonna kiss me.

Henrik Karlsson is *finally* going to kiss me.

He holds me in this eternal moment of waiting, our breathing shallow, chests rising and falling in unison. His hands hold me pinned to the car as he crowds my space, but he doesn't press himself against me. I wait until I can't bear it another second. Then I break, asking in a whisper, "What are you doing?"

He blinks, then swallows, as if coming back to his body. Then his gaze is trailing down from my eyes to my parted lips. "Not breaking any more of your rules."

My mind hums as I try to understand. Then I groan as he leans away. Goddamn it, he's talking about my "no kissing" rule. *Fuck.* I drop my hands to his shoulders, trying to keep him close, desperate to feel the weight of him pinning me to the side of this sports car. At this point, I'm beyond starving for the taste of his lips on mine. "Break it," I beg. "Henrik, it's okay. I want you to—"

But he's pulling away. He's shutting off, locking down. The moment is over. I've lost him, and now I wanna die. Like Icarus, I flew too close to the sun. I got a taste of his fire, and now I'm falling, wings melted, tumbling through the air.

"We're both just upset," he says in that reasoned tone. "Emotions are high. But you made your rules with deliberate care. And I made a vow I'd not break them—"

"We're already breaking them," I cry, tears of frustration stinging my eyes. I swear I'll never forgive myself for falling for a Capricorn. "You slept in my bed last night. It was my understanding we were doing it again tonight. Because you *want* to be on my list. You want me to comfort you. You want to come home to me, remember?"

"I do," he admits.

"Well, the home you want isn't the lifeless apartment we share—it's *me*." I press both hands to my chest. "It's my chaos and my moods and my body. You want me, Henrik. I know you do. And it's okay that I give you comfort. So let me. In all the ways I can, I want you to let me."

He closes his eyes, wincing as if my words are hurting him. "I can't."

"Will you give me one good reason?"

He considers for a moment. Finally, he glances my way, suddenly looking almost nervous. "Teddy, I know what you want from me. I see the way you look at me. You want our relationship to have a physical component. It's your rule to break, but you're the one who wants a kiss . . . Am I right?"

I cross my arms in this sparkly WAG jacket, branded with his number on my arms and back. "So what if I do? Just a moment ago, you did too. It's only natural for two people sharing a life to share intimacies as well. When they have the kind of chemistry we have, it's practically inevitable."

"I can't be with you in that way, Teddy."

I hold my breath, daring to ask the question sitting like a rock in my chest. "Because you're not attracted to men . . . or because you're just not attracted to me?"

Holding my gaze, he offers me a weak smile. "Because I'm not attracted to anyone."

"What does that even mean?"

He shrugs, sadness filling his eyes. "I'm broken, Teddy. Stay with me long enough, and I fear I'll break you too."

37

TEDDY

*H*enrik keeps his eyes on the road and both hands on the wheel as he drives us in the direction of the apartment. There's a low hum in my ears as I watch the streetlights flash overhead. The memory of getting in the car already feels hazy. I know Henrik opened my door for me. Then he was in too. Then the engine purred to life. He pulled us out of the garage, waving to the parking attendant.

Just down the street from the arena, we pass a row of bustling bars and clubs. The thumping bass of the music creates a discordant buzzing in my chest. Henrik slows the car to a stop at a red light. The Mexican restaurant on the corner is overflowing with late-night diners. Some of them are wearing Rays hockey jerseys.

The light changes, and the Porsche glides forward.

I can't take the silence for another second. "What did you mean when you said you're broken?"

Henrik sighs, flexing his hands on the wheel. "Honestly? I don't know. It's just how I feel. It's how I've always felt."

"But, like, broken how? Like, does it all work down there?"

"Teddy . . ."

I throw up both hands. "Hey, it's totally fine if it doesn't. Plenty of men struggle to get and stay erect. And there's a lot you can do to try to address it, from homeopathic remedies to over-the-counter stuff—"

"I can get an erection," he says over me.

"Okay."

"That's not the problem. Physically, it all works."

"So then what *is* the problem?"

His eyes stay locked on the road as he takes one of the last turns before we'll be back at the apartment. "It's my head."

"Your head is broken?"

"I don't know. My head . . . or my heart. Perhaps it's my spirit. A combination therein. All I know is that I've always felt that sex was something I was meant to want. It's something all men want, right?"

"Well, no. Not particularly." I glance his way, taking in his face in profile under the passing streetlights. He looks confused and frustrated, brow furrowed, hands clenched on the steering wheel. "Walk me through it. You say you feel like you're supposed to want sex. Why do you feel that way?"

He shrugs. "Look at my life. Look at what I do. Look at the men who surround me."

"You think because you're a professional athlete, you're supposed to be having lots of sex? Why, because your teammates are doing it?"

"All my life, I've watched as men around me have chased after women. I've heard the stories of their conquests in the locker room. I've caught countless roommates in shared hotel rooms bouncing a naked girl in their lap. I've been to the after-parties and the clubs. I've seen the open hedonism firsthand."

"Yeah . . . but, Henrik, most of that behavior is toxic as fuck. It's rooted in the misogyny and sexual exploitation of women that plagues the NHL. Sex scandals and payoffs, messy players getting their hookups pregnant, then marrying them, then divorcing them. Wash, rinse, repeat. Honestly, that you're not a part of that culture is a fucking relief. Do you wanna be like those assholes?"

"Not all of the players are like that," he assures me. "I've skated with plenty of good men. Family men, loyal to their partners. And even they all seemed to just *need* sex. I've seen teammates twitching with eagerness to get off the plane. It's like they ache with it, like the act of sex is somehow as essential as food and water."

"For some people, it is."

Henrik just hums, pulling the car into the garage under the apartment building. "Well, it's not for me."

"Can I ask . . . well, have you ever had sex before?"

He parks the car in his assigned spot and cuts the engine. We sit there in silence. "Yes," he finally admits.

"More than once?"

"Yes."

"With more than one person? Not, like, at a time," I quickly correct. "I mean that you've tried having sex with different people. Or maybe it *was* at the same time, who am I to judge?"

He narrows his eyes at me. "Yes, Teddy. I've had sex with more than one person. And no, it wasn't at the same time."

"And was this in relationships? Or just random hookups?"

"What does that matter?"

"Trust me, it totally matters. And I'll not judge you either way for your answer. I'm just trying to understand. Did you know the people you had sex with? Were they, like, your girlfriends?"

He considers for a moment. I brace myself to hear him admit to having past fiancées. Petty Teddy is not above some light internet stalking. I swear to god, if she looks anything like Hanna, I'm gonna walk into the ocean.

"I would call them acquaintances," he says at last. "Not strangers, but not girlfriends either."

Thank fucking god. I let out a breath. "And the sex wasn't any good? With any of them?"

"It was nothing," he replies, his voice sounding hollow. "Truthfully, I just felt numb the whole time. It was like I knew what I should be doing, so, in the moment, my body did it. But my mind? I felt so detached from the whole thing, so wholly disinterested."

Not gonna lie, he's describing what sounds like my literal worst nightmare.

Personally, I *love* sex. I love the passion that comes from sharing energy, time, and sweat with another person. I love the physicality of it all. I love the feel of my body pressed against another, muscles straining, hands trembling. God, I can't even imagine going robotically through the motions of sex and not feeling attached to the other person.

My problem is that sex typically comes first in all my relationships. It's only after I've let myself become addicted to their physical energy that I realize their mental and emotional energy is a total mismatch with me. My most toxic trait is that I'll usually stick around a month too long because the physical feels too damn good. I let it cloud my rationality.

Could I ever try it Henrik's way and go without sex altogether?

Perhaps for the right person . . .

I gaze across the car at him. Henrik and I really do seem to click in all other ways. We're a case study in opposites attracting. His quiet more than matches my loud. He's calm where I'm chaotic, rational where I'm emotional. But he's a quiet lion who still knows how to roar. Which is the turn-on of the fucking century. It looked so effortless for him to put the press in their place tonight. Even my mother looked a little rattled. God, I wish one of my sisters had been recording it.

Maybe it's possible.

As if he can read my mind, Henrik glances my way. "I won't lead you on, Teddy. If I have already, I'm sorry for it. You're just such a passionate person. I know you must be seeking that in your partner."

I turn in my seat. "But you're so passionate too."

"Right," he mutters.

"You are. Passion isn't only sexual, Henrik. You're fiercely protective of Karolina, and loyal to your teammates. You care deeply about justice and fairness. You saw my family treating me unfairly tonight, and you threw yourself toe to toe with my mom. And you held your own pretty good. Seriously, you have to show me how you did that. You have your convictions, and you stand by them. That's passion, Henrik. That's heart. What did you call me in Sweden?"

The corner of his mouth twitches with a smile. "Rent hjärta. Pure of heart."

I think he called me that again last night. He was tired, so it was sort of mumbled. I reach across the center console and place my hand on his knee. "You have a pure heart too. Don't let anyone dare tell you any different." An idea sparks in my mind, and I drop my hand away, not wanting him to think I'm making some kind of pass. "Have you ever been in love?"

His smile disappears. "No. Why?"

"Well, maybe that's your problem."

"What?"

"You've never been in love with the people you've had sex with. You never put in the work to have a deep, meaningful connection with them. You know, for some people, sexual attraction can only come after there's a relationship built first. Maybe you just needed a little more trust and emotional security. Only then could you start to see that person with an eye towards romantic interest."

"And you know people like this?"

"I do. My friend Carrie in college identified as demisexual."

"I don't know that word."

"To be demisexual is like . . ." I try to think of the right explanation. Latching onto an idea, I turn back to him, smiling. "It's like Caleb and Jake Price."

"How so?"

"Well, from what I've heard, Caleb has always been pretty confident in his sexuality. What do you think would have happened if he'd professed his love to Jake back in their bunny-wheeling college days?"

Henrik considers. "Jake probably would have turned him down."

"Oh, big time. Caleb's intensity would have sent Jake running for the hills. Because he wasn't ready for that kind of relationship with Caleb. They both had to put in the work first. They built a friendship for years. By the time they started sneaking around during my intern year, they were basically two gnarled trees, all twisted up and grown together. The team was already calling them domestic life partners. It's lucky there was any room left for Doc Price to squeeze herself in there."

He smiles faintly, his mind clearly humming with this new information.

"No one would ever say that Jake Price is broken," I add. "He just had to learn Caleb's language first. Once he did, they could finally communicate. And just look at them now, happy as clams."

"Clams?"

I snort. With how good his English is, sometimes I forget that it's not Henrik's first language. "All I'm saying is that it's possible. Maybe the way Jake is with Caleb is the way you are with all people. It's not that you can't enjoy physical intimacy—you just haven't found the right person who speaks your language."

He's quiet for a minute, still considering.

Taking a risk, I lean in a little closer. "Can I ask . . . back in the parking garage, you seemed like you wanted to kiss me. Was that . . . I mean, is there a chance you were feeling something for me then?"

"I don't know what I was feeling," he admits. "Angry, maybe? Ashamed. Defensive."

"It makes sense," I murmur, hiding the disappointment from my tone. "My mom had just tried to rip you a new asshole."

He leans to the side, propping his arm on the car door. "I'm not good at expressing myself. You already know that. And I don't like feeling pulled by my emotions. Any emotion—anger, lust, fear, embarrassment. I don't like . . ." He sighs, sinking into silence.

"Losing control," I finish for him.

He nods.

"Henrik, I'm sorry."

He glances my way. "Why are you sorry?"

"I'm sorry if I've been adding to your stress about all this. You've got enough on your plate. You don't need my drama added to it."

"You're not the problem."

"I am, though. Or I'm part of it. Because you're right, I'm a super passionate person. I wear my heart on my sleeve, and I just feel every feeling as loud as I can all the time. And I love sex. I love physical intimacy, and I love being in love. As a double Pisces with Leo rising, I was basically hardwired to be an emotional mess. So, I'm sorry. For sending mixed signals. For stressing you out. For letting my emotions get the better of me until you felt like you were the one spinning out of control."

Glancing his way, I smile, desperate to do something to ease this tension. "But in my defense, you are exceptionally good looking."

The hint of a smile crosses his face. "It feels strange for me to apologize for that."

I laugh. "Don't apologize. Own it. Henrik, you're so gorgeous, I wanna cry myself to sleep at night."

He chuckles. "Well, thank you."

"I'm serious. You in that suit? Stretched out in the front seat of this sexy little sports car like you're shooting a damn cologne commercial? It's the stuff of my wildest fantasies. But that's *my* problem," I quickly add. "Not yours. And I'm gonna do my best to cool it.

You've set your limits, and I'm going to respect them. Watch and see, I'm gonna be the most platonic fake husband you've ever had."

Now he really smiles. It brushes the soft freckles of his cheeks and lights up his eyes. He reaches over and takes my hand, giving it a squeeze. "Thank you, Teddy. Truly. For everything. I don't know where I'd be without your kindness to me."

I shrug, slipping my hand away. "Probably upstairs already, half asleep in your bathtub with some ancient history podcast playing too loud over the speakers."

He chuckles. "Fair enough."

I open my car door and step out into the quiet garage. Henrik follows. He keeps following me, all the way to the elevator and up into our apartment. Where we live. Together. Just like Bert and Ernie. Only they had separate beds, right?

Well, call me irrational if you want. Call me crazy. Call me a glutton for punishment. But our first rule is already broken. If I have my way, it's gonna stay fucking broken. Henrik and I may be husbands who are just friends, but that man is gonna keep sleeping in my bed.

As soon as Hanna is dismissed for the night, he returns to the kitchen, feet shuffling with fatigue. I was going to draw him a bath and bring him a beer, but I think we're too far past that now. "Go lie down," I say, nodding towards my bedroom. "I'll bring you a protein shake and the JetBoots."

With a grateful nod, he shuffles away, not even questioning my command. Because my mom is wrong. Henrik *does* want me. He may not want my dick. That's too much for him right now, and that's fine. But he wants me. He wants my comfort. He wants my support, my friendship, my advice.

And for now, that's enough.

In fact, it's oddly satisfying. Before now, sex has always been my crutch. I use it to soothe, and mask, and deflect. I use it to hide my deeper relationship problems. I mean, who has problems when you have orgasms, right?

But this is a new era. With Henrik, I get to be a whole new Teddy. I don't know what the hell I'm doing, but I'm curious to see where it will lead.

38

TEDDY

"Okay, and does this hurt?" I gently massage the side of Perry's knee with my thumb.

"Ahhh—*fuck*," he hisses through his teeth. "Yeah, Doc. It fucking hurts."

"I still think it's just sprained." I reach behind me and snag his compression bandage off the table and rewrap his knee. This isn't even a hockey injury. The asshole went running with his dog this morning and it took off after a squirrel. Nearly jerked Perry's arm out of his socket and sent him twisting down to the pavement. "I think you should—"

"Don't say it."

"Sit out a game," I say over him.

"Fuck," he mutters again.

"It's just one game. And we don't want to make it worse, right? For now, some ibuprofen should help reduce pain and inflammation. We can get you an ice wrap too. And elevate the knee tonight."

"Hey, Doc—" He grabs my arm as I step past. "Don't tell the guys how this happened, alright? Like, don't write it down. Tell them I did it doing squats or something."

I pat his hand on my arm. "Sure thing, man. It can be our secret."

He sighs with relief as I step away to wash my hands.

It's been a week since the epic fallout with my family. All my sisters have tried to call, but I haven't answered. Excuse the fuck out of me, but I need another minute. They sat back and watched as Mama tore into Henrik. They judged me. They doubted me. I won't leave them on read forever, but I'm not rushing this either. I'll answer when I'm good and ready.

For now, I'm throwing myself into work. And this has been one hell of a crazy day. The team leaves tomorrow for some away games, so most of them are taking it easy today. No gym time, no practice. But the staff is all here, and everyone seems to be putting out a fire.

Some of the new PT equipment was delayed, so Caleb Price has been storming around on the phone all afternoon, angrier than a tornado, calling out tracking numbers to a confused warehouse foreman. Apparently, our shit is somewhere in Jacksonville—it's just not here. And the PTs need to check it over so the EMs can get it all loaded. It's a mess.

I've been so distracted by all the walk-ins that I skipped lunch. My stomach growls as I tug a couple paper towels out of the dispenser and dry my hands.

"Hey, Teddy?" Caleb appears in the doorway.

"Yeah?"

"The PT shit is here. You free?"

I sigh, tossing my paper towels in the trash. I guess my cold chicken parm sub will just have to wait. "Yeah, I'm free. What do you need?"

T wo hours later, I've finally reached the end of my shift. I swear, this day has felt like ten. I'm putting away some of the stretching equipment when I hear a familiar voice and groan.

"Hey, there he is! Looking good, Teddy."

I glance over my shoulder to see Lukas Novikov strutting into the PT suite. "Keep walking, Nov. I'm headed out the door."

From the other side of the room, Brady chuckles, pushing his glasses up his nose, as he reviews my treatment protocols for the day.

Novy feigns innocence. "You don't even know what I want."

"I know exactly what you want, and my answer is no. I'm not massaging you. Ask Brady."

"Brady uses his thumbs too hard," he whines. "It feels like I'm getting massaged by the Terminator."

"You know I can hear you, right?" Brady calls from the corner.

Novy rounds on him. "Hey, if the skate fits, lace it up. Besides, it's not even an insult. Some guys like a firm hand. I just prefer Teddy's magic touch. It's like getting massaged with warm butter."

I frown. "Eew. Use a different analogy."

Novy considers for a moment. "It's like—"

"No." I hold up a hand. "I changed my mind. No more analogies. And the answer is still no."

"Come on, bud. My calves are so fucking tight. Do you really wanna risk me not playing my best? Do you want a big, fat 'L' on your conscience?"

"Novy, you are not my patient. And I was off the clock two minutes ago."

"I'll pay you. Come on, you know I'm good for it."

With a sigh, I drop my backpack down to the chair. Crossing my arms, I glare at him. "How much?"

"I am not hearing this," Brady mutters, tapping away on the tablet.

Novy stares me down like we're in the Wild West. "One hundred dollars."

I snort. "Nov, I'd pay *you* a hundred bucks just to let me leave."

"Fine. Five hundred dollars."

"You know I know your salary, right?"

He groans, dragging a hand through his short hair. "I've only got five hundred cash on me."

The man looks so pathetic. And I guess I do have the time. Henrik's home with Karolina. He took her to PT this afternoon. "Fine. Five hundred bucks. For five minutes." I hold out my hand and wait.

"Five minutes? Are you shitting me?"

"Hey, five minutes is plenty of time to get one good calf massage . . . or two kinda good massages."

Muttering under his breath, Novy digs in the pocket of his shorts for his wallet and pulls out the cash: five crisp one-hundred-dollar bills.

"Thank you." I pluck the bills from his hand. "Hop up on the table. You want one massage or two?"

"One," he growls. "Left calf. And you better make it good."

"I will do my absolute best work," I assure him, pocketing the cash. I make a show of setting my phone down on the table by his head before tapping the timer and starting his countdown. Oiling up my hands, I massage his calf. Following the lines of the musculature, I work to ease his tightness. He chokes back the sex noises as best he can, pressing his forehead to his folded arms.

"Pressure good?"

"So good," he mutters.

I smile. I really do take pride in my massages. And Novy's not the first client to tell me they prefer me to all the other PTs. He's just the most obnoxious.

My phone dings and Novy perks up. "Karlsson just texted."

"What's he saying?"

He props himself up on his elbows, my phone in his hand. "He's asking, 'Are you ready?'"

I go still. "What?"

"Hey, that was not five fucking minutes." He shows me the ticking timer on the phone. "Keep going or give me my money back."

I keep massaging. Did I miss something? Am I ready for what? My phone pings a second time.

"Karlsson again. He says he's outside. Want me to call him and tell him you're occupied?"

"I—"

"Oh wait, never mind. He's calling you." Before I can stop him, Novy answers my phone, turning it on speaker. He puts on an airy receptionist voice. "You've reached the office of Doctor Theodore O'Connor. May I ask who's calling?"

I groan as Brady chuckles again from his corner.

Henrik is clearly confused. "I . . . what? Who is this?"

Novy snorts, switching to his normal voice. "It's Novy, asshole. What do you want? Your husband's busy right now."

"I thought he was off at five."

"I was," I call out. "I'm being held hostage by a Canadian brute with tight calves!"

"He's mine for the next three minutes," Novy shouts into the phone. "You can have your precious husband when I'm done with him."

"But we have reservations," comes Henrik's voice.

Oh fuck, was that tonight? No, no, no. I wrote it down. It was next week.

"Oooh, reservations where?" says Novy.

"High Tide," Henrik replies.

FUCK.

How did I confuse the days for our first Poppy-orchestrated fake public date?! And what the hell am I supposed to do now? High Tide is a swanky seafood restaurant set right on the beach overlooking the ocean. It's the kind of place with white tablecloths, and glass stemware, and a cocktail menu as long as the regular menu.

"Oh, nice," says Novy. "Hey, get the whole branzino. And they do this dessert that's a flight of mini cheesecakes. It's so fucking good."

"We have to make our reservation first," says Henrik.

They keep talking about the menu while I totally spiral out. I didn't bring anything to change into. Henrik's probably out there in his Porsche in a suit, and I'm standing here with oil on my hands, rubbing Novy's calf while wearing a Rays polo, Nike athletic pants, and a pair of running shoes. Fuck me, this is gonna be our Swedish wedding all over again. Poppy has arranged for a cameraman to be there!

In the middle of my freak-out, my phone timer goes off. Novy's five minutes are up. He turns off my alarm, still talking to Henrik. "Hey man, we're done here. I'll send your guy out, okay? Don't call the police on me. Hostage crisis over."

I drop my hands from his calf and stand there like I'm frozen.

Novy rolls over, my phone still in his hand. "Man, I am so fucking jealous that you get the full Teddy treatment whenever you want. Coley likes to think he gives good massages, but honestly, he's as bad as old Iron Fingers Brady."

"Fuck you too, Novikov," Brady says in parting. "Teddy, I'll see you tomorrow?"

I just nod.

As Novy stands from the table, he tries to hand me back my phone, still talking to Henrik. "Well, you two lovebirds have a nice time tonight. Don't do anything I wouldn't do, especially with a camera there."

"I'm waiting outside," says Henrik.

Snatching my phone from Novy, I force out something that sounds like, "Great, I'll be right there." Then I hang up on him. Novy goes to step away, and I grab his arm. "Please tell me that by some miracle you have a suit in your locker or your car."

"What? Why?" He looks me up and down. "Aw, come on, you look dynamite."

"I look like a high school gym teacher! Poppy's gonna be spreading these pictures all over the fucking internet, and this is not how I want to present myself to the world. Novy, *please*. Do you have a suit or not?"

He narrows his eyes, flashing me the smirk that has devastated hearts in two countries and counting. "Give me my five hundred bucks back."

I gasp, glaring at him. "Seriously?"

He grins, holding out his hand. "Dude, you're gonna look so good. You might not even make it to the restaurant. Karlsson's just gonna jump your bones in the car."

Yeah, fat chance of that.

Seeing as I have literally no other option, I fish the money from my pocket and slap it back into Novy's greedy hand. "I hate you."

39

HENRIK

I don't like being late for things. In the hockey world, it gets drilled into us that being early is being on time. Planes don't wait for us. Neither do busses. Reservations typically don't wait either. And I didn't make these reservations. I don't even know the restaurant. My GPS says it will take us almost thirty minutes to get there. And Teddy still hasn't come out.

What the hell is he doing in there? Probably still laughing and joking with Novy. The man is such a showboat. He's my teammate, and he's a friend, but . . .

Fuck, I don't know what I'm even thinking. He's a teammate and a friend. Full stop. I'm sure nothing untoward is happening. Teddy is just dedicated to his job.

I think perhaps I'm just hungry.

And oddly nervous.

I'm going on a date with my husband. But it's a fake date, orchestrated by our PR director. There will be a cameraperson ready to photograph us entering and leaving the restaurant. And Poppy expressly asked that we "crank up the spice" to quell the nasty rumors that this is all just some kind of publicity stunt.

Well, I suppose this *is* a publicity stunt. The date, I mean. All part of Poppy's grand Operation Mighty Oak. But our marriage doesn't feel like a stunt. It may have been spontaneous, born out of necessity, but my affection for Teddy is very real, and growing stronger every day.

Poppy assures us that in a couple weeks, this will all die down. For now, the gossip machine is firing on all cylinders. My American agent, Laura, has been harassed by the press all week. They want an official statement about my press conference. But the conference *was* my official statement. I'll not be making another one. Poppy said it went viral, so why would I bother?

She was so touched by my including Novy and Morrow in my remarks that she baked me enough cookies to feed my entire apartment building. She brought them by last week, tears in her eyes, and stayed for two hours, letting her daughter play with Karro.

I fight the urge to check my watch for a third time just as the front doors of the practice arena open. Teddy comes striding out, and my eyes go wide. He's wearing a sleek forest-green suit, a black belt and shoes, and a white shirt, no tie. The shirt is unbuttoned halfway down his chest. His hair is pulled back, bundled at his nape.

Behind him, a few of the guys, including Novy, pool out of the open doorway, wolf-whistling and calling his name.

"Yeah, Teddy!"

"Get it, superstar!"

"That's my physical therapist!"

Teddy just laughs, his smile lighting up his entire face, as he waves them off and strides over to the car. He's almost reached it before I remember myself. I fling my door open and step out, circling the back of the Porsche to try to beat him to the other side. Like Teddy, I'm dressed in a suit with no tie, only mine is stone blue.

"Hey, Karlsson, have him back by ten," Novy shouts.

The others all laugh.

"Looking good, Karlsson!"

"Don't do anything I wouldn't do, boys!"

I brush my hand down the front of my crisp white dress shirt and open Teddy's door for him.

"Hey," he says, breathless. "You look great."

"As do you," I reply. "Is that my suit? I don't recognize it."

He just grins, slipping into the front seat. "Nah, it's mine."

We make it to the restaurant with less than a minute to spare. I give my keys to a valet. Offering Teddy my hand, I help him unfold his long legs and stand. This little sports car may not be practical for two men as tall and broad shouldered as we are, but that's not really the reason one buys a Porsche.

He presses into me as the valet rushes behind him to shut his door. "How we didn't just get a dozen speeding tickets, I will literally never know."

I just chuckle. I'm about to lead the way inside when Teddy stiffens, his hand wrapping around my arm. "Oh my god."

"What?"

"He's right over there—no—*don't look*," he hisses as I'm about to turn. "He's literally standing in the fucking bushes. Oh god, this is like something out of a bad movie."

"What do I do?"

"Don't turn around! Just act natural."

I sigh, feeling foolish. "We can't stand here, Teddy. Let's just walk in."

"Okay. But do we, like, walk in together? Like, hand in hand? Or do you sort of walk ahead? What will look more believable for pictures—"

"Not choreographing this will look *most* believable." I tug him along next to me, putting myself between him and the camera.

"Don't look so mad," he says through his fake smile. "You're supposed to be in love with me, remember?"

"I'm Swedish. This is just my face. I look this way when I'm happy too."

Teddy snorts a nervous laugh.

I do try to relax my shoulders a little. Then I nod to an older couple as they make their way out of the restaurant. The lady takes in our joined hands and Teddy's smile and frowns. Her lip curls up as if she just smelled something rotten. It stops me in my tracks. I know Teddy sees it too, because his hand tightens in mine.

He shocks the hell out of me by rounding on her. "What? You've never seen two men holding hands before? Take a picture. It'll last longer!"

Knowing there's a photographer in the bushes, Teddy and I both start laughing.

The older woman gasps, her hand flying up to clutch her literal pearls, as her husband, an old white man in a navy sport coat, wraps his hand around her arm. "Come on, Denise."

"Yeah, keep walking, Denise," Teddy calls after her. "Nothing to see here."

"Will you stop?" I say in his ear.

"Hey, later tonight, we're gonna go home and do gay stuff together," he adds, giving her a dramatic wave. "It's gonna be great, Denise! We'll Snapchat you photos!"

"Come on." I pull him away.

"Fuck, I feel better." He pulls the door open for me. "Shall we? I've heard the branzino is divine."

W̲e make it through drinks and the appetizer course before the subject of the photographer comes up again. Teddy is mid-sentence, recounting a progress update from Karro's tutor, when he stops, his shoulders stiffening. He sets his amaretto sour aside, eyes locked on the empty plate of mussels between us.

"What's wrong?"

"The photographer is in the corner by the bar."

Before I can say anything, my phone buzzes in my inside pocket. I reach for it and see a message from Poppy glowing on the screen:

POPPY: Squeeeee, you two look so cute together! I wanna melt you in a pan and serve you over ice cream!

I flash Teddy the phone and let him read the message. "Is this a good thing?"

He shrugs. "I guess. I mean, we *do* look good." He brushes his hand down his chest. "I lied in the car though."

"What?"

"This suit. It isn't mine. It's Novy's."

"You're wearing Novy's suit?" I note the way it fits a little too large in the shoulders.

He glances sharply across the table, eyes narrowed. "You better not be about to ask me if I traded sexual favors for it. The answer is no, asshole."

I raise both hands, leaning back in my chair. "I said nothing."

"I forgot my suit at home, and he had one. End of story."

I smile, sipping my beer. "You should keep it. It looks better on you."

He huffs, poking at the mussels with a fork, looking for one with the meat still inside. "Oh believe me, for five hundred bucks, I'm keeping the suit *and* the shoes."

I just hum, contentedly sipping my beer. Since our conversation in the car last week, I've felt a new kind of curiosity towards Teddy. And I've researched the term. *Demisexuality*. It's a rather broad term, covering everything from those who seek no sexual touch ever to people who engage in casual sex but may not express romantic feelings until a deeper relationship is established first.

The more I read, the more the label seems to fit me. The article last night talked of primary versus secondary sexual attraction. Apparently, primary attraction happens at first sight. You can look at a person, even a stranger on the street, and feel attracted to them. I'm not sure I've ever felt that before. Aesthetically, I may look at someone and admire their beauty. But I admire them with the same feeling of joy or excitement as seeing a sunset or a stag standing in the snow.

I glance across the table at Teddy again. Aesthetically, he's very pleasing. I've always thought that. He's a composition of sharp angles—broad shoulders, long legs, pronounced cheekbones. I particularly like his neck. I like watching how it twists and elongates as he looks around, as he laughs.

But I want to photograph his neck, not lick it.

The article had a lot to say about scent as a primary attractor too. As a Swedish person, I found it all very amusing. We Swedes enjoy having our own space, even with friends and family. It made me mindful. How often do I ever let myself get close enough to smell another person? Well, aside from the sweaty hockey players I encounter on the ice. But not one of them has ever sparked my sexual interest with their stench.

No, scent has only aroused me with one person. Only with Teddy.

I blame it on the fact that I'm still sleeping in his bed. I don't know why I haven't put a stop to it. Now that I'm admitting to myself that I'm curious about him, it feels like a line is being crossed. But I don't want to stop. I'm getting the best sleep I've had in ages. And I like it. I like lying in the bed and having him roll to me, hands seeking in the dark. Even in sleep, he'll curl around me, his head on my chest, our legs tangled.

If he doesn't roll to me, I seek him out. I lock my arm around his chest and press my face to his neck, breathing him in. I'm not sure what to make of his scent arousing me because he's using my body wash and wearing my cologne. Am I attracted to him? Or the scents? Or is this some kind of caveman hindbrain situation where I'm attracted to my scent *on* him?

"How are we doing over here?" says the waiter, removing the empty plates.

"Fine," Teddy replies, fishing the cherries out of his drink as he tries not to look in the corner.

I hate that the photographer is ruining this for him. "I'm sorry," I say as soon as the waiter leaves. "We can go if he's making you this uncomfortable. Poppy didn't say how long we need to stay."

"It's fine."

But I know it's not. He hates this performance as much as I do. I want to make it up to him. When I get back from this series of aways, I'm going to take him out again. No cameras. No falsity. Just good conversation and a good meal. We both deserve it.

He leans back as the waiter returns, placing down our main courses. We decided to split the whole roasted branzino and a plate of lobster and scallop risotto. He heaps some risotto onto my plate as I squeeze half a lemon over the branzino. He can't help but glance at the corner again. "Has Laura said anything else about the interview requests?"

"I told her to refuse them all," I reply, testing the flakiness of the fish with my fork.

"Will that cause problems?"

"I made it clear that would be my only statement. We'll let them take these pictures, and hopefully we can all just move on."

He nods, eyes on his plate as he tries the fish.

"Hey." I set my fork aside and reach my hand across the table.

He glances at it for a moment before sighing and placing his hand in mine.

"I'm glad you're here. Our voyeur notwithstanding, I'm having a nice time."

He snorts. "Seriously?"

"What?"

"You can use the word 'notwithstanding' correctly in a sentence, but you don't know the phrase 'happy as clams'?"

Feeling prickly, I switch to Swedish. "And you can't understand a word of Swedish, so let's refrain from throwing rocks at glass houses, shall we?"

The words roll over him like a wave, and he just purses his lips. "Fair point."

"I thought so," I say in English.

He chuckles, dropping my hand to resume his meal. "Oh, don't try to hide it now, Mr. Big Shot. That felt really good, didn't it? Foreigners love making Americans feel dumb by speaking languages they know we don't understand. How many languages do you speak, by the way?"

I consider for a moment. "Fluently? Or just enough to get by?"

He sighs. "Let's go with fluently."

"Three."

"Swedish, English, and . . ."

"French. I played three seasons with the Canadiens before I joined the Rays."

"Fuck, that's so hot." He takes a bite of the risotto. "And this is so fucking good."

It is good. Creamy and hearty with chunks of grilled scallop and a whole lobster tail. As we sit and eat, and as I watch Teddy try and fail to stop glancing to the corner, I get bold. This will be our last chance to be alone for several days. Even once I get back from these away games, our schedules mean I'll hardly see him.

In this moment, I feel greedy. I want his attention on me. And I want him out of his own head, not focused on how he looks being photographed eating this damn fish. "Can I ask you a question?" I say, setting my fork aside to sip my water.

"Sure."

"I've been researching demisexuality this week."

"Well, that's good, right?"

I nod. "I've learned a lot. I'm currently exploring what it means to feel primary versus secondary sexual attraction. I'll admit, I'm not sure I've ever felt primary attraction before. At least, not the way the article describes it."

"Well, I think that's actually common for a lot of people. Not just those who identify as demi. It's no big deal if you don't cross some rando on the street and think, 'Whoa, he's hot.'"

"Is it like that for you?"

He nearly chokes on his water. One hand to his chest, he lowers the glass. "Pardon?"

"Do you meet people and feel an instant sexual attraction based solely on their physical attributes?"

He shrugs. "I mean, sometimes. Depends on the person, I guess. And maybe a little on my mood. It's definitely happened before though, sure."

I wait until he has the glass to his lips again, and then I ask, "Did it happen with me?"

He doesn't choke this time. His eyes narrow, and he quickly sets the glass aside, lowering his voice. "Okay, asshole. Fuck you, I know what you're doing."

"What am I doing?" I reply, taking a bite of the grilled fish. It's crispy and flaky, with just the right hint of citrus.

Teddy rolls his eyes. "You're just trying to distract me from thinking about the photographer. Also, I think you're fishing."

"Fishing?"

"Yeah, you want me to get all flustered and admit that I think you're handsome."

I say nothing.

His eyes flash as he leans across the table. "You want my attention, Henrik? You always have it. And for your information, *yes*. From the moment I first saw you, I thought you were the most beautiful man I'd ever seen. I then spent one of the most sexually frustrated years of my life pining after you, so lost in lust with your beauty and poise and primary sexual attractants that, I swear to god, I don't know how I survived."

I forget to breathe as he holds my gaze, daring me to look away.

"Now that you're my husband, I spend every day agonizing over my attraction to you—when you press against me in your sleep, when you pant on your little stationary bike, when you step out of the shower, when you stand at the stove in those sleep pants that curve so perfectly to every inch of your ass and thighs. Get some bigger pants, Henrik. They don't need to be that goddamn formfitting. There. Is that what you wanted to hear?"

I smile as he lowers his gaze to the table, digging furiously into the fish with his fork.

"Hey, Teddy?"

He stills, not looking up at me. "What?"

"I think you're beautiful too."

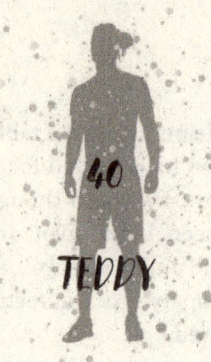

40

TEDDY

What the actual fuck is happening right now? I glare across the table at Henrik. "What are you doing?"

"I think the technical term is flirting."

I blink, my vision spinning like I just took a punch to the fucking head. There are a lot of thoughts and emotions swirling in my mind, but only one coherent word pops out. "Why?"

He shrugs, taking a sip of his beer. "This is a date, right? We've never been on a date before. I know it was orchestrated by Poppy, and I know we have an audience, but I'm still here with you, sharing this nice meal. It's customary to flirt on a date, no?"

I groan, sinking back in my chair. "Hen, come on. I don't need you to pity flirt with me. That's just fucking depressing."

He arches a brow. "What pity?"

"I don't want you flirting with me because you *have* to or because you think it's what you're supposed to do on a date."

"Then when am I allowed to flirt with you?"

I'm fucking reeling. "What?"

He gestures around. "If this setting is inappropriate, when and where am I permitted to flirt with you?"

Glaring at him, I rattle down my fork. "Am I getting punk'd right now?"

"What?"

"Is Novy listening to us on a hidden mic somewhere?" I glance all around. "Is he about to pop out dressed as a giant seagull or something?" Peering out at the patio, I look for any sign of a candid camera. It's full of other diners enjoying the seaside sunset. The sky is currently lit up in a spray of pinks and purples. Cotton candy clouds dot the horizon above the blue ocean.

Now poor Henrik is thoroughly confused. "Why would Novy be dressed as a seagull?"

"I don't fucking know. Why are *you* flirting with me? We don't do that, Henrik. We don't—it's too much, okay? I mean, my god. I can't be your crash test dummy."

"My what?"

I take a deep breath. "Look, I think it's great that we had our talk the other night. I feel like I know you so much better now. And I'm so thankful you trusted me enough to share that part of yourself with me . . ."

Reading between my lines, he frowns. "But?"

"But . . . well, I can't be your crash test dummy," I repeat. "I can't be the guy you experiment with, exploring the limits of your interest in sex and human connection. I'm so flattered," I add quickly. "And you have no idea how much I'd love to say yes. I think if you were anyone else . . . maybe if I were anyone else, I could say yes. I could sit here and flirt with you, and laugh, and tease, and pretend it doesn't mean anything at all. I could pretend we're just having harmless fun. But it's not . . ." I fall silent, trying to think of the right words.

"It's not an experiment for you," he finishes.

I nod.

"You know what you want from me, and you won't settle for less."

All I can do is shrug. "Can you blame me?"

He offers me a weak smile. "Never."

I glance down at my risotto, suddenly not feeling very hungry.

"Can I offer just one counterpoint?"

I look up, heart in my throat. He sits across from me, looking like my every dream in that fitted blue suit with the little yellow pocket square, no tie, shirt unbuttoned to expose his neck. He trimmed his beard for tonight. His sandy hair lies perfectly across his forehead. He wants to offer me a reasoned counterpoint on why we shouldn't flirt with each other?

"Sure," I say on a breath.

His gaze softens. "How will I know if I can give you everything you want, if you won't let me try?"

41

HENRIK

Teddy lets out a shaky breath, eyes on the half-eaten plate of branzino. "What would that even look like?"

"Me trying?"

He nods.

I consider for a moment. "The article I read talked about secondary sexual attractants too, things like personality and life experience, talents. Teddy, your personality has always attracted me. From the beginning, I've felt drawn to you as a person, your light, your energy. The more I've come to know you, the more I want to be where you are. I know there's nothing inherently sexual in that admission, but it's still an admission."

He reaches for his water glass, seemingly desperate to do something with his hands. "Fair enough. But I don't think I can be content just sharing space with you. I know we're doing that now," he adds. "But I don't know if you noticed that I'm not handling it all that well."

"I've noticed. I still make you uncomfortable."

"No, you make me turned on. There's a difference." Setting his water glass aside, he tosses his napkin on the table too, holding my gaze. "Hen, this has never once been about me feeling uncomfortable around you. You keep using that word. That's not it at all. Or if it *is* a feeling of discomfort, it's rooted in me being completely, irrationally, and irrevocably in love with you."

I blink. "What?"

He frowns. "Oh, did you not want me to go there? We're having the honest conversation now, right? So let's fucking have it."

Bracing myself, I nod. "Fine, proceed."

"From the moment we met out on that sidewalk six years ago, you crashed into my life, and into my heart, and literally swept me off my fucking feet. I looked up at you and felt like I'd just found the one. It's crazy, I admit that. But that's who I am."

He presses a hand to his chest and goes on, "Henrik, I can only be who I am. I can only feel what I feel. And what I feel for you is so far and away above what you feel for me. The imbalance here is fucking staggering. And now you're offering me crumbs while I'm over here literally starving. Don't get me wrong, I'm gonna take them. I will take every crumb you offer because I can't walk away from you. I certainly can't walk away from Karro. She's sunk her hooks in me all the way to my beating heart. I love that little girl. So now I'm twice as twisted up, wriggling like a fish on both your lines."

My mind races as I listen to his confession. His mother is right—he doesn't want things from me. He doesn't want my clothes or the comfort of my apartment. He doesn't want money or acclaim. He's not chasing me for status. He just wants me. It's a heady feeling. I'm not sure that I've ever felt wanted before. Needed, certainly. Everyone in my life always seems to need something from me. I give and give, offering whatever I can. I would give until there's nothing left for myself.

But Teddy doesn't need anything from me. He has a career and a life, a strong family of support, good friends. He could walk away and be fine. I never have to worry that he'll find what he needs. He's here because he wants to be here. He faced down the press with me, stood up to his family for me. He's embraced Karolina, treating her like his own child, loving her as she deserves to be loved.

All for want of me.

His expression is wary as he takes me in. "Henrik? Fuck, say something. I said too much, didn't I?" He groans, sitting back. "I shouldn't have said anything. Can we sort of, just, rewind?" He gestures with his fingers like he's spinning back the tape. "Let's just order the cheesecakes. Nov said we should try them." He cranes his neck, looking around. "Do you see our waiter?"

"But we *are* at this table."

He lowers his hand from gesturing for the waiter. "What?"

"We're at this table," I repeat. "There's no going backwards."

He opens his mouth to speak just as the waiter appears.

"Hey there! How are we doin' over here? Oooh, looks like we're still working on those mains. Can I get either of you a refresh on your drinks?"

"We need a minute," says Teddy, his gaze locked on me.

"But you called me over—"

"My guy?" Teddy cries. "We need a fucking minute. Please and thank you."

The waiter disappears, and I can't help but smile.

He groans, dragging a hand over his face. "Fuck, that was so rude."

"I'll tip him generously," I reply, still smiling.

Teddy doesn't smile. "You were saying?"

"We can't go backwards," I repeat. "Whatever hand of fate led us here, we *are* here. We're in this moment. We're married, sharing custody of a child . . . and you're in love with me. If it's all the same to you, I'd like to see if I could learn to love you too."

Slowly, he shakes his head. "What if you can't? Henrik, I won't survive it . . ."

I take some cash out of my wallet and toss it on the table. It's more than enough to cover the meal. "I'm not too worried. If anything, I think I'm excited."

He watches as I rise from the table. "What are you doing?"

I offer out my hand. "Come with me."

He places his hand in mine, and I draw him up from his chair. Lacing our fingers together, I weave out of the dining room, past the photographer sitting at the end of the bar. The man scrambles, digging in his wallet to pay his bill so he can follow us out of the restaurant.

Once we step outside, the ocean air fills my senses. The sun has set beyond the dunes, leaving a hazy blue twilight out on the beach. The waves crash into the white sand as a pod of pelicans goes drifting silently past. I cut right, leading us away from the valet stand.

Teddy follows behind. "Where are we going?"

I walk him over to the rickety stairs that lead down to the beach.

"Hen, these shoes are Italian leather. And not mine."

Smiling, I kick off my own shoes, leaving them by the stairs. Dropping his hand, I bend down and tug my socks off, stuffing them in my pocket. Righting myself, I extend out my hand again. "Live a little."

Rolling his eyes, he kicks off his shoes, cuffing the hem of his pants that are an inch too long. Then he places his hand back in mine, and I lead the way down the stairs. The wood is rough, but the beach is cool. My feet sink, sand pouring between my toes.

"Our shadow is following us," he says at my shoulder.

"Ignore him. He doesn't matter." I don't stop walking until we reach the water's edge. Bits of shell and other detritus litter the surf, dusted with frothy sea foam.

Teddy groans. "If I get this suit wet, Novy's gonna make me get it professionally dry-cleaned—" He gasps as I turn and reel him in. Our chests brush, feet sinking in the sand, as I sling my arm around his shoulders, keeping hold of his left hand. "What are you doing?"

"I'll buy Novy ten suits," I say in his ear. "One in every color. Just shut up and dance with me."

He goes stiff for a moment. Then he relaxes, his hand going to my waist. We shift in the sand, doing an awkward half turn. "Hen, there's no music."

I break us apart long enough to pull my phone from my pocket and tap the first song on my "Teddy" playlist. I turn the volume all the way up so we can hear it over the surf. Then I pull him back to me, my arm around his shoulders.

The music filters out and he relaxes, resting his forehead to mine. "I love this song."

"I know."

He leans away, searching my face. "How?"

"You listen to it all the time in the bathtub."

"Should I be flattered that you researched the artist? Or worried that you guard the door while I bathe?"

I shrug, surprising him as I spin him out and pull him back in. "You sit in there so long, I have to check that you're still alive."

He laughs as an ocean breeze blows a few of his locs loose. "It's called self-care."

I tuck the locs behind his ear, fingertips brushing down the column of his neck. His eyes go wide, unsure of what to make of my touch. "I know you're scared. You have every reason to doubt me, to want to protect your heart. I'm asking you to give me a chance."

Before he can reply, I spin him out again, letting him turn back into my arms.

"We'll take it slow," I go on. "You can say no at any time to anything. And I'll try to be clear if I think I'm ready for more."

Finally, he nods, letting out a breath. "Okay."

Okay.

A weight lifts off my chest as the word sinks deep. He's willing to let me try. He's willing to let me see where this can lead. Erick Baker's "Unbroken Promise" filters out from my pocket, as Teddy and I slow dance in the sand. I don't care that a photographer is taking pictures of us. I don't care that everyone else thinks we're crazy. No one can tell me this is a lie. Standing here, holding him, feeling him in my arms? Nothing about Teddy O'Connor is a lie. Even when he can't say what he means, he shows you in action. All you have to do is pay attention.

Teddy is the truth I never saw coming. The truth that I could want more from life, deserve more. But I don't know how to do this. I don't know how to open myself to another in this way. I don't know how to want someone. Christ knows I don't know how to be wanted.

I'm just going to follow Teddy's lead. I'm going to act on instinct. And my every instinct is telling me that, in this moment, what I want is to dance with my husband on the beach.

42

TEDDY

"Okay, what *exactly* did he say?" Colin takes the beer and two jumbo soft pretzels I offer him. All around us, rowdy hockey fans crowd in, laughing and chatting. It's the first home game for the Rays since their stretch of aways.

And since Henrik and I danced on the beach.

I thank the concession stand attendant, slipping our bottles of water and the bag of cotton candy into the backpack hooked on Karolina's wheelchair. Giving her a push, we weave through the crowd, heading for the VIP section. We're here early enough to catch the tail end of warm-up.

Colin walks at my side, resolutely being an asshole by wearing a Jags jersey to an NHL game. Why did I even invite him? He takes a bite of one of the soft pretzels, talking as he chews. "Did he give any indication of how slow he wants to take things?"

"None. We danced on the beach and drove home holding hands. When we got home, Karolina was in hysterics because her rainbow unicorn stuffie lost an eye, and Hanna couldn't find a sewing kit to put it back on. I had to run out and get one. By the time we got that sorted, Hen was exhausted and stressed, saying he had to go to bed because of his travel schedule. That was four days ago."

"But you told him you loved him?"

I groan. "Col, I spilled my freaking guts. I told him everything. It was so embarrassing."

"And you've said nothing to each other since?"

"No. I mean, we've talked every day. But it's just been about Karro and, like, 'Hey, good game,' and stuff like that. He got home yesterday, but I was at a fundraising thing. It's all just been a little crazy."

"Unbelievable." Juggling his beer and pretzels, he tries to show the attendant his lanyard pass.

"I got you," she says, scanning the pass.

Once she scans mine and Karro's, I wheel Karro up to the elevator. "Press the button, sweets. We're going down."

Shifting her pile of new Rays merch to the side, Karro reaches out with her casted arm and presses the Down button. When the elevator arrives, we wait for it to clear before stepping in. I wheel Karro in backwards. Colin stands at my side with a stupid smirk on his face.

"What?"

He just shakes his head. "You are so down bad. It'd be funny if it wasn't so tragic."

"How is that helping?" I try to keep my voice down as the elevator starts to move.

"Just talk to him, bro. Next time you see him, tell him, 'Henrik, my one true love, I wanna know you in the biblical way.'"

"Did you forget the part where I said *slow*? We're talking glacier pace here. And he might not even want that from me. Like, ever. Never."

Colin turns to me, a look of horror on his face. "And you're cool with that?"

"I don't know! This is completely uncharted territory for me, Col. I only ever do relationships where the banana bread comes first."

He swallows a sip of beer. "Banana bread?"

I gesture down at Karro with a dramatic nod of my head.

He snorts. "Ahhh . . . good old banana bread. I love banana bread. I know *you* love banana bread—"

"Don't."

"Wait. Does Karlsson not like banana bread? Or is he more of a sourdough bread eater?"

I grimace. "Can we change the kind of bread, please?"

He just laughs, leading the way out of the elevator. "What stupid metaphor would you prefer? Rye bread? A good slice of pumpernickel? Man, if Tracy was a bread, I think she'd be a nice, crispy French loaf."

I just shake my head. "Why did I think I could talk to you about this? Why did I even bother? I have only myself to blame."

He laughs again. "You're talking to me because I'm older than you, I'm wiser than you, and I have more success in relationships than you do. I'm basically Yoda."

"My god, does that make me Luke Skywalker?"

Before he can respond, Karro perks up in her wheelchair. She's decked out in a Karlsson jersey, glitter on her cheeks, and pigtails I've fixed with silver and teal streamers. "Morbror loves banana bread."

Colin and I both stiffen, eyes wide.

Fuck, I have *got* to remember that this girl understands English! And the longer she hangs out with my dumb ass, the better she gets.

"That's great, sweets," I say, patting her shoulder. "We should make some this weekend. Wouldn't that be fun?"

"Yeah!"

Colin just shakes his head at me.

"Shut up," I hiss, pushing Karro forward.

"You're going to hell," he mouths.

"You can leave now."

He just follows at my side, a new spring in his step. "Delusional Rejects, table for one."

"I'm unfriending you, effective immediately."

"Hey, when I meet your man later, should I refer to you as my Padawan or my hopeless case?"

"I'm gonna murder you in a lake."

"We've got a looooong way to go if you're gonna keep that attitude."

43

HENRIK

"**M**orbror!"

I turn to see Teddy and Karolina standing at the end of the rink up against the glass. She's wearing a Karlsson jersey so large, it falls past her knees. There are sparkly ribbons in her hair.

Smiling, I leave my teammates and skate up to them. "Hej, mitt lilla lamm." Glancing at Teddy, I offer him a smile too. "Hej, Teddy."

"Hi," he says on a breath. He's not wearing his WAG jacket tonight. He's in a black T-shirt, ripped jeans, and my leather jacket. His locs are pulled up in a bun, held in place with a teal Rays bandana. I had hoped to see him yesterday when I got home, but he volunteered to help at some rehabilitation hospital event the Rays were sponsoring. He didn't get back until after I was asleep. And I was out the door early this morning.

Karro presses both hands to the glass and says in English, "Teddy got me cotton candy!"

His smile falls slightly. "I will not be letting her eat it all."

I pull my glove off, press my hand to the glass over Karro's, and say in Swedish, "Did you have a good time while I was gone? Were you good for Hanna and Mr. Torres?"

She pouts. "He makes me do math."

I give her a solemn nod. "Math can be hard. But we want to be bright like Mamma, ja?"

Lindberg skates up on my left, popping his mouth guard free to smile at Karro and say in Swedish, "Hej, hej. Look at you growing so big and strong."

Her eyes go wide as she notices his missing front teeth. She's only ever seen him with his flipper. Laughing, I sling an arm around his shoulders. "See? This is why you practice your math. Otherwise, you have to become a hockey player, like Morbror and Mr. Lindberg, and then you'll lose all your teeth."

Leaning into the bit, Lindberg lowers his face to the glass, flashing his gummy smile. "Give us some cotton candy, little girl. We can't chew without our teeth!"

"No!" She covers her mouth with both hands, nearly toppling off the ledge.

"Wow," says Teddy in English, keeping her upright. "Great uncle-ing there, Morbror. Lindy, put your guard back in before you're eating steak through a straw."

With a chuckle, Lindberg pops his guard in and skates off, patting my shoulder as he goes.

A whistle blows, and I know I'm out of time. "I have to go," I say in English.

"We're gonna watch you play," says Karro in Swedish.

I switch back too. "I'm so happy you're both here, mitt lilla lamm."

"Hey, Ted!"

Teddy glances over his shoulder.

A handsome Black man in a Jags NFL jersey waits by the stairs, holding a beer. "I'm gonna head up to the seats," he calls with a wave.

"K." Teddy waves back at him. "We'll be right there!"

I watch as the man scales the steps, disappearing into the stands. "Who was that?"

"What?" Teddy glances over his shoulder. "Oh, that was Colin. I thought you met Colin before."

My shoulders tense as my smile falls. "No."

He gives me a puzzled look. "I was sure you had. I think he came to a beach thing once or twice during my intern year."

"Why is he here?" I say, trying to keep my tone light. I must be failing, judging by Teddy's expression.

He arches a confused brow. "To watch the game. I invited him. Wait, is that a problem?"

"Of course not." What else am I supposed to say?

"I mean, the WAGs gave us more tickets than I could ever use," he goes on. "And Colin was finally free tonight. Besides, I wanted backup in case this one became a sugar-crazed terror," he adds, kissing Karro's glittery cheek.

She smiles. "Can I have my cotton candy now?"

"Not until we get to the seats. Ask again, and I'm gonna give your cotton candy to Pelly the Pelican."

"No," she whines.

Another whistle blows, and I push back from the glass. "I have to go."

"Skate well," Teddy calls with a wave. "Say bye to Morbror, honey bunny."

"Bye, Morbror!"

"Kick Dallas's ass!" he adds.

I skate backwards, leaving Karro and Teddy at the glass.

This doesn't make any sense. I thought Teddy and I were making progress. I told him what I wanted before I left for Columbus. I couldn't have been clearer. I told him I was ready to try. He agreed to let me.

So why did my husband bring a date to my game?

44

TEDDY

Not gonna lie, the Rays are a mess tonight. The score is still 0-0, but they're losing pucks and missing shots. Henrik is definitely part of the problem. He, Lindy, and Langley just aren't skating as a line tonight. The only reason the Stars haven't scored is that DeGraw is having a great game. Actually, he's having a great season. He's already made two truly incredible saves, and we're only halfway through the first period.

"Where did y'all find this guy?" Colin says in my ear, cheering with the rest of the fans as DeGraw drops a caught puck to the ice. He was already in a full butterfly when he did this twisty, ballerina backbend, snatching the puck out of the corner of the net with his glove.

"Australia!" I jump up and down, clapping.

Next to me, Karro sits happily in her chair, swinging her feet, eating her cotton candy by the sticky fistful. Thanks to my friend Cheyenne in the ticketing department, we were able to snag three handicap-accessible seats in the lower VIP area. We're not right on the glass, but we're close enough to feel part of the action.

The Dallas goalie is hunched in the net right in front of us, watching the action as the puck is dropped for another face-off. Lindy gains possession and slaps it over to Henrik.

"Morbror has the puck!" I scoop Karro out of her seat and balance her on my hip. We got the all-clear from her doctor regarding the hairline fracture on her ribs, which has been amazing. She can get more comfortable sleeping, and we don't have to treat her quite so much like a glass doll. Really, it's just her casted arm and leg to worry about now, and she'll be able to bear weight on the leg in a few more weeks.

She shakes her bag of cotton candy in my face. "Go, Morbror!"

"Man, he's fast," says Colin.

Henrik cuts and glides, dancing around the Dallas players. They're closing in, and he doesn't have a clean shot. He drops the puck back to Jake, who passes it up to Lindy. The forward line re-forms, with Henrik trying to get clear for a pass. Lindy slips the puck around a defender, right to Henrik, but Henrik is too wide to get over to the goal. Instead, he races around the back of the net.

He's crossing right in front of us as a Dallas defenseman slams him into the plexiglass. There's a loud *crack* as the glass sways. Excited fans surge forward, pounding their fists on the glass in Henrik's face.

"Morbror!" Karro squeals in fright.

"He's okay," I soothe.

He grunts in frustration as the crowd screams. The puck gets caught between their skates as they scrap for possession. Then the other defenseman comes crashing in, slamming Henrik down to the ice.

Karro practically flings herself from my arms. "Nej!"

"Shh, he's okay, honey." I can hardly breathe as I watch him stumble to his feet and push off the wall, chasing after the puck that's now crossing the center line in the opposite direction.

Karro looks to me with anxious eyes. "Is he hurt?"

I kiss her cheek. "No, honey. See?" I point to him as he zips towards the Rays' goal. "He's still out there skating. Look how fast he is. Do you see him? Number seventeen?"

She nods, her bag of cotton candy still clutched in her fist.

There's a scramble in front of our net, and Jake whacks the puck free, sending it careening down the ice, three lengths ahead of Langley. He's skating as fast as he can, but the Dallas defenseman gets there first, claiming possession and pulling the puck back into his defensive zone. Langley flies around the back of the net, looking for his forward line to reset for a pass.

"He's not open," Colin shouts, all but strangling me as he jumps up and down, seeing the play unravel before it happens. The Dallas defenseman makes the pass, but the puck is intercepted by Henrik.

"Morbror has the puck again." I point him out on the ice, balancing Karro on my hip. "See him?"

She nods.

"Pass it! Pass it!" Colin shouts.

Henrik slides to a stop in a spray of ice and shoots the puck forward, right to a waiting Langley. Ryan barely has it on the tip of his blade before he whacks it into the back of the net. The cherry lights up, the horn blasts, and the crowd goes wild. It's Langley's point, but Henrik gets credit for the assist.

"Yes! Yes!" Colin jostles me as Karro covers her ears with her hands. Her cotton candy bag hits me in the face. I can hardly see Henrik down on the ice through the cloud of pink-and-blue plastic. Langley stops at the wall right in front of us. The rest of the team skates in, congratulating him.

"Morbror!" Karro shouts.

Through the din, Henrik hears her cry. His gaze locks on our section, focusing like a laser as he searches for her in the crowd. The second he spots us four rows up, I know something's wrong. His eyes burn like molten lava as he glares, first at me, then Colin.

Oh shit.

I know Colin notices, too, because he drops his arm from my shoulder and leans away. "Uhh . . . he knows I'm married, right? And straight? Like, as a fucking arrow?"

Heart in my throat, I brush Karro's cotton candy bag away from my face. "It's possible your sexual orientation has never come up."

Colin groans. "You really are a hopeless case, you know that?"

"Well, how often does that come up about a person you literally *never* discuss?"

"Okay, rude. I talk about you with Tracy all the time. By the way, she agrees that you're hopeless—"

"Not fucking helping!"

Karro keeps waving, trying to get Henrik's attention. But he only has eyes for me. And the feelings behind the look he's giving me are clear as fucking day: hurt and betrayal.

Oh, this is so bad.

"I thought you said he wanted to take things slow?" Colin says as Henrik skates off, called away by the whistle to return to the bench.

"He did." God, my mouth is suddenly as dry as a desert. I set Karro back down, hiding the rest of the cotton candy in the backpack. When I right myself, Colin is glaring at me. "What?"

"Seriously?"

I groan. "Col, if you've got something to say—"

"Did that look like the face of a man who wants to take things fucking slow?" He points down at the ice.

"I—"

"Christ, Teddy! If he catches me touching you again, he's gonna abracadabra that fucking glass, charge up here, and kick my ass!"

"Well, what am I supposed to do?"

"Fix it!"

"How?"

"Seriously?" He grabs at my lanyard, pulls up my arena pass, and flashes it in my face. "You work for the team. This period is almost over. Go down there and set him straight."

I gasp, jerking my lanyard out of his hand. "I can't just go down there. I can't distract him like that—"

"You've already distracted him. He's not gonna be able to think about anything else until you fix this. Dragging it out, waiting till the end of the game, it's just cruel, Ted. Go to your man. Let him sweep you off your feet."

"But Karro—"

"I've got the kid. She'll be fine without you for five minutes. We'll split a beer and some jalapeño nachos."

"I—"

"*Go*, Teddy."

I let out a breath, heart racing in my chest. "Colin . . ."

His eyes widen. "Ohhhh. You're scared?"

"Duh!"

"Well, that's fine. Go do it anyway."

Tears sting my eyes as I shake my head. "If he rejects me . . ."

"He won't."

"How can you be sure?"

Laughing, he grabs me by the shoulders and turns me around, giving me a shove towards the aisle. "I can't. So why don't you just go see for yourself?"

45

TEDDY

This is crazy. This is such a bad idea. Why did I let Colin talk me into this? I should go back upstairs, get Karro in the car, and drive until we hit Canada.

Okay, no, that's good. Get all the bad ideas out now, Teddy.

I jog down the concourse, weaving through the throngs of fans in line for the bathroom or concessions.

"Hey, Teddy," says Marjorie with a wave, guarding the tunnel access door.

I find her a smile. "Hey, Miss Marj."

"You on duty tonight too?" She's been a volunteer at the arena since long before I was an intern. She's this eighty-year-old white lady who weighs, like, ninety pounds. And she always has candy.

"Not tonight," I say, flashing her my access badge. "Just forgot something earlier."

She reaches a bony hand into her pocket. "Want some candy, honey?"

I pause. "Actually, you got any mints?"

She hands me a peppermint in a twisty plastic wrapper.

"Thanks. You're an angel." I give her a wave as I pop the mint in my mouth.

The break between first and second period is only seventeen minutes long. And the buzzer went off as I made my way over to Marjorie. The clock is already ticking. I hurry down the stairs, passing the last set of security guards with a wave of my access pass before I'm in the tunnels.

What am I even doing? Am I just gonna charge into the dressing room, lock eyes with Henrik, and shout, "Colin is straight!"

I round the corner and nearly crash right into Cody, one of the EMs. "Whoa," he says with a laugh, juggling a bundle of hockey sticks. "Close call. You on tonight?"

"Nope." I dart around him. "You seen Henrik anywhere?"

"Who?"

"Karlsson. Where is he?"

"Uhh . . . beats me." He shrugs, rattling the jumble of sticks. Someone calls his name down the hall, and he takes off. "Later, Ted!"

This is a sign, right? Cody doesn't know where he is, so I should just give up now. Probably head back upstairs. This was a bad idea anyway—

"Teddy!"

I flinch, turning around. Brady is in the hall, waving me down. "Hey, what's up?"

"I thought you weren't on shift tonight." He looks me up and down. "What are you wearing?"

"Umm . . ."

"Whatever. Look, if you're working, go hunt down some ice packs. Someone moved all our shit around. When I find out who, there's gonna be hell to pay."

"What do you mean?"

"I mean, they literally came in and moved a whole goddamn freezer. And apparently no one on my staff fucking noticed until now! It's gone, replaced with a fridge full of electrolyte water."

"Well, I'm not actually on shift—"

"Whatever. Just find me that freezer and get some ice packs to the guys waiting in the PT suite. Help me out with this, and I'll give you all the cash in my pocket, you greedy fuck."

I laugh, crossing my arms. "Why do I get the feeling there's no cash in your pocket?"

"Teddy, *go!*"

"On it." Spinning on my heel, I'm emboldened with my new mission: Find Freezer.

Actually, this is helping. I'm not even thinking about the devastation that could come when I go to Henrik and throw myself at him. Again.

This has to be some kind of record, right? It's only been four days since the man of my dreams confessed to feeling not nothing for me. Since he said he's willing to try feeling something. And then I had to go and invite Colin fucking Holliday to a game. Now the something Henrik is feeling is pain and regret, thinking Colin is here as some kind of date.

My god, as if. Colin Holliday? The man eats yogurt with a fork. He wears boot-cut jeans. He thinks Lunchables are an acceptable form of charcuterie. I quite literally would never.

I duck into the first room I find with an unlocked door. There's nothing remotely freezer-shaped in here. Just some janitorial equipment and dusty boxes of who-knows-what. I slip back into the hall and try the next room. This one is packed full of folding chairs.

"If I were a freezer, where would I hide?" I say to myself, hurrying back out to the hall.

Down around the corner, there's a food prep room. It's kind of out of the way, and too small for the needs of the team. As an intern, I'd go in there sometimes and use the microwave. Worth a shot, right? Maybe some asshole decided the freezer was lonely and needed to be reunited with a proper kitchen.

I break into a jog, taking a left, then a right, sliding to a stop in front of the door labeled, "101-A." Reaching out, I jiggle the handle. It opens. I shove the door with my shoulder, step inside, and turn on the lights. They hum to life in that way fluorescents do.

"Aha!"

Sitting under a flickering light panel, right next to an industrial fridge, is a small deep freeze. There's even a peel-and-stick Rays logo stuck to the front. I flip open the lid. Stacked inside are a ton of gel ice packs in a range of sizes. There's no way I can just drag this whole freezer down the hall. It's not on wheels. Someone's gonna need to get a dolly.

Looking around, I hurry over to the sink and open the lower cabinet.

"Yes!"

I snatch up the roll of garbage bags and tear one loose. Opening it with a furious shake, I grab several different sizes of ice pack and shove them in the bag. The plastic strains with the weight of the packs as I sling the whole thing over my shoulder like some kind of sporty Santa Claus. Dashing from the room, I cut the light and run down the hall towards the PT suite.

"'Scuse me," I call out, ducking around the guys milling in the hallway.

Around the corner, the EMs are furiously sharpening skate blades, getting ready for second period. The high-pitched squeal of the sharpener pierces the senses, leaving the faint smell of burning metal in the air.

"Coming through!" I shout. "Hey, open that door!" Someone pulls the PT door open, and I stride in. "I have ice packs!"

There's a flurry as the other PTs rush forward, digging into the bag as I set it down on the first empty massage table.

"Sweet!"

"Where the hell did you find them?"

"You're our hero, Ted."

"Karlsson, you want some ice for your knee too?"

I freeze, heart in my throat. Slowly turning, I see Henrik sitting on the farthest massage table. He's got the top half of his kit off. His shoulders look pink, like someone was just massaging him, loosening his tight muscles. I knew he took a hard hit out there. First into the boards, then down to the ice. I told Karro he was fine in the moment, but I saw the way it zapped his speed.

"I got it," I say, taking the ice pack from Jeremy's hands.

Henrik looks as tense as a cornered lion as I walk up to him, my humble offering of ice in hand. He says nothing as I step up to the table and drape the ice pack over his shoulder. I grab a wrap and gently secure the pack in place. He lets me, still saying nothing.

I can't bear this fucking silence. I'm crawling out of my skin. Leaning in, I whisper, "Henrik, Colin is just a friend."

He stiffens, leaning away.

"We're not—we've *never*." I place a hand on his unwrapped shoulder. "He's straight. Plus, I'm totally out of his league," I add with a weak smile.

He looks up at me with those sad eyes, the denim blue of his irises looking so faded and tired.

On instinct, I cup his bearded cheek. "Please don't look at me like that. It's not fair, okay? I didn't do anything wrong. Meet Colin after the game, and he'll tell you himself. He barely tolerates me. He calls me 'hopeless.'"

Lifting a hand, he covers mine on his cheek. "I don't know how to do this," he admits, his voice low.

"Do what?"

"Want you."

My gaze darts to his beautiful, sad eyes. "Henrik—"

I gasp as he wraps his arm around me, slipping his hand up under my leather jacket. His fingers splay possessively across my back. Then he reels me in until I'm practically straddling his leg. He's still in his skates and hockey pants. His other hand drops to grip the front of my T-shirt. He pulls me closer. I can smell his faint athletic musk, practically taste the salt of his perspiration. Our noses brush as he breathes me in. "Du är *min* man," he growls.

Then he's kissing me.

Oh my god, Henrik Karlsson is kissing me. I can't even process it. His hands are on me, I'm practically straddling his thigh, and he's kissing me. And what did he say? Fuck, why did I never learn Swedish? Two semesters of Latin utterly wasted.

His lips press to mine, his beard prickling my chin. The second I stop thinking and actually start kissing him back, it's like a volcano erupts in my chest. I'm molten with need, fingers gripping his face, as I press back into his kiss, lips parted, eager for more.

Both his hands go around me, splayed on my back as he pulls me in. My cock is pressed against his padded hockey pants. Thank god. Maybe he won't feel how hard I am. When you've been wandering in the desert for as long as I have, that first drop of water was always bound to send the senses haywire.

I try to memorize this moment—the feel of his iron hands at my back, the bitter taste of salt in his kiss, the warmth of his breath panting with mine. I groan against his mouth, my fingers brushing down the column of his sweaty neck. With a tease of my tongue, his lips part for me, and then we both detonate. I gasp again as he pulls me in tighter, arms banded across my upper and lower back. I'm on my toes, straddling his thigh. My hands brush into his sweaty hair, and I'm flying. He tastes so good, like power, and strength, and raw fucking passion.

"What are we doing?" he groans against my lips.

"Flying too close to the sun." I kiss him again, never wanting to stop.

"Alright, break it up you two!"

"Yeah, jeez. Keep it in the bedroom."

I gasp as Henrik suddenly pushes me back. I'm left reeling as he locks his elbows, placing me firmly away from him. Oh fuck, what did we just do? I glance over my shoulder to see everyone in the PT suite staring at us. Yeah, I definitely just climbed onto my half-naked husband's lap and rode his thigh while he choked me with his tongue. In front of a live audience.

That just happened.

That was our first kiss.

Henrik drops his hands away from me, and I'm left swaying on the spot. Thank god I'm turned away from the room so no one can see my raging hard-on. Stage fright already has it deflating fast. Some people are into public displays, but that's never been me. I was just so desperate for Henrik to see me, hear me, that I didn't care that we weren't alone.

Henrik.

He sits on the edge of the table, ice pack wrapped around one shoulder, hair a mess from my hands. His lips are parted, still wet from my claiming kiss. And he's looking at me like I'm the answer to every question he's never thought to ask.

I have to remember this moment. I want it tattooed on my brain. The way he's looking at me now? He's not seeing Teddy the intern, who once walked into traffic, or Teddy the PT, who wraps ice packs on shoulders. He doesn't even see Teddy the caretaker, who over-bakes cookies and braids Karro's hair. For the first time in six long years, the man I've loved and longed for sees *me*.

And I think he likes what he sees.

This is all too much for my brain to handle. I feel like Icarus again, tumbling through the air, feathers flying. "Good job out there," I say, offering him my hand like a total asshole.

Confused, Henrik shakes it, his hand calloused and warm as it wraps around mine.

I pull away, stepping back. "So, anyhoo . . . I guess I'll just see you at home. Glad we could get that cleared up. Okay, bye."

He stands. "Teddy . . ."

I turn around, heart in my throat. "Yeah?"

He towers over me in his skates, and it's such a fucking turn-on. In reality, the skates only add, like, an inch or two. But I'm still fighting the desperate urge to blurt out the words, "Hold me."

Instead, he only holds my gaze, uncaring that the room is full of his teammates. "I asked for two ice packs."

I grin, heart flipping. "Get the intern to help you. I'm off the clock."

Feeling like that's a much cooler line to use as my exit, I flee the room to the sounds of the laughter and whooping cheers of our friends.

46

TEDDY

"That's a pretty dress." Karolina traces her finger over the lines of a purple ballgown in her favorite princess book.

"It *is* a pretty dress. I like this white one too." I point to the Black girl on the page. She's wearing a strappy gown with glitter on the bodice.

"Som en brud," Karro murmurs, her eyes heavy with fatigue. I always know she's exhausted when she stops translating her Swedish.

I'm sitting on the edge of her bed, reading to her by the glow of her twinkle lights. We got home from Henrik's game about forty minutes ago, having left before it was over. Karro was getting pretty cranky. When she dropped a piece of popcorn to the ground and burst into tears, I knew it was time to go.

Her Karlsson jersey is slung over the top of her Barbie playhouse. She wouldn't let me take the streamers out of her hair. But I got most of the glitter off her cheeks. And we brushed her teeth. If this girl gets cavities, it won't be my fault.

Now she's snug as a bug, surrounded by her stuffed animals.

"Hey." I brush a hand over her hair. "What does 'Door minman' mean?"

She blinks her eyes open, fighting sleep. "Vad?"

"What does 'Door minman' mean?" I repeat, trying to say it the way Henrik did. I'm probably getting it wrong. When I plugged it into Google Translate earlier, it asked me if it was Dutch.

She mumbles something in Swedish, which is completely counterproductive. But then why am I asking the five-year-old?

"You know what? Never mind." Closing the book, I slip off the side of her bed. I glance down at her and smile. She's toast. Lips parted, she breathes in and out, totally lost in dreamland. I put her book back on the shelf, click off her twinkle lights, and tiptoe out, leaving her door cracked.

I stand in the corner of the living room and look around at the mess of the day. Toys everywhere, coloring books, the apple peels from Karro's snack. I click on a few lamps and dim the overhead lights.

The apartment feels too quiet after the roar of the arena crowd. And I feel like I have a hive of bees in my chest. I check the time on my phone. Henrik should be coming home soon. Any minute, really. And then what?

He wants to practice wanting me, whatever the fuck that means. And tonight, he kissed me. Did he even like it? I think he did, but maybe I'm just projecting how much *I* liked it. He said he's never felt sexual attraction before. When he's gone through the motions in the past, he said he felt nothing.

My god, nothing?

I can't even imagine—

Wait. What if he was kissing me and he was, like, running back game tape in his head? What if he was counting by fives or making a grocery list? What if he felt *nothing*? I don't think I can let him tell me. We'll have to develop some kind of hand signal instead, and I'll just disappear into the sunset.

Squashing down my scary thoughts, I try to make myself busy by cleaning up Karro's art supplies. We've been working on her fine motor skills in therapy, so I got her a gem art set. It comes with all these premade designs, like rainbows and five-layer cakes. She uses a stylus to pick up the gems and place them in the right color order to make a picture. She's obsessed.

And yes, we used some of the gems to make fairy wings on our faces while I introduced her to the magic that is *Spirited Away*.

I shuffle all the papers together, put them in her art box, and close the lid on the gem kit. I'm still on my knees, reorganizing her colored pencils, when I finally hear the click of a key in the lock.

Oh god.

I refuse to do anything but act cool, even if inside I'm aching to be at the door when it opens, shouting, "What does this mean?!" Instead, I start separating the coloring sheets, setting aside the ones she's already finished.

The door opens, and Henrik is there, looking like a god in a tan linen suit, white shirt, and no tie. His eyes lock on me, and my heart starts to thrum. "Hey," I say on a breath.

"Hej," he replies, hanging his keys on the hook by the door.

"Did y'all win?"

"No."

Fuck. I was really hoping they'd pull out a win so his mood would be elevated. A good thing with Henrik is that he's not the type to wallow. Wins happen, and so do losses. Even as an intern, I admired his ability to just focus on the next game.

"I looked for you after the game."

I wince. "Yeah, sorry. We left early. Karro was turning into a pumpkin, and Colin had an early morning. The Jags play tomorrow."

He glances down the hallway towards her room. "Is she well?"

"Oh, she's fine. Just too much sugar. I washed most of the stickiness off her hands and put her to bed. And I'm throwing away the rest of the cotton candy . . . unless you want it?"

"No."

Okay, this is easy. I can do this all night. But talking about Karro is always easy. It's talking about *us* that has me feeling like I want to take a running leap through the glass wall. I keep shuffling the papers, separating the clean coloring sheets from the scribbled-on ones. Penguin in a scarf. Owl reading a book. Kitten on a rainbow.

Maybe Henrik doesn't want to talk about us. Maybe the kiss was barely tolerable, and if it's all the same to me, he'd like to forget it ever happened. Maybe he's thought about it, and practicing wanting me just doesn't fit in his busy schedule right now.

Sensing my mood, he sighs. "Teddy . . ."

I stare down at a photo of a smiling chicken holding a balloon. Its stupid, beady eyes look up at me as it waves with one wing. Oh my god, I feel so called out. Clutching the papers to my chest, I look up at him. "What does 'Door minman' mean?"

"What?" He steps around the end of the couch, shrugging out of his suit jacket and tossing it on the chair.

I'm instantly distracted, trying to ignore how cut his shoulders look in that fitted shirt. "The thing you said in Swedish before you—I mean, before we . . ." I groan, pinching the bridge of my nose. "Just what did you say?"

"Ah." His mouth quirks with a smile as he sinks down onto the end of the couch. "Is that what has you acting so strange? I assumed you were dissecting every aspect of my kissing technique, not my Swedish mumblings."

Oh god, he said it first. I mean, yeah, I threw the door wide open. But he said the word "kiss." Which means we are *so* doing this now. "What does it mean?"

Leaning back against the cushions, he holds out his hand. "Come here, and I'll tell you."

Did Henrik Karlsson just spread his knees and say, "Come here"? There are a lot of ways I can play this. I could rise to my feet and saunter over like Billy the Kid. Or I could pounce like the needy puppy I am, curl up in his lap, and beg him to hold me.

My body chooses secret option three. Setting the stack of clean coloring papers aside, including the judgy chicken, I crawl around the end of the coffee table and settle myself between his spread legs. Hands on his thighs, I push up, bringing my face almost even with his.

He reaches out, his fingertips ghosting over my lips. I can't breathe, can't break this moment. He sits forward, his warm gaze locked on me, both hands cupping my face. Desperate for more touch, I lift my hands from his thighs, wrapping them around his wrists.

The corner of his mouth lifts with a tired smile. "Du är min man. That's what I said."

I nod, lost in the blue of his eyes. I can see just how tired he is. Like Karro, he's past the point of endurance. He always leaves everything on the ice. Night after night, he gives it his all. He doesn't know any other way. He's always giving everyone his all. I won't push him for more tonight, but he has to give me this. "What does it mean?"

"You tell me."

I lean away, brows furrowed. "How am I supposed to—"

"Listen." He presses his fingers to my lips. "Hear the words, mitt hjärta. Are you listening?"

"Okay," I say against his fingertips.

He lowers his hand. "Du är," he says, rolling the *r* ever so slightly.

"You are," I translate.

He nods. "Du är *min*." Like in the locker room, he puts the emphasis on this word. As he says it, he brushes his fingertips down the column of my neck.

I close my eyes, leaning against his leg. "Mine," I whisper. Opening my eyes, I look up at him. "'Du är min' means 'You are mine.'"

"Almost. I said, 'Du är min man,' so the meaning changes a little."

Heart in my throat, I drop my hands back to his thighs. "I'm your man?"

"Not quite."

"Then what does 'man' mean?"

He cups my cheek again, his thumb brushing over my freckles. "To say it is to break a rule. Saying it in Swedish is already a cheat." He drops his hand away from me, leaning back. "And I vowed I'd not break your rules."

I follow him, pressing myself between his legs. "We're already breaking all the rules. You sleep in my bed. Tonight, you kissed me. Now, look me in the eyes, and tell me who I am."

He holds my gaze. "If you want the rule broken, *you* break it."

Oh, this is so fucking happening. I can ponder what a mistake it is later. Climbing into his lap, I straddle him, wrapping my arms around his neck. His intoxicating, shower-fresh scent hits my senses, setting me on fire. His hands brace my hips, and my fingers weave into the damp hair at his nape as I tip his head back. "You are my husband. Henrik, you're *mine*."

We crash together in a fierce kiss. It's hot and needy, our hands seeking. In his starched dress shirt, he reaches the limit of his flexibility, trying to wrap an arm around my shoulders. But I'm just in a T-shirt and sweatpants. I wrap myself around him, grinding on his lap. "Tell me what you feel," I pant against his lips. "Please, *god*, tell me you feel something more than nothing—"

He pulls away, breathless, his blue eyes searching my face. Slowly, he nods. "I feel." Taking my hand, he presses it to his chest.

I lean in, fingers brushing over his dress shirt as I feel the erratic pulsing of his heart under my palm. "Do you like it? I mean, do you like kissing me? Fuck—don't answer unless the answer is yes—"

He silences me with another kiss, his beard tickling my mouth as our faces tilt, our bodies seeking more closeness. I'm about to grind my dick against him again, but then I'm groaning, all but stumbling out of his lap. "Okay—*fuck*—new rules." I back away, shoulders heaving, adjusting my dick in these formfitting briefs. "Henrik, we need new rules."

He sits forward, shirt untucked, hair a mess. With a practiced flick of his wrists, he undoes the buttons at his cuffs. Which is so fucking hot, I could probably come without even touching myself.

Focus.

No more pouncing. No more kissing. New rules, Teddy. This man is your fucking kryptonite.

"Teddy—"

"I need a minute," I bark, raising a hand to warn him back. I swear to god, if he gets off that couch, I'm gonna be dropping to my knees, and then it's all over. "Just . . . *stay*."

He sits back, watching me pace in front of the TV.

So, here's the deal. Intern Teddy would have done literally anything for this man. Because Intern Teddy was weak, hopeless, and desperate for love. But I'm Doctor Teddy now. There *will* be ramifications if and when this falls apart. And I have a career to think about. I have a custody agreement with the little girl asleep in the next room. And my family's voices are all screaming like a klaxon alarm in my head: *Protect yourself*.

I mean, my god, we don't even have a signed prenup agreement. Or a postnup. There are no nups! No protections in place. For me, for Karro. Worse, there are no protections for Henrik, and he has the most to lose. The man is a multimillionaire. He owns real estate in two countries. And don't ask me how I know, but Florida is a no-fault state. If I divorced him now, I could walk away with half his earnings. And alimony. And if I took full custody of Karro, we could throw in a little five-figure monthly child support.

Not that I would *ever* do any of those things. But we've never even talked about it. And now he wants to practice wanting me? He wants us both to be more deeply, emotionally entangled? What, so this can blow up even more spectacularly in our faces?

"What new rules do you require?" he asks, watching me pace.

I stop, spinning to face him. "Oh, don't even pretend these rules are only for me. They're for you too. Because apparently, we can no longer be trusted to be alone in the same room. I mean, fuck! If you tell me kissing is finally on the table, I'm never gonna stop. And *you* said you wanted this to go slow," I add, pointing a finger at him.

God, I'm worse than the judgy chicken!

"I do," he assures me. "Teddy, I don't want to hurt you. I don't want to ever say or do the wrong thing."

"Well, that's not possible for anyone. We're both gonna say and do the wrong thing eventually. More than once. That's just what it means to be human." I spin in my socks, facing him again. "But there's shit we definitely have to discuss, before this can go any further."

"Like what?"

I cross my arms, staring him down. "Like, a postnup."

"What?"

"A postnuptial agreement. It's a legal contract that outlines how our assets will be handled in the event of our inevitable divorce. Because that's where this is still going, right? This was all only meant to be temporary, right?"

He leans away, his expression impossible to read. "I said I wouldn't trap you with me, and I meant it."

Awesome. Ripping that arrow from my fucking spleen, I go on. "Right, well you have to call Laura. Tomorrow. I want a draft of a postnup on our kitchen island by end of day. We walk out of this marriage only with the assets we each brought into it. I want nothing from you."

He sighs. "Teddy—"

"The only sticking point will be custody of Karro. Because I'll be fucked if you think I'm walking away from that little girl," I add, pointing a finger at him again. "She's mine too, Henrik. What's the Swedish for that? I'm gonna tattoo it on my fucking chest."

A smile flits across his lips. "Karolina är mitt barn."

"Right. Mitt barn, Henrik. You asked for my help, and now you've fucking got it. For life. Because that little girl deserves to have people in her life that love her and are gonna fight for her. And I will *fight* you, Henrik. I will fight you for her—"

He stands. The move is so sudden and deliberate that it stops my rant in its tracks. Sweeping around the coffee table, he descends on me, pulling me to him with both hands. But he doesn't kiss me. Instead, he just wraps me in his arms, hugging me with his whole body.

I suck in a breath, my hands going up to brace against his back. We stand like that for a moment, clinging to each other.

"Thank you," he murmurs, pressing a chaste kiss to my cheek. "Thank you, Teddy."

I blink back tears as he pulls away. He puts a little space between us, his hands brushing down my arms, until he lets me go. "What else do you need from me? What other rules?"

My mind is spinning. What other rules do I need in place before I can let Henrik Karlsson practice wanting me? "I'm on PrEP," I blurt out. "Are you?"

"What's prep?"

So that's a no then.

"PrEP is pre-exposure prophylaxis," I explain. "It reduces the risk of contracting HIV. And before you and I have any sex, I'll want to get a clean STI scan as well . . . even if I haven't had sex in, like, six months. Better safe than sorry."

"I haven't had sex in over six years. When I did, I only ever used a condom."

As I hear him say it out loud, the reality of our situation hits me like a ton of bricks. Backing away from him, I sink down onto the opposite couch. "Well . . . so then maybe you can skip the STI screening."

"And the other thing?"

"I mean, you don't have to be on PrEP. That's totally your call. Maybe talk to a doctor? I've never really considered going off it because I've never settled down with just one person. Condoms alone are definitely more convenient, but it was never worth the risk for me."

He considers for a moment. "This prep is for having sex with many people?"

I shrug. "I mean, that's a bit derivative, but sure. That's one good use for PrEP."

He glares at me, his arms crossed. "I'll not share you, Teddy. You are my husband, or you're nothing."

Wow. How often have I fantasized about Henrik Karlsson saying those words to me? Swallowing my nerves, I offer a weak smile. "So, obviously that's one of your conditions we need to renegotiate."

"What?"

"When we married, you said I'd be free. You said you'd never hold me back. You said I can do whatever I want with whomever I want. It just can't happen in this house. Would you like to renegotiate those terms?"

He stalks over to me and drops to his knees. Mirroring my position from moments before, he places his hands on my thighs, his dark blue eyes fierce in their intensity. "Look at me, mitt hjärta."

I look at him, heart in my throat.

"Jag vill ha dig. Do you know what that means?"

I shake my head.

His hands smooth up my thighs in a natural gesture of possession. "It means, 'I want you.' Teddy, I want *only* you."

I melt for him, folding forward until our foreheads touch. "Henrik . . ."

"But I cannot want what can't be mine." Holding up my hand, he lets the gold of my ring glint in the lamplight. "So long as you wear this, say only I will know your touch." He takes that hand and presses it to his cheek, holding it there. "I may not know much about intimacy, but I know I need this from you."

"Only you," I assure him. "Henrik, I only want you."

He groans, wrapping his arms around me. The familiar weight of him pressing me back feels so goddamn good. I want to wrap my legs around him and stay like this forever. He nuzzles gently against my neck as he breathes me in, and I crow with happiness.

Digging my fingers into his hair, I pull his head back, desperate to see his eyes. "Say you're mine too. Maybe with another, I could have shared. But not you, Henrik. Never you. You're mine, or you're nothing."

He leans away, touching my face with searching fingers. The tips brush featherlight over my brow, down the bridge of my nose, along my jaw. It's like he's committing me to memory. It feels primal. Sacred. Finally, his hand drops away. "Whatever else I am, I'm yours."

"Min man," I whisper.

He nods.

"So . . . we should do away with that rule too? In English and Swedish?"

"I think it would be best."

"And the kissing rule?"

He considers. "I meant what I said before. I want to take my time with you. Nothing needs to be rushed. Can it be enough? Can my vow to you be enough? A vow to try?"

Here we come to it. What if he tries and he doesn't like it? What if all I ever get are a few *really* good kisses? Can it be enough for me? Can I accept him for who he is and love him in whatever capacity he'll allow?

I take a deep breath and let it out. "I have one more new rule."

He tenses. "Name it."

I place a hand on his shoulder, mooring us together with a more platonic, familiar kind of touch. "No sex in the bed."

His brow furrows as I'm sure he's second-guessing his own translation. "What?"

"I mean it, Henrik." I push him until he's rocked back on his ankles and I'm fully sitting up. "The bed we share is not for sex. That has to stay sacred. Because, regardless of whatever else happens, I have to stay here. For Karro, for the custody review. And the bed is where we sleep. It's where *you* sleep," I add more gently. "I won't rob you of your safe space. So . . . no wanting me in the bed. Agreed?"

He considers for a moment. "Agreed. Thank you, Teddy."

"But the others go," I repeat. "The no-kissing one, and the no sleeping in my bed, and the no saying husbands in English and Swedish." I tick them off on my fingers. "But I still want to pay rent."

He groans.

"I'm serious, Hen. I have to have some small feeling of autonomy here. Either accept my money, or I'll start getting *real* creative with the shit I buy for the apartment. Ever heard of Dadaism?"

Using my knees, he pushes up from the floor and rises to his feet. Bending over, he brushes a kiss to the top of my head. "Keep your money, mitt hjärta. I am not afraid of your ire. Besides, a print of *jeune homme triste dans un train* would look wonderful next to Karolina's retrospective on rainbow unicorns." He leaves me there, clicking off one of the lamps as he walks away.

Did that gorgeous professional hockey player just weave English, French, and Swedish into a clever comeback about Dadaism?

Well, if I wasn't already in love with my not-so-fake husband, I am now.

Rising from the couch, I click off the other lamp and follow him to bed.

47

HENRIK

"**S**top fidgeting," I mutter.

"I'm not fidgeting." Next to me, Teddy tugs at the collar of his sweater again. My lips purse, and he curses under his breath. "Fucking stop, alright? Just let me fidget."

Cheryl, our representative from the child welfare office, finishes her phone call, turning back to face us. She's a middle-aged white lady with greying hair cut in a blunt bob. "So sorry about that. Never a dull moment, as they say."

"Oh, that's totally fine," says Teddy.

She checks her notes on her tablet. "So, you were walking me through her daily routine."

"Yes." He drops my hand and sweeps forward, gesturing all around the living room as he shows her Karolina's art wall and craft station. He's talking fast, clearly nervous. "And this has all been great for retaining her fine motor skills. Once her arm cast comes off in a couple weeks, we'll be starting on the manipulatives, like molder's clay."

Cheryl nods, taking notes.

Teddy takes her on the grand tour, leading her down to Karolina's room and showing her the modifications we made to ease her care, like the adjustable bed and the child monitors. "And she sleeps a solid six hours every night," he goes on. "Sometimes it's closer to eight. But she really does come by it naturally. Henrik is a light sleeper too. He only needs, like, four hours, and he's good to go play professional hockey. So, I think we're doing pretty good if we balance out at an even seven—"

I take his hand, giving it a reassuring squeeze. "Breathe."

He huffs out a breath, and Cheryl gives him a consoling look. "You're doing great."

He groans, cheeks blooming pink with embarrassment.

"I know this can all feel stressful," she goes on. "My job here is just to listen, observe, and document. I'm not making any judgments. And I'm not here with any agenda, other than assuring the welfare of a child." She holds up her tablet. "Do you mind if I take some photos?"

"Of course not," I reply. "We'll wait for you in the kitchen." Tugging on Teddy's hand, I pull him from the bedroom, leaving Cheryl alone to take her photos.

He's been on edge for the last three days, feverishly cleaning and reorganizing the house in preparation for this visit. I only just got back this morning from another away game. The apartment looks unrecognizable compared with the sterile, white-walled unit of a month ago. The walls of glass still let in great light and views, but now there is color and life everywhere.

Like an anxious magpie, Teddy has turned this place into a cozy nest. We now have books (and the shelves to hold them). Karolina has a full craft center in the corner, complete with a little desk and chair. Electric candles glow on the coffee table next to a decorative wooden tray he's filled with fall pumpkins and gourds.

And the whole house smells like cinnamon, because Teddy made kanelbullar. They're a bit misshapen and a little burnt on the bottom. But he made them, which makes them perfect. He even sprinkled them with pärlsocker.

Dropping my hand, he paces into the kitchen, not stopping until he reaches the far wall of glass. Gasping, he turns. "Oh—I forgot to mention her bath routine—"

I grab his arm as he tries to dart past. "Stay."

He groans, jerking his arm free. "How are you so calm about this?"

"Because we have nothing to fear. We take excellent care of Karolina. Either Cheryl will see that, or she won't."

"Well, we can help her along. You know, *tell* her all the ways we care for Karro and not just leave it to her imagination."

I reach out a hand and press it over his chest. I just want to see if his heart beats as fast as his racing thoughts.

He slaps my hand down. "What are you doing?"

"Touching you," I reply with a smirk.

"Don't you dare distract me right now, Henrik. This is too important."

He's right. We need to focus. Besides, Hanna will be back with Karro at any moment. We asked her to take Karro down the street for ice cream while we gave Cheryl some time to ask her questions and take photos. We already completed all the required questionnaires.

"Fine," I say. "I won't distract you while she's here."

He huffs, craning his neck to see if she's coming around the corner. "Good."

I step in behind him, smoothing my hands up his sides until he stiffens. I like seeing how he reacts to different kinds of touch. His body just seems to know when what I want is the comfort that comes with sleep or the casual touches that come with sharing a life.

But in a moment like this, when I tease? When I caress? His body comes alive like nothing else. It's intoxicating. I press in behind him, daring to whisper in his ear, "But the moment she's gone, I'm going to distract you some more."

Within thirty minutes, we say goodbye to Cheryl at the door. She took all her photos and asked all her questions, including a few directly to Karro. Cheryl warned us that we wouldn't hear anything for a few weeks. For me, that's a relief, and I'll push the case from my mind. No action needed. For Teddy, it's something to fixate on and worry over every hour of every day until she contacts us again.

We all have our own coping strategies.

Almost as soon as Cheryl leaves, Teddy lets out a gasping breath.

"Fuck, why did I think it would be a good idea to wear a sweater?" He tugs it off over his head as he dashes away.

Hanna just laughs, following him as far as the kitchen, while I finish getting Karro set up on the couch with her coloring books. Hanna is staying through the evening because Teddy and I are being forced by Poppy to continue with Operation Mighty Oak. Tonight is date two, wherein I will join Teddy at dinner with all the other queer players on my team.

I'm dreading it. I have such limited free time now that we're in season. Any moment not spent on the ice or traveling for a game, I want to be home. I want to be with Karolina and Teddy. Sharing him with my teammates tonight feels like a chore. Doubly so, because we all know we're being photographed.

But, as Poppy said, this matters. We're sending a signal that will hopefully reach far beyond the hockey world. We're telling people it's okay to live, and love, and build families in different ways. The love Jake shares with Caleb and Ilmari is no less sacred than the love Langley shares with Tess.

And we all have children to protect and raise. Tonight is as much for Karro's future as it is for mine and Teddy's present.

That's a lot of pressure to place on one plate of sushi.

"So, where are you all going tonight?" says Hanna, taking a bite of one of Teddy's cinnamon rolls.

"I'm not sure," I reply. "Jake Price picked it. I believe it's a Japanese restaurant."

"Yum!"

Offering her a weak smile, I step around the island. "Will you excuse me a moment?"

I duck into the bedroom and find it empty. My side of the bed is pristine, with nothing on the side table except a phone charging cord and a glass of water. Teddy's side table overflows with books and electronics in various states of charge, vitamin bottles, reading glasses, his retainer case.

He tried to hide his retainer from me at first, only putting it in when he thought I was already asleep. It was charming the first time he woke in a daze, forgot it was in, and spoke to me with slurred speech. He only stopped fretting about it when I let him catch me making a mess with my water flosser.

The bathroom door is wide open. Our unspoken rule is that an open door means the other can enter. I step through into the bathroom and immediately see Teddy back in the closet, one foot in the air, tugging on a pair of rust-colored chinos. He's shirtless, his sweater and T-shirt left in a pile on the floor.

"Hej."

He jolts upright, tugging the chinos up around his hips. "Do you think she hated us?"

"What?" It takes me a moment to even think of Cheryl. "No. You heard her; she forms no opinion of us. The facts will speak for themselves."

He snorts, buttoning his pants and zipping the fly. "Yeah, right. And you believed her? Everyone forms opinions about everyone."

I step into the closet, watching the way the muscles of his torso twist and flex as he moves. There's hardly an ounce of fat on him. He's long and lean, yet more angles to add to his composition. He turns around, showing me the muscles of his back, as he searches in the drawer for a fresh T-shirt.

Not for the first time, I wish I didn't leave all my photography equipment in Sweden. I've never really felt inspired here. My work is so all-consuming that I don't often pause to mourn my lack of other hobbies. But in this moment, with the closet lights casting shadows across the planes of his back and shoulders, my fingers itch to capture him.

Luckily, there are other ways to capture a moment. I step in behind him, smoothing my hands up his sides.

He jolts again, standing upright. "What are you doing?"

Is it fair to say I don't know? Up to this point, we've limited our experimentation to kissing, which I've enjoyed. Quick kisses in the car. Slow, burning kisses on the couch, Teddy in my lap. We accidentally kissed in front of Karolina last night, which sent her doubling over in fits of squeals and laughter.

I've felt ready to try more, but I haven't known how to express it. Part of me wishes Teddy would just take charge, shove me against the wall, and have his way with me. Call it extreme exposure therapy. But he's been so obliging, always asking if I like it, assuring me we can take things at my speed.

But I don't know what speed I want. And I have no sexual experience with a man, so I'm not really sure what to do. I would take what I like and try to replicate it, but I've never enjoyed sexual touch before Teddy. Each time, my senses went into overdrive until they went numb. Things always felt too wet. There was too much friction. The scent of the latex condom made it feel all the more clinical, coldly procedural. Too much panting. Gripping hands, whispered moans.

I shut it all out, until I felt cut off from my body. Floating somewhere in a dark ether in my mind, I concentrated on just one sensation: coming. That's what my partner wanted from me, right? That's what I was supposed to want? To come into the condom? With my eyes closed tight, I made myself come.

Then I thanked them.

And they left.

I always stood alone in the shower after, hands shaking, wondering why I felt so broken.

With Teddy I finally feel different. I feel *more*. His body is a tether that keeps me grounded in the moment. I don't try to escape. When he's touching me or I'm touching him, I feel curious. I like watching him react. I want to learn his body better.

I glide my hands over his ribs and up his back, brushing them over his bare shoulders. His skin is so warm. And smooth. And there's not a single hair. I circle my thumbs over his upper trapezius muscles, pressing down lightly.

He pushes the drawer closed with his hips, his hands lifting to grip the shelf above. "What are you doing?" he repeats on a groan.

"Touching you. Do you want me to stop?"

"No."

I've slept next to him for a couple weeks now. Usually, he wears a T-shirt to bed. I think it's his way of keeping our touch platonic. I've spent my nights wrapped up in him, breathing him in. Before, he was my life raft. I needed him. He kept me afloat.

But I don't want to need him anymore. I want to *want* him. I want to crave him like he so clearly craves me. I want to memorize his every line and curve so I can picture them in my mind when he's away from me. I step in, my hands slipping under his arms to brush down his chest.

He sucks in a breath, his head sagging forward.

I press my front against his back, heart pounding as a sensual feeling races through me. It's like a fluttering of wings in my gut. I feel fevered, but it doesn't repulse me. His skin warms under my touch, and my skin warms to match. This is a natural reaction. It's nothing to fear.

He groans again, dropping his hands to a lower shelf, as I skate my fingertips down the rigid muscles of his abdomen, letting them glide across his hips. He has hair on his stomach. A faint dusting, hardly anything. I'm much hairier across my chest and abdomen. I've never noticed it before. Never given it a second thought. Does it bother him?

"I have hair on my chest," I whisper.

Teddy stiffens. Then he snorts a laugh. It shakes his shoulders. "I know. I've seen it."

"Does it bother you? You have very little hair by comparison."

He spins around to face me, grabbing my wrists before I can drop my hands away. He presses my hands back to the flat planes of his chest, smiling like he has a lantern glowing inside him. "I have some hair. See?" He moves my wrists, letting my palms brush over the fine, soft hairs of his chest.

"I have more hair," I remind him. "Does it bother you?"

Still smiling, he drops his hands to the bottom of my T-shirt and slips them up and under. It's my turn to stifle a gasp as he glides his hands over my stomach and up to my chest, lifting the hem of my shirt as he goes. I feel my skin heat under his smooth palms. His thumbs brush circles against my coarse chest hair. "It doesn't bother me, baby." He leans in, his lips by my ear. "It turns me the fuck on."

Before I can respond, Karro's voice comes from the bedroom, shouting in Swedish. "Teddy, Morbror, look, it came, it came!"

Teddy and I break apart as Karro comes scooting into the

bathroom on the new walker/rider toy we ordered for her last week. It's purple and shaped like a puppy and will let her zoom around the apartment using just her weight-bearing leg. Her smile is dazzling as she shoots forward three feet, almost hitting the side of the tub.

"What are you doing?" she says in English, glancing between us.

"Nothing," I say in Swedish, stepping away from him.

With a laugh, Teddy pulls two sweaters off the shelf. "Morbror was just helping me get dressed for our big date." He holds up the sweaters for me. "Blue or tan, babe?"

I can't help but smile as, from the bathroom, Karro shouts, "Blue!"

48

TEDDY

"This is so weird." I let Henrik take my hand as we make our way towards the restaurant. Trust Jake Price to find an authentic, Japanese-style izakaya in Jacksonville, Florida. It smells good, even from the outside. And it looks cute. A string of red lanterns glow above the door.

"What's weird?" says Henrik. "You don't like Japanese food?"

"Are you kidding? I love Japanese food. No, I'm saying it's weird that I'm here, going out with your teammates."

He holds me back, searching my face. "Why?"

I shrug. "I don't know."

"Teddy . . ."

"Okay!" I brush his hand away. "I guess part of me feels like I never really shed the label of 'the intern,' you know? I still feel like that lanky kid who tripped over my shoelaces and fumbled with ice packs. Going out to dinner with 'the guys' feels a little like sitting at the big kids' table. Am I crazy?"

"I think you're giving Novikov entirely too much credit."

"But he still has a seat at the table. He's *in*, Henrik. He's an assistant captain. And I'm just . . . me."

He smiles. "Chin up, mitt hjärta."

"Well, just cover for me, okay?"

He leads the way inside the loud, bar-like restaurant. "Cover you? Like pay for you meal? Of course I will."

"No, cover *for* me," I say, raising my voice to be heard over the

Japanese pop music. "Deflect attention. You know, ask questions and stuff. And keep them from teasing me."

"All will be well."

As we weave between the tables, I look around for our voyeur. Poppy said a guy would come by with a camera and maybe even ask for a sound bite. They're posting this to all the team's social media accounts tonight.

The photos from our first date night went even more viral than Henrik's press conference speech. Fans freaked out at the pictures and video of us dancing on the beach. Not gonna lie, the pics are fucking swoon-worthy. Not as great as the actual memory of slow dancing in the surf. But I definitely saved them all to my phone, showed them to a squealing Hanna and Karro, and set one as my phone screen saver.

I'm curious to see what tonight's action will bring.

"Hey, there they are," Novy shouts, waving us over.

All the guys get up to greet us. Caleb and Jake dragged Mars along. Novy sits with Morrow on the other side of the table. Henrik and I make seven. All the men shake my hand, with Morrow adding a sideways, one-armed hug.

"Fucking finally," says Jake, climbing back onto his stool. "We started the first round without you."

Henrik shoots me a sidelong glance before accepting the empty seat by Novy.

Okay, fine. We're a little late, and it's all my fault. And, yes, I know how much Henrik hates being late. Like, *hate* hates it. But he's married to me now, so he'll have to just deal with it.

I take the only remaining seat at the end of the table.

"Help yourself." Jake passes us a basket of edamame and some chicken skewers.

Mars quietly slides over two sharing plates while Novy waves his arm to catch the waiter's attention.

"Sorry we're late," I offer in greeting. "My fault."

"No big deal," says Jake. "Just gave us time to gossip about you before you got here."

I smile nervously, accepting a plate of beef-wrapped asparagus bites. "Oh, yeah? What's the gossip?"

Caleb shoots Jake a glare, and Jake snatches up his beer and takes a sip. Morrow covers for him, gesturing to the baskets of food. "Everyone, dig in."

"Oh—here's the waiter," says Novy. "Hey, Kiko. We've got two more here."

Henrik and I give Kiko our drink orders, and Jake orders four more dishes for the table to share. He rattles off the Japanese like a pro, adding, "I made Amy highlight everything on the menu she knew we'd like."

I almost forgot he had a sister. I saw her once, the night the Prices got married in L.A. She flew over from Japan for it. She does something cool with engineering, like robotics or space or something. I was too starstruck being in Hal Price's house to dare try to chat with her. But I got to touch a Grammy that night. And I saw Al Pacino.

The guys settle into an easy rhythm with each other, picking up their conversation from before we arrived. They practically share a hive mind, finishing each other's sentences and starting a new topic midstream that has them all laughing and pointing at each other. I try to follow along, but a lot of the conversation is hockey jargon. They're talking about trades, and the draft, and stats that go way above my head. I've learned to like hockey over the years, but I'm no expert. And Henrik does nothing to help me. He just sinks into a sort of stupor, drinking his beer, eating his food, and passing things around to the others while they talk.

After about twenty minutes of this, the waiter brings over a fresh round of drinks, trading out some of the empty baskets for more delicious bar snacks. As the guys all dig into the new dishes, divvying them onto the sharing plates, Jake leans down the table. "So, Karlsson, how's the kid?"

"She's well," Henrik replies, passing a plate of fried tofu across to Mars.

The table waits for him to say more, but he doesn't.

"Cool," says Jake.

Novy and Morrow snort into their beers, and Caleb elbows Jake in the ribs.

"*Ow*—what?" Jake glares at his husband. "Poppy said we had to ask him a question. I asked him a question."

I glance around the table. "What am I missing?"

Novy slings his arm around Henrik's shoulders. "Oh, Poppy just said we have to try to draw Karlsson out of his shell tonight. But we all know there's no cracking open this clam."

"Yeah, some leopards just don't change their spots," says Jake, popping a piece of chicken karaage into his mouth. "Which is totally cool," he adds at Henrik. "You know we love a strong, silent type. Hell, I'm married to one." He jabs his thumb around Caleb at Mars.

Henrik just smiles good-naturedly, sipping his beer.

The conversation turns to fantasy football, but I'm stuck thinking about what Jake said. Didn't I used to think the same thing about Henrik? Now that I know him so much better, it's easy to see all the ways he's willing to change. He twisted his life inside out to make room for Karolina. He's made changes for me too. He's not so prickly about me making him something other than overnight oats for breakfast anymore. He shares his closet, his bed, his coveted bathtub.

Not, like, at the same time. It's definitely big enough, but you know . . . not that.

Not yet.

God, Teddy, get a fucking grip.

I wrap both hands around my beer glass, staring down at the amber liquid. It was unfair of me to judge him then, just as it's unfair of his teammates to dismiss him now.

The topic has switched to football and Novy and Jake are arguing over a quarterback trade when I hear myself say, "Henrik and I talk all the time."

The table quiets, all eyes glancing my way.

"What?" says Novy.

Feeling flustered, I sip my beer. "I'm just saying, we talk all the time. He's full of interesting conversation," I add, setting the beer aside.

"I'm sure he is," says Morrow, which somehow makes me feel even more awkward.

I glance to Henrik, giving him a pleading look. If he's willing to change, I need this to be an area where he puts in a little more effort. I mean, is this how he makes his way through all the team dinners? Offering nothing? No anecdotes? No engagement? Am I supposed to just sit at his side as his silent plus-one?

Picking up on my unease, Henrik clears his throat, setting his beer aside. "Jake, how are your children, Jamie and Tuomas?"

I wince. Okay, so his delivery could use a little work. But I'm giving him an A for that effort. He's come a long way from not knowing any of the children's names to getting them right on the first try. Reaching under the table, I squeeze his thigh.

Across the table, Jake stifles a grin. "My children, Jamie and Tuomas?" he repeats, using Henrik's robotic cadence. Caleb very unsubtly elbows him again, and he adds, "They're good, man. Thanks for asking."

"They're looking forward to meeting the new babies in a couple months," adds Caleb.

"Can you believe there's gonna be three more Li'l Rays soon?" says Novy. "Man, how did we all get so lucky?"

The conversation turns to their kids and comparing the status of their pregnant wives.

I lean in towards Henrik, giving his thigh another squeeze as I lower my voice. "Everything okay?"

"It's fine."

"But you're not saying anything."

He shifts away from my touch.

I let my hand drop to my lap. "Well, am *I* allowed to talk?"

He raised a confused brow at me. "Of course. My silence should have no bearing on your participation in conversation."

"See, but you just said more in that sentence than you've contributed all night."

He just shrugs. "Leave it, Teddy. We have a rhythm."

Well, from where I'm sitting, the only rhythm he's a part of is circulating the air around the table with his breathing. I always knew he was the 'strong, silent type,' as Jake called him. But the Henrik I know has only ever been easy to converse with. He can talk about anything from hockey to current events to Dadaism. Hell, he can do it in three freaking languages!

So, why is he content to sit here like a house plant?

And why do I feel like if he's not talking, I shouldn't be either?

He sets his beer aside, rising from his stool.

I sit up a little straighter. "Where are you going?"

"Restroom," he mutters.

I watch him walk away, locking eyes with an older man he passes. The man holds up his camera, giving me a knowing nod. Oh fuck, our voyeur is here, ready to take pictures of this supremely awkward evening.

41

HENRIK

I jerk a few paper towels out of the dispenser, roughly drying my hands. Behind me, a toilet loudly flushes. Christ, this is such a disaster. Why did I agree to do this? I didn't want to. I should have said no the minute Poppy proposed the idea of a group date. I like my teammates, and I enjoy their company. And I really do care for their families. But their lives are their own. I've never been one to interfere or engage.

And Teddy is different. Who I am *with* Teddy is different. Is it so wrong that I like the Henrik I am with Teddy to be different than the Karlsson I am with my team? At this point, the two versions of me feel all but irreconcilable.

We should leave. We can still salvage the rest of this evening. I should go out there, drag Teddy off his stool, and take him back to that hot dog stand on the beach. We went there on Karolina's first day in Jacksonville. We can eat hot dogs and drink more beer, and I'll let him ask me as many questions as he wants. We can talk until the sun rises. Then I'll take him down to the surf and kiss him in the waves.

This is a good plan. This is safe, and comfortable, and intimate. All things I like when I'm with Teddy.

I toss my used paper towels in the trash and head for the door. I only get it halfway open before Ilmari Price pushes his way in, towering over me with his massive 6'5" frame. There's a reason he won an Olympic gold medal and two Stanley Cups. The man is built like an iron giant, and he has the flexibility of a gymnast. Even retired, he's still in pristine shape.

He slips inside the bathroom, but he makes no effort to go to the urinal or a stall. Instead, he folds his arms and stands with his shoulder slightly in front of the door. "Why are you acting so odd?" he asks in Swedish.

"I'm not," I reply defensively.

He just stares down at me, leaning against the wall.

I groan, rubbing the back of my neck. "Is it really that bad?"

"Worse," he mutters. "I think Teddy is close to tears."

My gut churns at the thought. "I don't know how to do this."

"Do what?"

"*This.*" I gesture towards the bar. "I know what Teddy wants from me. He wants me to laugh, and tell jokes, and be the center of attention as easily as Jake or Novikov. But I don't do this. I'm not that man."

Ilmari just shrugs a shoulder. "Maybe you are. Maybe you'd enjoy it if you tried."

I glare at him, crossing my arms too. "Like you've tried? You haven't said a word all night. You're just sitting across the table, watching me drown."

"But I'm here," he reasons.

"What?"

"Six years ago, I wouldn't be. Six years ago, I was like you are now, living only for myself."

This has me feeling even more defensive. Cursing under my breath, I step into his space. "I *live* for others. My every thought is for others."

"You *provide* for others," he corrects. "You live for yourself. Always in your own head, always wanting your own way. You were just the same out on the ice. You play as part of a team only when it suits you. And I say that with no judgment," he adds. "As I say, I was exactly the same."

"What happened for you to change?"

The corner of his mouth tips with a smile. "Rachel. Then Jake. Eventually Caleb. Now the children we share. I am forever changed by the people in my life who made changing feel not only possible, but desirable."

I fight a smirk. "Jake before Caleb? That's surprising."

He shrugs again. "It shouldn't be. Jake is the beating heart of our family. I knew I needed him in my life long before he ever knew he needed me. I would follow him to the ends of this earth. He's the reason I'm here tonight. He wanted me here, so I'm here."

"Jake Price calls, and the Mighty Mars comes running?"

"I would do anything for his happiness," he replies with a solemn nod. "Including spending an evening having an awkward dinner with you."

I groan.

"What would you do for Teddy's happiness? What is he worth to you?"

A lightness grows in my chest at just the thought of him. His smile, his laugh, the way he's always anxiously twisting his wedding ring on his finger. "Anything," I reply. "Everything." I look up, staring into Ilmari's bearded face. "I want to give Teddy everything."

He raises a scarred brow. "So, it's not fake then?"

"What?"

"Your marriage. The rumor is that it's fake . . . as much as I'm privy to team rumors, retired as I am."

I scoff, dragging a hand through my hair. "You're married to the head of PT, the head of equipment management, and the team captain. *And* you've been the President of the WAGs for four years. I doubt there's a person alive who hears more Rays gossip than you."

He dares to shrug again. "Caleb and Tess think it's funny to keep nominating me. I've begged them to stop. Besides, it's a title in name only. I have no real power. And I pay no attention to the gossip. But I'm pleased for you." Reaching out, he squeezes my shoulder. "Teddy is a good person. He's good for you."

I brighten a little. "You think?"

"A man like Teddy is loyal to the grave. He's like my Jake. Pour into his cup and watch as he returns your effort tenfold."

His words send a chill down my spine. All I can picture are the red frames of Keziah Wilson's bespectacled face as she voiced her grievances that hummed with the power of prophecy. She called me an empty glass with no bottom. Those words have haunted me ever since. Now Ilmari Price is standing here, telling me I need to pour back into Teddy the bounty he shares with me.

"What if my cup is empty? What if I have nothing to give him? Or what if what I have isn't enough? What if *I'm* not enough?"

His eyes narrow. "You think his faith in you is misplaced? You think Teddy would pick his life partner poorly?"

"No."

He steps in closer, making me lean away. "Do you intend to break his heart?"

"No!"

Another step has me backing away from him. "In my official capacity as President of the WAGs, if I know you intend to break his heart, I'm required by my oath of office to kick your ass."

"No—" My hip hits the sink and I raise both hands in surrender. "Fuck—Mars, stop."

"We can take this outside right now." He points over his shoulder towards the door. "Caleb will hold your arms for me—"

"*No*," I all but shout.

He holds his glare for another long moment before finally nodding. "Good. Then go back out there and salvage the rest of this miserable evening."

All my breath leaves me on a heavy exhale. "How? What do I do?"

"Try harder."

"Well, do you have any ideas?"

His lips purse with a smile, and I perk up, pushing away from the sink. "Do you have one?"

"I have one."

Hope blooms in my chest. "What is it?"

He just chuckles, shaking his head. "Come with me."

50

TEDDY

Just as I'm about to slink away from this table and check to see if Henrik dined and freaking dashed on me, he and Mars come striding back across the bar. Henrik is in front, carrying a tray of what looks like shots.

"Oh god," I mutter, eyes wide.

"Hey, there they are," calls Jake.

"We thought maybe you both fell in," Novy teases. "Is that bathroom actually *in* Japan?"

Caleb eyes the tray warily. "Oh, what the fuck are those?"

"Make room," says Henrik, wielding the tray of shots. Novy and Caleb scramble to shuffle the plates and baskets aside.

Jake leans back, catching a basket before it falls off the table. "I didn't know this was that kind of party. Someone wanna explain?"

Henrik slips back onto his stool and starts passing out a round of shots. "We're celebrating."

Novy takes his shot. "Celebrating what? Don't get me wrong, I'm always down for shots. Just tell me why. Is it Arbor Day or something?"

"Arbor Day is in April," says Caleb.

Novy glares across the table at him. "Can you fucking not?"

Caleb raises both hands, leaning away.

"This one's for you, Aarre," Mars says at him, sliding him a shot glass.

Caleb takes it.

"Just club soda," Ilmari adds, kissing his cheek. Then he reaches forward and takes a shot offered by Henrik with a soft word of thanks in Swedish.

Now, everyone's eyes go wide.

"Okay, what the fuck?" says Jake. "What is going on? Mars, you don't drink."

"I do tonight," he replies.

Novy sniffs his shot. "Why? What are we celebrating? Wait, is this sake?"

"Yeah, they didn't have schnapps," says Henrik. "But this will work the same."

He finally hands me a shot. Then he surprises me by cupping my cheek. The touch is so gentle, almost loving. He smiles at me, and my heart does a freaking backflip. Then he turns to the group. "As you all know, shortly before the season started, I had the honor and privilege of making Teddy my husband."

"Here, here," says Morrow, raising his shot.

"Poor bastard," adds Novy, and the others laugh.

Henrik drops his hand to my shoulder. "Teddy was there for me in a profound moment of grief. I lost my sister, my best friend. Everyone here knows what it feels like to lose, or think you're about to lose, someone precious to you."

The mood at the table sobers in an instant. I watch as Novy places a hand on Morrow's knee. Across the table, Jake wraps an arm around Caleb's shoulder.

"But in that darkness," Henrik goes on, "Teddy was the light. He guided me back to life, back to living. The rings we wear became a tether. So long as I have him, I can keep fighting."

"I picked those rings," Novy fake whispers, making the other guys smile.

Tears burn my eyes as Henrik looks to me again. Then he clears his throat, turning back to the table. "In all the chaos of the last several weeks, there's been no time to pause and celebrate our marriage. Typically, in Sweden, a wedding reception would begin with a toast."

"Yes!" Jake is smiling from ear to ear. "Ohmygod, this is gonna be so fun. Do we get to give the toasts? As team captain, I get to go first, right? Can we use props?"

We all laugh.

"Ilmari had a good idea," Henrik says. "He thought it might be fun to bring a little of my Swedish culture to this moment, as a nod to where our story began."

"It's perfect," I say through my tears.

Novy pounds his fist on the table. "Teddy loves it! What do we need to do? Is there a Swedish toast we can learn? Isn't it just 'Skål' or something?"

Henrik lifts up his own shot. "I'm going to teach you all a snapsvisa."

"I heard the word 'schnapps,'" says Jake.

The guys all laugh again.

Henrik smiles. "I'm going to teach you a Swedish drinking song."

Fifteen minutes later, we've drawn the attention of most of the patrons in this restaurant as we collectively lose our shit, laughing and trying to sing this damn drinking song in Swedish.

Jake slaps his hand on the table. "Wait, wait, wait. One more time—"

"Come *on*," Caleb groans.

"Boo!" Novy shouts.

Morrow and I just laugh.

Ilmari mutters something in Swedish that has him and Henrik smirking.

"I've almost got it," says Jake. "It's the last line. Just do the last line again."

Taking a deep breath, Henrik holds up his shot glass and chants, "Han heller inte halvan får."

Jake repeats it twice under his breath as the rest of us laugh again. "Okay! Alright, I got it. Let's go."

Henrik holds up his shot glass a little higher. "Ready?"

"We're ready," says Morrow.

"Let's fucking do this," Novy shouts.

"Wait—" Jake's eyes are wide as he stares down the table. "Mars, you're really gonna do a shot with us?"

At my left, Mars is holding up his shot glass. "If I'm singing 'Helan Går,' I'm taking a real fucking shot."

Cheers go up around the table as he looks to Henrik and nods.

Henrik pounds his fist on the table. "Right. This is for Teddy O'Connor, my husband, min kärlek, mitt allt . . . and the best-looking man in any room!"

Novy lowers his glass an inch. "Hey now—"

Henrik launches into the song, and this time we all sing along. To either side of me, Henrik and Mars both have rich, baritone voices. The words flow off their tongues with ease. I'll admit, I just feel like I'm along for this wild ride. The whole restaurant turns to watch us as we sing at the top of our lungs:

"Helan går,
Sjung hopp faderallan lallan lej
Helan går,
Sjung hopp faderallan lej."

Then comes the tongue twister that has us all gasping for breath:

"Och den som inte helan tar,
Han heller inte halvan får.
Helan gååååår!!!!"

As we hold out the last note, drumming the table with our free hands, Henrik holds his glass high. "Now, drink!"

As one, we all down our shots of sake, slamming our empty cups onto the table.

With a wave of Henrik's hand, we finish the song with one more chant of, "Sjung hopp faderallan lej!"

All around the restaurant, the other patrons cheer for us. Some shout their congratulations. Several of them have their phones out, taking pictures and videos. I know our trusty voyeur is doing his job. Surprising the heck out of me, Henrik leans over and kisses me right on the lips. "Well done, min älskade."

I'm smiling, breathless, high on this moment. Not wanting him to get away so quickly, I wrap my hand around his neck and pull him back to me, kissing the taste of the sake from his lips while our friends all pound their fists on the table and cheer.

Two hours later, we stumble out of the elevator, nearly tripping each other as we try to kiss and walk at the same time. I'm drunk, but I don't care. Henrik is in my arms. He's alive and kissing me, and I never want him to stop. He backs me up against the door, my ass slamming into the doorknob, as he fumbles and drops his keys to the floor.

"Fan i helvete," he mutters.

Okay, maybe he's a little tipsy too. By the end of the night, I lost track of how many times we actually sang "Helan Går." Things really got out of hand when our waitress, Kiko, taught us a Japanese drinking song. Caleb called us all Ubers, piling his drunk husbands into the back of their truck. Henrik and I kissed all the way back to the apartment. Now his English translator seems to be on the fritz. He mumbles something in Swedish, looking for his keys.

"Leave them," I pant, tugging on his shoulder. "Just fucking kiss me."

Abandoning his hunt, Henrik rights himself. Pressing in with his hips, he pins me to the door. I groan with aching need, my hands fisting tight to his shirt as I pull him to me. Our lips meet, and we both just sink into each other, taking what we need.

It's not air. It's certainly not more fucking sake. I just need more of *him*. More of this taste. More of the feel of him. I want us naked. Undone. I want him pressing me down, making me bear his weight, as he claims me again and again. Fuck, I want him to ruin me more than I'm already ruined. I am so lost to this man.

But we can't do any of that in this hallway.

With a groan, I break our kiss. "Baby, get the keys."

"Va?"

"Keys, Henrik. Keys for door. Come on, I don't speak enough Swedish for this."

Swaying slighting, Henrik steps back, once again searching for his keys on the floor.

I hear a click, but I'm too tipsy to register what it means. The front door swings open from the inside, and I go falling backwards.

"Teddy!" Hanna shrieks.

I'd like to say I catch myself, but that would be a lie. I land on my back on the entry rug, staring up at a shocked and dismayed Hanna.

"I'm so sorry!" She reaches for me with both hands. "I heard a noise. I thought maybe you forgot your keys!"

"Found them," says Henrik, holding up his key ring. He finds me on the floor and lifts a confused brow. "What are you doing on the floor, mitt hjärta?"

Hanna giggles, helping me to my feet. "Seems like you two had a nice time tonight."

I slip my shoes off, leaving them by the door. "Henrik taught us all a snapsvisa."

"Uh-oh." She steps back, holding the door as Henrik enters. "Do you need me to stay the night?"

"Not necessary," I reply with a wave, stumbling my drunk ass towards the kitchen.

Henrik says something in Swedish.

"English, babe," I call over my shoulder.

Hanna laughs. "Actually, I speak Swedish, remember?"

I just groan. "Why does everyone speak Swedish but me?"

Over by the door, Henrik now seems to be having trouble removing his shoes.

Hanna just smiles. "Well, you both seem good. So, I'm gonna go. Have a great rest of your night, okay? Maybe take some aspirin."

"I'm gonna make us some coffee," I call from the kitchen. "We'll be totally sober in, like, an hour." She stifles a giggle that has me turning towards her. "What's so funny?"

"Oh, nothing," she says with a wave. "Just, Henrik said almost the exact same thing in Swedish just now. You two enjoy the rest of your night."

I'm busy stuffing coffee grounds into the brew basket when I hear the front door finally shut. I set a mug on the cup rest and press the On button. The machine hums to life just as Henrik steps in behind me, pressing me to the counter with his hips. "I don't want coffee," he growls in my ear, his hands wrapping possessively around me to splay across my chest.

"You will," I assure him, patting his arm. "In about thirty minutes, when this warm cloud of drunkenness wears off and the sake headache sets in."

He groans, pressing his face to my neck. "Then we still have thirty minutes."

I grab his wrists and squeeze. "Not here."

"Tell me where."

The command in his tone sends a shiver through me. Taking his hand, I lead him deeper into the back of the apartment. Call me paranoid, but this would be the perfect moment for our niece to wake up and come rolling into the damn living room on her new puppy scooter.

Henrik looks around as we walk into the bedroom. "I thought you said no bed?"

"Just come with me." Feeling confident in my drunken mobility, I turn, walking backwards through the bathroom and into the closet. The lights blink on, illuminating Henrik's gorgeous rows of designer suits. Other lights glow in the cubbies for his shoes, dress shirts, denim, and sweaters. "You started something earlier in here," I tease, backing until I press myself up against the shelf of sweaters. "Come finish it."

Wasting no time, Henrik boxes me in. One hand grips the shelf by my head while the other cups my face as he kisses me, parting my lips with his tongue. I sigh into the kiss. Fuck, he's so good at this. He may not have had much practice, but he's a quick study. His kisses are soft and firm at the same time. Deliberate. He likes to change his approach, learning my reactions when he nips at my lips or flicks with his tongue.

Desperate for more, I slip my hands under his shirt. It's a short-sleeve linen button-down. The top of the collar is open, showing just a hint of that chest hair he was teasing me with earlier. He groans as my hands brush over the warm skin of his stomach. He's like a furnace. I've noticed that when we sleep too. His metabolism is so high, always working in overdrive. He's like my own personal sun.

Not for the first time, I accept that I'm the Icarus in this relationship. I don't know when, and I don't know how, but I'm going to fall. Harder than I've already fallen for him. In this moment, there's only one thing I want: I want to fall to my knees. Brushing my lips to his, I push him gently away. "Do you want more?"

He opens his eyes, panting for breath. "Vad?"

I smile against his mouth, wrapping my hands around to stroke the small of his back. "Do you want more, baby? Do you want me to make you feel good?"

"Teddy." He says my name like a plea.

I drop my hands to the top of his pants, making my intentions clear. "I wanna make you feel so fucking good. Do you trust me?"

Holding my gaze, he nods.

We keep our eyes locked on each other as I undo his belt. "Say stop, and it stops, okay?"

He nods again.

"Teach me in Swedish." I press a kiss to his lips. "Teach me, baby. Say 'stop.'"

With one hand, he cups my face. "Sluta."

My drunken brain tattoos it to my memory. "Easy enough. Say it in English or Swedish, and it all stops."

He kisses me again. "Don't stop." As if to prove his eagerness, he drops his hands to my shoulders and pushes gently, guiding me down to my knees.

My senses are going haywire. I'm on my knees in Henrik Karlsson's closet, and I'm unbuttoning his pants. I'm about to suck his dick. Gazing up at him, I slowly work his zipper, opening his fly. Then my fingers hook into the top of his khakis, and I pull them down around his muscled thighs.

His hardness is right there, waiting for me. Henrik is hard for me. He *wants* me. I can't wait another second for what I want. I press my face to his crotch over his briefs, breathing him in. The scent of his raw, masculine energy has me dripping in my pants. Fuck, he smells so good.

Grabbing his hips tight with both hands, I nuzzle his crotch, letting my parted lips brush over his shaft through the fabric of his briefs. He groans, sinking back against the closet shelf. "Teddy . . . tell me what to do."

I smile up at him, cupping him with my hand over his briefs. He twitches with eagerness. I can see it in his eyes. I feel it in his touch. He wants more. Knowing it has me flying. "You don't have to do a thing. Just feel it all, baby. And enjoy."

Hooking my fingers into the top of his briefs, I slowly pull them down, freeing his cock. It hangs in my face, uncut and ready. Fuck, it's so beautiful. I've waited for this for so long, and here it is, hard and aching, already dripping for me. I just know that getting him off is gonna get me off harder than I've ever come in my life.

But this isn't about my pleasure. This moment is all about pleasing Henrik, showing him how this can feel. Holding to his hips, I do the thing I've been dreaming of doing for six long years. Eyes closed in bliss, I lick along his cut V-line from above his hip, down to his crotch. Pressing my face into the soft thatch of his pubic hair, I breathe him in again.

Henrik groans, one hand dropping down to fist my hair tightly. "Sluta inte."

"What?"

"Don't stop."

51

HENRIK

I can't breathe. Can't think. Teddy's face is pressed against my crotch, his warm breath is fanning over my hard cock, and it feels so good. My legs feel like they're made of jelly as I hold tight to his hair. "Don't stop," I say again. Who knows if I'm speaking English or Swedish?

This is good. Whatever he's doing, this feels good. He peppers warm, open-mouthed kisses across my hip bones and over my thighs, his hands soft and caressing. He hasn't even touched my cock yet.

"Please," I whisper.

Surely, he knows what he's doing, right? As much as it makes me irrationally upset to think of him with other men, it must be a virtue in this moment. Teddy knows what he's doing. I can trust him. Nothing he's done so far has made me feel uncomfortable.

"Can I make you feel good, baby?" he whispers.

"Do anything. Just don't stop."

At long last, he wraps a warm hand around the base of my shaft. We both groan as he pants his warm breath over my aching tip. At the first touch of his tongue, I feel like I've been zapped by lighting. I cry out, all but collapsing against the wall of the closet.

He smiles, humming low in his throat as he licks me again, tasting my precum with his tongue. The sound he lets out is feral with need. I can hardly breathe as he sinks his mouth around me completely, swallowing my length.

"God—" I can't breathe past the feeling of his warmth mouth sucking me. And watching him is intoxicating. I can't look away. He bobs on my cock, swirling his tongue around my tip. His hands hold my hips, caressing as he sucks. The moment he drops a hand down and cups my balls, I feel like I'm going to burst into a thousand pieces. "I can't," I pant.

He pops off me with a gentle sucking sound. Then he gazes up at me, his eyes dark with desire. "Do you want me to stop?"

Dropping my hand to his mouth, I brush my fingers over his parted lips. "No. . . but I think my legs are going to give out."

Smiling, he holds out a hand. "Then come down here."

"What?"

"Lie down." He tugs on my hand.

I drop down, not caring that my pants are wrapped around my knees. He gets me on the floor. With a practiced hand, he strips my lower half naked. Then he shifts me until I'm reclining against the drawers, my bare legs stretched across the carpet.

"I don't want you horizontal," he says, pressing a quick kiss to my lips. "I want you watching me." He crawls over my leg, situating himself between my knees. Folding himself over on all fours, he licks along my shaft, leaving my hands trembling again. Now that I'm not thinking about standing, my every sense is locked on the feel of his mouth on me. It's warm, and wet, soft and so smooth. His tongue feels inviting as it licks and teases, and his hands are strong, bracing against my hips. I'm torn between wanting to close my eyes and never blink.

He takes me to the back of his throat, humming and sucking, and I feel my soul leave my body. It's floating somewhere in this closet, as the sound of his soft gagging has me gripping his shoulders with both hands. They brush over the fabric of his T-shirt and I grimace. I want it gone. I want to feel his skin.

"Don't stop," I growl.

Fuck, I'm so close.

He whines, slipping a hand back between my legs to play with my balls as he sucks on my tip, flicking with his tongue. The mix of wonderful sensations has me levitating off the closet floor. I feel warm all over. My breath catches. "I'm gonna—Teddy—should I—"

This feels far and away better than anything I've ever

experienced. But I've never come during sex without a condom. What should I do? I want to come. I *need* to come. "Teddy—"

"Come in my mouth," he pants. "Baby, please. I'm fucking dying for it—"

"Fuck!"

He doesn't even get his mouth back on me. His words are enough for me to release. He groans with relief, mouth open, as he pumps my cock with slow, languid pulls. My release shoots from my tip, landing in his open mouth. It's beautiful to see the joy on his face, the absolute peace he feels in this moment, tasting me, claiming me in this way. I'm trembling as I let him finish.

"Fuck, yes." He drops his mouth over me once more, pulling back my foreskin to suck my tip. "Baby, you taste so good. Fucking love your cock." He kisses my tip one last time. Then he sits up, his lips and chin shiny with my mess. His eager eyes search my face, and I already know his question before he asks it. "Was that good for you? Did you like it?"

Wrapping a hand around the back of his neck, I reel him in. "I loved it."

Teddy closes his eyes, mouth moving as if he's praying a word of thanks. Then I kiss him, tasting myself on his lips. The taste is sweet, and musky, and not unpleasant. I want more. I want more of Teddy, and kissing, and experimenting in closets. Pushing him back, I hold his gaze. "Teach me. Show me what to do."

His smile is radiant as he nods. "I'll show you everything."

52

TEDDY

"**M**ommy said I have to ask you if Lina can come to my sleepover!" Emma Langley stands in front of me, hands on her hips, fiery red hair in a halo of curls around her head.

"Oh, well, I . . ." Setting the salad tongs down, I give her my full attention. "This is sort of uncharted territory for me," I admit.

She tilts her head to the side like a confused owl. "What?"

I snort a laugh. "Can I think about it, honey?"

Her brows crease in frustration. "The sleepover is tonight."

"Then I'll think *really* fast."

In a perfect imitation of her mother, she huffs and stomps away.

It's game day, intermission time. The Rays are up by two, and the WAG room is buzzing with excitement. All the little kids are playing over in the corner. They've got a great setup, including age-appropriate toy bins and a TV that can play movies.

The rest of the room is set up for the adults, with tables for eating, a couple couches, and the infamous WAG room buffet spread. Today it's Caesar salad with grilled chicken or salmon as a protein, homemade mac and cheese with the curly noodles and a crispy baked topping, and a build-your-own sundae bar.

I glance over my shoulder, checking on Karolina. She's sitting with Emma and Grace Morrow, all three of them furiously coloring. Nearby, Doc Price is hunkered down with her boys, feeding them bites of mac and cheese while they play. I offer her a smile and a wave. Once I got back from Sweden, she was finally able to go on maternity leave. It's been weird around the gym without her. Brady is cool, but he just doesn't have the same energy. Rachel Price always comes with just a little touch of chaos that makes each workday fun.

I turn back to the buffet, juggling mine and Karro's plates. I add a little salmon for her and some chicken for me.

I should just say yes, right? To the slumber party? As one of her legal guardians, I'm allowed to make this kind of decision on the fly. But it still feels odd. As much as I've fallen into a rhythm with Karro and I like thinking of her as partly mine, there's still a wall there. It's the "they're family, and I'm not" wall. Henrik is her blood relation. They speak the same language. They both knew her mother. God help me, they both like Kalles Kaviar. It's this awful, fishy paste made from salted cod roe. It's pink, and it comes in a tube like toothpaste, and it ruined my breakfast last week. They love it. Can't get enough of it.

What I'm saying is I still feel like an outsider. Henrik and Karro, even Hanna, are firmly over *there*. And I'm over *here*, wondering exactly where I fit into this long term. Because I want a long term. I don't want this marriage to only be temporary. Henrik and I have something. I knew it from the moment we met on that sidewalk six years ago. It's taken time for that spark to grow into a flame. But this last week has taught me to hope like I've never really hoped before.

And that's saying a lot, because I'm a delusional double Pisces.

Henrik's been in and out for travel. But when he's home? God, the man is undeniable. Now that he's discovered he *has* passion, he's unafraid to show it. But he's like a babe in the woods, unsure of what to do or how to express what he feels. And he's still not great at the verbal communication thing either.

Here's one thing: I don't know how much longer our "no sex in the bed" rule can last. We're still taking it slow, but our kissing is getting more adventurous by the day. We're each exploring more terrain, if you know what I mean. He got back last night, and once we got Karro in bed, he had me stretched out on the couch, shirt off, hands seeking, teasing my nipples and kissing across my chest until—

Okay. Cool it, psycho. The WAG room buffet line is not the place to reminisce about the time you came in your pants from a little nipple play.

Because, yeah, that happened.

And, yes, Henrik noticed.

I think he's curious to try more. He certainly doesn't object when I suck him off, which has been every night that he's been home. Twice on Tuesday. I've made it clear that he can do more to me too, but I think he's nervous. He likes the kissing, and he definitely likes touching me.

I don't know, maybe he's a bottom? He gives such quiet lion energy that I just thought his instincts would take over and he'd pounce. Maybe he's vers. Maybe he *will* be a top, but I have to show him how first. I've always preferred bottoming. But with Henrik? If he needs me to top him to show him how things work, he only has to ask.

"Hey."

I practically jump out of my skin as Tess steps in behind me. "Jesus, you scared me," I say.

"How did I scare you? I was standing right here."

I force all thoughts of Henrik from my head. "What do you need, Tess?"

"Emma just told me you said Karolina can't come for a sleepover. And that's totally fine. But if you're worried about her because of the injuries—"

I hold up a hand. "Whoa, I did *not* say that. I said I needed to think about it."

"What's there to think about? Three little girls having a sleepover, watching *Mulan* in my living room. I'll be there the whole time. No rough play, and no sugar after eight. Lights out by nine."

I groan. "Look, I just need to clear it with Henrik first, okay? I can give you an answer by the end of the game."

She eyes me critically. "How's all that going then?"

"All what?"

Before she can respond, Poppy comes breezing up to us. "Teddy, honey, there you are." She looks a little breathless, her cheeks flushed pink. "Can I talk to you for a minute?"

"Uhh . . ." I glance over my shoulder to where Karro plays.

"I got her," says Tess. "Go."

Poppy wraps a hand around my arm. Apparently, I have no choice but to set aside my plates of food and abandon this buffet line, letting Poppy lead me towards the door. "Hey, Tess?" she calls over her shoulder.

"Yeah?"

"You're taking Gracie tonight, right?"

"Yep! Sleepover."

"Thanks, honey. Hey, be a dear and take my Bennett too, won't you? Thanks so much!" She waves with her free hand, not giving Tess a chance to say no, as she tugs me into the hallway.

"Something wrong, Pop?"

She lets go of my arm. "Oh, nothing much. I'm just gonna go ahead and give you these." She fishes something out of her pocket, holding it in her closed fist.

I reach out on instinct, and she places a set of car keys in my hand. "What are these?"

"Those are the keys to Lukas's truck."

"Why do I—whoa—" I glance down, eyes wide. "Uhh . . . Poppy, you're—are you leaking?" I point to the water on the floor.

She lets out a breath, rubbing a hand over her pregnant belly. "Oh, that's just my water breaking."

"Your—oh god—" I step back. "Poppy!"

"It's okay," she says, breathing through the pain. "All totally okay. Totally normal. A little early, but okay. That's why I'm gonna go ahead and head on over to the hospital now."

I'm officially fritzing. "Jesus. Well, do you need any help?"

"Nope. Colton is bringing the car around as we speak. I just need you to tell Lukas where we've gone once the game is over. Drive him to the hospital for me. Okay, sweets?"

"Poppy—"

"We're going to Jacksonville General. Labor and Delivery is on the third floor. After two babies, he knows the drill."

"Oh my god." I follow her as she waddles down the hall in her designer wrap dress and stiletto heels. "Poppy, just tell Novy now."

"Are you kidding? He has a game to finish. Rays are up, and he's playing so well tonight. Besides, who knows if this little kiwi is even coming out today? This could be fake labor."

"Your water breaking seems like real fucking labor."

She just laughs. "I know, right?"

I'm fucking reeling. Is this happening? This woman is crazy. "Poppy, I can't be the one to tell Novy."

Turning, she grabs me by the shoulder, one hand still bracing her heavy baby bump. "No, you *have* to. Teddy O'Connor, you look at me."

I groan, trying to look anywhere else.

Her hand on my shoulder tightens. "*Look* at me."

With a huff, I stare into her Barbie blue eyes.

She smiles. "Good. Now, I love that man more than my own life, but he's not great in a crisis. If he has things his way, he'll storm into that hospital, parking his truck in the dang lobby. He is not to be given those keys, do you hear me? You're the only one on staff I can trust not to give in to his demands."

"This is bullshit."

"You are the solid rock, Teddy. Lukas is the wave that will crash upon you. And yet, you will remain unmoved."

"Unbelievable," I mutter.

She groans, patting her stomach. "I know, but it really can't be helped. Teddy, honey, do this for me, and I'll send you a fruit basket. Don't worry, it'll be a big one. And if Lukas tries to knock your lights out, I'll throw in three tickets to Disney on Ice." Letting me go, she continues down the long hallway.

"Is that a likely possibility?" I call after her.

She just waves over her shoulder, shuffling down the hall in her clicking heels.

In moments, Morrow comes jogging around the corner, determined to intercept her. After a quick word with her, he locks eyes with me, pointing with the finger of destiny. "Do *not* let him fucking drive!"

Oh, this is so fucking fucked!

53

HENRIK

The whistle blows, and the crowd roars in outrage. My heart races, my breath heavy in my chest. I saw the whole thing like it was happening in slow motion. Number thirty-two on the Golden Knights has been goading Lindberg all game. He's a young hot head, fresh off the draft, and Lindberg just scored on him. Again. In a fit of petulant rage, the kid shoved Lindberg after the play, sending him face-first into the boards. His helmet hit with a crack, and Lindberg went down to the ice.

Now the kid is standing over him, shouting something as the ref skates in. But I'm closer. Surging forward, I drop my glove and punch the kid right in the fucking face. My hand instantly burns with the pain of the contact, the muscles clenching tight. The kid drops to the ice, scrambling to get back up as blood flows down his chin. "Bro, what the fuck!"

"Play fair or get the fuck off my ice!"

"Bro, man, fuck you!" The kid swings at me, and I duck.

I lose my footing as a second Golden Knight comes crashing in to defend his teammate. I trip over Lindberg's legs as I'm pressed into the boards. With a growl, I elbow whoever is behind me.

The whistles are going crazy now as the refs swoop in. Jake grabs me by the arms, pulling me back. A Knights defenseman does the same to thirty-two.

"I'm gonna kick your ass, man," he shouts at me. "Try me! Fucking try me, man!"

"Go back to the beer leagues, you piece of shit!" That's all I can get out in English before I switch to Swedish, profanity pouring from me like a fountain.

"Hey," Jake growls in my ear, skating me backwards. "It's done."

"Did you see what he did?"

"I saw. The punk was asking for it. But stop while you've got the upper hand. He's the one who looks like an ass, not you."

The whistles are still blowing as the linemen try to pull Novikov off the defenseman who hit me into the boards. He has him pinned down on the ice, grappling with him.

"Lindberg!" I turn in Jake's arms, looking for my injured teammate.

"He's fine," Jake assures me. "Just got the wind knocked out of him."

I glance up, catching the replay footage on the jumbotron. The crowd watches too, screaming and pounding the plexiglass. Their thirst for bloodlust knows no bounds. Not for the first time, I feel like a gladiator in the Colosseum. This is a dangerous sport and accidents happen. Would they even care if we died? Is that how I might meet my end? To their thunderous applause?

I didn't fight that kid because I wanted to. I fought because behavior like that can't be tolerated. He could have seriously injured Lindberg, taken him out of the game. If a broken nose encourages him to play fair, I'll break his nose every day of the week.

There's not enough time on the game clock for me to wait out my penalty, so the ref sends me back to the bench with Novy. Coach Johnson doesn't even spare a harsh word for us. The Rays are up, and he knows exactly why we did what we did. Down the wall, that punk-ass kid marches into the tunnel to the jeers of the Rays home crowd, holding a bloody towel to his face.

The game still ends with a Rays win. My job done for another night, I make my way down the tunnel, back to the dressing room. As I'm untying my skate laces, Lindberg sits next to me. "Hej."

"Hej, hej," I say. "You okay?"

He nods, placing a hand on my bare shoulder. "Thanks."

I just shrug. "You'd do the same for me."

"That was a solid punch," says DeGraw from my other side. He doesn't speak Swedish, but he intuits what we're talking about. "The EMT said you broke his nose."

"Good," Lindberg mutters. With a heavy sigh, he shakes his head. "He's my replacement."

"What?" says DeGraw.

"When the Rays traded for me, the Knights took that kid and gave him *my* center position. He's the new me."

"Which is why he thought he had something to prove tonight," says DeGraw. "Instead, he proved the opposite."

Lindberg glances up. "What opposite?"

DeGraw smiles. "There is no replacing you."

F resh from my shower, I'm slipping back into my suit when Teddy appears in the doorway of the changing room. He looks around before rushing over to my side. His anxiety instantly sets me on edge. "Teddy, what—"

"Help me."

My heart stops as I reel him in. "What happened?"

"I need you to help me. Now. Come on."

He tries to pull me forward, but I twist my arm free, reaching for my dress shirt. "I'm half dressed, mitt hjärta. I will come," I add. "But just tell me what's wrong."

He lowers his voice, clearly trying to avoid being overheard by the other men in the changing room. "Okay, so Poppy totally just screwed me over. I need you to come run interference for me with Novy."

"What?"

"She's in early labor, and she took his keys so he can't chase her to the hospital and, like, get in an accident or park his car in the ambulance bay," he explains with a wave of his hand.

"Well, that sounds sensible."

"Yeah. Only she gave his keys to *me*." Reaching in the pocket of his jacket, he pulls out a set of car keys.

"Shit."

"Right? Apparently, I'm the only one on staff she trusts to handle him."

I shrug into my dress shirt and work the buttons closed. "What do you need from me?"

"Help! Hold him back if he tries to hit me. Or, you know, get between us and take the hit for me."

My fingers pause on my middle button. "You want me to fight Novy because his partner is in labor?"

"God—*no*—I want you to stop him from fighting *me*." He presses a hand to his chest, fingers splayed. "I am your husband, Henrik. For better or worse. That was in our vows, right? They were in Swedish, so I don't even fucking know. But you should know that most wedding vows come with a 'for better or worse' clause. Well, this is the 'for worse' part." He shakes the keys at me. "You can protect your teammates out on the ice all you want. Off it, you have to protect *me*."

His panic is charming. It's all I can do not to sweep him in my arms and kiss him right now. "Novy is a grown man," I say with a shrug. "Surely he'll see reason."

"He's Lukas Novikov! Did you see him out there? You punched a man once, Henrik." He holds up a single finger to emphasize his point. "Novy tackled a man to the ice, straddled him, and wailed on him for a full sixty seconds before three grown men had to pull him off. If he'll do that to protect a teammate, what do you think he'll do to get to Poppy St. James?"

I consider for a moment, arms crossed in my half-open dress shirt. "Fair point."

"Thank you." He drops his hand to his side. "Now, finish getting dressed, and get ready to defend my honor. I know I look tough, but I bruise like a peach."

I smile as he hurries away. If I weren't already married to Teddy, this outburst would definitely convince me to give it a try.

54

TEDDY

Heart in my throat, I stand just inside the doorway of the changing room. Most of the guys have cleared out. The rest are toweling off from their showers and dressing back in their suits. Novy stands across the room at his stall. He's all but dressed. Only thing left is to slip on his shirt, button it, and grab his jacket.

My gaze darts left, and I give Henrik a nod. He's already dressed and ready, his arms crossed as he leans against his stall. Fighting a smile, he nods back. Whatever. He can think this is funny all he wants. For as much as I tease Novy and put him in his place, I've never really had to stand up to him. Not about something that mattered.

"Novy," I call out. "I need to talk to you."

He pats down his pockets, not turning around. "Uhh . . . can it wait?"

Oh shit, he already knows.

I step fully into the room. "Novy, this is important."

His head swivels, his gaze locked on the ground. "Has anyone seen my goddamn keys?"

"Novikov," Henrik shouts.

All the guys in the room stop their yapping and look to Henrik. Novy is one of the last to turn, his brow raised in question.

"My husband is talking to you," Henrik says, pointing at me.

Novy turns, giving me his full attention. The man is built like a freaking tree. He's a few inches taller and several pounds heavier than Henrik. He's a wall of muscle, with broad shoulders and a barrel chest. It's what makes him such an excellent enforcer. "What, Ted?"

I clear my throat. "I need you to calmly get your things and come with me. Please."

"What? Why?"

"I can't tell you that."

His eyes narrow. "Why not, Ted?"

I swallow, taking a step back. "Because I don't want you to hit me."

He frowns in confusion. "Why the hell would I hit you? Come on, man, knock it off. I can't find my damn keys." He turns around, ready to tear his stall apart.

"I have your keys," I call out.

The silence in the room deepens as he turns back around. "Why do you have my keys?"

"Poppy gave them to me during intermission with strict instructions that I'm to drive you to . . . the place where she is."

He quickly does the math, his eyes widening. "Oh shit. Fuck." He pulls his phone from his pocket, checking it for messages. "When did it happen? When did she leave?" He grabs his dress shirt and tugs it on, leaving the jacket hanging in his stall. Crossing over to me, shirt unbuttoned, he holds out his hand. "Teddy, give me my keys."

Tipping up my chin, I stand firm. "No."

His face becomes a mask of rage as he leans away. "No? Teddy, come on, you just said Poppy is in fucking labor. Give me my goddamn keys!"

"Just give him his keys," one of the guys calls.

"Yeah, man. Before he knocks out all your jibs."

On instinct, I raise a hand to shield my mouth. Oh god, I love my teeth. They're straight and cute, and they have the thinnest little gap in the front. "She thought you might react this way. Which is why she instructed me to keep your keys and drive you to the hospital myself."

He storms forward, getting right in my face. "I don't need a goddamn babysitter!"

"And I totally respect your position. But I made a promise to— *ah*—" The shriek that comes out of me as he grabs me is totally involuntary. "Violence will avail you nothing!"

He wraps an arm around me and squeezes like a goddamn boa constrictor. With his free hand, he digs in my pocket, searching for his keys. "Where are they, Ted?"

I flop like a fish out of water. "No—I promised Poppy!"

"Is a promise worth your goddamn life?"

"I'm more afraid of her than I am of you," I squawk, twisting in his hold as he checks my other pocket. "Just let me drive you, asshole!"

"Gimme um—*ouch*—"

"Let him go," a new voice growls.

"Ow, ow—fuck—you're gonna rip it off," Novy snarls.

"Let my husband go, or I twist."

I'm panting, room spinning, as Novy's iron arm loosens around my middle. I wriggle out of his clutches to see Henrik behind Novy, gripping so tightly to his ear that the tissue is already turning reddish purple.

Novy growls like an angry bear. "Let me go, Karlsson!"

"Knees," my husband replies.

"Ouch—*fuck*—let go—"

"On your knees, and it stops."

Cursing, Novy sinks to his knees. The moment they touch the carpet, Henrik lets him go. Novy's ear is bright red and shiny. He reaches up and rubs it. "Motherfucker." He glares at Henrik, eyes narrowing. "Teddy doesn't even have the keys, does he? He gave them to you."

Henrik just glares back. "Touch my husband again, and your keys will take up new residence in your colon."

Around the room, the guys let out chuckles and sounds of "Oohoo" and "Don't hurt him, Karlsson."

Taking a deep breath, I right my mussed jacket, smoothing down the front. "Right, well if you're quite ready, Henrik and I will be more than happy to drive you to the hospital to welcome your newest bundle of joy. Shall we?"

Novy gets slowly to his feet, shaking his head in disgust. "Betrayed by my favorite PT. Lemme guess, she promised you a goddamn fruit basket?"

I smirk, holding his furious gaze. "Yeah, and your anaconda attack just added three tickets to Disney on Ice. So, thank *you* for being so predictable. Now, get your shit. We're leaving."

N ovy makes us park at the hospital, demanding we leave his truck in the lot.

"How are we supposed to get home?" I call as he snatches his keys from my hand and takes off running across the lot, dressed in half a suit.

"I don't give a fuck," he calls over his shoulder.

I cross my arms with a huff. "Well, this is what I get for letting Poppy corner me at a buffet table. I am never doing her another favor again. I don't care how much she flips her hair."

Chuckling, Henrik drapes an arm around my shoulders. "He'll be alright. Once the baby is born, he'll forget how he even got here. All that will matter is that he's with his family."

I glance around this dark hospital parking lot. "I guess we have to call a car to come pick us up. Both our cars are still back at the arena."

He takes out his phone, already pulling up the app. But then his shoulders stiffen. "Wait—where is Karro?"

I wince. "Uhh . . . yeah. So, I figured we should probably keep her out of the way of the great, fire-breathing Novikov."

"Where is she?"

"I let her go have a sleepover with Emma Langley." Turning to him, I brace my hands on his shoulders. "And I'm sorry, okay? I *know* I should have asked you first. You have final say on all matters Karro, and this was her first sleepover, and I know that's big. But I feel like you have to trust me with at least a few things when it comes to her care. It doesn't have to all be on you, Hen. And Tess is totally reliable—"

"Teddy . . . *Teddy*," he says over me, gripping my arms with both hands.

I take a breath, waiting.

"I'm not mad. You have every right to help make decisions about Karro's care. And if you trust Tess Langley, then so do I."

"You're really not mad?"

"I'm not mad," he repeats, his mouth tipping with a smile. "You know what I am?"

I lean away. "Uhh . . . hungry? Tired, probably. That was a crazy game. I—"

His eyes flash with secret meaning, which has my stomach flipping.

"Oh. Wait, seriously?"

Stepping closer, he wraps an arm around me. "Know what I was thinking earlier? Watching you hold your own against Novikov?"

I fight a blush, remembering the way I squealed and flopped like a fish. I was raised by three sisters. They taught me to fight with words, not fists. "I don't know if I'd call it holding my own . . ."

His hands smooth across my back as he turns me, pressing me up against the side of Novy's truck. Leaning in, he kisses my jaw, his beard soft and bristling. I roll my neck, giving him more room. His kisses are soft, seeking, but then his fingers dig into my locs and he jerks my head back. "He had his hands on you," he growls in my ear. "And I wanted to *rip* them off."

"Henrik—"

His teeth scrape over my skin, drawing a sound like a whimper from my throat. "No one touches you but me, mitt hjärta. *Say it.*"

"No one," I pant, moving my hips against him, desperate for some friction.

He drops a hand between us, cupping my dick, and I wanna die. Oh god, he's never been so deliberate before. His hold on me is firm as he presses in, practically lifting me off the ground. His other hand stays twisted up in my hair. I'm on my toes, pressed against the side of this damn truck, with Henrik holding my cash and fucking prizes like a dragon clutching his treasure.

"Baby, please."

"What do you want?" He kisses along my neck, nipping and nuzzling my ear. "Speak. Tell me what you want from me."

"I want more."

"What more?" He squeezes my crotch tighter, and I think I might just come. Is there such a thing as a seismic orgasm? Because this isn't biology anymore—it's geology. Like how compression makes diamonds.

Fuck, I can't even think.

I cling to his shoulders. "Henrik, baby, please. I want more. I want *you*. I want—god, I want everything. Anything you'll give me."

His hold on me relaxes a little. "I've never been with a man before."

I turn my face to his, my nose brushing his cheek. "I know. But you're already so good at everything we've tried. And you can't fake chemistry like this," I add, pressing my hand over his heart. "What we have? How this feels? Do you know how fucking rare this is? Not to get too cheesy, but in the immortal words of Kiss, I was made for lovin' you, baby."

He chuckles, leaning away with a shake his head.

"What?"

He cups my cheek, smoothing his thumb over my freckles. He likes to do that, following the line of my cheekbone. "Du är så vacker."

I grin, feeling nervous. "What does that mean?"

Leaning in, he kisses me. "It means, I'm taking you home now."

I perk up. "Yeah? And then what?"

"And then I'm taking off all your clothes," he says against my lips. "And I'm putting you in my bathtub."

55

HENRIK

Teddy sits naked in my lap, straddling my legs. His hands are braced on my shoulders while mine frame his narrow waist. This bathtub is meant for total immersion, so there's a seat inside, wide enough for us to fit comfortably. Hot water covers us to mid-chest, steam misting our cheeks. His locs are tied up on the crown of his head. A spray of thin end pieces stick out on the sides. I wish I had a camera now. I would capture him just like this—naked, and glistening, and perfect.

This feels like a timeless moment. You get so few of them in life. Moments when every part of you is set to record. It's not just something you see with your eyes or feel with your hands. Your soul takes a picture too.

And human memory is such a fickle thing. Mom taught me that. You can't rely on just your eyes and ears to record the passing of time. That's all we get in this life: memories that fade over time. Like photographs, the edges become warped and discolored, sometimes damaged beyond all repair.

But a truly timeless moment? Moments even your soul sits up and takes notice of? Those make an imprint deeper than a photograph. Those last forever.

Reaching my hand out of the bath, I touch Teddy's face. Water slips down my arm, dripping back into the tub. All the while, he looks at me, breathing with me, *being* with me. This beautiful man, made of sharp angles. His hard cock waits in the water. I haven't touched it yet, but I'm going to. Tonight. And soon.

For now, it's enough just to look at him.

This man came crashing into my life with all the subtly of an earthquake. He shook me to my very foundation. In the span of weeks, I've been remade. There was the Henrik Karlsson before Teddy. And there will be the Henrik Karlsson after.

"What are you thinking?" he whispers, breaking our silence. He lifts a hand too, his wet fingertips brushing over my brow.

I lean back against the wall of the tub, smiling up at him. "I'm thinking I want to photograph you, sitting here just like this, looking down at me with that look in your eyes."

He shifts on my lap, water sloshing. "Do you do that a lot?"

"What? Take pictures of beautiful naked men on my lap? No. Never."

He grins. "I just meant take pictures in general. I saw all the camera stuff back in Stockholm."

I let my eyes feast on him, dropping my gaze to his shoulder as I trail my fingers slowly down his arm. "Sometimes."

"What do you like to photograph?"

He's nervous talking, trying to distract himself from the feel of my hands on him, trying to keep this moving slow. I allow it. "I like macro photography. Not that I'm any good at it. I don't have the time to do it properly."

"Macro photography is fitting for you, the man who pays attention to every detail."

"Life is in the details," I murmur, slipping my hand under his arm to brush my thumb over his dark nipple.

He shivers, leaning closer rather than away. Bracing himself with one hand on the tub, he runs the other through my hair, giving the roots a tug until my head tips back. "Do you ever photograph people?"

I like the feel of his hands on me, the tension on my hair as he tugs at my roots. "Only at family functions. Petra would shove a camera at me and demand pictures on holidays. I like portraiture too. I've just never experimented with it much."

Smiling, he reaches over the side of the tub and plucks his phone off the stool. Norah Jones pauses as he turns on his camera app and hands me the phone. "Take my picture."

"Teddy ..."

"Hey, it's a good camera. With the sexy lighting in here, I'm gonna look hot," he adds, nodding around at the electric candles. He strategically placed them around the room while the tub was filling with water.

I take the phone, and he stays leaning over me, shifting his hips until our cocks touch. I stifle my groan as he grins. "You did that on purpose."

He laughs, sobering as he focuses on the camera. "Tell me what you want. If you don't like this angle or—"

"It's perfect. Hold still." I place the phone low, near my chin, angling it up at him. I want to capture the feeling of him floating over me, the light around him golden. I take the shot and check it. The candles cast shadows over the sharp angles of his shoulders, his muscled chest, his jawline. Golden light warms the fair brown hue of his skin.

He sits up. "Well?"

Turning the phone, I show him the picture.

He actually blushes. He's naked in my lap, eager for more intimacy, and a photo makes him blush. He glances down at me. "Do you like it?"

Taking the phone from him, I set it aside, never breaking our eye contact. With my free hand, I cup the back of his neck and pull him down to me. Our lips lock in a kiss, and then he's melting into me. I've never felt this with another person. This level of trust, this feeling of intimacy. Teddy was right—this is chemistry. There's something about our chemical makeups that just works.

Strange, because on paper we make no sense. He's loud and chaotic, always changing his food order. One day he wants banana pancakes stacked with syrup. The next it's breakfast tacos. And he likes movies that make him cry. He'll watch them *so* he can cry. He feels everything at once, all the time, with no filter and no pause button. He ought to drive me crazy. He *does* drive me crazy.

And yet, I can't seem to get enough.

With Teddy, I fear there is no enough.

All the while, here I am, quiet and contained. I could eat the same thing for breakfast every day for the rest of my life without complaint. I overanalyze everything. All things ordered, everything in its place. Teddy once accused me of being so good at compartmentalizing that I put living in a box.

He was right. Before he and Karro came into my life, I wasn't living. I was merely existing. I was biding time on this earth.

No, I was *wasting* time.

Well, I don't want to waste another minute. This beautiful man is in my arms, and he loves me. With all my faults, all my fears and over-rationalizations. He's been biding his time for years, just waiting for me to notice him.

I see him now. I can't look away. And at the end of my life, I don't want a handful of moments to look back on and treasure. I want a library of cataloged prints. I want messy stacks of memories, too many to fit on the shelves—with Karro, with Teddy, with the people who make our lives full. I'm starting now. Teddy is in my arms, and I'm not letting go.

"Mitt hjärta," I whisper against his lips. My strong heart. My Teddy. Breaking our kiss, I frame his face with both hands. He smiles down at me, drunk on my affection. My fear of intimacy means nothing with him in my arms. With him, I am safe. With him, there will be only pleasure. Only love.

"What's wrong?" he whispers.

"Du är min nu," I say with a smile. "Du betyder allt för mig."

He runs both hands through my hair, returning my smile. "I'm gonna assume you just said that I'm a really good kisser and that you'd like me to keep going."

I pull him back to me. "Never stop."

He's so eager, wrapping himself around me, pressing in with his hips until my hard cock is pinned against my stomach. We kiss some more, hands seeking. But the warm water is affecting my senses. It's a distraction I don't need. I want to feel just Teddy—his skin against mine, his warmth, his pulse.

"Up." I pull on his arms, and he leans away, distracted.

"What?"

"Stand up."

"Hen—"

"Trust me."

Scooting back off my lap, he rises out of the water until he's standing. The water sluices down his abdomen, dripping from his fingertips. His hard cock waits right before my face, nestled in a thatch of soft black hair. Engorged as it is, it's a shade or two darker than his fair brown skin.

He must know I'm looking because he wraps his hand around it, giving it a slow stroke. "Keep looking at me like that, and I'm gonna have an eyegasm."

"A what?"

"You know, it's like an orgasm, but I'm getting off because your eyes are on me." His smile falls. "It was a joke, but it sucked. Are we getting out or—" He gasps as I reach out and wrap my hand around his on his cock. "Henrik—"

"Let go."

His hand drops to his side, and then it's only me stroking him. He tips his head back, eyes closed.

"Look at me."

He curses, his head rolling on his neck to look down at me. He blinks his eyes open. They're glassy with desire as I stroke him. Slow. Measured. Deliberate. Those are all the things he loves about me, right?

"I'm gonna come," he whispers, biting his bottom lip.

I stop moving my hand. "Wait."

He groans. "Fuck. Seriously? You're finally fucking touching me, and now you're gonna edge me?"

"What's edge?" I give his cock another caress.

"Seriously? You don't know?"

"Not in this context."

"Well, I'm not telling you."

"Why?"

"Because I don't want you to fucking do it to me," he says on a breath.

I smile. This feels good. I feel in control. I reach out with my other hand and reel him in by the hip.

"Oh, fuck," he whines. "Fuck, fuck—*ah*—"

I wrap my mouth around him, sucking on the tip of his cock. I've never done this before, but he seems to like it. He certainly seems to enjoy doing it to me. Thanks to him, I know how good it feels to receive this kind of pleasure. I try to replicate the motions he's made on me, luxuriating in the feel of his soft skin, the glide of my lips along his hardness.

"Slower." He fists a hand in my wet hair, moving me how he wants. "Slow, baby—*fuck*—"

I slow down, opening my mouth to lick the side of his shaft.

"Henrik, I'm gonna—"

"No," I growl, moving my mouth away from him.

"Oh, fuck you. Don't tease me."

"I want us to come together."

He blinks down at me, fingers still twisted in my hair. "What?"

I stand, sloshing the water.

His eyes go wide. "What are you doing?"

"Get out."

"Like, of the tub ... or your life?"

Using the seat as a step, I climb out of the tub, not caring if I get water on the floor. I grab a towel, making quick work of drying off. Teddy follows me out and I hand him my towel, watching as he dries himself off. His cock bobs as he rubs the towel down his legs.

I can't keep waiting. I want this too much. I want *him*. I pull him to me, my mouth seeking his as we kiss again. He sighs, dropping the towel at our feet. His hands are gentle but strong as they wrap around my back. I step into him as he smoothes his hands down, down, until they're gripping my butt. I groan, biting his lip as I do the same to him, hands flexing over the tight globes of his ass.

"Fuck," he pants against my mouth. "How am I supposed to stop touching you, huh? You're so beautiful, Hen. Feel so good."

I kiss down his neck and across his collarbone. Dropping a hand between us, I take his cock, aligning it with mine, and stroke us together. His forehead drops to my shoulder. Then he rocks against

me with his hips, sliding his cock in and out of my fist. There's a riot
of sensations—the friction of my calloused hand, the warmth, the
glide of our sensitive skin.

Teddy wraps his hand around mine, fucking harder into our
fists. "I'm gonna come." He lifts his head off my shoulder, chasing a
kiss.

"No."

"Don't say no," he cries.

"I want mouths," I say against his lips.

"What?"

"I want to taste you. I want to come into you as you come into
me. Du är min, Teddy. Jag behöver det här . . . . behöver dig."

He huffs. "Your translator—"

"It's not broken," I say over him. Leaning away, I hold his gaze.
"My emotions come from the deepest part of me, and the deepest
part of me is Swedish. Accept my words as they are."

Slowly, he nods.

"Jag är kär i dig."

He groans. "Fuck, I've gotta learn fucking Swedish."

"Later. I'll teach you everything, mitt hjärta. For now, get on your
knees."

He drops to his knees so willingly. He always goes so willingly
for me. I surprise him when I drop to my knees too. "What are you
doing?"

I smile. "I'm going to suck your cock as you suck mine. We come
together, or not at all."

56

TEDDY

Oh god, is this really happening? Henrik is lying me back on this plush bathroom rug, chasing his filthy words with a kiss. Anything. He can have anything. "Have you done this before?" he asks, his naked body stretching out alongside mine.

I wrap my hand around our dicks, aligning them as I scoot closer. I can't help but sling a leg over his hip and grind a little. He fucking loves it. He's growling like a bear, gripping my ass as he kisses me again. It's messy and frantic. We're both nearing the edge of our control.

"Teddy . . ."

Right. Fuck, he asked me a question. He wants to sixty-nine with me, but he's not sure what to do. "I'll show you," I say, unwilling to confirm or deny to my possessive husband whether I have the requisite experience.

He says something else in Swedish, gripping my ass and rolling onto his back. I roll with him, straddling his lap again. Smoothing my hands over his hairy chest, I smile down at him. I love the power trip that comes from bottoming from the top. And I *know* Henrik is a top. Once he gets the hang of this, I just know his possessive side will come out to play. And then there will be nowhere for me to hide.

I can't fucking wait.

But that's not what tonight is about. Tonight is about slow and sensual. It's about building to a point of mutual euphoria. He wants the give-and-take, the push and pull of intimacy that feels like sinking into a warm bath.

Well, we already took the bath. Now, let's slow burn the fuck out of this orgasm. He wants a little mutual edging? Baby, I can do this all night. Folding over him, I brace my hands to either side of his head and start kissing across his chest. He's been edging me with action. I want to try edging him with words. "You want my cock, baby?"

His hands splay across my upper back, coaxing me to continue. "Yes."

I hum against his warm skin, nuzzling his chest, flicking my tongue over his nipple until he curses in Swedish. "You're so sensitive," I praise. "Look how well you react to me. You like when I tease you, baby? Like when I kiss you?"

"Yes."

"Where?"

"Här." He turns his head to expose his neck.

I crawl up his body, lowering to my elbows until he's carrying most of my weight. "Här?" I tease, rolling the *r* in a way that I hope sounds sexy as I brush a finger over his pulse point.

He nods.

Smiling, I plant an open-mouthed kiss to the point, sucking and teasing, scraping with my teeth until he wraps himself around me and rolls me under him again. I gasp, landing on my back with Henrik between my spread thighs. He grinds down with his hips, our dicks pinned between us. Yeah, he knows what he's doing. His instincts are taking over.

Tipping my head back, eyes closed, I ride the moment with him. This works for me. I can definitely come like this. It'll shoot all over our stomachs. So primal. So high school. "God, baby, don't stop."

"No." There's a smile in his tone this time as he fucking stops again.

"No," I echo. Mine comes out much more of a petulant whine.

He grins down at me. "Is this what the edge is? Telling you no?"

I snort a laugh. "It's not a noun. It's a verb. To edge. Edging. And yes, you're fucking edging me, and it's the fucking worst."

He pulls away slightly. "Do you really not like it?"

I stifle a groan, running my hands down the taut muscles of his back until I can grab two handfuls of his perfectly sculpted ass. Then, because I'm a brat, I give both cheeks a hard smack.

This man is so fucking perfect. He clenches for me, choking on a gasp. "Teddy!"

I laugh again. "I fucking love it, you caveman. Are you kidding? Literally any attention from you, I'm gonna eat with a spoon. You're my kryptonite, Henrik. You're my fucking sun."

His brow furrows. "I understand the kryptonite reference."

I lie back with a smile. "Good. Otherwise, this relationship is over."

"What do you mean by the sun?"

Fuck. I'm not sure if I want to explain that one. "Uhh . . . it's from mythology. The fall of Icarus. It's no big deal."

He pushes up with both hands, the corded muscles of his arms taut. His denim-blue eyes search my face, looking past all my walls in that way he does.

I clear my throat, focusing my own attention somewhere around his chin. "Do you know it?"

"I know it."

Of course he fucking does. He listens to ancient history podcasts while he exercises. He speaks three languages. He knows about macro photography and Dadaism.

"You think I mean to harm you?"

I blink back my tears, staring up at the ceiling. "The sun doesn't mean to harm anyone. The sun just is."

"But you think I'm harmful. Proximity to me is dangerous for you. That is the story of Icarus, yes?"

"Henrik—"

"Icarus flew too close to the sun, and the sun melted his wings. He crashed into the sea and drowned, Teddy."

"Yeah, I know the fucking story."

He tips my chin, forcing me to look at him. "That is not our story."

I hold his fierce gaze. "I don't want it to be."

"If I am the sun, you are the sea."

"What?"

"In the story," he presses, "Icarus is warned not to fly too close to sun or sea. It's not the sun that kills him, Teddy. It's the sea. Both are wild and untamed. Both are strong. You're not a victim of the forces that surround you. You *are* the force. Depthless, endless, ever reaching. You're not Icarus. You're the sea."

I lie beneath him, chest heaving, mind shattered. I'm not Icarus. Is that possible? And I'm not the sun that shines too bright, damning others to fall from the sky. I'm the sea. I take the sun's light and reflect it back. I let it warm me but not devour.

God, this feels like a revelation. My mother was wrong about us. I'm not pouring into him, giving my soul away. I'm just reflecting light back to him. What I give is freely offered. It's okay that we're different. It's okay that he's quiet and I'm loud. It's okay that I overreact and he overthinks. We can balance each other. We can build something together: a partnership, a marriage, a beautiful life shared.

I press a hand over his heart, resolve burning in my chest. Looking up, I open the floodgates of my own heart, letting him see into my fullest depths. "You're mine. Henrik—"

"I know," he groans, collapsing atop me as we kiss. "I'm yours," he says against my lips. "And you're mine."

Yes. *His*. Please, god, make this last.

He rolls to the side, pulling me with him, our legs tangling together as we keep kissing. The slow burn is over. Now we're both on fire. "Show me what to do. Teddy—"

"Lie on your back." I push his shoulder. "That's it, baby." Once he's on his back, I roll up to my knees and turn around, straddling his face. My hard dick is ready for him. Slipping a hand between my legs, I angle my dick down. "Take it," I command. "Put me in your mouth—*yes*—"

My praise comes out on a hiss as Henrik wraps his mouth around my tip, groaning out his own relief. *This*. We need this. You can't just mess around with this kind of soul connection. We need to be joined. Whatever else he wants from my body, he can have. I'll show him everything. But first, we share this.

Balancing my weight on my hands, hips canted up so I don't choke him with my dick, I suck his proud length into the back of my throat. I take him to the root, moaning with want as I breathe in his masculine scent. The sensation of giving and receiving quickly has me spiraling. I feel like a firecracker about to burst.

Henrik's hands fist my ass as he sucks the tip of my dick. With my hands trembling, it's all I can do to keep upright. "More," he growls, pulling on my hips. "I'm close. Give me more."

He's close? I'm closer. This is the edge. In this moment, we're both Icarus. Hand in hand, we're about to fucking leap. I lower my hips, giving him more, and he takes. He's so goddamn eager. His mouth is wet and warm, and I can't help myself from rutting into him. This feels too good. There's candlelight, and the room is warm and steamy from the bath. Our energy is primal. It's a goddamn bacchanal.

"Yes!" My adrenaline takes over, and now I'm balancing on one hand. The other goes between his legs to cup his balls, squeezing as I hollow my cheeks, sucking his length. I slip my hand lower, my fingers seeking. All it takes is the gentlest of pressure with two fingers on his asshole and he's rocking up with his hips, crying out around my dick as he releases.

His cum fills my mouth, and that's all the urging I need to leap. I'm spiraling through the air, orgasm shattering through me as I come down Henrik's throat. God, I've wanted this for so long. It's beyond euphoria. His hands hold me tight enough to bruise as he swallows what I give him. He hums wordless sounds of praise, unable to speak with my dick choking him.

Spent and exhausted, I start to sink. This is a different kind of fall than the one I feared. Best of all, Henrik is there to catch me. He turns me and rolls with me until we're both on our sides, curled around each other, holding one another in a tangle of limbs.

We breathe together, floating down like a pair of autumn leaves. The room comes back into focus and I grunt, shifting the bundled edge of the towel out from under my hip. Henrik watches me with a glassy, contented look on his face. He's calm now, at peace.

"Thank you," he whispers, his fingers trailing down the line of my shoulder.

"For what?"

I feel his smile as he leans in, kissing my brow. "For waiting for me."

57

HENRIK

Stepping into the closet, fresh from my shower, I sigh. On the valet hook, Teddy has set out a cherry-red T-shirt and a pair of matching tracksuit bottoms. On the shelf, there's what looks suspiciously like a googly-eyed crab hat and a pair of matching, mitten-like claws.

Exiting the closet with all haste, I hold the top of my towel in place with one hand as I march through the apartment. I find Teddy and Karolina in her bathroom. She's balancing on her good leg at the mirror while he stands behind, styling a red wig on her head with a curling iron. She's chatting in an animated mix of English and Swedish that has him laughing.

"I'm not wearing a costume," I declare.

He catches my reflection in the mirror, eyes narrowing. Slowly, he sets the curling iron aside. Kissing the top of Karro's wig, he leaves her at the counter. "Hold still a minute, honey bun."

"Morbror, look! We have shells for my hair," she calls in Swedish, holding up a pair of colorful starfish.

"Very pretty," I call back.

Teddy comes out of the bathroom, his gaze taking me in from the wet hair on my head to my bare toes. He stops right in front of me, his hands on his hips. "You have something to say?"

Why do I feel like I've already lost this argument? I dare to hold my ground. "I'm not wearing a costume."

It looks like he's already wearing his costume. It's a T-shirt with yellow and blue stripes and a pair of matching blue shorts. Behind him, Karolina stands at the counter dressed as a red-haired mermaid. It's not hard for me to put the pieces of this tableau together. But I will not go before the whole of the sports world dressed as Sebastian the Crab.

"I'll still go," I quickly add. "I want to go."

He crosses his arms, waiting.

I groan. "Teddy, come on."

He raises a brow, still waiting.

Perhaps he'll allow a compromise. It's worth a try. "Fine, but I'm not wearing the hat."

He glances around the room. "Who do you actually think you're talking to right now?"

Rubbing the back of my neck, I stifle another groan. "Teddy . . ."

"No, because I'm confused. What part of this seems open to negotiation?"

I stand here, utterly defeated.

He knows it too. Smiling, he steps forward and wraps his hand around the top of my towel. Reeling me in, he presses a soft kiss to my lips. My hands can't help but reach for him. Leaning closer, he makes a hungry sound low in his throat that sharpens all my senses. "You know I can't resist you in a towel," he whispers, his tone full of heat. "So, here's my compromise: Be a good little crab for me, and later tonight, I'll suck on your balls until you scream. Deal?"

Fuck.

My husband really doesn't know how to play fair.

"Hey, Karlsson!" Langley waves me down. "Whoa, fun costume, guys."

I wave back.

He's dressed in a medieval-looking costume, with a short red cape and a red hat. Behind him, Tess wanders closer, walking hand in hand with their daughter, Emma.

Ah, *Sleeping Beauty*. I see it now. Tess is the witch, Maleficent, complete with horns and a walking staff. Emma drops her hand and comes running up in a pink Aurora dress. "Wow, Lina!"

The girls talk excitedly as Karro shows her all the decorative pieces of her costume. Teddy went all out for this, covering Karro's wheelchair to make it look like a rock in the ocean. Karro is perched on the chair in her mermaid costume, red hair flowing down her back. It's charming.

And, yes, I'm in my full crab costume. Dressed as Flounder, Teddy pushes the chair while I fumble at passing out candy with these damn mitten claws.

We're at the Rays' annual Boo-tacular Trunk-or-Treat event. Poppy and her team have been hosting it for years. Each year, they pick a community to support, and the whole team comes out to the parking lot of the practice center. We invite members of that community and do a mix of trunk-or-treating and food banking. The kids go home with candy, and their parents get a month's worth of groceries.

"Smile, everyone!" A photographer holds up a camera, and Tess and Langley step in to either side of us, posing for a picture.

"Have you seen the new baby?" asks Tess.

"What new baby?" I reply.

"Poppy's new baby."

Next to me, Teddy stiffens. "Oh god, they're here?"

"Yeah. She said they're not staying long though," Tess replies. "But you know Poppy. She can't resist micromanaging an event, even with a newborn."

Two weeks have already passed since we drove Novy to the hospital. NHL players don't get anything resembling paternity leave, but he's been a ghost when he's not at practice or on the ice. I know they had another little girl, but I haven't heard her name yet.

Teddy looks around, eyes wide. "Ohmygod." He grabs my arm. "Babe, they're right over there."

Langley follows his gaze, clearly confused. "What's up?"

"He thinks Novy still hates him," I tease.

"Shut up. You didn't see the look of haunted betrayal in his eyes."

I pat his arm. "Why don't you be a good little guppy and go say hello."

"Are you kidding? Flounder is a total coward."

Grinning ear to ear, Tess shouts, waving them over. "Poppy! Girl, hey!"

"Seriously," Teddy hisses at her. "That staff better be able to do actual magic, you witch!"

Tess just laughs.

With a wave from Poppy, the St. James-Novikov-Morrow clan comes wandering our way. I try to make sense of their group costume. The families always come dressed in theme. Somewhere, the Prices are here dressed as all the characters from the board game Candy Land. It's one of Karolina's favorite games, so I recognized them on sight. Rachel is dressed as the kindly old Gramma Nutt. Caleb is the Peppermint Prince, Ilmari is King Candy, and Jake is strutting around, swirling the ends of a red velvet cape as Lord Licorice. Their boys are dressed as the Candy Land kids. I spy Caleb and Jake down the row of open car trunks, waiting in line to help their boys into the bounce house.

"Hey, Poppy," Tess says again. "Girl, you look great."

Poppy huffs out a breath, shifting her hold on the newborn bundled in her arms. She's dressed as a witch in a lacy black dress with a black pointy hat. "I don't know how much fun we have left in us today."

Novy looks relaxed as he gives me a nod. I let him take one good swing at me when he first came back to work after the baby's birth. Since then, he's been cordial. Next to me, Teddy is vibrating with nerves.

"What are you supposed to be?" I say.

Novy's wearing a black cowboy hat and a black suit with a grey vest and a red ascot. "I'm Doc Holliday," he says, spreading his arms wide. "You know, from *Tombstone*?" He narrows his eyes at Poppy. "Only someone wouldn't let me bring the shotgun. The costume kind of falls apart without it."

She huffs. "This is a children's trunk-or-treat event. The toy shotgun will be staying in the car."

I glance between them. "What does the cowboy have to do with a witch?"

"Absolutely nothing," Poppy relies.

"But I thought we all had to come in theme?"

Hanging back, trapped in conversation with some fans, Morrow is dressed as Spider-Man without the mask. Their son darts around in a ninja costume while their daughter stands over by Emma and Karro dressed as what looks like a cat wearing an astronaut helmet.

Poppy just huffs. "I live in a house with six chefs, Henrik, honey. Not a line cook in sight. So, the only theme here is chaos. I at least tried to match with Gracie when she said she wanted to be a cat. I thought, 'Right, I'll be a witch.' But then she informed us she wanted to be a 'space cat' right as we were all headed out the door. It was all we could do to fashion her that helmet to stave off a complete meltdown."

"Well, you look great," Tess assures her.

"Yeah, I love a little chaos," says Langley.

"Only adds to the fun," echoes Tess. "Plus, this way everyone is happy and wearing what they want."

"Hear, hear," I mutter, flexing my hands in these itchy crab mittens.

"So, uhh . . . what's the baby's name?" asks Teddy, finally breaking his silence.

Novy crosses his arms, glaring at him. "Tell the traitor nothing."

Poppy sighs. "Lukas, honey, you have to forgive Teddy. He was acting on my orders. If you need to be mad at someone, be mad at me."

"I can't be mad at you. You birthed my baby."

She flashes him a dazzling smile. "She's a good one, isn't she?"

He softens, his shoulders relaxing. "She's perfect."

"Okay, so show her off to your friend Teddy and bury this hatchet, while I go to the ladies' room." She shuffles the baby into his arms as Novy mutters a grunt of protest. Then she sweeps off to collect Grace. "Space Kitty, let's go. Potty break!"

"We gotta go too," says Tess, giving my anxious husband a pat on the shoulder. "But y'all have fun with this."

"Tess, come on," he pleads.

"Let's go, Aurora," she calls to her daughter. "We've got pumpkins to carve!"

In the Langleys' absence, Novy and Teddy stare each other down. Nov sways slightly to soothe his fussing baby. Slowly, Teddy holds out his arms. "So, uhh . . . can I hold her—"

"No," he growls.

"Oh, come on, man. This is total bullshit. I only did what your partners thought was best. Morrow told me not to give you the keys too. And it all worked out. Look." He gestures at the baby. "She's perfect, right? And you didn't even miss a thing. So, you have to forgive me already."

"I don't *have* to do anything."

Teddy flaps his arms. "Well, so what then? What do you want from me? What'll it take, huh? Name your freaking price."

Novy's eyes flash with interest. "Seriously?"

"Yes! What, do you want your suit back?"

"I—" Novy's mouth snaps shut as his eyes narrow. "Wait, you still have that?"

Teddy shrugs. "Maybe."

"Then, yes, asshole. I want that back."

"Fine. What else?"

He smirks as he considers. "Oh, I think you know what I want."

Teddy points a finger at him. "Only within reason. Don't be a greedy fuck."

Now, Novy smiles, and I feel the need to inch in closer to Teddy's side. "What do you think is fair, Doc?"

Teddy considers. "Ten minutes?"

"Try an hour. Every week. For the rest of the season."

"You know what? Maybe I'm fine with you being mad at me." Crossing his arms, Teddy glares at the baby. "Maybe I don't even want to know her name."

Novy gasps, pulling back, as Morrow finally steps in behind him, one hand on his shoulder. "Hey, guys. Ted, Karlsson." He smirks at the stupid crab claw mittens on my hands. "Whoa, nice costume there, bud." Sensing the mood, he glances between Novy and Teddy. "Wait, what's happening right now?"

Teddy holds Novy's stare. "Your partner is setting the terms for his forgiveness. In this moment, I'm forgetting why I'm even sorry."

"What are you negotiating?" I ask.

"My time," Teddy replies, still staring Novy down.

I glance between them. "Your time?"

"Yeah, he wants another massage. That's the price of his forgiveness."

Heat prickles the back of my neck. The thought of Teddy putting his hands on one of my teammates for any length of time has me itching to jerk these stupid crab mittens off and punch something. Which is completely irrational, because that's his job. And he's good at it. The guys all praise him for how skilled he is as a physical therapist.

But it's been six years since he's massaged me. Back then, I wouldn't have considered what it feels like to have his hands on me as anything other than providing therapeutic pain relief. Now? His every touch sets a fire under my skin. I've never felt this way before. What once held no interest for me now feels like all I can think about. The possessive part of me doesn't like the idea of his hands on anyone but me.

I have to get over this.

All the same, I inch closer, trying to make it look casual when I put my arm around his waist, my mitten-clad hand resting on his hip.

"Fine," he says at Novy. "I will give you three one-hour massages, redeemable at a time of your choosing. But I get full forgiveness for driving you to the hospital. And I get to hold her," he adds, nodding to the baby.

Now Morrow is the one narrowing his eyes. "Do I get a say in this?"

"No," Teddy and Novy say at the same time.

Interesting. Perhaps Morrow and I have a little possessive jealousy in common? As if reading my mind, he just gives me a subtle shake of his head, his jaw clenched tight.

Teddy reaches out his hand. "Are we agreed?"

Grinning, Novy shifts the baby to one arm and holds out his hand to shake.

Teddy squeezes tight, pulling Novy in closer. "But you make any creepy noises, I am duct-taping your mouth shut. Nonnegotiable."

Novy tips his head back on a laugh. "Come on, Doc. Don't threaten me with a good time."

Groaning, Teddy drops his hand. "Shut up and let me hold the baby."

Novy shifts the baby over to Teddy's arms, and Teddy lights up like a candle. He's gentle, cooing at her. "Well, isn't she just the prettiest thing? Babe, look."

Leaning in, my hand still braced on his hip, I glance over his shoulder at the newborn. Her face is scrunched in a frown as Teddy sways with her. She's wearing an outfit dotted with jack-o'-lanterns and black cats.

"What's her name?" Teddy asks.

"Fiona Lane Morrow," says Novy. "We've all been calling her Fi."

Teddy coos over her some more. "Hi, Miss FiFi." He glances up. "What's the Lane from?"

"My grandmother," Morrow replies, his arm around Novy's shoulder. All his jealousy from a moment ago has evaporated as he looks lovingly at his daughter.

Teddy hands the baby back over to Novy. "She looks just like her sister."

Novy is gentle for such a giant, cradling her close. His eyes practically glow as he looks down at her too. "She's our angel."

Leaning in, Morrow kisses his cheek. "You two make beautiful babies."

Nodding once at me, Novy turns to Teddy. "I'm cashing in my first massage next week. Be ready."

Teddy salutes him, giving Morrow a wave as they turn and head off in search of Poppy. Clapping his hands together, Teddy calls out to Karro. "Okay, Miss Ariel, I think it's time we all go get our faces painted to look like fairy unicorns!"

"Yes! Then pumpkins!"

"Then more candy," he teases.

"Yay!"

Teddy takes my hand and gives it a squeeze. "Come on, Sebastian." Leaning in, he speaks so only I can hear him. "You're being such a good crab for me."

His words ping inside my brain like a loose puck hitting the walls. He *did* promise a reward for my good behavior. Stuffing all my irrational jealousy inside one of the many mental compartments my husband is so fond of, I follow wherever he leads.

58

TEDDY

"**D**id you have fun today, min lilla mermaid?" I tuck Karro into bed with her stuffed animals, and she nods, her eyes bleary with fatigue.

Henrik and I washed the rainbow tiger stripes from our faces as soon as we got home, but Karro cried when Henrik told her she had to wash off her glittery unicorn. With a gentle nudge from me, he relented. Our new deal is that Karro can wear her face paint to bed tonight, and we'll wash it off in the morning. Also in the morning, she has to eat two eggs and take her vitamins without complaining. It feels like an even trade.

"Are you leaving?" she murmurs.

"I don't have to. I can sit right here while you fall asleep. Want me to sing 'Part of Your World' again?"

Her mouth turns down into that little pout I've come to love so much. She reaches for Teddy the Bear, wrapping her casted arm around him. "They said you're leaving."

I'm distracted, fluffing her pillows. "Who said what, honey?"

"A mommy. At the apples. She said you're leaving."

I go still. We stopped by a caramel apple booth just before we left the event tonight. The kiddos could all dip and decorate their apples with different fixings. The two that Karolina and Henrik made are sitting on the kitchen island. "Honey, who said that? Can you remember what she looked like?"

Karro shakes her head. "I don't want you to go."

I drop down on my elbow. "Oh, honey, no. I don't know why that mommy said that, but it's not true, okay?"

Tears well in her eyes. "You won't leave?"

My protective instincts flare. Some of the other WAGs were definitely milling around with their kids. I swear to fuck, if I find out who was talking about us like that in front of my little girl, I'm gonna sling her around by her goddamn hair. Swallowing my anger, I focus on Karro. "Honey, look at me."

She glances up, her bottom lip still quivering.

"I will never leave you. Not ever. You and me? We're friends for life, right?"

Slowly, she nods.

Bending down, I kiss her brow, avoiding the unicorn paint. Then the words spill forth, like I've been dying to say them all my life. "Oh, honey, I love you."

Her eyes brighten as she smiles up at me. "You do?"

"Of course I do. Can you teach me in Swedish? I want you to know in both languages. Say 'I love you.'"

"Jag älskar dig."

"Jag älskar dig," I repeat. "Karolina, you're my best little friend, and I love you. I want to always be in your life."

She squeezes her bear. "And Morbror?"

"He loves you too, honey. So much."

But she shakes her head. "You won't leave him?"

Fuck. How did I ever think this could go any other way? There's no faking a marriage when a child is involved. There is no temporary. There's no "just helping out a friend." Henrik may have first caught my attention, but Karolina reeled me in. The two of them have me bound. I'm in this now, to whatever end. I take her hand in mine, giving it a kiss. "When I married your morbror, I made him a vow. I'll not break it. I'm here for as long as you both want me to stay. Is that okay?"

Sighing, she settles back against her pillows, a frown still on her face.

I brush the wisps of blonde hair off her brow. "What's wrong, honey?"

"Mamma said I could be flower girl."

"What?"

"At Morbror's wedding." She looks down at her bear. "I would be flower girl, Mamma said."

I glance to the framed picture sitting on her nightstand. It's a picture of Petra with her arms around Karro. Both are laughing, smiling at the camera, as Karro holds up a bunch of freshly picked flowers.

This admonishment from this five-year-old stings worse than any questions about me leaving ever could. Deep down, I know it's the same reason my family is still so upset with me. They're worried about my choices, sure. And they're right to be worried. I was emotional, irrational, and rash—all my worst traits—multiplied by, like, a thousand.

But I'm also their Teddy. They fed me, raised me, helped me with my homework, got me to swim meets and track practice. They went to every graduation, every award ceremony. Then I go and get married, and I don't even send them a picture. I don't *have* a picture. I just had a spouse they'd never met and a faxed copy of a marriage certificate in Swedish.

I denied them all something critical. I denied them the chance to support me, cheer for me, love me out loud. And I'm not alone. Henrik did the same thing. His parents understand. They wished us well in their way. But Karro? The girl who loves princesses, and dresses, and happily-ever-afters? The girl who picked flowers with her mom and still believes the world is bright and perfect? She had a dream too, a dream of being the flower girl at Henrik's wedding.

We took that from her.

"Let me talk to Morbror," I whisper, not sure what else to say. "We'll fix it, okay?"

She doesn't answer. She's already fading, her eyelids fluttering, heavy with sleep.

Clicking off her twinkle lights, I slip from her room. But I don't go in search of Henrik. Instead, I take my phone from my pocket and head out to the balcony. I dial Shae's number and wait as it rings. I would understand if she didn't take my call.

She finally picks up on the fourth ring. The line is quiet as we connect. Then comes a voice I know as well as my own. "You got something to say to me?"

Sinking down onto the deck chair, I hold the phone to my ear. "Shae, I'm *so* sorry."

"For what?"

I frown down at the ground. "For . . . god, everything."

She sighs. "That's not how this works. You can't just go passing out sorrys like they're candy and expect us to tell you they taste sweet."

"I know."

"Well, so try again." She waits, not hanging up on me, not yelling.

Folding myself forward, my elbows on my knees, I groan. "Okay, well, can I at least tell you what happened at my wedding?"

She's quiet for a moment. Finally, she extends the olive branch I know I don't deserve. "What happened?"

I take a deep breath let it out, and start talking a mile a minute, spilling out all the truth I've kept bottled up for weeks. "Oh god, Shae, it was a disaster. First of all, I was wearing a T-shirt and athletic pants. At my wedding."

She gasps. "No."

"Yes! Shae, I had zippers at my ankles. And I needed my something old, new, borrowed, and blue, right?"

"Obviously."

"Yeah, so I tried to steal a blue ink pen from this secretary, but then he caught me. He was super nice and actually let me borrow his dad's old watch too. And did I mention the whole thing was in Swedish?"

Her side of the line crinkles and I'm sure she's opening a bag of chips. She likes to snack while she's on the phone. "Swedish, huh? So, you might have signed away all your organs or something."

"That's exactly what I said! Right after I freaked out and called the officiant a Swedish C-3PO."

She laughs. "A C-what? Ted, start from the beginning."

This time, I do. I start over, and I start from the beginning. The *real* beginning. I start from the moment I was walking down the sidewalk six years ago, checking our group text on my phone. I start from the moment I first met Henrik. And I leave nothing out.

59

HENRIK

Teddy's been outside on the phone for the last two hours. He started sitting on the chair. Then he took to pacing. I can't hear him through the glass. He's equal parts animated and reserved, sometimes gesturing wildly with his free hand, sometimes sitting quietly, nodding as the other person speaks.

Who is he talking to? Someone from his family? I hope he can mend those fences. It's clear how much they care for him. Even clearer that they care not at all for me. In fact, it's safe to say they hate me. Perhaps I have some grace left with the husbands. But his sisters? His mother? I imagine they'd all like to see me cast into the fiery pit.

I try to keep myself busy while he's outside, checking Karro's progress reports from Mr. Torres and answering the pile of emails from Laura and Elin. Laura has new endorsement deals for me to consider, and Elin did some research on elderly care facilities.

Even after his fall from the ladder, Dad is still being resistant to any change. He doesn't want more help, and he definitely doesn't want to move. He's afraid moving Mom will mean he loses her faster. She has so many memories rooted to that house and the land. Some days, the familiarity of her kitchen and her garden is all that keeps her grounded.

The instability of their situation eats at me night and day. I'm afraid the decision will fall to me and I'll have to enforce it with an iron hand. I want to be ready. I'm scrolling the website of an assisted living facility when Teddy comes back in. "All good?" I call.

He heaves a sigh of relief and drops down next to me on the couch. "So good."

I set my phone aside, wrapping an arm around his shoulders. Now that we've crossed the barrier of intimate touch, casual touch just feels natural. Teddy must feel the same because he sinks against me, propping his feet up on the coffee table. Then he pulls my arm tighter around his neck, banding my forearm across his chest.

I kiss his brow. "Who were you talking to?"

"My sister."

"Which one?"

He hums contentedly, brushing his fingers down my arm. "Shae. I called her. We had a good talk. Finally."

"Finally?"

"Yeah, it was time I came clean."

"About what?"

He laughs. "Like, everything."

"Everything?"

"Yeah. You, me, this whole crazy situation."

"I thought you told them what we did and why."

"Yeah, but before I just told them the basics. This time I filled in the gaps. I told Shae everything. Like, down to the details of my shoes on our wedding day. It helped, you know? To finally get it all off my chest. I hated feeling like I was keeping secrets."

"You felt like you were keeping secrets by not telling your sister the shoes you wore to our wedding?"

"Well, not secrets, I guess. But those details, yeah. By keeping everything quiet and rushing like we did, I denied my family a lot. I hurt them, Hen. I think I'm really only just now realizing how much I hurt them. Something Karro said tonight opened the wound fresh."

"What did she say?"

He brushes his hand down my arm again. "She said Petra promised her she could be the flower girl at your wedding."

I go still, my heart clenching tight. The picture is so easy to paint in my mind. I can all but hear Petra's voice saying the words, followed by Karro's little cheer of excitement. "Karolina would have made an excellent flower girl."

"Yeah, I feel bad," he goes on. "We really messed up that part, I think. Shae said again how much she wished she could have been there. I wish we could make it up to all of them."

I hum in understanding. "What if we hosted a party?"

"A party?"

"Many of my teammates in the past have had weddings abroad in the offseason, then they host parties once the season starts again. Would that help soothe hurt feelings?"

He sits up, an excited look in his eyes. "Like a reception?"

I shrug. "If you want."

He bites his bottom lip, leaning away, his mind clearly racing.

Reaching out, I brush my fingers lightly over the locs on his shoulder. "What are you thinking?"

"Could we maybe hire a photographer too? We just don't really have any pictures of us—I mean, the ones on your phone definitely don't count. I can't send those to my sisters in a Christmas card."

I chuckle. Since our little photoshoot in the bathtub, we've added a few shots to the password-protected folder on my phone. "Of course. A photographer for Teddy, a dress for Karolina—"

"And maybe a kiss?" Once the words are out of his mouth, I can see he regrets them. He groans, shifting away.

I prop my feet next to his, tucking him against me with both arms around his chest so he can't get away. "What do you mean?"

"Nothing. It's fine."

"Teddy . . ." I wait, not letting him go.

After a moment, he relaxes against me with a sigh. "Okay, well we didn't even kiss at our wedding. Like, I married you, and . . . nothing."

I sit with that truth for a moment. He's right, of course. It hadn't even occurred to me that he would want that. If my memory serves, he was panicking, and I was just trying to have it all over and done as quickly as possible to spare him any discomfort or embarrassment.

"I had a stolen pen in my pocket, Felix's dad's watch on my wrist, and the whole thing was in Swedish," he goes on. "I could have been vowing to give you all my organs."

I chuckle again, brushing my lips to his shoulder. I resent the feeling of his cotton T-shirt, blocking me from touching his skin. "You didn't," I assure him.

"But that's the thing, I don't know. No one does but you and that snobby officiant guy. We didn't even have a witness. And I'll be fucked before anyone sees those mugshot pictures they took of us to submit with the license."

I must admit, I'm a bit distracted from all this talk of weddings and parties. I blame Teddy. His loc oil smells so good, like a soothing peppermint tea. And he's wearing some of my cologne. The mix of peppermint with the woodsy cologne has him smelling like a crisp winter morning. I press my face in at his neck, breathing him in until he squirms.

"Fuck, babe, come on," he says on a groan. "I can't think when you do that."

"Do what?"

"Breathe me in like that."

"Like what?"

"Like you're a wolf or something. It's so primal."

I smile, nuzzling the soft skin behind his ear. "Stop smelling so good then." He just hums and my arm tightens around him. I kiss his neck, right at the point where the scents merge. When I flick with my tongue, he gasps. "You smell like me. It's intoxicating."

"Well, I've been using your cologne, so that tracks." I don't need to see his face to know he's smiling. My distraction is working. He's coming back to me, floating out of his panic spiral and back into my arms.

"Do you wear it to drive me crazy?"

He huffs. "No, I wear it to drive *me* crazy."

Loosening my hold on him, I let my hands roam over the firm planes of his chest. "What do you mean?"

His body goes slack as I caress him. "I just like smelling like you."

"Why?" I nip his ear, and he hisses, trying to hold still.

"Makes me feel like you're there, even when you're not, like your skin was just touching my skin. It turns me on."

"So primal," I tease, slipping my hand up under his shirt. My calloused fingertips trace over his warm skin.

He melts against me. "God, Hen, I seriously can't think with you touching me, and I need to say something else."

I go still, both hands under his shirt. "What?"

Pushing away from me with a frustrated groan, he sits up. "Okay, so don't freak out, but someone said something nasty about us tonight and Karolina heard them."

I sit up, good feelings gone. "What was said?"

He shifts away slightly so we can face each other. "They said I'm leaving you. Which totally isn't true," he quickly adds. "But they said it, and Karro heard, and she was definitely upset."

My protective instincts surge at the thought of someone upsetting her. "Who said it?"

"Karro doesn't know." He places a hand on my shoulder. "But it doesn't matter. People think it's true. Whether the guys are gossiping to their wives or the media is still stirring the shit, people still think this marriage is just, like, a publicity stunt, a means to an end. And that end is you getting full custody of Karro. And maybe that is how this all started, minus the interest in publicity," he quickly adds. "We both just wanted to do whatever we could to protect Karro. But getting married as our solution was impulsive and reckless and—"

"And we didn't even kiss," I say over him, squeezing his hand. "Yes, I'm seeing more and more how unfair our rushed wedding was for everyone on all sides."

He sits back. "Right. Well, I assured her I'm not leaving. Not—like, that I'm not leaving her," he quickly amends. "I made a vow to her as much as you, and I'll not break it, Henrik. And I may have . . ." His words trail into silence as he bites his bottom lip again.

I feel his anxiety spike, and I sit forward. "What, mitt hjärta?"

He lets his breath out. "Okay, I may have said something. It was in the moment, and it felt right, but I don't wanna feel like I crossed any lines. I mean, you don't make kids promises you can't keep.

That's, like, rule number one. And I *know* I should have checked with you first—"

"Teddy, just tell me—"

"I told her I love her. I told her in English and in Swedish. God, Hen, it was eating me up not to say it," he adds with a groan. "She needs to know how serious I am. Karolina's my little girl now too. She's mine, and no one is gonna say shit that will make her doubt my intentions to stay in her life."

"I'm not mad," I assure him, one hand on his thigh.

He raises a dark brow. "You're not?"

I shake my head, smiling with relief. "No, I'm glad."

It's not as if I didn't know. Anyone can see the way they are together—laughing and singing and making jokes. In those moments of play, he reminds me the most of Petra. They're so different in personality in all other respects. But loving Karolina brings out the best in both of them. Teddy is just the sort of joyous, fun-loving parent Karolina deserves.

I've been finding my own way into parenting, shifting from being the morbror she only saw on video calls and holidays to being a daily fixture in her life. Ours is a quieter kind of love, the love of stillness. Arms to hold her, words of comfort to share. She goes to Teddy when she wants to laugh and play. She comes to me when she's tired, when she's sad and grieving, when she needs the world to stop spinning quite so fast.

Both kinds of love are worthwhile. And Karolina deserves nothing less. I smile, glancing at Teddy. We really do make a good team. "She's a very blessed little girl," I say, giving his thigh a squeeze. "To earn your love is a gift not to be taken for granted."

He inches closer. "Hen, I . . ."

"What?"

He swallows, his nervousness now like an aura around him. "I said it in haste to you before . . . at the restaurant. I kind of threw it at you, actually. Classic, Teddy, right? My emotions get the best of me, and I sort of just blast everything I'm feeling, like a firework."

I can't help but smile. A firework. It's such a fitting analogy for my Teddy. He burns hot, spiraling in the air, bursting in a kaleidoscope of colors. He's everywhere at once, requiring all my senses to fully take in his radiance.

"But I *do* feel that way about you," he goes on, a giant blush on his freckled cheeks. "I mean, I still do. I did then, and I do now. But I definitely should have finessed it better. I can't just go around blurting those things out. To Karro or to you. I need to be more measured, more controlled, more—"

"Teddy." I squeeze his thigh again and he stops, my breath held tight. Still smiling, I lift my other hand and brush my fingertips down the locs on his shoulder. "Never make yourself smaller. Not for Karolina, and certainly not for me."

He flashes me that nervous smile. "You gotta admit, I'm a lot. Especially for Swedish people."

"You are just enough. You're my partner, my husband. And you're Karolina's fiercest guardian. We're lucky to have you, Teddy. I for one mean to continue earning the trust you've put in me. I will put you first—"

"And I'll put *you* first." He scoots closer, his hand covering mine on his thigh. "You and Karro. I mean, this can work, right? It's crazy. How this all started is so crazy. It's no wonder people gossip about us."

"Let them gossip." My anger still threatens to peak at the thought of someone saying cruel words where Karolina or Teddy can hear. "They mean nothing to us."

He nods. "Yeah, they don't matter."

"Nothing matters but this." I take his hand, placing it over my heart.

He splays his fingers, his body relaxing as he sinks closer to me. I reel him in, one arm around his shoulders. Yes, *this* is what I want. Everything else can be fixed. This may have all started in a haze of grief and panic, but that now feels like another life. Our families will forgive us. The press will ignore us. So long as I have Teddy, it will all be fine.

In this moment, I just want him close to me. I want him sharing my air. I want to *be* his air. Pulling him to me, I kiss him, my lips parted and seeking. He hums with relief, as if he too is starving for my affection. I cup the back of his neck, breaking our kiss. "I believe you promised me a reward for my good behavior today."

He grins, his hands braced on my chest. "I did, didn't I?" He leans closer, kissing me again. "You were such a good crab for me, baby. So patient." Kiss. "So helpful." Kiss. "And I can't believe you actually let us paint your face like a rainbow tiger."

I huff. "That's what has you most surprised?"

"Attending the Rays' annual Boo-tacular Trunk-or-Treat doesn't seem like your jam," he says with a shrug.

I let a glare seep through my contented expression. "You should be more impressed with how I made no comment while you made plans to stroke my teammate from head to toe. Thrice over."

"Ooooh." His grin widens. "Is *that* why you were being so weird with Novy? I thought it was some kind of protective thing, like you were trying to intimidate him for me."

"Impossible. The only person alive who can intimidate that man is Poppy St. James."

"But you were jealous," he presses. "You're jealous that I'm gonna give Novy a massage?"

"Three massages." I hold up three fingers, still glaring at him.

Laughing, Teddy grabs my wrist and climbs into my lap. With my fingers still held up, he reverently kisses the tip of each one. Then he takes my hand and slips it back under his shirt, rubbing my palm up his bare chest. He arches into my touch, his hips grinding over mine. Letting my wrist go, he places both hands on my shoulders. "Trust me when I say there's no reason to be jealous of me massaging Novy. Or anyone else on the team."

"Is there not? I'm your husband, so you're not allowed to massage me, remember? It's hard not to feel like I'm being punished for having the audacity to make you mine."

He rocks on my lap again, teasing me with a groan, as my cock hardens against my thigh. Then he runs his fingers through my hair, tipping my head back. "The rule is no massages *at work*. Novy was right. You're the one to be jealous of here, not him."

"Oh, yes? Why?"

He moves atop me, setting the fire in my chest burning brighter.

Then he folds over me, kissing me, hands stroking. "Because you can have the full Teddy treatment anytime you want. All you have to do is ask."

Weaving my fingers into his hair, I tug him gently back, breaking our kiss. "You would massage me too?"

"Baby, 'too' implies I'm gonna massage you like I massage your teammates. And I don't typically massage my clients naked. You're an exception."

Stifling a growl, I sit up. Hands on his ass, I hold him to me as I stand. He gasps, the sound coming out like a laugh, as his arms wrap around my neck, legs around my hips. "Ohgod—"

Walking him forward, I don't stop until we hit the wall. He groans, his head tipping back. Pinning him with my hips, I free a hand, wrapping it around his throat. "I'm the *only* exception. Say it."

His smile is incandescent as he leans into the pressure of my hand. "You say it. Say the words, Henrik."

I grind him against the wall. Christ, my heart is racing. I feel desperate. He makes me want to lose control. Or cede it. I know if I do, I'll feel nothing but pleasure.

As he reads my mind, his smile is triumphant. "You're aching for it, baby. You think I can't feel your hard cock pressed against mine? You need release. Say the words, and I'll give you what you need. Let me show you how good we can be."

My senses are spinning as I try to remember how to form words in English. He does this to me. He twists me up, leaving me breathless and voiceless, completely incapable of thought. To go from feeling all but numb to life to this vibrancy? It's almost more than I can bear.

Every moment with Teddy has been something new—joy, curiosity, anxiety, lust, need, peace, frustration. He feels so much all the time. Like an electrical conduit, he transfers all his emotion into me. When we touch, we become a completed circuit. Feelings overflow from him into me. In this moment, I'm that cup with no bottom. I want him to pour into me and never stop.

But his family is wrong about us. There's no fear of me draining him dry. There is too much of Teddy to ever claim all of him. He'll give me only what I need. He'll take such good care of me. Someone as precious as him can do no less.

"Say it," he teases again. "Say, 'Massage me.'"

Those are the words he wants, but they're not the words I give him. It's time. I'm ready. I want to be his in all ways. I squeeze my hand at his throat and lean in, holding his adoring gaze. "Fuck me."

60

TEDDY

I lean into the pressure of Henrik's hand at my throat. "What?"

"I want you to fuck me," he says, grinding against me with his hips. "Teddy, please."

At the sound of his begging, I gasp, squeezing his shoulders. "Put me down."

He leans away from the wall, and I slide down his front, feet touching the ground. Only an inch or two separate our heights, but I still always feel like he's gazing down at me from on high. "You're serious? You would want that? Like, you know what it means and where stuff goes, and . . . you still want that?"

He rolls his eyes, which relaxes me a little. An eye roll is such a me thing to do. I've officially become a bad influence on this polite Swede. Now he sings drinking songs, and rolls his eyes, and says lewd things, like, "Fuck me."

Dropping a hand between us, he cups my dick. His hold is firm, possessive. "I want you to take this cock and put it inside me," he says against my lips. "Paint my insides with your cum; drag your nails down my back. Don't stop until I'm marked inside and out. Everyone will know why I call you min man." He leans away, and I see the glint of excitement in his eyes. "Is that clear enough for you?"

Groaning, I pull him to me in a fierce kiss. I break away first, pushing on his chest. "I swear, I was about to give you the best massage of your fucking life. I was gonna make it so good, relax you from head to toe. Then I was gonna suck your cock and swallow all your cum like the good little whore I am."

His eyes widen, cheeks blooming pink, as I match him dirty word for dirty word. It's adorable. "And now?"

I grin. "Now? I'm gonna bend you the fuck over." Squeezing his ass in those stupidly snug lounge pants, I lean in closer. "I'm gonna take your tight hole, spread it with my fingers, and fuck you till you're screaming my name. We don't stop until you're dripping with me."

He drops his forehead to my shoulder, both hands clinging to the front of my shirt, as he mutters something in Swedish.

"What's that, baby?" I tease.

"Do it," he says in English. "Take me, Teddy. Show me what this can be."

Oh god, his submission is such a fucking turn-on. I'm usually the one who likes to play the brat and then get railed. Henrik's request feels like a gift, something precious and rare and so delicate. I have to be careful. I can't mess this up.

As if he can sense the swirling shift in my thoughts, he tips my chin up. The blue of his eyes is so warm and inviting. "The time for hesitation between us has long passed. We need this, ja? We're ready."

I nod, tears in my eyes. "Yeah—or—I mean, ja. Whatever. Fuck, Henrik, I'm saying *yes*." I chase the words with another kiss, his soft beard hair bristling against my lips.

Our hands are everywhere as we pull at each other's clothes, dropping our shirts to the floor. God, his skin feels like a furnace. He runs so hot. I brush my hands over his hairy chest, groaning with relief to feel him in my arms. Fuck, he's *mine*.

"Mitt hjärta—wait—"

At first, I don't register his words. I just keep kissing him, shoving my hand inside the tight band of his lounge pants until I feel the warm silk of his dick in my fist.

He groans, his forehead pressed to mine. "We can't do this here. We'll wake Karolina."

The utterance of her name has me pulling away, gasping for air as I glance around. We're standing half naked in the living room with my hand down Henrik's pants. Now that Karro is using crutches to get around the house, she could come out here and investigate. Knowing our girl, she will. She's too damn curious for her own good.

I push away from him. "Bedroom?"

"Yours or mine?"

"Yours *is* mine." I pull him forward. "Did you think I wouldn't notice when you moved all your stuff back into the closet? By the way, we're renovating your perfect bathroom."

"Oh, are we?" There's amusement in his tone, but there's an edge too. My quiet Swede is very particular about having everything just so.

When we get into the kitchen, I turn to him and stop. He all but collides with my chest. Hands on his shoulders, I hold his gaze. "There's only one sink, Henrik, which screams bachelor pad. And if you haven't forgotten, you're married now." I wiggle my ringed finger in his face. "And you gifted that bathroom to *me* as a wedding present."

His smile widens. "Oh, did I now?"

"You did. And if you think I'm gonna share a sink with you, you're crazy. I may share clothes and colognes, and, yes, once in Sweden, I accidentally used your toothbrush. But if you love me, you'll invest in a second sink."

He leans away in surprise. Then his brow furrows as he clearly considers my words.

Shit, there I go again, letting my mouth run away with me. And Henrik is too damn literal. He takes me at my word every time. He's never actually said the words yet, even if I think he might feel them. Did I just set him a test? Some bar he has to jump over? If he loves me, he'll get me a sink.

Seriously? Why the hell didn't I tell him to get me a Porsche? Or a trip to Southeast Asia?

God, I can't think about love sinks now. My husband just asked me to paint his insides with my cum, which is a memory I'll be replaying in my mind until the end of time. Groaning again, I grab his hand. "Come on."

He follows me down the hall and back into our bedroom. The lights are off, but a glow of yellow light stretches across the carpet from the bathroom. His side of the bed is so orderly and minimal.

Mine is a mess of books I only pretend to read. I'm always too tired at night to focus on the words on a page. My new eye massager is plugged in atop the teetering pile. That I do use. It's amazing—

Focus, Teddy!

I don't even know what we need. I'm so out of practice. Henrik and I are definitely sexually active now, but up to this point, we've restricted everything to hands and mouths. I don't think I have any condoms. Lube, yes. I introduced Henrik to the wonderful world of lubed hand jobs last week. He doesn't like fooling around in the shower, something about the water confusing his sensations. But he definitely liked the feel of my lube-slicked hand pumping his cock until he blew a load on my face.

We should use a condom, right? I don't bottom for anyone unless they're wrapped. But I haven't bought any condoms while I've been living here. It felt too much like a jinx. Wish and plan too hard for something, and the universe makes sure it doesn't happen, right? Goddamn it, these stupid, superstitious hockey players are rubbing off on me. Now, my version of the Stanley Cup playoffs is finally here, and I'm unprepared?

I turn to Henrik. "Please tell me you have condoms."

He leans away. "What? No, of course not. Do we really need them?"

"Honestly, we've been a bit lax when it comes to protection. Everything just sort of happened, and then I wanted it to keep happening, and it felt so damn good." I close my eyes, relishing the memory of the first time we came together on the bathroom floor. "But safety matters. I mean, I got tested. I showed you the results."

"You did, but—"

"And we both know you're fine," I keep going. "So, I guess I just let it go in my head that we should be using condoms during blow jobs too. But we totally can. We should definitely . . . Yeah, let's take a breath, and let's talk about this—"

"*Teddy*." Henrik grabs me by the shoulders.

I lean away. "What?"

He fights to hide a smile. He lifts a hand and brushes his knuckles along my cheek. "Breathe with me."

I suck in a breath as he places his hand back on my shoulder.

"There's no one else. You are safe with me, as I know I'm safe with you. But would using a condom make you feel more comfortable?"

His question makes my brain skip like a busted CD player. "I—would *you* be more comfortable?"

He just shakes his head, all calm, cool, and collected. "I'm asking what you want, mitt hjärta. Be brave now and tell me."

I let out a heavy breath, my eyes locked on the man in my arms. This is up to me? He would trust me to choose? Lost in the blue of his eyes, I say the words on my heart. "Oh god. Henrik, baby, I wanna take you bare." I smooth my hands over his naked chest, loving the feel of his warm skin against my palms. "I don't want to use a condom." I drop my gaze to somewhere around his collarbone. "Is that . . . would you be okay with that?"

It's a huge ask, I know. I've never done this with anyone. Well, not since I was a sixteen-year-old kid messing around at a swim meet. In my adult life, I've always been a paragon of health and safety. I'm even still taking my PrEP. But with Henrik, this doesn't feel like a risk. God help me, it feels like coming home.

He tips up my chin, a soft smile relaxing his features. "Min Teddy . . . jag är din och du är min."

His voice is a tad lower when he speaks in Swedish. I've learned enough of his repeated phrases to intuit what he said this time. *I am yours, and you are mine.* The words wrap around my heart, and I close my eyes, trying to memorize the feel of this moment. His everything. I'm Henrik's everything. Opening my eyes, resolve burns in my chest. "Get on the bed."

He hesitates, glancing over to the rumpled sheets of the bed I only ever allow us to sleep in. Our sanctuary, our safe space. If we do this on the bed, there's no more pretending this is anything but what it is: a full relationship with hearts and bodies entangled.

God, we've been fooling ourselves for weeks. Nothing about this is fake anymore. Henrik is my husband. We're going to be married in every sense of the word. Slipping my fingers into the top of his pants, I reel him in, pressing a firm kiss to his lips. "Take these off and get on the bed. Lie on your back."

He holds my gaze, daring me to break first, as he shucks his pants down to the floor. He stands in front of me, naked, our marriage bed framed behind him. I press a hand to the middle of his chest and push him back. Smiling, he lets himself be guided. His calves hit the edge of the bed, and he sinks down.

Reaching out with both hands, he reels me in by the hips, not stopping until I'm standing between his spread legs. He presses his face to the crotch of my pants, letting out a hungry sound that sends a shiver of need coiling up into my chest. I'm all instinct as I weave my fingers into his hair, tipping his head back. "Take my pants off, baby. You want my dick? Want me to make you my man?"

He groans out a muffled "yes" as he drags my pants down my thighs, releasing my aching dick. It's hard and so ready for him.

"Get it wet—*fuck*—" He doesn't need my command before he's sinking his warm mouth around my length. He hums with relief, his hands gripping my ass, as he bobs on my cock, taking me deep. I can hardly breathe. He looks so beautiful with my dick in his mouth. "Slow," I say, tugging on his hair. "We need me to last a little while longer. Baby, lie back."

He fights the push of my hands on his shoulders as I try to guide him back. Instead, he eagerly sucks my tip, dropping a hand down to cup my balls. It's my turn to groan as I push him harder. "That's enough. You asked me to take charge, and that's what I'm gonna do. Now, be my good little crab, and lie back on the bed."

His teeth gently scrape the top of my shaft as he lets me go. He leans back, bracing against the mattress with his hands. "Does all cum taste as good as yours?"

Desire burns through me as I follow him onto the bed. He scoots towards the middle, lying back. I kneel between his spread legs, my hands brushing up his thighs. "Hmm, let me see." Folding myself over him, I claim his lips in a kiss. I press in with my tongue, flicking and teasing, seeking out any flavor of me.

After a moment, I hum my approval. The taste isn't as heady as when he's swallowed a mouthful of my cum, but there's a hint of me there. The primal part of me crows with triumph to know I've marked him. It's not nearly as satisfying as blowing a load on his chest and rubbing my cum into his skin.

And nothing will be more satisfying as what we're about to do. My man will take me where no one else has ever claimed him. God, I'm already dripping just thinking of his body giving way to mine. The push and pull of it, the heat, the thrill of him clenching me tight. Desperate to get started, I break our kiss and make my way down his chest, sucking his nipple until he gasps, teasing with my hands.

"Tell me what to do," he says, no less eager than I am to be joined. "Teddy—"

I reach up, pressing my fingers to his lips. "Now who's impatient?"

He groans, rocking up with his hips as I lick along the length of his hard shaft. I'm not used to being with a guy who is uncut. His foreskin fascinates me. It's so soft and silky. I love the smooth glide of it up and down with each slow pump of my fist. I draw my fist down, exposing his shiny head. Precum wets his tip, just waiting for me to get a taste.

But I have another idea. With a swipe of my thumb, I collect the cum. Rising over Henrik, I press my thumb to his lips. "Taste."

His expression heats as he flicks his tongue out, tasting himself. My cock twitches as he sucks my thumb into his mouth, nipping the pad with his teeth. "You taste pretty good too, right?"

He lets me go with a satisfied nod. Then he lies back, his hands gliding along my ribs and over the curve of my hips. "More."

"Baby, we're just getting started." Using my hands, I massage and soothe, helping him relax, while my mouth continues to tease. I taste every inch of him, breathing him in. His skin is so warm. The scent of his body wash is soft on his skin—citrus and salt, with a soothing middle note I can't quite place. "You smell like the sea," I practically moan into his stomach.

He makes a sound like a hum of laughter, one hand braced on my shoulder. "Well, that's fitting for a crab."

I smile, nipping the soft skin at his hip. The combination of my hands and mouth quickly has him rocking on the bed, trying to thrust with his hips. "Teddy," he begs. And I swear, there's no sweeter sound.

I kiss lower, letting a hand slip between his legs to caress his upper thigh. "What do you need, baby?"

"More," he says again.

With a turn of my wrist, I cup his balls, letting them rest warm and heavy against my palm as I stroke his taint with two fingers. He gasps, legs spreading like he's inviting me in. Fuck, it's so beautiful. I reach down a little further, touching the bud of his asshole with the pad of my middle finger. I give it a press, feeling his body's natural reaction. He tenses, even as he groans with need. "Have you ever been taken here?"

He shakes his head, eyes shutting tight. "No."

"Do you like when I do this?"

"I like when you do anything," he says on a breath, stifling a groan as I give his balls a little squeeze.

His admission has my confidence soaring. He wants me in charge. He said he wants me to show him what this can be. I know part of him meant it metaphorically. But he also means it literally. He's never been with a man. He doesn't know what this can be. Henrik literally wants me to show him. "Turn over," I say, pulling on his hips. "Hands and knees, baby."

There's no hesitation in him as he does what he's told, rolling first to his side, then up on his knees. His trust in me is absolute. It's the most powerful of aphrodisiacs. I'm practically whimpering to get my first taste of him.

The muscles of his shoulders flex as he glances back at me. I sense his nerves, warring with his resolve. "Tell me what to do."

"Nothing." I smooth my hands up his sides as I kiss his warm back. "Just enjoy. Tell me to stop, and it stops."

He rocks back into the press of my hands. "Don't stop."

Fuck, he's so perfect. So strong, yet so willing to give. Stroking my hands over the curves of his ass, I spread his cheeks, taking my first look at his tight hole. Reaching a hand between his legs, I curl my fingers around his hard shaft, giving it a pull. As he arches into that touch, I descend, kissing his ass cheek.

He gasps, body stiff as he takes in the new sensation. With my free hand, I press in at his asshole, testing the tightness. "You have to relax," I say against his warm skin. "I'm gonna work you up to taking my cock. But let's just start with fingers, okay? Can I taste you here?" I press in at his hole again, even as I stroke his hard length.

He groans. "Too much."

I still. "What's too much? Tell me what to stop."

He taps my hand on his dick, and I let him go. Smiling I give his ass cheeks a slow, firm squeeze with both hands. "One thing at a time then, yeah? Henrik, baby, I'm gonna play with your asshole now. Just say stop and—"

"Don't stop," he commands over me.

Still smiling, I spread his cheeks with both hands and descend, licking his tight bud. He cries out something in Swedish, rocking away. But then his hips press right back towards me, and I lick him again. "Hold still," I growl.

He moans, muttering something unintelligible as my grip on his hip tightens and I start to play. I lick and suck, massaging his cheeks with my hands. Then I dribble some spit onto his hole and work him with my fingers, loving the way his body responds. "Feel good?"

"I hardly know," he says on a breath. "What are you doing?"

Chuckling, I replace my fingers with my mouth and moan low, letting him feel the vibrations against his ass as I prod with my tongue. I flick and tease, rimming his tight bud, pressing in until I feel the muscle give. "What does it feel like I'm doing?"

His only response is a desperate, muffled groan.

Sitting up, I run a hand up his spine, pressing his shoulders down as I push inside him with one finger.

"Oh, Christ," he pants, his body instantly tensing.

Fuck, he's so tight, I wanna scream. I want to pull my finger out and shove my dick in. I wanna pound his tight hole, fill him to the brim. But I wait. I go slow. "That's it, baby," I soothe. Grabbing his shoulder, I push my finger all the way in. Then I kiss along his collarbone, up his neck, to his ear. "How does it feel?" I slowly slide the finger in and out, flexing the tip along his prostate until he groans.

"Teddy—Christ—how can it feel so good?"

Smiling, I pull my finger out to the tip. "Want more?"

He nods.

Rocking back on my ankles, I squeeze his ass cheek and spit onto his hole, pressing in with a second finger. He drops down to his elbows, forehead pressed to his arms, as I push in past his tight ring of muscle with both fingers. "So good," I praise. "Baby, you're so fucking tight. Relax a bit more for me, okay?"

He grunts something in Swedish. It doesn't sound like the word "stop," so I keep going, using my spit to work the fingers in deeper, massaging his tight ring of muscle to help him relax. I pull my fingers out and he groans in frustration. "Want more?"

"Yes," he groans, his voice muffled by the bed. "Teddy, please."

I swear to god, if this man keeps begging me, I'm not gonna last until I'm inside him. Already, my cock aches with the need for release. Scrambling off the bed, I dart to the bathroom.

He pushes up on all fours, watching me go with a mix of longing and confusion. "Teddy, what—"

"I'll be right back," I call, rattling open the drawers under the sink until I find my small bottle of lube. I hurry back into the bedroom, already squirting some of the lube into my hand.

"What are you doing?"

"Trust me." I climb back onto the bed behind him. "I'm not saying I've got god's gift to dicks, but it's bigger than anything you've ever taken, right?"

He actually looks confused, the precious man. "Teddy, I've never—"

"I know," I say over him, stifling my laugh as I rub my lubed fingers over his hole. He swallows the rest of his words, rocking back against the pressure of my hand. Smoothing my free hand down his back, I work two fingers inside him again, letting him flex and press against me. "Babe, you're a natural. You're gonna make such a tight fit for me."

"Feels so good," he manages in English.

The give of his body is making me feel high. He's so eager to let me fill him. I don't know how I'll ever get enough. "I need to be inside you," I say on a breath. "Please, let me take you. Need to fill you, make you mine."

"Do it."

I work my fingers in and out a few more times, twisting them until I press down on his prostate. His body spasms. "Teddy!"

"I know, baby. God, fuck, I know. Just give me a sec." I pull my fingers free and fumble with the cap of the lube, slicking the cool liquid all over my dick. Shifting forward on my knees, I grab him by the hip, inching closer until my tip is in position. "Push against the pressure, baby. Bear down on me. And if it's too much—"

"Christ, Teddy, just put your dick in me!"

The thrill of being treated like a bottom while I top him has my shaft twitching with eagerness in my hand. I slick my tip over his lubed hole, marking what's mine. Doing this bare is such a rush. I can't even imagine what the wet heat of his channel will feel like without the barrier of a condom to dull my senses. Taking a deep breath, I start to press in. I'm a groaning, eager mess as I feel my tip slip past his tight ring of muscle.

Henrik grunts, pushing up on his hands. "Christ in heaven."

I try to laugh, but it comes out as a whine as I sink in another inch. Watching him take me is going to finish me too soon. Tipping my head back, I close my eyes and let myself feel everything instead—the warmth of him, the tight squeeze. God, I'm flying.

Is this real? I'm half a dick deep inside Henrik Karlsson. We're married, and he just told me I'm his. Better yet, he just told me he's *mine*. Crying out, I start to move my hips. My instincts command it. I pull him back to me, letting his heat swallowing me inch by inch as I stretch him to take me. Remembering myself, I smooth my hands all over him, tethering us with as much touch as possible. "Are you okay? Does it feel good?"

He nods, unable to speak, eyes shut tight.

I slip my hand around to stroke his hard cock as I press in again. "You like my dick in your ass? You're so tight for me. So fucking perfect. So beautiful. Min man." The words come out in a stream as I stroke him slowly. His tip is dripping for me. Desperate for a taste, I swipe my thumb across his head and bring it to my lips, sucking on his essence with my tongue. "Oh god—"

Grabbing tight to his hips with both hands, I bury myself all the way inside him. Spots of light dance in my vision, and I'm seconds away from blowing my load. I've wanted this for too long. Now it's here and I can't make it last. "Oh—*fuck*—" Dropping a hand between us, I grip my balls tight, trying to stave off this aching need to come.

Beneath me, Henrik moans, his ass clenching around me tight enough to make me see fucking stars. "Teddy—I can't—"

I kiss his shoulders as we move together. Sliding in and out, I take him again and again, stretching his tight hole, burying myself inside the man I love. My husband. My Henrik. Oh god, how did we ever finally get here?

"Teddy," he says again, his voice breathless and low.

"What, baby?"

Anything. I'll give him anything.

"Stop."

61

HENRIK

Teddy stills behind me, his hands gripping my shoulders. It's all too much—the feeling of him inside me, the heat, the friction, the overwhelming need to come. I'm breathless and shaking, hands trembling. It's too much . . . and not nearly enough.

"What's wrong?" he pants, his hands caressing my sides. "Am I hurting you?"

"No," I manage to grit out. It's pressure more than pain, though there was some pain at first. Now, it's the feeling of being so full that dwarfs everything. Feeling full and feeling something foreign inside me—but it's not foreign, is it? It's Teddy. *My* Teddy. Christ, he feels so good. I never knew sex could feel like this. My thoughts are all a jumble. Do I really want him to stop?

"Use your words," Teddy pleads. "Henrik . . ."

He pulls out of me, and I'm suddenly empty. It's like he's ripped the very soul out of me, and now the room feels like it's spinning. I'm gasping for air, hands gripping the sheets in tight fists. "Teddy." It's the only word I can sensibly get out.

His hold on me gentles. "Was that—I mean, did you not like it?" He's breathless too, worried, confused.

I glance over my shoulder and see the look of rejection on his face. Desperate to make it go away, I roll up to my knees and take him into my arms. "Oh, min älskade," I murmur, kissing his brow. "Mitt liv, no." I soothe him with my hands, rubbing them up his arms and down his back. I kiss away his fears, holding him to me with both hands. I'll never let him go.

"Did you not like it?" he asks again, as I trace the curve of his neck with my lips. "Because we don't have to do it like that. We can do other things."

Weaving my fingers gently into the locs at his nape, I pull his head back, forcing him to look at me. The only light in the room comes from the bathroom, but it's enough to see the soft dusting of freckles on his cheeks and the green of his eyes. I see more too. I see his wariness, his fear. He wants this so badly for us. He needs it.

His need spirals mine higher. I feel so possessive of him. No one can hurt my Teddy, not even me. The very idea that my hesitation hurt him has me growling in frustration as I pull him down with me.

"Hen, what—"

"We continue." I lie back, pulling him atop me, kissing away his protests until he's breathless again. I know he wants this because his hard dick is pressed against mine. I may be the one pinned by his weight to the bed, but I take charge, moving my hips. "More," I pant, biting his lip until he gasps.

"Fuck—" He arches back, licking his abused bottom lip. His expression no longer looks haunted. It looks heated.

"Mark me," I command. Grabbing him by the back of the neck, I pull him down. "Do it."

Groaning with need, he comes alive atop me. His hand burrows into my hair as he pulls, jerking my head back. The sensation sets a fire in me as his mouth latches onto my neck and he begins to suck, scraping with his teeth, leaving his mark on my skin.

I'm a live wire. In Teddy's arms, I spark and flare. This aching need has to go somewhere, this wild feeling of release that coils inside me. I want to mark him too, crawl inside his skin. I said it earlier as a tease. I was trying to sound daring, whispering lovers' words. Acting with total abandon, I drag the stubs of my nails across his shoulders with both hands.

Crying out, he arches back. "Fuck—Henrik!"

I like the way he cries out my name, so desperate and needy. I run both hands up his naked front, smoothing them over the planes of his stomach, brushing my thumbs over his dark nipples. He tips his head back, lost to the bliss of my touch. With a grin, I rake both hands sharply back down.

"*Yes*," he chants. "Fuck, baby, do it again."

I pull on his arms, desperate to feel his weight atop me. He comes so willingly, the hesitation from moments ago now obliterated. "I want you back inside me," I pant against his lips, surprising us both.

He shakes his head. "Henrik—"

I kiss away his protest. "Can we do it like this? Can we try?"

"We don't have to."

"I *want* to. Teddy, do it. No more walking around this world as halves. Make us whole."

He groans, dropping his head down to my shoulder as he catches his breath. Then he pushes up with both hands, rocking back on his knees. I lie on the bed, gazing up at my husband, who kneels between my spread legs. I'm completely exposed to him, but I feel no shame. The marks from my fingers are faintly visible on his chest. Seeing them centers me.

This is what I need. The other position felt good, but I want the feel of him in my arms. I want to look at him, and hold him, and kiss him as he fills me. Reaching out with both hands, I pull him down to me. "Mitt hjärta," I whisper. "Please."

My quiet plea breaks his last ounce of resolve. Dropping down, he wraps his mouth around me, taking my length to the back of his throat. I cry out, arching on the bed, as he hums low, sucking me hard. He's so good at this. With tongue and teeth, he knows just how to tease me.

He cups my balls, squeezing gently as he sucks, and I feel myself thrust out onto the edge of a great precipice. Eyes shut tight, I'm unprepared when he grabs me by the thighs and rolls my hips back, exposing more of me. I cry out again as he sucks one of my balls into his mouth, fingers pressing in at my ass. His hold on me is firm as he licks and teases, making my body his. If I were being dematerialized, I could feel no less undone than I do in this moment.

"Teddy," I pant, hands gripping the sheets. "More. God, please, don't stop. Need more."

His mouth descends on my hole, and I moan like a dying man as his tongue prods. The sensation is odd but thrilling. I feel warm and achy, all my muscles contracting, even as I try to relax.

"Fuck, baby, you taste so good," he says on a breath. "I'll never get enough. Never." He sinks his fingers deep inside me, moving them with slow, even strokes that have me all but levitating off the bed.

"Teddy," I cry again. I feel full, but not in the way I want.

"I know." His fingers slip out of me, and I'm a whimpering mess. I feel so empty. He scrambles for the bottle of lube. I hear the slick sound of him prepping his cock. Next time, it will be *my* hands that prep him. "Oh, god, baby, just hold on," he groans, shifting his hold on my thighs.

How can he know how desperate I feel? How panicked and aching?

I smile, eyes closing in bliss. Of course he feels just as desperate and aching as me. He wants this just as badly. He wants *me*. His tip presses in at my stretched hole and I brace for the feel of his cock sliding back inside me.

"Henrik," Teddy's voice is soft, gentle. "Look at me."

I blink my eyes open, looking up at him. He's so beautiful, my man of sharp angles. He hovers over me, and my mind flashes to that first night in the bathtub, the night I first tasted him.

"Eyes on me."

Reaching up, I cup his cheek. "I see you."

"Don't look away," he pants.

"Never."

We both suck in a breath as he sinks in that first inch. He rolls with his hips, stretching me. It doesn't take much before he's pressed all the way in again, his hands lovingly caressing my thighs as we settle together. "Oh fuck," he says on a breath. "Feel good?"

"Move," I plead.

He thrusts a few times, slow and even, both of us groaning at the slick sound of his lubed cock moving inside me. The pressure is glorious now. The heat, the tension. There's a feeling of being stretched, a slight burning. Lost in the look of lust and awe in his eyes, I pull him to me, desperate for a kiss.

He all but moans with relief as he falls forward, bracing with his hands on the bed as we kiss. His thighs slap against my ass as he pounds into me with wild abandon. With each thrust, I begin to forget where my body stops and his begins. He shifts a knee, lifting my left hip. The change in angle has me gasping. I break our kiss, wrapping an arm around his shoulders to keep him close. "Like this. Move just like this."

His movements become more erratic as he presses in, grinding his hips against mine. The tip of his cock presses in at just the right angle, finding some secret place inside me I never knew was there. Like striking a match to the touch paper, I ignite. Every thrust stokes the flames higher. Crying out, I hold him to me. "Oh, Christ, don't stop."

He slams into me, grinding hard, and a noise escapes me that doesn't sound quite human. Somehow, I manage to get out the word, "More."

And my Teddy delivers, slipping a hand between us to stroke my cock. "Henrik—baby—I'm gonna come."

Yes, *this* is what I crave most. I see him now. I have him in my arms. My kiss is branded to his lips. But this will make me feel less empty, less adrift. I'm tethered in this moment to my body through Teddy. He'll give me what I need. He always gives me just what I need. "Come inside me," I beg. "Teddy—"

"Ahh!" Teddy unleashes, slamming his hips against mine, sinking his length as deep as it will go inside me. I drop my hands to his ass and pull, holding him to me as his back arches and he finally releases. The heat of him fills me, and I sigh with relief, even before I've come. I feel myself clench around him, and he groans, all but collapsing atop me.

It takes me a moment to come back to my senses. Our bodies are slicked with sweat. He trembles in my arms, and I mumble soft words of gratitude in Swedish, my fingertips tracing down his arm. This is what I needed, to be claimed by Teddy, filled to the brim.

But then he's pulling away. The loss of his weight feels like a physical tearing of part of me. "What are you doing?" I can't conceal the hint of panic in my tone.

"Not finished," he grunts. "Got too distracted. Wanted us to come at the same time." He crawls back between my legs, offering me a satisfied smile, but I'm suddenly self-conscious. I can feel his cum leaking out of me.

"It's okay," I mutter, shifting away. "Teddy, I'm fine."

"You will be fine," he says in that teasing tone. "Once you've choked me with your cum." Then he reaches a hand low and presses two fingers back inside me. I gasp at feeling so full again. At the same time, he wraps his other hand around my hard shaft and pulls down my foreskin, lapping at the head of my cock like it's his favorite lollipop. It's obscene, almost comical. It makes me smile.

I tuck an arm behind my head and watch him, luxuriating in the feel of his fingers inside me, his mouth around me. "You're far too happy with my cock in your mouth," I say on a groan.

He just grins. Pulling his dripping fingers from my ass, he wipes a streak of his cum down the length of my shaft. I stare at it, watching as he licks it up. My breath catches as he does it again. He moans, as if the taste of his cum is the sweetest ambrosia. My cock hardens as I reach for him. "I want to taste it too."

His gaze heats as he slicks his fingers over my sticky asshole. "I made such a mess of you, baby. Will you try something for me?"

I sit up on my elbows. "What?"

He slips his two fingers back up inside me and parts them in a V. "Squeeze for me."

I squeeze, gasping again as I feel more of his release leak out of me.

"Fuck." The heat in his tone has my every nerve ending sparking. "Look at you." His gaze lifts to mine and I see the passion there, the love and adoration. "We said we wouldn't stop until you were dripping with me."

"Jag är din," I say on a breath, meaning every word. It sounds strange to me in English. In Swedish, it just makes sense, like the sky being blue or ice being cold. I'm Teddy's now. Cherished, claimed. I think I've been his for far longer than I knew.

He smiles again, slipping his fingers from inside me. "That's right, baby. You're all mine. Min perfect man." He smears his cum-slicked fingers across my lips, chasing the action with a kiss. "How do you say 'perfect' in Swedish?"

I grin, holding him to me. "It's 'perfekt.'"

He blinks, leaning away. "Wait, really?"

I nod and he sighs with relief. "God, I'll finally get one right on the first try." He steals my laugh with another kiss. Then I groan into his mouth as he fists my cock tight, stroking me hard and fast. His tongue flicks with mine. I taste his release, mingled with the soft tang of the lube. "Come for me," he begs. "God, baby, come all over me. Make me drip too. So fucking perfect."

I cry out, my hips pressing up into the furious stroking of his hand.

"I'm yours," he pants against my lips. "Show 'em, baby. Show 'em how you claim your man—fuck," he shouts on a laugh, rocking back and angling my cock up as I come. It spurts from my tip, landing on his abs. He doesn't stop stroking me and I just keep coming.

"Oh god," I cry, rocking into each stroke of his hand.

"Yes," he praises. "Fuck, you're so beautiful." Ducking down, he catches the last of my release in his mouth, sucking my tip until I'm begging him to stop. I finally lie back, breathless and boneless, completely wrung out.

There's a satisfied smile on his face as he rubs my release into his skin. In the light from the bathroom, I catch the glint of gold on his finger. His wedding ring. I didn't even put it there. He slipped it on himself while we were sitting in Poppy's office. In that moment, he wore an expression like he was attending his own funeral.

No ring. No kiss, No family in attendance.

Teddy is always so worried about what others want and need. He worries for Karro, for his sisters. But what about what he needs? I know now how much he loves weddings. He and Karro watch reruns of *Say Yes to the Dress: Atlanta* by the hour. What did our rushed wedding truly cost him? I've never stopped to consider what he needs to make it right, to put it in the past, so we can all look to our future.

Grabbing his wrist, I pull him to me, sucking two of his fingers in my mouth, tasting my release against his skin. He watches, his gaze still smoldering. Then I roll to the side, taking him with me. We're a tangle of limbs as our sweat-slicked bodies twist in the sheets of our marriage bed. Gone is the hesitation I've felt these long weeks. Now

I want to pull him closer in the night, want him to wake with his cock in my mouth. He is my husband, and this is our bed. I mean to please him in it.

Once I have him on his side, I sling a leg over his hip, wincing slightly at the new stretch and burn from where I've been used.

"Was that good for you?" he whispers. "You liked it?"

I brush my finger down the tip of his nose, doing my best to memorize the pattern of freckling on his cheeks, as I nod. "Give me a minute to catch my breath, and we'll do it again."

His eyes go wide as he laughs and leans away. "Oh god, what have I unleashed?"

I smile, rolling with him until he's pinned under me. Each moment with Teddy is a gift, and I intend to take none of them for granted. I kiss my way down his chest. "I think I've got the idea of it now. You just lie back, mitt hjärta. Leave the rest to me."

61

TEDDY

"Okay, now stir, stir," I chant, holding the bowl while Karolina moves the whisk in a jerky pattern. "Keep stirring. Tight circles, remember?"

"Here, like this," says Henrik, trying to reach in and take over.

I playfully slap his hand away. "Babe, she can do it. Just give her a sec."

Karolina furiously churns the eggs into the top inch of cinnamon roll mixture, an excited smile on her face. "Am I doing it?"

"Dig deeper," I say on a laugh. "You gotta mix the whooooole bowl."

We've finally made it to the last day of her wearing the arm cast. The last scans of the break look great, so she gets the cast off first thing tomorrow. To celebrate, we're baking some cinnamon rolls as a gift for Hanna. Karro stands at the counter on her kitchen stool. She's perfected the art of balancing on one foot, keeping the weight off her healing leg. That cast will be on for another few weeks, at least.

Henrik checks the time on the oven again, offering me a pained wince. "I must go."

"I know." Leaning around Karro, I wipe a smudge of flour off his forehead. Baking with a five-year-old who only has one good arm is always a bit of a messy adventure. "Give me a kiss before you go, and I might consider saving you a cinnamon roll."

It's game day today, an afternoon game against the Chicago Blackhawks. Henrik has delayed for as long as he can, but it's time to head in. He pulls me in by my shirt and kisses me. "They're called kanelbulle in this house. Get it right, or I eat them all." With a last quick peck, he lets me go.

I feel dizzy, lost in a haze of sappy love and contentment. I can't remember a time when everything in my life felt more perfect. Henrik says something in Swedish that has Karro nodding. Then she starts digging deeper into the bowl, properly mixing the dry and wet ingredients. "Yes," I praise. "Good girl. Keep going, min lilla chef. Once you get it mixed, I'm gonna knead it for you. But once that cast comes off tomorrow, you'll be kneading your own dough balls."

She giggles, still aggressively whisking.

About fifteen minutes later, I'm setting the freshly kneaded dough into a bowl, covering it with a damp towel, when Henrik walks out in a crisp, charcoal-grey suit. "Whoa," I blurt. Schooling my expression, I offer him a cool wink. "I mean, hej, snygging."

Henrik's eyes go wide. "Who taught you that?"

Karro can't hold it in a moment longer. She cracks up with a loud "Me!"

Chuckling, he shakes his head, holding his arms out. "Well? How do I really look?"

Sitting on the edge of the counter, her sticky fingers dusted with pärlsocker, she gives him a once-over. "You need a pink suit."

He smiles. "I'm sure you must be right. For today, will this do?"

She just shrugs, content to turn her attention back to eating all the pärlsocker.

He looks to me, one brow raised in silent question. "You think me handsome?"

I shrug too. "You know how I feel about you in a suit."

His smile widens, reaching his eyes. He steps around the island and gives me a last parting kiss. "I'll see you both later."

"We'll be there. Go play hockey. Skate fast, win pucks."

He gives Karro a forehead kiss before he slips his protein drink from the fridge and a banana from the hook. Then he heads for the door. As soon as I hear it click shut, my phone starts buzzing on the counter. I check the screen to see Brad Brady's face smiling up at me. I tap the green button. "Hey, Brad, what's—"

"Help!" he shouts over me. "Ted, you gotta help me out, man."

My heart leaps into my throat. "My god, what happened? What do you need?"

"I need you to cover for me at the game. Like, now. Like, pronto. Pregame stuff is starting, and Cassidy already called off. She's in France or something. Without me, they'll be scrambling for PTs. Please, Ted."

"What happened?" I say again. "It sounds like you're in your car."

"I am! My stupid husband only just got himself into a stupid motorcycle accident. I hate fucking motorcycles!"

"Oh my god." I sink down onto one of the island stools. "Well, is he gonna be okay?"

Brad groans into the phone. "They think he broke his clavicle. And he all but degloved his right elbow from the road rash."

"Jesus."

"Well? Can you do it?"

I take a deep breath, thinking through all my options at warp speed. "I mean, I have Karolina with me, and Hanna's in Orlando—"

"Just bring her! Come on, you know one of the WAGs will take her. Please—"

"I'm coming," I say over him, rising to my feet. "It's all good. We'll get ready now and go."

"Oh god, Teddy, you're a lifesaver."

"Not a problem. Just go take care of Dylan."

"Yeah. Hey, why did I have to fall for a biker, huh? Why couldn't I find myself a nice birdwatcher or a guy who collects stamps?"

I laugh. "We can't help who we love."

"Can't we? If this man tests my heart like this one more time, he and his leather pants are gonna take a long freaking hike back to Nebraska."

"Uh-huh." We both know Brad is crazy about Dylan. I shift the phone to my shoulder as I start cleaning up the cinnamon roll mess. "Look, I need like fifteen minutes here to get organized, then I'll head to the arena. Tell the others?"

"Thanks, Teddy. You've really saved my bacon."

"Shut up. You'd do the same for me. Hanging up now."

We both hang up, and I turn to Karro, now busy on her tablet playing a finger-painting game. "Well, min lilla honey bun, I guess it's take-your-niece-to-work day."

"Yay!"

"Feeling better?" I say. "Nice and loose?"

DeGraw rolls his shoulders. "Right one is still feeling a bit tight, Doc."

I give him a little more deep-tissue stimulation, pressing in with my thumbs. I haven't had much one-on-one time with our new starting goalie. He's having an amazing season, with no injuries, so he's been off my table. "How are you adjusting to life as a Ray? The other guys treating you well?"

"Yeah, everyone's been great," he says, speaking in a thick Australian accent. I read somewhere that he's only the second Australian to ever play in the NHL. His recruitment was all down to Mars Price. Something about a chance encounter in Japan, which led to the team flying DeGraw out for a trial.

Tess ducks her head into the PT room, waving to grab my attention. "Hey, we're heading out," she calls. "Just pick her up whenever tomorrow."

"Thanks," I call back. "It'll be early. Cast is coming off!"

"Cast is coming off," she echoes in a singsong voice.

She came straight over with Emma when I called her from the car. The Langley girls will take her home for another slumber party. Which means I now get to watch my man play hockey *and* I get a child-free evening with him after the game.

I shift my hands to DeGraw's other shoulder. "Are you going out with the guys tonight?"

He just shrugs. Some players, especially goalies, get way inside their heads as part of their pregame ritual. But DeGraw isn't like that. He always seems happy to chat. "Yeah, probably. Cap says he wants us all there, win or lose."

The "win or lose" threat is valid. Apparently, Jake worked it out with the Hawks' team captain that the teams are going out together. It's karaoke night at Rip's, which is practically a religion with the Rays at this point.

I pause my massaging. "Any better?"

DeGraw rolls his shoulders again, then his neck. "Yeah, Doc. Wow, you're good."

I smile. "Well, they didn't give me a DPT for nothing."

He chuckles.

"Need anything else? Help stretching?"

"Nah, I'm good. Gonna go get kitted up." He hops off my table, bouncing on the balls of his feet. He has nothing like Ilmari's massive 6'5" frame, but he's still a big guy. Most goalies are these days. DeGraw is easily over six feet tall, but he has more of a swimmer's physique, compared to Ilmari's thick rugby build.

He turns slightly. "Hey, do you know if any of the other staff are going out tonight?"

I raise a brow. "What staff? Like the PTs and the equipment managers?"

"Yeah, them. Or others."

I shrug. "I mean, maybe. Caleb Price is kind of the king of karaoke night. He's usually always there. Who were you hoping for exactly?"

"No one," he replies quickly. *Too* quickly.

My gossip antenna perks up. "Come on, you can tell me."

"I'm all good, Doc. Thanks." The poor guy is actually blushing.

"Hey," I call as he walks away. "Maybe if you ask, I'll know the answer . . . or I can find you the answer."

He stops, his shoulders stiff. Slowly, he turns back around. Then he walks back over to me, lowering his voice to a conspiratorial whisper. "Okay, do you know Roshni?"

I scrunch my brow, trying to place the name. "Is she . . ."

"Analytics."

With that point of connection, a face flashes before my eyes: pretty, bespeckled, and oh so serious. Roshni Varma is one of the Rays' new statisticians. They review game-day tapes and come up with stats for the team's shooting and save percentages. They also handle the draft and playoffs, and they calculate zone start ratios. It's all very technical, and number-crunchy, and way over my head.

I don't want to paint with a broad brush, but the analytics department here is just . . . well, they all fit the stereotype. There was a stats intern back when I was an intern. His name was Travis, and he arranged his Cheetos from largest to smallest before he ate them. The last head of their department retired as a multimillionaire, having invested early in the cryptocurrency craze. The only other guy I know designs his own video games and sells them to developers. He only keeps this job because he's such a big hockey fan.

Roshni only just started. She's a gorgeous South Asian woman, with curly black hair, walnut-brown eyes, and a little diamond stud nose ring. I should reserve judgment, right? Until I learn whether she categorizes her socks by fabric type?

I look to DeGraw. "Want me to see if she's going tonight? If not, I'll try to invite her."

His eyes go wide. "I—no. Thanks, Doc." Spinning on his heel, the poor guy flees the room like his ass is on fire.

I don't get a moment to ponder his odd behavior before Paulie taps me on the shoulder. "You free, Doc? I could really use some help stretching my hammies."

"Sure." I pat the empty table. "Hop up."

63

TEDDY

I forgot how exciting it is to be behind the scenes on game day. The energy below the stands is just as electric as above. Everyone hurries around, setting the stage for the first intermission with snacks, electrolytes, fresh sticks and blades. Some of the players have quirky habits where they change their gloves or skate laces between every period. Lindberg likes to slurp on a jar of pickle juice. Some of the defensemen swear by mustard shots. They down packets of Heinz yellow mustard like they're tonic shots. It's revolting.

Thank god Henrik's only habit is his obsession with some obscure Swedish sock brand. They make the only socks he'll ever wear with his skates. I snort, remembering how I was ready to judge Roshni for doing the same thing. Maybe everyone involved with hockey has to be just a little bit weird.

Maybe that's why I feel so welcome.

In the last seconds of the first period, the game is tied at one point each. Chicago got a lucky score within the first three minutes, which set a rather ominous tone. But a brilliant shot by Langley brought us back even, renewing the fans' spirits. The buzzer sounds, ending the period.

"Here they come," someone shouts.

It's pandemonium as all the guys come rushing in off the ice. I work with the other PTs to do a quick round of check-ins. We assess each guy for any aches or pains they need addressed. Jake took a hard hit into the boards, but he has no complaints. And Henrik took a stick to the side of the face.

I pat his thick shoulder pad. "Hey, babe, you okay?"

He glances up, his hair wet with sweat. His temple looks slightly pink and puffy, but there's no broken skin. "I'm fine, mitt hjärta." He snakes his arm around me, pulling me closer.

"Hey, hey," Langley teases. "None of that now, boys."

"Great score," I tell him.

"Someone had to," Henrik mutters. He's had three shots on goal, all caught in the goalie's glove.

"You'll get one in," Langley assures him, taking a crunch out of an apple.

"Let's go, Ted! We need you!"

Henrik drops his arm from my waist, but I can't help brushing my fingers through his sweaty hair as I race away, ducking back into the PT room to help some of the guys limber up for the next period. I'm finishing with DJ Perry when my phone buzzes in my pocket. I open a new message from Brad and almost retch. "Oh god—"

It's a picture of Dylan's elbow injury.

DJ peers over my shoulder. "Whoa. That's gnarly."

I grimace. "Yeah."

"Is that Dyl?"

"Yep."

My phone pings with another message.

BRADY: They say he's gonna need a skin graft

"Well, duh," says Novy from my other shoulder. "The guy's got no skin left."

One of the forwards, Flash, steps in next to him. "What are y'all looking at?"

From there, my phone gets passed around to every person in the PT room, each one exclaiming in disgust and surprise at the state of Dylan's injury.

"He could be an extra on *The Walking Dead*," Paulie mutters.

Jake just waves his hands, leaning away from the phone. "No way. I don't wanna see that shit."

Caleb takes a look, then hands the phone to Henrik as he appears in the doorway, kitted up and ready except for his gloves and helmet. The others are all talking and moving around, so I don't hear it when my phone pings with a new message.

I definitely hear it when Henrik glares at me from across the room and says, "Who the hell is Fish Lips?"

64

HENRIK

I stare down at Teddy's phone and read the message again. Someone named "Fish Lips" texted him just as Caleb handed me the phone.

FISH LIPS: Hey, beautiful. Someone said you were back with the Rays. Had to see it to believe. Perfect timing, eh? Let me take you out after the game. You know I can show you a better time than that old lump Karlsson.

Teddy crosses the room to my side and reaches for the phone. "What's up?"

There's a ringing in my ears as I hold the phone away from him. "Who is Fish Lips?" I say again.

His expression shutters and I have my answer. "No one."

"Uh-oh." Flash hops off the closest PT table. "Daddy looks mad."

I glare at him, pulling the phone in close to my chest.

He raises a brow, glancing between us. "What? I just assumed that would be y'all's vibe. You strike me as the rough, spanking, 'call me daddy' type, Karlsson."

"And with that, I'm gonna go empty my bowels," says Tremors, stepping past me through the open door.

Teddy holds out his hand. "Babe, give me my phone."

I have no right to keep it from him, even though I want to squeeze it to powder in my fist. I hand it over.

He snatches it quickly, reading the message with a low groan of annoyance. "Fucking seriously?"

"Who is it?"

"It's literally no one," he says again, stuffing the phone in his pocket.

The ringing in my ears gets louder as the room clears out. We're running out of time. I see the seconds ticking down on the game clock. I have to head back out to the ice. But suddenly, hockey doesn't matter. I need Teddy to answer the goddamn question. "Teddy . . ."

He huffs, flapping his arms. "Fine. You wanna do this here? We'll do this right here. He was a guy I matched with on a dating app six freaking years ago. And we never even hooked up," he quickly adds.

Absorbing this information, I cross my arms. "What did you do?"

Jake steps past me, clapping a hand down on my shoulder pad. "Karlsson, bud, a bit of free advice? Never ask that question."

I ignore him, my eyes only for Teddy.

"Your funeral," Novy mutters, following Jake out.

Teddy just shakes his head. "Henrik, I swear it was nothing."

"Tell me the nothing," I press. "It can't be worse than what I'm imagining."

"Oh my god, we matched on the app and flirted a little. He took me out after a game in Chicago, and it sucked. He was pushy, and he kissed like a fish, and I bolted from the bar. End of story."

I tense, eyes narrowing. "You met him in Chicago?"

"Yeah, six *years* ago."

"And now he says he sees you here. He's here now?"

His eyes go wide. "I—maybe. I don't know. Because I don't *care*," he adds emphatically.

"Did he play for the Blackhawks?"

He lifts his chin, holding my gaze. "Yes."

I know this is ridiculous, and irrational, and fifty other words synonymous with completely inappropriate, but that doesn't stop my mind from filling with images of *my* Teddy in the arms of one of the men now out there skating around in a Hawks jersey.

I'm not upset that Teddy has a romantic past. We all have one, even me. Teddy has never judged me for having taken lovers before him. That Teddy flirted with another man, even kissed another man, can easily be excused.

It's the indignity that I cannot excuse, the outright insult to me as Teddy's partner. This man *knows* we're married. The news of our wedding has been blasted everywhere for weeks. Not to mention Poppy's Operation Mighty Oak campaign, and all the images of us on dates—drinking cocktails at High Tide, dancing barefoot on the beach, laughing with friends in that Japanese pub. He knows Teddy is mine. And, still, this man dares to send such a message? He thinks, with a crook of his finger, Teddy will go running to him? Fall into bed with him?

That has me seeing red.

"Tell me his name."

Teddy leans away. "Babe, it doesn't matter."

Gripping his Rays polo shirt tight in my fist, I pull him closer, burying my face at the crook of his neck. I'm desperate to catch a hint of my scent on his skin, the physical reminder that he's mine. It's there, waiting for me, that scent of peppermint oil and wooded spice. I groan, dragging my teeth over his skin until he gasps, hands braced on my padded shoulders.

"Karlsson, let's go," someone shouts.

"Yeah, you can make growling noises with Teddy later!"

"Henrik," Teddy says in my ear. "Look at me." He pulls away, both hands gripping the collar of my jersey. "I'm not gonna do some shitty 'other man' drama with you right now. Until you said the words 'Fish Lips,' I forgot he even existed. Please, tell me you believe me. I'll block him. He's blocked, okay?"

I wrap my hands around his wrists and pull them down. "I believe you."

The relief on his face is so instant and so complete. Then he leans in, pressing his lips to mine. "God, I love you," he says against my lips. "Henrik, I love only you."

Before I can reply, someone jerks on the back of my jersey from out in the hallway. "Jesus, man, let's fucking go! Kissy time can wait!"

Teddy steps away from me, still smiling. "Go. I'll be here when it's over. Karro is at the Langleys', so Rip's tonight, okay? It's karaoke night."

I groan. The last thing I want when I'm feeling this tense is to sit on a stool at Riptide's Bar and Grill and watch other people sing. I want Teddy under me, inside me, shouting my name. No one can show my husband a better time than me. Tonight, I mean to remind him of it.

65

TEDDY

The moment Henrik turns the corner and heads back out to the ice, I jerk my phone from my pocket and craft a scathing response to Fish Lips, aka Corey Lamont, middle-string forward on the Chicago Blackhawks.

I meant every word I said to Henrik. Corey and I were nothing. Less than nothing. I was a lonely college kid, and he was a handsome professional hockey player, arranging gay hookups on the sly. We matched in Chicago, and I was stupid enough to agree to meet up with him.

Online, he was charming, but that was only to get me to say yes. In person, he was arrogant, rude, and clearly only interested in a quick fuck. After the game, he took me way outside the city center to some seedy bar and grinded on me for half an hour.

I finally ducked away to use the bathroom, and he followed. He cornered me and stuck his tongue in my mouth, slurping at me like a fish until I made some excuse about actually needing to use the bathroom. Then I bolted out a side exit and took a taxi back to the hotel.

That's it. That's the epic love story of Teddy O'Connor and Corey "Fish Lips" Lamont.

Henrik doesn't need to know about that chapter of my life. I was a horny, reckless kid. I went with a man I'd just met to a part of town I didn't know to a bar where I felt unsafe. And all for what? A chance at a love connection? It was dumb. And so fucking dangerous. And the taxi back to the hotel cost me, like, forty bucks.

In truth, that disaster of a date with Fish Lips was the last time I ever took that kind of risk. I deleted my account on all the dating apps. I just hated the way he made me feel. So small and dirty. Utterly disposable.

Thumbs flying, I type out my message, then read it back.

TEDDY: You stupid fucking fuck! My husband just saw your message. You better thank your lucky stars I didn't tell him your name, otherwise the Zamboni would be cleaning you off the ice in tiny, bloody pieces. I wasn't interested six years ago, and I'm not interested now. Fuck off forever. I'm blocking this number *middle finger emoji*

There. No room for misinterpretation, right?

Feeling better, the righteous indignation flows through me as I hit Send. Then I block Corey's number with a muttered, "Goodbye, Fish Lips."

I didn't conceal his name to protect him. I did it to protect Henrik. My husband means far too much to me to see him get in trouble out on the ice over something as trivial as a bad date six years ago—

"Oooooh!"

"That's gotta hurt."

"Hey, Ted, Karlsson just got checked pretty bad!"

Zapped out of my stupor, I look around the PT room. "What?"

All the guys are huddled around our TV. The second period has already started. Dustin Evers, one of the athletic trainers, steps back, pointing at the screen. "Chicago just did a shift change, and number nine came busting out like a freight train. Slammed Karlsson down to the ice. He's okay though," he adds as I dart across the room.

"What?" Heart in my throat, I catch the tail end of the replay footage. Henrik takes possession of the puck, but he only gets in one good stride towards the goal before a flash of white and red barrels into him, knocking him down to the ice. The player has a big number nine on his jersey. Above the number, his name is stitched in thick black letters: "LAMONT."

"Oh . . . fuck."

The game ends 4-1 with a Rays win. Corey chased Henrik all over the ice for two periods, scrapping like he had something to prove, but Henrik still earned two of the goals. My throat feels like it's on fire from how much I cheered for him, even if I was only watching it on the TV in the PT room.

The second goal was wild. Henrik hooked it on the end of his blade, a lucky pass from Lindberg, and did a kind of pirouette around Corey, flicking the puck into the top of the net. To my surprise and delight, he's kept "Money Maker" as his goal song all season. It's ridiculous and makes me love him so much I fear I might literally pass out each time I get to watch him skate around the rink in a victory lap.

The game ended twenty minutes ago, and I'm deep into all the cooldown routines. I've got DeGraw back up on the table, helping him stretch out.

"Well, Doc?" he asks. "Did you hear?"

"Hear what?" I say, putting pressure on his hip as he turns.

"About Roshni," he grunts, breathing through the stretch. "Is she coming?"

Oh, fuck me. With all my personal drama, I forgot to even ask. "I . . ."

He must read my face. "It's okay, Doc. I'm sure she's not coming. She doesn't come to anything."

"Does she know she's invited? Meaning have *you* invited her?"

He just grunts, rolling to his other side.

"I'll take that caveman sound as a no?"

"She's so far out of my league," he mutters, gazing off at the poster-clad wall. "Plus, workplace romances, eh? Who needs 'em?"

I snort a laugh, helping him into a deeper hip flex. "Uhh, judging by the dynamics of this team? Like, literally everyone. Myself included. I was so head over heels for my workplace crush, I went off and married him. So, careful with that talk, DeGraw, or you might just be next."

He chuckles through his deep exhale. "Yeah, Doc. Good advice."

By the time I get DeGraw off the table, most of the other guys are clearing out, fresh from their showers.

"Hey," Novy calls over to me. "Rip's tonight. I'm bringing Coley. You guys in?"

"We're coming," I say with a wave.

"Any chance you'll get Karlsson on the mic?" says Paulie.

I just laugh. "Doubtful. But, hey, if you can find someone to be our Chilli, I'm up for singing 'No Scrubs.'"

"Cool. Do I get to be T-Boz?"

"Hell no. I'm T-Boz. Always."

Laughing, he waves me off.

I find Henrik waiting for me in the hallway, dressed in his charcoal suit. He's fresh from a shower, the hair at his nape still wet and curling slightly. "Hey, babe. You ready? Karaoke time."

Once I'm close enough, he pulls me in with his free hand and kisses me rough. I sigh with relief, opening my mouth to take his tongue. The kiss is powerful and claiming, leaving me in no doubt of where his mind is at in this moment.

"Hen," I gasp as he pulls away.

"We're going home."

"But karaoke—"

"I'm taking you home," he says over me, his voice practically a growl. Then he loosens his hold on me, his shoulders relaxing a little. "Teddy, please."

I nod, brushing my hands down the lapels of his jacket. "Yeah, okay."

"Hey, you two lovebirds," Jake calls from down the hall. He wanders closer, one arm around Caleb's shoulder. "Karaoke starts in twenty. Don't be late."

"Uhh . . . I think we need a rain check," I say.

Caleb just snorts. He definitely knows what's up. But Jake shakes his head. "We must be noble in victory, just as the Hawks will now be generous in their defeat." Seeing the looks on our faces, he rolls his eyes. "Come on, guys. Just stay for two songs. Then you can go. Captain's orders," he adds with a stern finger point at Henrik.

"Fine," Henrik mutters.

I brighten a little, equally as excited by the prospect of a little social time with Henrik as I am alone time. This way, I'll get both. Sounds like the perfect night to me. Before he can change his mind, I weave my fingers in with his and pull him along after Jake and Caleb towards the parking garage.

66

HENRIK

Rip's is bursting at the seams. The outside bar area is packed with Rays, Hawks, and all the fans who caught wind of our karaoke night. More people seem to be arriving every minute. The waitstaff are so overwhelmed that it's taken twenty minutes just to get our first round of drinks. At this rate, it'll be midnight before I get my garden burger and fries.

Teddy sits on a stool at the bar, and I stand behind, my hands bracing the bar to either side of him. Call me possessive, but Hawks are swarming all around, and I know at least one of them has their eye on him. If Teddy would just tell me who, I could stand here brooding and watch the man until we leave.

I asked again in the car, but Teddy just groaned and told me to drop it. Now he's deep in animated conversation with DeGraw, who sits on the stool next to him. They're discussing the merits of some statistician who works for the team. I get the feeling Teddy is trying to boost his confidence enough that he'll ask the woman out.

"But what if she's perfect for you?" Teddy cries with a wave of his hand.

"What if she's a lesbian?" DeGraw retorts.

Teddy snorts into his beer. "Oh god—I think I just got beer up my nose."

Reaching between them, I grab a napkin and hold it up for him.

He takes it, dabbing at his chin. "Thanks, babe." Then he's turning back to DeGraw. "All I'm saying is that you won't know until you *ask* her."

DeGraw's eyes go wide. Then he grabs Teddy's arm. "You could do it."

"Do what?"

"Ask her for me."

"Ohmygod." Teddy wrenches away from him. "Ask her out for you? Or ask her if she's a lesbian? Honestly, both are super pathetic, Hunt. You need to just be a big hockey player and ask her yourself."

Groaning, DeGraw folds his arms on the bar top and slams his head down with a thunk that rattles their beer glasses.

Teddy laughs, giving his back a consoling pat. "Cheer up. Maybe you'll find out she's a lesbian with an exhibitionist kink. That could be fun, right?"

Whatever DeGraw replies is lost to the sound of someone strumming an electric guitar on stage. All around us, the crowd starts to cheer.

Teddy spins around on his stool and leans in, shouting in my ear, "I'm gonna go use the bathroom before karaoke starts. Save my stool. And order DeGraw another beer so he can drown his sorrows." Patting my shoulders, he pecks my cheek and darts away.

I take his place on the stool, gesturing at the bartender for another round. Glancing over my shoulder, I watch Teddy weave away through the crowd. As he passes the corner booth by the door, one of the Hawks slams down his beer, rises from his table, and follows.

My heart drops from my chest.

DeGraw leans in and shouts, "So, what are the chances you're gonna sing tonight?"

"Save Teddy's stool," I reply, already on my feet.

"Everything alright, mate?"

For professional hockey players, there are moments on the ice when you feel outside of your own body. The rhythm of the game is instinct more than anything. My muscle memory takes over, my senses sharpen, and I just flow with the energy of the game. In those moments, I just *know* what will happen next. I see it play out in my mind, like a case of déjà vu.

Weaving through this crowded bar, I feel it.

"Hey, Karlsson, where you going?" DeGraw calls after me. "Karlsson!"

I can't stop now. My feet are taking me where I need to go.

And I know exactly what will happen next.

TEDDY

"**C**ome on, man, did you die in there?" I pound my fist on the bathroom door again. I'm standing in this dark hallway as a fluorescent bulb flickers overhead. The wall behind me is covered in a sea of faded posters for everything from beach events, to missing pets, to items for sale. The music starts up outside, and the crowd surges with a cheer. I just barely hear the door lock click before the door is swinging open, nearly catching me in the face.

"Sorry 'bout that," says Jake, stepping out of the bathroom. His cheeks are flushed, eyes glassy, hair tousled.

Caleb steps out behind him, looking a little more put together. He pats me on the shoulder with a smug, "All yours, man."

My mouth opens in shock as I watch them both saunter away. "Oh, fuck both of you!"

Caleb waves over his shoulder, giving Jake's ass a swat as they both turn the corner to head back outside.

Grumbling, I step into the bathroom and take care of my business. I jerk a few paper towels free, dry my hands, and toss the papers atop the already teetering pile in the trash can. I barely have the door open before someone steps into my space, blocking me from getting out.

"Hey, Ted. Long time, no see."

I glare up into the face of Corey Lamont. He's tall and broad shouldered, with a *Mad Men* haircut and a little cleft in his chin. I'd still call him handsome if I didn't know he was such a pompous prick. "Fuck off, Corey. Forever. Or did you not get my last text before I blocked your number?"

"Oh, I did." He grips my arm, stopping me from slipping past. "So feisty."

I jerk away from him. "No touching, asshole."

"I heard you got married," he says in a teasing tone.

"And you still just had to shoot your shot, didn't you? You're pathetic. Let me go."

He leans in, a sweep of his dark hair crossing his brow. "I also heard it was a publicity stunt. Something to do with Karlsson's kid, right?"

Seriously, who the fuck is still out here saying our marriage is fake? Because I'm about to kick them in the fucking cunt. If it's Corey spreading the gossip, I'll kick him twice. "There's nothing fake about my marriage."

Corey leans in, his other arm bracing against the open doorway. "Come on, you can tell me the truth. I know that stiff Karlsson can't possibly keep you satisfied."

"You wouldn't know the first thing about what keeps me satisfied, seeing as we never fucked." I twist my arm out of his grip. "Now, get out of my way, before I knee you in the balls."

He just grins, baring his teeth like a wolf. "You thought you were so cute, slipping my hook the last time. You left me standing there with my dick in my hand."

Fuck, the asshole is already drunk. His breath is hot, reeking of beer. I grimace, leaning away. "I imagine it's not a foreign sensation for you, right? Alone with your dick in your hand?"

He inches closer. "Teddy the Tuna. The one that got away. Well, I caught you now, little fish. Come on, baby. Just one taste."

Heart racing, I dare to try to duck under his arm just as he grabs for me. He pulls at my shirt, and I stumble as he turns. We both fall against the wall. The faded posters for missing cats and used jet skis crinkle behind my head as I twist around and push on him hard with both hands. "Get the fuck off me."

His eyes flash with anger as he recovers his balance, still trying to block my way. "You're a fucking whore, you know that?"

"And you're a bad loser."

"Oh yeah?"

"Yeah. I watched Henrik best you out on that ice all night. My man beat your ass, and now you're being petulant, trying to take what isn't yours."

"You owe me for being a dirty fucking tease," he snarls. "Should be quick now that you're putting out for that clumsy Swedish asshole—"

Crack.

"Ouch," I cry, shaking out my fist. "Oh, fuck, that fucking hurt!"

Corey reels around, one hand rising to catch the blood now dripping from his nose. His expression is all surprise. "You hit me, you little bitch."

"Talk shit about my husband again, I'll do more than hit you," I shout, adrenaline pumping. "And you ever touch me again, I'll run you over with his goddamn Porsche. Then I'll let Henrik fuck me on the hood while you scream. Is that clear enough for you? Teddy the Tuna is off limits."

The moment he digests my words, he lunges, surprising us both with his drunken violence. I scramble backwards, crying out as Corey goes stumbling past me and into the wall. But he's not actually stumbling. He was shoved from behind.

"Henrik!" I step back, eyes wide. "Oh god, stop!"

Henrik and Corey wrestle down to the floor in a great storm of grunts and curses. Their fighting tips over a stack of boxes. Plastic cups and lids go rolling around on the floor. Corey fights to break free as Henrik wails on him with both fists. Corey's legs kick about, but Henrik keeps him pinned.

"Babe, stop," I beg, trying to grab Henrik's arm.

He shouts something in Swedish as Corey wrestles an arm free and starts hitting him back. "Did you touch him?" Henrik switches in English. "Did you fucking touch him?"

"Getoffme—fucking asshole—"

"Guys, stop!"

All the commotion gets the attention of people down the hallway in the main dining room. A woman screams.

"Someone, call the police!"

"God, no police," I shout. "Henrik, *stop!*" I dive for him in earnest, pulling on his arm. "Just leave him."

"He attacked you!"

"He's drunk." I pull on him harder. "Come on, baby. Just leave with me. *Please*."

"Hey!" Hunter DeGraw comes running down the hallway, followed closely by Flash and Paulie. A Hawks player is there too. "Break it up," Hunter shouts. He barrels in next to me and grabs Henrik by both arms, lifting him bodily away from Corey. "Let's leave this kind of fighting for the ice, eh, fellas?"

The other Hawks player ducks around me and pins a bleeding Corey to the wall with his forearm, keeping him from lunging at us again. "Come on, Core, calm down."

Corey laughs, blood in his teeth. "What's the big deal, huh, Karlsson? Your boyfriend and I were just talking—"

"He's my husband!" Henrik shouts, now restrained by Hunter and Flash.

In moments, Jake appears, all his mirth from minutes ago gone. He storms down the hallway in full team-captain mode. "What the hell happened?"

"Karlsson and Lamont were fighting," Paulie explains.

Jake glances from Henrik, his clothes disheveled and his chest heaving like a rhinoceros, to Corey, who looks like he'll have two shiners and is still bleeding from the nose. "Jesus. Why?"

"It was me," I admit. "Corey's drunk and he wasn't taking no for an answer."

"We were just talking," he sneers, dabbing at his bleeding nose with the back of his hand.

Henrik jerks under the hands restraining him. "Don't talk to him—talk to me!"

"Hey, he *wanted* to talk to me," Corey taunts.

"Oh, you're such a fucking liar," I shout. "I was minding my own business, and you know it."

"Please, you wanted me to follow you. Practically begged for it—"

"Say another word to him, and I kill you," Henrik bellows, fighting against his teammates.

"Okay," Jake shouts over him, stepping between them and putting up his hands. "Fuck's sake. Ryder, get Lamont in the bathroom and clean him up," he says at the other Hawks player. "He doesn't get to walk out of this hallway to a bunch of cameras looking like the victim of a bear attack. None of us needs that kind of bad press."

My heart drops out. Cameras? Of course everyone out there who heard the shouting will have a smartphone. And someone shouted something about the police. Oh, fucking fuck.

"I got him," Ryder mutters, pulling on his teammate. "Come on, Core."

Corey just smirks. "But Teddy and I weren't finished."

Jake rounds on him. "You got a fucking death wish, asshole? 'Cause with a snap of my fingers, my guys let Karlsson go to finish your drunk ass."

"No," I plead, adding my hands to the ones holding Henrik at bay.

"I can take him," Corey slurs. "I could take any of you pansy-ass bitches—"

"Jake, he's sorry," Ryder says over him, pulling him away. "If not now, he will be in the morning."

"He's dead," Jake growls. "Clean him up, and get him out of here, Ry."

With a nod, Ryder shoves Corey into the bathroom, slamming the door shut.

As soon as the Hawks are gone, Jake lets out a breath. "For fuck's sake. Seriously, guys? Bar brawling on karaoke night in our own backyard?"

Tears fill my eyes at the look of rage on Henrik's face. "We shouldn't have come. I knew Corey would be here. I just thought he wouldn't care enough to do or say anything stupid. I was wrong."

Jake raises a brow at me. "You and Lamont have history?"

"Barely," I mutter, chest filling with white-hot shame.

He sighs, nodding to the guys to let Henrik go.

Hunter and Flash loosen their hold on him.

I step in. "Jake, someone said they were calling the police. Please, Henrik can't get arrested. We have Karro—our custody case—"

"It won't come to that," he replies, squeezing my shoulder.

"Straighten up," he says at Henrik. "You and Teddy will walk out with us. Get to the parking lot and keep going. Don't say a word to anyone, understand? Just go home."

Henrik nods, running his hands through his mussed hair and straightening his shirt.

"I'll come back and deal with Lamont. We'll put the fear of god in him to keep his mouth shut. It'll be fine." He turns to the other defensemen. "Paulie, Flash, stay with them."

The guys both nod.

"I can go too," says Hunter.

Jake shakes his head. "Sorry, man. You're way too valuable if this turns into a brawl in the parking lot."

"It won't," I assure them all. "We'll go straight home." I look to Henrik, heart in my throat. "Right, babe?" I hold out my hand, desperate for him to take it.

After a moment's hesitation, he does, his fingers wrapping possessively around mine as he reels me in. I let myself be pulled, not stopping until my arm is around his waist, face tucked in at his shoulder. I fight the urge to cry, clinging to him. God, I think I'm trembling.

Paulie leads the way with Hunter. Henrik and I follow. The other two take up the rear. The dining room is ready for us. Half the room is looking our way. Some people are standing. There are definitely phones out. A few of them flash. Henrik tucks me in tighter at his side, trying to shield me.

"Just keep walking," Jake says from behind us. "Don't look at them. Smile and keep walking."

The crowd buzzes like a hive as the karaoke music outside hums. The whole building feels like it vibrates with an excited energy that doesn't match our somber group. Henrik keeps me tucked in tight at his side as we walk right through the restaurant, past the hostess stand, and out the front doors into the parking lot.

Jake and Hunter wait under the lights of the front porch as Paulie and Flash walk with us out to the car. All three men have their heads on swivels, looking for more trouble.

"Where'd you park?" says Flash.

"Back of the lot," Henrik replies, guiding me that way. We get to the Porsche, and he opens my door, not letting me go until I'm safely inside. I can't hear what he says to the others before he opens his door and slides in, closing it with a snap.

The sounds of the karaoke band filter out on the night ocean breeze. It sounds like Caleb is singing a Billy Idol song. I feel like I'm outside of my body, not really part of this moment. The car purrs as Henrik puts it in reverse. With two quick turns, we're rolling down the A1A highway.

"Henrik, I'm sorry," I finally blurt.

"Don't."

"Don't what? Apologize? I have to if I feel like I've done something wrong. And I have—"

"He attacked you!"

I shake my head, tears stinging hot and heavy. "You didn't hear it all."

"I heard enough."

"I goaded him. He pissed me off. I said things to stir him up, even when I knew he was drunk. I did this—"

"Just stop." Henrik shifts gears and the Porsche picks up as we race down the beach highway. "No more talking. I need quiet."

I bite my bottom lip, heart racing faster than the car. Each breath sits shallow in my chest. Henrik passes the first turn that would lead back towards our apartment. Then he passes the second. "Henrik—"

"It's fine."

"But that was the exit." I glance over my shoulder. "Babe, we're driving in the wrong direction."

"We're not going home."

My heart races faster. We're going in the wrong direction to get to Karolina too. "Then . . . where are we going?"

"Out."

"Out where?"

He just keeps driving.

68

TEDDY

After about fifteen minutes of silent driving down the A1A, Henrik pulls off onto a dark sandy road that looks like it leads right into a damn sand dune.

I sit up in my seat, looking around. "Babe, driving on the dunes is all kinds of illegal."

The car takes a sharp turn around a row of low palm trees, and then we're in a small, six-car parking lot, all but tucked away from the main road. Ours is the only car here. The Porsche's headlights gleam on a large sign at the end of the lot that clearly states there's no parking after dark.

"Babe, we can't park here—"

"Get out." Henrik turns off the car, opens his door, and steps out.

I have no choice but to scramble out after him. I stand next to the car, breathing in the crisp beach air. It's salty and a little sweet, with just a hint of brine. I look up, spying all the stars overhead. "Man, it's beautiful out here," I say, still looking around. "How did you even know about this place?"

Henrik steps around the front of the car and pulls me to him, taking me with another rough kiss. I melt against him, arms going around his neck. His kisses are fevered and claiming. He nips with his teeth, all but bending me back until I'm pressed up against the side of the car.

"Hen—"

"I heard you."

I search his face by the light of the stars, hands brushing down his chest. "Heard what?"

"In the hallway. With him. I heard what you said."

My mind races as I think back through all the horrible things that were said. Corey was the drunk asshole, but it certainly wasn't my finest moment either. I grimace. "Which part?"

Henrik leans in, his hips pressing against mine. "The part where he called me a clumsy Swedish asshole."

My heart skips a beat as he lowers his hands to the top of my athletic pants. "Henrik . . ."

"What did you say, Teddy?"

I lick my lips, my breathing shallow as he slips a hand inside my pants, stroking my dick over my briefs. I groan, bracing him by the arms. "Oh, fuck."

His thumb presses over my head until my precum makes a little wet spot I know he can feel through the briefs. He hums his approval. "I'm waiting."

"I said . . ." My mind is reeling, too distracted by his proximity, the feel of his hands on me. I can never think when he's touching me. "Fuck, I think I said if he talked shit about you again, I'd do worse than hit him."

He smiles, giving my dick another teasing squeeze. "And if he touched you? What then?"

I swallow the nerves sitting high in my throat, holding his fiery gaze. Oh, this is so fucking happening. Feeling bold, I wrap my hand around his wrist, keeping his hand in my pants. "I told him I'd run him over in your car and let you fuck me on the hood."

His gaze is equal parts proud and triumphant. I feel awash in the glow of his approval. "He called you my boyfriend."

I fight a growl, my grip on his wrist tightening. "We're not boys, and you're not my friend. You are *mine*, Henrik. Flesh of my flesh, and bone of my bone. I mean to pass through this life as your other half."

He nods, his smile tender and beautiful as a fucking sunrise. "Two halves made whole."

I sigh, my forehead dropping to the middle of his chest.

"What do you need?" His free hand strokes my shoulder as his thumb circles the tip of my dick again, making me twitch. "Say it."

Leaning away, I hold his gaze, hoping he can see how desperate I am, how needy for him. "Make us whole? Right here. God, baby, this time I'm the one begging for it." I work both hands up under his shirt, feeling the warmth of his skin against my palms.

His smile falls, and my hands stop their caressing. "You knew he was there tonight. You knew he was watching you."

My heart stops and the words to an apology are on the tip of my tongue. It takes everything in me to swallow them back. The old Teddy would have fallen over himself to smooth it over, make it right. Even in the car, I was ready to apologize. But in Henrik's arms, I am remade. He makes me feel confident and in control. With him, I am my truest self. With him, I *trust* myself. No compromises, no making myself smaller.

Squaring my shoulders, I hold his gaze. "I won't apologize, because I've done nothing wrong. His shitty, drunken behavior is his own problem. And I told you he means less than nothing to me." I cup Henrik's face, desperate for him to see me in that way only he can. "I would never risk what we have. Not ever. Do you believe me?"

His gaze is molten as he tips his chin, kissing my palm. "I believe you, mitt hjärta. There is only me for you."

At his endearment, I groan with relief, sinking against him. "God, baby, *yes*." I cling to him with both hands, seeking a kiss. He obliges, his lips warm and inviting. I feel fevered, like I'm suddenly crawling out of my own skin.

"Tell me what you need."

"I need you to touch me everywhere he tried to touch me. Burn his memory from my skin—"

He swallows my plea with another heady kiss. Mouths open, we devour. Gone is all finesse. Like twin fires, we burn. His hands are everywhere, touching every part of me. Our kisses turn into mutual panting as we fight to get closer, pulling at our clothes.

"You're mine," he growls against my lips. "My Teddy, my pure heart."

"Yes," I chant, jerking my athletic pants down. "Yours." I don't care that my bare ass is pressed against the side of his Porsche. I just need my dick out. The cool air is a relief against the fire in my blood. I'm gasping, fisting his hair tight, shoving him to his knees. "Suck me. Suck my dick. Baby, please."

My man goes so willingly. He drops to the gravel with a hungry groan and grabs me by the hips, sucking my hard length to the back of his throat.

"Fuck!" I tip my head back, lost to the sensation of him pleasuring me. His mouth is so warm and wet, his beard bristling against my sensitive skin. I weave my fingers into his thick hair, gripping tight. He likes a little roughness, likes when I guide and pull. When I start to rock with my hips, fucking his face in earnest, I'm rewarded with the most perfect humming moan that vibrates down my shaft and licks like fire up into my chest.

Oh god, I'm gonna come.

The stars blink overhead. Just beyond the dune, the ocean laps at the sand. Too many cadences at once—my racing heart, the lull of the waves, Henrik sucking and bobbing on my dick like he's trying to win a goddamn medal. He reaches a hand between my legs, his fingers brushing along my taint, and I buck into his mouth. "Oh, fuck!"

I feel like a desperate teen about to get caught. I mean, we *are* out in the open, exposed to the wilds. My god, I think there are pumas in this part of Florida. And another car could come along at any moment. I hear them rushing past out on the highway. I see the flicker of their headlights through the fronds of the shrubby palms.

We should stop. We have a perfectly good bed at home where there's no risk of getting caught—

Henrik pops off my cock and stands, panting for breath. Grabbing my arm, he tugs me over to the front of the Porsche. "Turn around," he growls. "Hands on the hood."

Gazing up at him like he's the answer to every unsolved problem of the universe, I smile. "Make me."

He blinks twice, translating both the words and my intention.

Then he lunges. An excited laugh bursts out of me as he grabs me around the middle and turns me to face the car, shoving my shoulders down. I'm practically preening as my husband bends me over the hood of his sexy sports car, my hands splayed against the sleek blue paint.

I'm so full of my own gloating, I don't even register the first slap. A surprise gasp escapes my lips as I rock forward. Then I feel the sharp, nettling sting on my ass cheek. Eyes wide, I glance over my shoulder.

My husband looks just as surprised. Slowly, he shakes his head. "Teddy, I—"

"Oh fuck, baby, do it again."

His eyes flash, his split second of panic replaced once more with need. Groaning low in his throat, he slaps my ass again. Hard. It stings like a motherfucker, even as it makes my cock twitch and drip. I can't help but grab it, giving it a stroke. God, it's still wet from his mouth.

"Don't come until I say," he commands. "I'm not nearly done with you."

Whimpering, I rock into Henrik's touch as he massages my ass cheeks, giving each a firm caress. "Baby, please, I want you inside me. Fuck me. Want your cock—*ah*—" I choke back a laugh as he slaps me again, this time on the other cheek.

Folding himself over me, he wraps a hand around my throat, pulling me up until my back is flush with his chest. "You'll take what I give you," he growls in my ear, nipping the lobe until I hiss. "I'll fill your ass with my cum when I'm good and ready, and not a moment before. Rush me, and we'll end the night here."

I flex my hands on the hood of his car. "Flash was wrong earlier. You're not the 'daddy' type. But clearly, spanking is on the table. Which, thank fucking god."

He raises a brow. "You really like it?"

"Getting spanked? Fuck yes. Baby, it's so hot. I like getting choked too, but we can work our way up to that. When you really feel like having some fun, you can chase me." At the flash in his eyes, I crow inside. "Oh yeah, look at you. I bet you're dripping at that, aren't you?" Being the brat I am, I rock back with my hips, pressing my bare ass against his crotch. "Imagine getting to chase me, pin me down, and fuck my brains out like we're two wild animals—"

Growling, he slams forward with his hips, rubbing his hard cock against my ass cheek as he pushes down on my shoulders. "Stop trying to distract me. You don't want me to fuck you on the hood this car?"

"I do," I cry, turning back to face the windshield. "Fuck, baby, I do. God, anything. I'm yours." I'm a mumbling mess as he finally undoes his belt. He's still in his game-day suit, just without the jacket and tie, shirtsleeves rolled up.

"Do I need to stretch you out first?"

I would answer him, but he's got his hard dick in his hand, tapping it against my ass cheek, so my brain is putting all its effort into standing right now.

"I have lube," he goes on.

I blink, glancing over my shoulder. "Wait, seriously?"

He fishes a little packet of lube from his pocket, holding it up.

I smile, feeling all warm and floaty. "Well, aren't you Mr. Prepared? Eagerly anticipating a beachside fuck, are we?"

He just shrugs. "The guys put a hundred pack of these in my locker as a joke shortly after our wedding."

"Look who's laughing now." My mirth settles as I sense the barest hint of his unease. He's still pretty new at this. "You won't hurt me," I assure him. "I trust you. Make me feel so good, like only you can."

Turning around, I'm content to watch our shadowy reflections in the windshield. I hear the soft *crick* as Henrik opens the lube packet, then I'm gasping at the feel of his slick fingers pressing in at my asshole. Huffing out a breath, I let myself sink into a cozy little sub space. Henrik is in control now. He'll take such good care of me.

He presses in with two fingers, stretching me open. "You're so tight, mitt hjärta."

The burn of that first stretch has my dick twitching. I moan, rocking back against his hand. "You'll fit. Please, baby, give me your cock. God, I need it."

His fingers slip out as he mutters a soft curse in Swedish. Then he's fisting his thick shaft, letting it glide slick and heavy between my cheeks. We both groan as his tip breaches my tight outer ring of muscle.

"Slow," I say on a breath.

He holds my hips tight enough to bruise as he rocks against me, stretching me with each thrust. Every inch of him I take has me feeling more anxious and breathless. I need to come. That's what this is. The anticipation is killing me. I need him to unleash himself on me—use me, fill me, tear me apart.

"I can't," he pants.

I hold still, trying to search his face in our reflection. "What is it? Talk to me."

"Can't bear it," he grits out. "Need to come."

I smile, triumphant. "Baby, look at me."

He grunts, looking down at where we're joined. "God, help me."

"Look at *me*," I press. "In the windshield. Look at my reflection."

He glances up, seeing the shadows of us reflected by the moon and stars above. His hands on my hips soften their crushing hold.

"There you are," I say with a smile. "Just breathe for a sec. Keep looking at me and breathe."

Slowly, he begins to thrust again. I can hardly bear the pleasure of being filled so full. I brace against the hood of the Porsche with both hands as he sinks all the way. Tension coils in my gut as my own urge to come presses in on me.

"You're in control," I pant, moving my hips against him. "No one comes until you say. Just take me. Take your pleasure from me. God, take anything."

With a desperate groan, Henrik wraps his hands around me, bracing against my chest. I feel his warm breath at my ear as he pants. "You feel so good, min kärlek. I can't bear it."

I tip my head back, exposing my neck to his lips as he fucks me in earnest. Our hips slap together as he claims me over and over.

Deeper. Harder. His hand grips tightly to my shoulder, then he's rocking back on a shout. Oh god, he's fucking pounding me, and I can't get enough. His energy is so chaotic and beautiful.

Speaking of chaos, I feel like a lit fuse, seconds away from detonation. The spark is sizzling closer and closer to the pile of TNT that is my waiting orgasm. My fingers are tingling, balls twitching. He's not even touching my dick yet. When he does, it's all over. "Henrik!"

His hand shifts from my shoulder to around my neck. Then he's pulling me back, the pressure at my neck firm. My hands wrap around to reach any part of him I can. I pull on his shirt, his hair, seeking any purchase.

"Touch yourself," he commands. "Pinch your nipples."

"Oh fuck." Breathless and trembling, I brush my hands down my chest, rubbing my thumbs over the fabric of my shirt. My nipples are peaked beneath the fabric.

Then his hand is gone from my neck, and he's clawing my shirt up my torso and off, tugging it over my head. I feel like I'm free-falling, arms in the air, pinned by the calves to the Porsche as he keeps his dick buried inside me. He tosses the shirt into the dirt and pulls out of me.

Gasping for air, I fall forward, catching myself with my hands on the hood. My pants are wrapped around my knees, keeping me trapped.

"Off," he commands. "Take them off."

I'm dizzy with lust. God, he's fucked the sense right out of me. "My pants? You want me buck naked where any passing pelican can see me?"

"I want you spread wider," he growls in my ear. "I want to get deeper."

Swallowing an eager whimper, I kick off my left shoe, tugging my knee up until it comes free of my pant leg. Then Henrik grabs my thigh and spreads me wider, bending me forward back over the hood of his goddamn Porsche. My left knee balances on the sleek surface, fingers of both hands splayed. I cry out as Henrik buries himself to the hilt inside me. "Fuck, fuck—"

He begins to thrust again, his hands on my hips jerking me back and back. He sinks deeper and we both moan. The glide of his cock against my prostate has me squirming. Forget the box of TNT. Forget Icarus shooting towards the sun. I'm a fucking meteor. There's no stopping this. I told Henrik he was in control, but nothing will stop me coming now.

"Henrik—" I chant his name, my own prayer.

His hand snakes around my hip, and he finally takes my dick in hand, stroking it from root to tip. "Come for me, mitt hjärta. Fill my hand."

His permission unleashes me. Clenching tight on the dick in my ass, I roll with my hips, thrusting my hard shaft into his lubed fist, once, twice. My orgasm overtakes me, and I'm coming on a garbled shout. My warm release fills his hand as he strokes me hard, making a sticky mess all over my shaft that drips down from my balls onto the hood of the car.

Taking his cum-soaked hand, Henrik roughly grabs my chin, twisting his hold on me to sink two fingers into my mouth. "Suck."

Groaning, I lick and suck my jizz from his fingers, crying out when he finally unleashes inside me. His hot cum fills me and he rocks against my ass, keeping himself buried deep, slowly thrusting as he rides out the last cresting wave of his orgasm.

My jaw hurts, my arms are shaking, and my asshole has its own heartbeat from the pounding it just took. But I feel so happy, and so incredibly full. Henrik's dick slips out of me, his cum leaking down my thighs. He pulls me to him, turning me around to wrap me in a hug. I cling to him, my face pressed to his shoulder. I don't care that I'm naked with only one shoe, my pants twisted around my ankle. I'm Henrik's. Claimed, body and soul. Nothing else matters.

I pull away just long enough to kiss him. "I love you," I whisper against his lips. "Henrik, baby, I love you so much."

He smiles down at me, his hands moving all over me, soothing every ache and pain. He cups my cheek, and I know this is the moment. He's finally going to say it, my man of few words. But these are words we both need. God, how I've waited for them. "Teddy, I—"

He goes tense. Then he curses in Swedish, spinning me around to block me with his body. I see the bright headlights before I hear the crunching of the gravel under tires. "Oh, fuck!"

"Stay behind me," he shouts, tucking his dick back in his pants.

"Babe—I only have one shoe!" And my pants are inside out at my ankle. And I have no shirt. But I'll be fucked if I let whoever's in that car get a shot of me hopping around on one foot with my dick flapping in the wind, trying to get my pants to go outside in.

A big SUV rolls to a stop at the mouth of the parking lot, blasting rock music, headlights shining. I feel like an idiot hiding behind Henrik, both my hands on his shoulders. He stands before me, shirt ripped open, pants unbuttoned. At least his dick is tucked away. He lifts a hand, guarding his eyes from the sharp glare. He's so tense, ready to slay this steel dragon for me.

The music cuts, and the passenger door opens. Someone pops out the side, standing on the rails. A wolf-whistle cuts over the sound of the roaring engine. "Hey, Karlsson! Hey, Ted! Having fun there, fellas?"

I relax, stifling a laugh. It's Chris Woodson, Henrik's teammate.

"Fuck, Woody," Henrik shouts. "Cut the goddamn headlights."

"Nah, we'll head back out," he calls back with a wave. "Leave you two lovebirds at it. Jake just wanted to make sure you weren't out here burying bodies or some shit."

"Wait, *we*?" I shout. "Who the hell is we?"

"Paulie's driving," he calls back as Paulie taps the horn. "And we brought Flash, Bouche, and DeGraw just in case."

Someone waves out the other window. "Hey, Ted!"

Yep, I think that's Hunter.

Fucking perfect.

"How did you even know where to find us?" Henrik shouts.

"Phone GPS," Woody calls back. "Jake has us all linked, remember? You two have fun!"

"Don't get caught," one of the guys yells from the back seat. "You know . . . again!"

Woody slips back into the SUV, and the rock music blasts up again. Paulie whips them around in a tight circle. Then they shoot back out onto the beach highway in a crunch of gravel, leaving Henrik and I standing here breathless, mostly naked, and covered in cum.

I give Henrik's shoulder a squeeze. "Any chance of them ever letting us live this down?"

Henrik shakes his head. "No. Never."

It only takes a moment before we're both cracking up, laughing so hard we cry, as we find the rest of my discarded clothes, stumble back into the Porsche, and race away from the scene of our first crime.

69

HENRIK

"How do you feel?" I ask in Swedish, watching Karolina flex her hand, newly without its purple cast.

"Strange," she murmurs, rotating her wrist the way the doctor showed her. "My bone isn't broken anymore?"

"No. Your body healed itself." I brush a hand down her thick Dutch braid, kissing the top of her head. "You're so strong, mitt lilla lamm."

"But not my leg, right?"

"Not yet. But soon."

"And then I can do ballet again? And go to school?"

"Of course. Mr. Torres says you're doing wonderfully well with your English lessons. He thinks you'll be ready for American school in January."

"And ballet?" Her brow furrows with that serious look of a child determined to have her way. Emma Langley is doing a recital with her ballet school of *Swan Lake* this Christmas. The Langleys invited us to attend. It's all Karolina has been able to talk about for days.

I nod again, offering her a patient smile. "As soon as your doctor clears you for athletic activity, we'll enroll you in ballet. Miss Maria is saving a spot for you in Emma's class."

"Emma says they do classes for daddies and daughters too. Would you go with me, Morbror? I can show you how to plié. It's not hard."

I chuckle. "Of course I will. Can Teddy come too?"

He was supposed to be here with us this morning, but he agreed to help cover for Brady through the end of the week. He should be home by lunchtime. We're celebrating Karolina's big milestone tonight with Hanna and Torres. Hot dogs and ice cream at the beach, Karro's choice.

Her smile falls as she drops her hand to her lap.

"What's wrong, lamm?"

She glances up at me through her lashes. "Do you love him?"

"Teddy? Of course I do. Why would you ask me that?"

Her bottom lip quivers. "He told Miss Shae you don't."

My heart stops. "What? When did you hear this?"

"On the phone. He says you won't say it, and it makes him sad."

I groan, crossing my arms. It's possible she misheard their English. Or, if she only heard Teddy, then she only heard one side. But why would Teddy talk of such things where Karolina might hear? And why discuss it with his sister instead of talking with me directly? I glance down at Karro. "And why were you listening to his private conversation?"

She pouts. "Are you mad?"

Sighing, I sink back in my chair. "No, lamm, I'm not mad."

"I didn't mean to listen. Honest. I just . . . woke up."

I place a hand on her shoulder and give it a squeeze. "Karro, look at me."

She looks up, bottom lip still quivering. "If you don't say you love them, they go."

"What?"

"Prince Derek didn't say it, and Odette left. Then the monster got her. If you don't say it, Teddy will go. I don't want Teddy to go. He has to stay."

"I'll say it," I assure her, brushing my hand down her long braid again. I'm getting better at braiding. My skills are nothing near as accomplished as Teddy's, but I can now manage a passable French braid, a Dutch braid, even a fishtail.

"You *have* to," she says again, her eyes narrowed at me.

"I will," I repeat, feeling very much like I'm being chastised by my bossy older sister. Thinking of Petra, I sigh. "Your uncle is an old Swedish fart, Karolina."

She giggles.

"I'm not used to saying what I feel," I admit. "Your mother was always so much better at it than me. And Mormor. She always says exactly what she thinks and feels. You and Petra get that from her."

"I miss Mormor," she murmurs. "And I miss Mamma."

I wrap my arm around her. "I miss your mamma too, lamm. Every day. So much. And Mormor. We'll go visit her in the spring, ja? As soon as my hockey season is over. We'll show Teddy the lake and the beach. We'll take him looking for mushrooms."

She sits up with an excited smile. "And Junibacken!"

I smile. "Of course." She and Petra had season passes to the little children's discovery center in Stockholm. I got them for Karolina as a third birthday present.

"I want Teddy to stay forever. He won't leave if you tell him he can stay."

My smile widens as I picture the two of them laughing and playing together, practicing ballet in the mirror. Years from now, they'll argue over homework, and he'll complain she drives too fast in my car. I can see it all. I see a future for the three of us, warm and bright. It's not the future any of us expected. But now it's the future we all deserve.

I glance down at her, nudging her with my elbow. "And me, lamm? Do you want to stay with me forever too?"

She takes my hand. "I have to."

"Why?"

She shrugs. "You were sad before I came, Morbror. You're not sad anymore."

Wiping away my unexpected tears, I look to the ceiling and say nothing, letting my niece hold my hand.

T he elevator doors open on our floor, and I push Karolina out to see Hanna waiting for us at the end of the hall. She scrambles off the floor at first sight of us, phone in hand. Her eyes look puffy, like she's been crying.

"Hanna, look," Karro calls in Swedish, waving her uncasted arm in the air. "It's all better now!"

"Look at you," Hanna coos, finding her a smile. All the while, she casts me a look of warning that has my stomach sinking.

"What is it?" I say, reaching in my pocket for the keys. "Why are you here so early?" I pause, glancing around. "And why are you waiting in the hall? Did you lose your key?"

"I umm . . . no. I guess I didn't feel right about just going in." She clutches to her phone. "Is Teddy not with you?"

"He had to cover someone at work."

She steps back. "I can—I think I'll come back later then."

"No. Stay."

Her eyes go wide at my command, giving me all the proof I need that something is definitely wrong.

"Come in," Karro calls in English as I push her inside the apartment. "We were gonna make you kanelbulle, but then we had to go to the hockey, because someone lost an elbow glove. And then I went to play with Emma!"

Hanna glances from Karro to me. Sometimes, between the constant switching from English to Swedish, things get a little lost in translation.

"You're welcome to come in," I assure her, gentling my tone. "Then you can tell me what's wrong."

"So you haven't seen then? You don't know?"

"Seen what?"

She glances from me to Karro again.

Groaning, I take the hint. "Start the coffee. I'll get her settled in."

By the time I have Karolina on the couch with a plate of apple slices and a princess movie, Hanna is in the kitchen, clutching to a mug of coffee. "What happened?" I say again, taking the other prepared cup.

"Oh, Henrik," she cries. "It's so awful. How have you not heard?"

"Show me."

Setting her mug of coffee on the island, she unlocks her phone and hands it to me. On the screen is an article:

"On Thin Ice: Inside the Public Free Fall of the NHL's Most Private Player"

My frown deepens as I read. It's a scathing exposé article on me. In the first paragraph, the author calls me a "loose cannon" and a "PR liability." There are pictures from Rip's last night—Teddy tucked under my arm, grainy photos of Lamont exiting the bar with a bloody face.

Between my fight on the ice with that rookie during the Golden Knights game—yes, there are pictures of that too—and my brawl with Lamont last night, they're calling me "violent" and "dangerous."

Somehow, the author even tracked down evidence of my recently broken endorsement deal. They argue "inside sources" say the brand broke ties with me because I was bad for their image. No mention at all of our scheduling conflict. Every word of the article is malicious, salacious, and completely unfounded.

"There is no truth to any of this," I say, holding the phone out for Hanna, but she shakes her head.

"Keep scrolling."

I flick with my thumb, letting more of the story zip past. I stop on a new set of images. One is of me, Hanna, and Karro at the ice cream shop a few weeks ago. We meet there all the time for her to take Karro before I headed off to practice. The pictures make it look like I'm kissing her.

Well, I *am* kissing her, but only her cheek. And only in greeting. There's a shot of us laughing together. Us smiling, each holding one of Karro's hands as we walk down the pier. We look like a happy little family. Our outfits are different in every shot, which plays perfectly into the narrative that Hanna and I must be secret lovers, engaging in a weeks-long tryst.

I sigh. "Hanna, I'm so sorry."

"Why are they doing this?" she says through her tears.

"To make money, I imagine. Why else?"

"But it's not true. None of this is, right?"

"Of course not." I hold out her phone. "I'm only sorry you were dragged into it."

She takes the phone and steps away, wrapping her arms around her middle. "But why are they taking pictures of us? Of Karolina? Can it even be legal?"

"Yes, it's legal. They've blurred her face out of the pictures they published."

"But it's so cruel. So irresponsible."

My frustration rises. "I know."

"It all just feels so violating," she goes on. "I didn't know what to do. I woke up to all these alerts from family and friends. Those pictures are everywhere, Henrik. Someone tried to tag me in them on Instagram. On the way over here, I got a request to do an interview."

My anger flares. "Say nothing. You will only fuel their fire. Best to let this all die out."

She shakes her head. "Teddy must hate me."

"He doesn't. Or he won't when he finds out. He knows it's not true too."

As if speaking his name is a summons, the front door opens, and Teddy comes charging in. His locs are a mess, half up, half down, and he looks like he sprinted here from the parking garage.

"Teddy," Karolina cries in welcome, waving with her whole arm. "Look, I got my cast off!"

He rattles his keys down in the tray and kicks off his shoes. "That's great, honey, but I gotta talk to Morbror for a second!" He jogs into the kitchen, letting out a breath as he lowers his voice. "What the actual fucking fuck is going on?"

I sigh. "I take it you know?"

"Of course I know. My phone went crazy with all my sisters calling at once. They were ready to come down here and barbecue you until I called them off."

Hanna bursts into tears. "Teddy, I'm *so* sorry!"

His eyes go wide as she stumbles into his arms on a stifled sob. He tries to soothe her, patting her back. "Hey, it's okay. Hanna, we know this has nothing to do with you, okay?"

"They made me look so awful," she says through her sniffles. "But I would never—Teddy, I'd *never* break up a marriage. My dad cheated on my mom and left the family when I was nine. So, I know that pain. You have to believe me—"

"We *do*," I assure her, stepping closer.

But Teddy holds up a warning hand, keeping me back. Best to just let her have a good cry. Proximity to me will likely only make it worse.

"You saw the article?" I say at him.

"Oh, I saw. The articles, the videos, the stupid fucking photo diaries. Who knew he had such a 'bad boy' streak, huh?" he teases, still patting Hanna's back. "I guess I bring it out in him. We'll have to get him a motorcycle to go with his leather jacket."

Hanna makes a sound between a laugh and a sob.

"You need to call Poppy," he says over her shoulder. "She needs to know, if she doesn't already."

I lean my hip against the island, sipping my coffee. I've resigned myself to taking it with milk and sugar. Teddy and Hanna won't prepare it any other way. "At this point, I don't know what else we can do, other than let it all die down naturally. The fires of controversy always flame out."

"But this isn't just idle gossip now. Hen, this is serious. They have pictures and 'inside accounts.'"

"All meritless," I growl.

"Idle gossip about us is one thing. Proof that you're violent? That you're a dangerous liability? This could ruin your chances at future endorsement deals. Hell, it could get you traded. The Rays won't want to carry the weight of your new 'bad boy' reputation if it will reflect poorly on them. Neither will any brands looking to keep a family-friendly image."

Hanna pulls away from him, her mascara running as she turns to me. "Oh god, this could get you traded?"

Teddy winces, patting her shoulders. "Still not your fault," he assures her.

Before I can respond, my phone starts buzzing in my pocket. I check the caller ID and see my dad's name. I look to Teddy, holding up the phone. "I have to take this."

His eyes go wide. "Is it Poppy? Elin?"

"My dad." Turning away from the kitchen, I walk down the hall and accept the call. "Hej, Dad."

"Oh, Henrik, what have you done?"

Closing the door to the bedroom, I sit down on the edge of the bed and try for a tone of levity. "I take it the story about my new devilish reputation has arrived in Sweden?"

"This is no laughing matter, son. A reporter came to the house this afternoon."

My heart stops. "What?"

"He asked all kinds of questions, upsetting your mother, confusing her with rumors of your infidelity. The questions played with the holes in her memory. She told him you weren't married. She's been crying all evening. Now she keeps asking for Petra."

My rage surges. "Why did you let him in? Why did you speak to the reporter at all? I told you, never talk to the press!"

"I didn't," he retorts. "Your mother let him in while I was out in the yard. The man said he was writing an article about your hockey career. He asked for pictures from your time in the SHL."

I groan. "Dad, any pictures he could ever need are already publicly available. Or he could contact the teams I played for directly. Same for the NHL. He doesn't need to go to my mother."

"Yes, well, you know how she gets confused. By the time I came inside, she'd already sat him down with coffee. She denied you were married. I assured him that you were. But then he kept asking whether you had a violent nature as a child, which upset her greatly."

"He was just trying to get a new angle on the story making the rounds in the American papers."

"He showed us the pictures of you and that poor nurse," Dad goes on. "Henrik, infidelity is so distasteful. I'll admit, I'm surprised at you."

"It's not true," I shout. "Dad, I am very happily married to Teddy. Hanna is our employee. She's Karolina's nurse. Nothing inappropriate has ever taken place. Not even close."

"Well, why put yourself in the position to be compromised in the first place?"

"If greeting someone on a public street is proof of infidelity, then we are all unfaithful every day of our lives!"

We're both quiet for a moment. My chest rises and falls with each breath as I clench my fist, trying to calm down.

"Son, we're just worried about you," he finally says. "You've been so careful to keep your reputation all about hockey."

I huff a laugh, shaking my head. "No, Dad. All I *had* was hockey."

"What?"

Rising to my feet, I pace into the bathroom. "Before Karolina came to stay with me, before Teddy, all I had was hockey. It was my whole life."

"Well, you were dedicated."

"I was a ghost! Practice and games, practice and games. Planes, busses, hotel rooms. I had no life, Dad. No friends. No focus, no dreams, no plans. Nothing outside of hockey and the four of you. Then Petra died, and I wanted the earth to swallow me too. But then Teddy and Karro came into my life, and now . . ."

Dad waits. "And now, son?"

I smile, looking around at the mess in my bathroom. Teddy's hair products are piled on the edge of the counter. Karro's bath toys litter the floor of the shower. My gaze settles on the lonely sink, and I laugh, dragging a hand through my hair. "God, Dad, now I have so many plans."

10

TEDDY

Well, we're right back where we fucking started, sitting on the couch in Poppy's office, waiting for her to tell us how she's going to make this all go away again. The only difference is that her lovely Chaddy receptionist has been replaced by a highly competent Korean college student named Yoon Hee.

Henrik sits next to me, looking as relaxed as I've ever seen him. Why is he not more upset about all this? Why isn't he freaking out? It's been two days, and Hanna is still a mess. Now Poppy is pacing, and I feel like I have gravel churning in my stomach.

But he's just sitting there, sipping the coffee Yoon Hee brought us, looking like he doesn't have a care in the world. He catches my anxious stare and smiles, placing a hand on my thigh.

"Can't even go away for three weeks without it all going to hell in a hand basket," Poppy mutters, still pacing.

"Sorry, Poppy."

She spins around in her heels. "Oh, Teddy, don't you apologize, honey. This isn't your fault. It's not your fault either," she quickly adds at Henrik. "The press is just . . . well, the worst. But what else is freaking new?"

"But you have an idea?" I shift to the edge of the couch. "Some plan to get us out of this? Some way to spin it all in Henrik's favor?"

She huffs, dropping down in the chair opposite us. "I'll not deny it, boys. This really is a rotten kettle of fish. These tabloid vultures aren't doing you any favors, and the story we were trying to avoid got out in the end."

"Which story is that?" I say.

Over the last couple days, more articles have been published. Internet sleuths even pulled pictures from my time as an intern. I didn't know they existed. Action shots of Henrik on the ice, me watching from the bench. There's even one of him walking off the bus on game day, me a few steps behind. He's stoic and aloof, completely unobtainable. While I look like a puppy, panting at his heels.

Frankly, they're embarrassing. More embarrassing than half the guys finding us with my pants around my ankles. At least at the beach, I was thoroughly fucked. The intern-era photos show just how hopeless and desperate I really was.

Poppy gestures to the spread of articles on the coffee table between us. "These photos act as a sort of timeline. At best, the stories make it look like Henrik took advantage of you, preying on your innocence as an intern."

I snort. My innocence? Yeah, I lost that back in middle school.

"At worst," she goes on, "These new articles are still painting your quickie marriage as a sham, designed to help Henrik gain custody of Karolina. Your mother saying you're not married hasn't helped."

"My mother is unwell," Henrik replies. "The Swedish press already issued a retraction, correcting her words."

"I know," she goes on. "But pair that little speed bump with the infidelity rumors, the proof of violence, and the broken endorsement deals, and it's not looking good . . ."

She pauses at Henrik's ringing phone. It buzzes on the coffee table, and I see Elin's name on the caller ID.

Oh fuck.

He glances sharply at me before looking to Poppy. "I have to take this."

"Please." She waves her hand. "Be my guest."

He brings the phone to his ear and answers in Swedish, his tone clipped. In moments, he's turning it on speaker and setting it on the coffee table. Then he switches to English. "Poppy, this is my lawyer in Sweden, Elin Ågren. Elin, I have you here with Teddy and my team publicist."

"Hello," comes her soft voice.

"Hey, Elin." I wave at the phone, even though she can't see me.

"What update do you have for us?" says Henrik.

She sighs, and my heart drops from my chest. "I'm sorry, but it's not good news."

I grip his knee.

"What news?" he presses, covering my hand with his.

"I've just been on the phone with Karolina's case worker. There are concerns about your suitability to be her primary guardian."

"Based on what?" he challenges. "Fabricated articles in sports tabloids? The manipulation of my mother? Social media posts?"

"There are concerns about your recent displays of violence. On and off the ice."

"My god, violence on the ice is his literal job," I cry. "He's a professional hockey player for Christ's sake!"

"And off it?"

Henrik sits forward. "Elin, the stories have it wrong. It wasn't a drunken brawl between rival teams. I stepped in when a drunken Blackhawks player attempted to sexually assault my husband. Does the Swedish government now hold with assault?"

"He assaulted you, Teddy? There is proof of this?"

I glance from Poppy back to the phone. "He tried. But, like Henrik said, he was drunk, and his team had just lost. It doesn't excuse anything, but I don't want to press charges."

"We have five witnesses to the altercation," Henrik goes on. "Including the team captains of both the Rays and the Chicago Blackhawks."

Clearing her throat, Poppy sits forward. "Miss Ågren, Poppy St. James here. I've spoken to the head of PR over at the Blackhawks personally, and they assure me Mr. Lamont will not be pressing any charges. To do so would mean legal retaliation, and Mr. Lamont is the one at fault here. Not Henrik, and certainly not Teddy. There's not a judge in the state of Florida who would rule otherwise."

"Can you get me something in writing to that effect, including witness statements?"

"I can," Poppy assures her.

Elin is quiet for a moment. I think she might be taking notes. "By sharing your marriage license publicly, we've put the gossip about you not being married to rest. But there's still the matter of the rumored infidelity. You must know how serious this is in cases of child welfare. The rules about paramours being introduced to children are quite strict—"

"There is no infidelity," Henrik says over her. "Miss Nilsson works for us. She's our in-home nurse for Karolina."

"Yes, I have that noted here. But she stays in the home with you? She shares guardianship of Karolina?"

"No, she *works* in the home," I clarify. "But she's no more a guardian than Karro's teacher, Mr. Torres. Or is he part of this dark web of infidelity too?"

Henrik squeezes my hand.

Poppy sits forward again. "Miss Ågren, how serious is this? They can't really be considering revoking Henrik and Teddy's custody, can they? It's too cruel for words."

Heart in my throat, I slap my other hand atop Henrik's on my knee, bracing for the tsunami wave.

"They can," Elin replies. "They are."

"Oh god." Tears burn my eyes.

But Henrik lunges forward, grabbing the phone off the table. "Elin, clarify. They're *considering* revoking custody, or they *are* revoking custody?"

"They're still just considering," she replies.

I let out a breath, my hand pressed to my chest. My heart is racing, and I feel sick.

"Elin, tell them to come again," Henrik declares.

"What?"

"They must come again and interview us all."

"Henrik—"

"I will not have the custody of my niece determined by baseless tabloid articles and meritless speculation! They will come, and they will interview everyone in Karolina's life, everyone who has been close to her these past months—Nurse Hanna and Mr. Torres, the Langleys, Frank at the ice cream shop, her doctors and PTs. Everyone will tell you what you already know: My niece is happy and loved."

"Surely, there must be a way," Poppy chimes. "Given the public nature of Henrik's job, these are certainly unprecedented circumstances. A second home study seems only fair. The team would cooperate in any way you need."

Elin is quiet for a moment. "I'll ask them to schedule another home visit."

Henrik lets out a breath, sinking back against the couch. "Thank you. All we want is a fair chance. In the end, these media stories will play themselves out. When the dust settles, Teddy and I will still be here, loving and caring for Karolina. Because we're a family. And I will fight for my family. I'll do whatever it takes."

I still have tears in my eyes, but now I'm smiling, looking at my husband with such pride glowing in my chest. He's so good to us. Good *for* us. So quiet, and principled, and strong. It's crazy to think that just a few months ago, I was more worried about Burning Man and trips to Thailand. Henrik and Karro have taken every single one of my life plans and flipped them inside out. I don't care what we do, so long as we're together. I'll move to Sweden and dance around a maypole. I'll eat pickled herring with my breakfast. Hell, I'll even learn to knit.

Okay, I won't actually be doing the second one. But the other stuff sounds cool. In the end, Henrik's right. It only matters that we're together.

He switches to Swedish, his voice measured and controlled as he plans with his lawyer. All the while, he keeps one hand on my thigh. Firm, unwavering.

For six years, the idea of Henrik Karlsson was a fantasy. I painted him as perfect in my mind, timeless and untouchable. I still can't believe I now have the real thing. But he's no longer perfect to me. He's moody and taciturn, slow to change. Sometimes he leaves his beard trimmings in the sink. He's completely tone deaf and annoyingly prompt. He's perfectly imperfect.

And he's *mine*.

He was a dream. Now he's my home. And I will fight for him too. I'll fight for our little girl and the life we're building. Because he's right—we belong together, the three of us. Family.

11

HENRIK

*C*heryl, the social worker, sits at the kitchen table across from me, her fingernails clicking on her keyboard. She wears rings on all her fingers and bangles on both wrists that clink faintly each time she moves. She's interviewing us for our second home study report. We've been at this for an hour, with no end in sight. Teddy has already refilled each of our coffee mugs twice. On his third attempt, Cheryl covered the top of her mug with her hand. "Any more java, and I'll be cartwheeling out of here."

Now he sits next to me, his knee bouncing with nervous energy. He had his time in the hot seat yesterday. She interviewed him for over three hours, asking a range of questions about his early life, his upbringing, his current relationship with his family. She quizzed him in detail on his connections to his nieces and nephews, his experiences as a parental figure.

They talked of Karolina, of what she means to him. I listened with pride as he spouted off everything from her favorite food to her second-favorite ballet position. He then provided Cheryl with a rank order of Karro's preferred stuffed animals, which included all their names and magical abilities.

So far, she's asked me similar questions. I've spoken of my young life in Sweden, my relationship with Petra, my early hockey career.

"From what we've found, your sister made no will," she goes

on. "In the event of her passing, did Petra want you to have custody of Karolina? Do you believe that was her wish?"

"Without question," I reply.

"Why?"

I consider for a moment, unraveling the threads of my grief from the facts of the case as best I can. Next to me, Teddy squeezes my hand in encouragement. "I loved my sister with all that I am. She was the older sibling, but she relied on me."

"How so?"

"She never had the patience for organization. And she loathed anything so mundane as the routine of paying bills or planning ahead. Even before her death, I was already caring for them both."

"In what ways?"

"I paid for her apartment, her car, Karolina's school. I made sure they wanted for nothing. As our parents' health has declined, I've cared for them too. Petra knew that if anything happened to her, I would continue to care for Karolina. Since her death, all that has changed is geography. Now, Karolina lives in the home with me."

"And how are you liking the change?"

I swallow a sip of my coffee. "Pardon?"

"To go from being her uncle, paying the bills, to becoming her live-in guardian is a huge step for you both. I'm asking how you've weathered the change. Have there been disruptions to your life, your patterns of behavior?"

"Every pattern of my life has been completely disrupted. But it doesn't follow that such disruptions are unwelcome. And they're not all her fault," I add, glancing at Teddy.

"Can you give me an example of how a pattern has changed and how you've reacted?"

I consider for a moment, setting my coffee aside. "My nighttime routine has certainly changed."

"Can you explain?"

I smile, leaning back in my chair. "Before Teddy and Karolina came to live with me, I lived alone. My nights not traveling or playing hockey were spent quietly in my apartment. I may have listened to a podcast while I exercised on my stationary bike. After which, I stretched and showered. Then I brushed my teeth, and it was lights out by ten o'clock."

"And now?"

I glance to Teddy again and he chuckles. "Just tell her, babe."

I turn back to Cheryl. "Now, my nights home are full of baking, bedazzling, and bath time, in that order. And Karolina and Teddy each have a nightly hair- and skincare regimen that would rival a Hollywood starlet."

Cheryl laughs. "And do you participate?"

"Oh, yes. I've been enrolled in the Teddy O'Connor School for Uncles Who Can't Do Hair."

She laughs again. "My, that sounds serious."

"It's grueling," I reply. "Compared with learning to braid hair, competing in the last Winter Olympics was a breeze."

"Would you consider these new routines an unwelcome change to your daily life? Do you ever resent them?"

I stare down at the table, my mind filling with the sounds of Teddy's and Karro's laughter and singing, echoing around my bathroom. Teddy standing at the sink, spritzing his locs. Karro sitting in the shower with Barbies on her lap, her casted arm and leg carefully wrapped to keep out the water. "No. The chaos they bring to each day is now more precious to me than any cheering crowd, any professional accolade."

Cheryl smiles, her eyes going misty. "That's a lovely thought, Henrik."

"It's the truth. Before Teddy and Karolina, I lived to work. My apartment was a place where I marked time, waiting to go back on the ice."

"And now?"

"Now, I work to live. I'm one of the last in and first out. I do my job, and I do it well. And I still love hockey, don't get me wrong. But my life is so much more now." I look to Teddy, squeezing his hand. "I could never resent them. And I'll never take them for granted."

Teddy's smile is dazzling as he looks at me, tears in his eyes. His love shines out like a beacon.

Across the table, Cheryl furiously types on her tablet. "Would you consider yourself a violent person, Henrik?"

I go still, my cup of coffee halfway to my lips. "What?"

Cheryl looks up over her tablet. Her tortoise shell–framed reading glasses have slipped to the tip of her nose. "There was recently a report made about an incident that happened at Riptide's Bar and Grill. You were involved in an altercation?"

"No one pressed charges," Teddy is quick to say. "It was all a big misunderstanding."

I grimace, setting my coffee down.

Cheryl looks to me. "You became violent with a man who was being violent with Teddy. Is that correct?"

Teddy sucks in a breath, his bouncing knee freezing to stone.

"That's correct," I reply. "Teddy was cornered coming out of the bathroom by another hockey player who was trying to press sexual advances on him. Teddy rebuffed the man, and the man got agitated. He pushed Teddy against the wall and called him a whore and a tease . . . among other things."

"And you attacked him?"

"I stopped him from further attacking Teddy," I correct.

"Why not call for help? Surely, the restaurant manager could have intervened. Or you could have called the police."

I huff, shaking my head. "You know nothing about the situation."

Teddy winces, giving me a pained look. But I won't feign politeness. Not about this. It's too important.

"What don't I know?" she replies. Her tone is open, nonjudgmental. She's genuinely seeking my answer.

I take a deep breath, and let it out. "You're assuming there was time for me to go through the motions of seeking out a higher authority, like a manager or the police. But have you ever heard your partner cry out in fear, Cheryl?"

"No," she murmurs. "I haven't."

"Then you don't know what you would have done in my position."

She nods, conceding the point.

"And my partner is a Black man, Cheryl. Add to that, he's gay. Do you really think it would have been safer for me to sit back and call in the support of a police officer while my Black gay husband was being attacked by a white man? A man with a multimillion-dollar contract on the line and the might of an NHL franchise at his back? You really think that would have deescalated the situation?"

"Probably not," she replies, eyes on her tablet.

"I knew I could handle it," I go on. "I've been handling men like Lamont all my life. There's violence inherent to a sport like hockey, it's true. Sometimes, the quickest way to solve a problem on or off the ice is just to tackle the man and wail on him for thirty seconds. I've found it's a useful tool for behavior modification. But we're all grown men, usually wearing protective equipment. And I promise you, he gave as good as he got."

I lean forward, elbow on the table. "But if you're questioning whether I know where the line is, if you're implying I may turn the violence of my sport onto my own family? I'll have to politely tell you to go fuck yourself."

She blinks, leaning away.

Next to me, Teddy groans. "Henrik . . ."

"I love my niece," I say over him, shrugging his hand off my shoulder. "I love her more than my own life. I would never raise a hand to her in anger. Not ever. Just as I would die before I'd raise a hand in anger at Teddy. They are my reasons for breathing. I will protect them from any harm. But I will never be the harm. Karolina is safe with me. So is Teddy. In that moment in the bar, tackling that brute to the ground with my own two hands was the most effective way to keep my Teddy safe. And before you ask, yes, I would do it again."

Smiling weakly, Teddy places his hand on mine on the table and gives it a squeeze.

"Understood," Cheryl replies, typing down a few notes on her tablet.

I glance to Teddy, and he gives me a nod of reassurance. I squeeze his hand back, and we wait. After a few tense moments, Cheryl looks up over her tablet. "Tell me about how you two first met."

Teddy is all smiles as he stretches back in his chair. "Do you want to start, or should I?"

I pick up my mug of coffee, taking a sip of the lukewarm brew. "I'll start."

Cheryl looks to me, her fingers poised over her keyboard, ready to type.

"The first thing you need to know about Teddy is that he has expensive and terrible taste in coffee."

HENRIK

"**P**ressure good?"

Lying face down on the massage table, I grunt something that sounds like assent as the PT intern, Cassidy, glides her thumbs up the column of my neck.

"You're carrying quite a bit of tension," she explains as she works.

Astute observation. It's been a week since the social worker interviewed us all again. A week and we've heard nothing. Before, it would have been in my nature to sit and wait. Having Karro has changed that in me. Now there can be no waiting quietly while our fate is decided by other people. I have to do something. I have to fix this. I can't just lie here with my head metaphorically in the sand.

"If you could just try to relax," Cassidy says in a soothing tone.

But I can't relax. If anything, my shoulders tighten as she pushes down with her thumbs.

"Why don't we try taking a few deep breaths?" she offers after another minute.

It's no use. Lying here is only making me more frustrated. I'll get no relief from a massage today. I have to get up. I can't call Cheryl and it's too late to call Elin in Sweden. Perhaps I'll go for a run.

"Is something wrong, Mr. Karlsson?"

Before I can reply, the door opens.

"Knock knock, asshole." Novy lets himself in, turning up the dimmed lights. "Hey, you almost done in here, bud?"

Flustered, Cassidy steps back. "I—we have this room reserved for another thirty minutes, I think."

"Really? Hmm, well, by my watch you're done."

"But I—"

"Tell you what," he says over her. "I keep an open tab down at the coffee cart. Why don't you go get yourself a little afternoon pick-me-up? Leave me and Karlsson here alone to talk hockey for a minute. Assistant captain stuff. Very secret."

My groan echoes in the face hole. "Both of you can go."

"Thank, Cass. You're a treasure," Novy calls, ushering her from the room and closing the door with a snap.

I sit up to find him leaning against the door, arms crossed. Muttering a curse in Swedish, I swing my legs off the table. Neither of us cares that I'm dressed in nothing but my boxer briefs. "What do you want, Novikov?"

He stares me down. "Do we have a problem, you and me?"

"No."

He chuckles, dragging a hand through his hair, still damp from his shower. We finished up practice less than an hour ago. "Yeah, see, only I don't believe you."

"Why not?"

"Because you just called me Novikov. You guys only do that when you're pissed at me for something . . . except Mars. He only ever called me Novikov. But even you call me Novy."

I sigh, my shoulders prickling with all this unresolved tension. "It's not about you."

His eyes narrow. "Then what is it?"

I've skated with this man for six years now. And while I wouldn't say we're friends, we've always been friendly. He doesn't mind my awkwardness, and he always invites me to things. And yet, we've never shared in each other's confidences. Not once in over six years has he sought me out to ask me about my feelings or the state of our relationship. So why start now?

I cross my arms over my naked chest, glaring at him. "What's your game, Novikov?"

He chuckles. "Aaaand we're right back to Novikov. See what I mean? Okay, so spill. What did I do?"

"Nothing."

"Sure. Except Coley has the emotional sonar abilities of a freaking dolphin, and he thinks you're upset with me. I told him he was crazy, and he told me I had to come set a few things straight. Are you listening?"

I grunt with annoyance as he holds up a finger in my face.

"Number one, what's happening with your niece fucking sucks. I don't know how you've been able to stay so calm about it. If someone was threatening to take my kids from me, I'd already be in jail for going full Punisher on their asses."

I lean away, surprised by the vehemence in his tone. After a moment, I sigh, giving him my truth. "If I appear outwardly calm, you should know that it's a thin mask I wear, growing thinner by the day."

"I can well fucking believe it. Which leads me to point number two: I'm sorry about the massage stuff."

"What?"

"You know, yanking your chain about Teddy and his magic massages. It's no mystery that I like to tease. Coley and I sort of get each other off on the whole jealousy kink thing. Usually, it's super fun. I swear to god, when that man gets wound tight enough, he can pound me into another fucking dimension—"

I scowl at him. "Fast-forward, Nov."

He snorts, checking the time on his watch. "Right. Well, that's my point. It's just teasing. I have no interest in Teddy, Karlsson. It's important to me that you know that. Coley's the only man I've ever been with. He's fucking it for me. He and Poppy are my world. The rest is just my excess flirting energy," he adds with a wave of his hand. "It has to come outta me, or I'll fucking burst, you know? And you and Ted have just been easy targets. But with everything else you've got going on, I don't think you need to be teased right now. By me or anyone else. So that leads me to point number three."

I sigh. "Christ, you have a third point?"

He grins. "I do." His smile falls as he points beyond the door. "Whatever else happens with your kid, don't fuck this up."

I glance to the door. "Fuck what up?"

"What else, asshole? Teddy."

Despite myself, my jealousy bristles at the look of intensity in his eyes. "Just say what you really came to say." I can sense we've finally come to the heart of it.

He crosses his arms. "Alright, I will. When I look at you, Karlsson, do you know what I see?"

I hold his glare. "No."

"I see myself. I see who I was six years ago, before Poppy and Cole flipped my life inside out. When I get scared, when things feel too heavy, I run. I've always been a runner. My running is a physical flight. You're a runner too. But you run *here*." He taps the side of his temple with a finger.

My racing mind trips at his accusation, and I let out an audible breath, leaning away in surprise.

Novy smirks. "Yeah, I see you running in there. You've been running for weeks. Thinking, plotting, scheming, second-guessing. But you and I are lucky, Karlsson. We picked partners who will run with us. Hell, I imagine Teddy's anxiety can run circles around yours all damn day. But there's something I've learned sharing my life with Poppy and Cole."

Apparently, I'm now accepting life advice from Lukas Novikov. "What have you learned?"

"The gift isn't that they can keep up with us," he explains.

"It's not?"

He shakes his head. "Nope. The gift is that they're the only thing in this life we wanna run *to* . . . not from. So run to him, Karlsson. Whatever else happens, never stop."

Before I can respond, there's another knock on the door and Novy leaps to pull it open. "Hey, there he is!" One-armed, he pulls Teddy into the room.

Teddy sees me all but naked on the table, and his eyes go wide. He glances between us, clearly looking for the other PT. "I . . . you told me to meet you here. Am I interrupting something?"

"Nope," Novy replies, his tone cheery. "I only beat you here by a minute. Cassidy just left. Actually, this is a bit of a bait-and-switch situation. Classic Novy, right? I'm a scoundrel. But hopefully this time you won't mind because I've decided to donate my last Teddy massage to Karlsson. Poor guy begged and pleaded with me for long enough that I just had to give in."

Teddy and I both stiffen, glancing from each other back to Novy. "But I can't massage Henrik at work," he says, his tone wary.

"Which is why the schedule will still read that it's me in here with you," Novy replies with a wink. "When, in fact, I will now be sneaking up to Poppy's office to fuck her on her desk. It's her own fault for wearing those heels with the ankle strappy things. She knows I can't resist. We'll all taste a bit of afternoon delight, and no one needs to ever know. Deal?"

Teddy waits for me to make the decision. Novy's last words fill my mind, taking up all the space I was using for worrying and over-thinking: *Run to him. Never stop.* Locking eyes with my Teddy, I hold out my hand. "Come here."

He steps right past Novy, so easily drawn in by my quiet command. I part my knees and lure him closer. He doesn't stop until his thighs hit the table. Then he's in my arms, his hands brushing over my bare shoulders as I cup his face and kiss him, staking my claim.

I barely register the door closing as Novy leaves the room. After a few more moments of kissing, Teddy pulls away. "Wait. What really happened before I came in here just now? What did he say?"

I smile, brushing my thumb over his parted lips. "He apologized for teasing us."

"Really?"

I nod. "I think he's grown a conscience since Poppy and Morrow broke into his home and moved themselves in."

He grins. "Hard to believe, but I think you might be right." He glances around the room. It's little more than a repurposed closet, barely big enough for the massage table, with overhead lights set on a dimmer switch. There are four of these rooms situated along the same wall in the PT suite. "Should we . . . I mean, he was obviously joking, right? We can't do a massage in here. We could get in trouble."

Teddy speaks sense. Rules are rules. But now I have him in my arms, and all that worrying I was doing has finally eased. My god, Lukas Novikov is right. With Teddy, it's like the chaos of the world stops and my racing thoughts quiet. With Teddy, I find stillness. Only with Teddy do I find peace. I smile, brushing his locs off his shoulder. "No more trouble than fucking you over the hood of my car at a public beach."

He blushes. Exactly the reaction I wanted. I love the way the warmth blooms in his cheeks under that soft spray of freckles. Each one is a fleck of caramel I want to taste. As he notes the hungry look on my face, a nervous smile spreads on his. "What's gotten into you?"

"Hopefully you," I tease. "After my massage, of course."

He snorts a laugh, pulling away. "Are you serious right now? You're finally gonna let me massage you?"

Feeling lighter than I have in days, I flip onto my stomach and place my face back in the cushioned cutout. "Lock the door and dim the lights."

I listen to him move around the room. The soft *click* of the door lock already has my cock twitching. I regret lying so eagerly on my stomach, pinning it to the table with my hips. Music starts up on the Bluetooth speaker. Cassidy was playing something that sounded like spa music. Teddy plays smooth, soft jazz.

"Novy and I had agreed on an hour-long, full-body massage. Is that what you'd like as well?" His tone is clinical. My sweet man, he's trying so hard to be professional.

Determined to rattle him, I shrug a shoulder. "Let's just see how long we last."

"What does that mean?"

"I can't imagine we'll make it more that fifteen minutes before you're asking me to suck your cock—*ah*—"

I wince as he twists his fingers into my hair and pulls my head up and out of the face cradle, forcing me to look at him. He doesn't bother hiding his smile or the heat in his eyes. "Keep pushing me when I'm just trying to do my job, and we won't get to the part where I ask. I'll just flip you over right now, jerk that ass to the end of the table, and make you take me."

Before I can respond, he lets me go, and my head flops back into the cradle. I chuckle, adjusting my hips so I'm not crushing my hardening cock.

"I'll start with your shoulders," he declares, rubbing his hands with oil. "What level of pressure would you like?"

"Hard."

He steps up to the head of the table where I can see his shoes. "Let's begin."

The moment his warm, oiled hands start to touch me, I relax. He moves them methodically over my shoulders, his pressure firm as he follows the line of each muscle, finding each nerve bundle, every knot and ache. His pressure is divine as he works the knots loose in my left shoulder first. I mutter a curse in Swedish and he eases up a little.

"Feel good? Not too much pressure?"

"'Sgood," I mumble, my eyes closed in bliss as my body goes slack.

"I had no idea you were carrying so much stress in your shoulders," he says after another minute or two. "Babe, you're riddled with knots."

"I know."

"I'm gonna talk to Brady. We need to finesse your cooldown routine. There's stretching we can modify, heat therapy, and you need to swim more."

"Swim?"

"Mhmm. It's great recovery for you. Hockey is so high impact. I know you love to run, but you need your therapies to do less damage, not more."

His comment about my love of running makes me smile. But I can't fight the relieved groan that escapes me as he starts to really dig into the knots on my lower trapezius muscle.

"I don't know if Novy told you, but I have a strict 'no sex noises' policy on my massage table," he teases, still digging in deep with his thumbs.

"That sound was involuntary," I grunt.

His pressure lightens as he works a knot loose, each movement so measured and controlled. "Hmm, well, just don't do it again. Second warning."

I stiffen. "Second warning? What was the first?"

"Seriously? You boasting that I'd be begging to suck your cock within the first fifteen minutes of this massage. Now, lie there like a good little hockey player, and let me do my work."

With a heavy huff, I exhale, relaxing back onto the table.

"Karro starts aqua aerobics for her leg in a couple weeks," he says after a few minutes. "We could both go with her and get in some laps at the pool."

I smile. "You know if we both go, she'll demand we get pizza after."

I've been traveling so much lately. Karolina has determined that any time all three of us are able to make it to her PT together, it's a party that must be celebrated with pizza and chocolate milk.

"I'll concede to the pizza if you promise to take better care of yourself," he replies.

I reach for him. I can't help myself. Dropping my arms from the table, I brush my hands up the back of his thighs.

Now it's his turn to groan as he tenses, but he doesn't step away. "You know, I'm really trying to be professional here. I want to make this good for you, baby. I want to help you."

"You do help me. You're so good to me."

He swats my hands away, moving to the side of the table to work on my middle back. "Okay, so then let me *really* help you. I could start massaging you more at home. I hate to feel like you're not getting what you need just because we're married. I'm more qualified than Cassidy, and I have gentler hands than Brady or Jeff—hey—"

I push off the table up to my elbows, grabbing him by the wrist before he can step away. "You *do* help me."

He looks down at me, shaking his head. As I watch, tears spring to his eyes. Then his shoulders sag.

"Hey . . . what is this now?"

"I just feel so helpless," he admits. "There's nothing else I can do. How can there really be nothing else?"

We're not talking about massages now. "I know," I say. "I feel the same."

Sighing, he takes his free hand and cups my cheek. "Oh, Hen, you've done everything you can."

"As have you," I assure him. "All we can do now is wait." Turning my face into his hand, I kiss his palm, breathing him in. His skin smells faintly of warm honey from the massage oil. "What do you need from me?"

"What?"

I hold his gaze. "We can't keep running, mitt hjärta. Not from this. We have to stay, and we have to wait. So let me distract you. Take what you need from me."

He lets out a shaky breath, his gaze darting around the room as he tries not to look at the long lines of my all-but-naked body lying on this massage table. Why is he holding himself back from me?

Fighting a smile, I raise a brow. "You're allowed to look at me, mitt hjärta. You're allowed to enjoy what you see."

"I feel guilty," he admits. "Is that crazy? Like I'm not allowed to have good things while there's this constant threat of the one big bad thing—"

"No." I sit up, swinging my legs off the table as I pull him to me. "No, we can't live like that. Whatever happens with Karolina, there's still you and there's me. That doesn't change."

He bites his bottom lip, shaking his head. His gaze is focused somewhere near my clavicle.

I brush my hand over his hair, trailing my knuckles along his cheek. "Talk to me."

"I'm only in your life because of Karolina," he murmurs. "If she goes . . . if I can't help you keep her—"

"Stop." I cup his face with both hands. "Christ, is this the weight you've been carrying for weeks? You think this is all on your shoulders?"

"Months," he admits. "Since Sweden. And it is all on me. Elin said it; the judge said it. But, Henrik, what if I'm not enough—"

"You are."

"Yeah, but what if I'm not?"

I sigh, pressing my forehead to his, my eyes shut tight. Slowly, he relaxes a little, his hands lifting to wrap around my wrists. "You make my world stop," I whisper.

"What?"

I lean away. He needs to see me, needs to see the truth in my eyes. "That's what Novy and I were in here talking about just before you arrived. He called me a runner. He told me I should run to you because you're where everything stops for me."

His eyes widen. "He really said that?"

I nod. "I know that you only came into my life for Karolina. I'm asking you to stay in it for me. Not because I want your help with Karro. I don't want your massages or your smoothies or your interior decorating skills either."

He fights a nervous smile. "Okay, so I think you're trying to be sweet right now, but to me that just sounds like a whole lot of rejection . . ."

I chuckle, brushing his cheek with my thumb. "I'm trying to say that you're enough. Badly, apparently." His smile flickers and I can't help but reach out and touch it too. "It's not about what you do for me," I go on. "Or what you do for Karolina. It's who you *are* that I care about. I want you, Teddy. Just as you are. I want you in my life. Stay."

He steps back as I slip off the edge of the table and stand. Operating on instinct, I drop down to one knee, reeling him in by the hips. He drops his hands to my bare shoulders. "Henrik, what are you doing?"

"I want you to stay with me." Pressing my face to his hip, I breathe in the cool scent of his athletic body spray. He squeezes my shoulders, his breath catching on a gasp as I cup his crotch, feeling the hardening of his cock beneath my hand. "Stay with me," I repeat.

"Henrik . . ." He whispers my name with the reverence of a prayer.

Slowly, I tug his pants down, relishing in the sight of the cut lines of his hips, the lean, banded muscles wrapping his thighs. He's my perfect work of art. Powerful and beautiful. His cock hangs hard and heavy for me, waiting. He's always waiting for me. My patient man.

I take him to hand, and he curses, one hand shifting to brace the back of my head. I look up, needing to see his face as I wrap my lips around his tip and taste that first essence of him. He groans, lips parted on a breath, as he watches me suck and tease.

He's fooling no one with this hesitancy. His hand is like iron on the back of my head, keeping me in place. I push back against him, loving the struggle, as he finally steps in with his hips, making me choke. I hum with relief, hungry for more, my hands gripping tight to his ass. "Make it stop," I pant the moment he lets me up for air. "Teddy, please."

"I know," he soothes, all his hesitancy shattered. "Eyes on me. Don't look away."

I drop down to both knees, rocking back on my ankles, as Teddy takes over. He's gentle but direct, guiding my actions with soothing words. "Just let go . . . I'm right here, baby. I'm not going anywhere. Look at me."

I groan with relief, taking his cock to the back of my throat again and again. He sets a punishing pace, fucking my mouth like he owns it. God help me, he does. We both know it. Every part of me is his now. These last few months have changed us forever. How did I ever live without him?

"Baby, I'm gonna come," he pants, making shallower thrusts with his hips. "Open your mouth. Show me. Wanna watch you take my cum."

I tip my head back and open my mouth. Teddy keeps one hand fisted tight in my hair, holding me just how he wants me. Then he curses softly as his other hand makes a tight fist around his shaft. He jerks himself hard and fast, just a few quick pulls before he sighs with relief. Our gazes hold as warm cum jets from his tip, landing on my waiting tongue. Like a fiend, I devour, claiming every drop.

But it's that look of ecstasy I was really chasing. *This* is where the world stops. In this moment, lost in the look of love in his eyes. There is no worry, no stress or pain. There is nothing outside the marrow-deep knowledge that Teddy is here with me.

Sated and drowsy, I lean forward, all but slumping against him. "Stay," I say again, eyes shut tight as I press my face to the bare skin of his hip and breathe him in. "Please stay with me."

His hands are gentle as they touch and soothe, his fingertips brushing through my hair. "Where the hell am I gonna go, huh? You've ruined me, Henrik. One look at you, and I was done. Just say the word, and I'll follow you anywhere."

13

TEDDY

"**W**as it always this cold in here?" Jayla blows hot air into her hands, trying to warm them up. "I feel like it wasn't this cold last time."

On my other side, Natalie wears a puffer coat zipped up to her chin. "Serves you right for always thinking you need to dress with your tits out."

Jayla tugs on the bedazzled V-neck of her Rays T-shirt, which only makes her ample cleavage more pronounced. "Don't be jealous 'cause you got Auntie Deb's flat chest."

Nat scoffs. "Me jealous of you? Don't make me laugh."

Sandwiched between them, I can only groan. "Come on, no fighting. Please? We're in full Operation United Front mode, remember?"

Jayla rolls her eyes, flicking her braids over her shoulder. "We know."

"We're here, aren't we?" Nat adds.

It's game night. Nat left the baby at home with Darius, bringing only her older girl, Evie. She and Camila sit in the row in front of us, showing Karolina how to play a bubble-popping game on a tablet. The intermission between the second and third periods is almost over. Rays are down by one, but it's been an exciting game. They're playing the Panthers, so the arena is a pretty even mix of red and teal. And completely sold out.

Checking the time left of the game clock, Nat grabs her purse. "I'm gonna go get the girls more popcorn. You two want anything?"

I shake my head. I'm too nervous to eat or drink.

"Get me some chicken tenders," Jayla calls as Nat starts jogging up the stairs. "And French fries! Hey, and some of those roasted pecans!"

As soon as Nat is gone, Jay nudges me. "You okay?"

I just shrug, looking out at the ice as the Zambonis do their final pass, smoothing the surface back to shiny white glass. Am I okay? It's been a whirlwind two weeks since Henrik and I sat in Poppy's office, feeling like our life was imploding. In those two weeks, we've dealt with the second home visit, four away games, new PT regimens, and moving a full-time caretaker into the boat shed to live with Henrik's parents.

It turns out that having a reporter take advantage of Maria's confusion was the last straw for Henrik. His dad fought it at first, but Alma is a retired nurse who plays cards and likes to garden. She's the perfect helpmate for Maria. It's not a permanent solution, as Alma has plans to move in with her daughter over the summer. But it's a temporary fix that seems to be easing everyone's minds. Alma is there during the waking hours, helping around the house and in the garden. She stays with Maria if Gunnar needs to go to the shops. And she monitors their medicine intake.

We don't have the results of our home study yet, but the whole team and all the WAGs were willing to be put on an interview list for the case worker. Hanna and Sam Torres were each interviewed again. As were Tess and Ryan, Brady, Poppy, even Novy. His interview was the only one we received immediate feedback on. Cheryl blushed, shuffling her paperwork, and called him "quite a character."

Cheryl also asked to interview my family. They stepped up without hesitation. Shae said Cheryl interviewed Mama for over two hours. When I expressed concern that Mama might sabotage the custody arrangement, Shae all but reached through the phone and smacked me. "She loves you, Teddy. And she's sorry for how that first meeting went down. Return her calls, and she'd tell you herself."

Shae was right—I was being a coward. I was afraid not talking to my mother would somehow save me from hearing something I didn't want to hear. But all it really did was make me sad and frustrated. It was Henrik who finally stepped in. Two nights ago, he pulled the jar of olives from my hand after dinner, replaced it with my phone, and pointed to the balcony door. "Call her. Now."

I called my mom, and we talked late into the night. It's not all fixed by any stretch, but it's a start.

God, just when everything in my life was starting to feel settled, it's all up in the air again! We can't think, can't plan, when our life isn't our own. I mean, will Karolina even be with us for Christmas? Or will they come and take her back to Sweden? It'll kill us both if they take her away. I can't even think what it will do to Karolina.

No, but Henrik's right. We've done everything we can. It's out of our hands. All we can do now is wait. Which just happens to be one of the many things I'm terrible at . . .

Jayla nudges me again. "Hey."

I glance her way.

"You know we're with you, right? Maybe we gave you a hard time at first, but that's only because you surprised us. If you say Henrik is the one—"

"He is," I say over her. "He's the one, Jay. He's my only one."

She smiles. "Then I'm happy for you."

The players skate onto the rink to the applause of the fans. Jayla claps along with the music, watching them warm up. It's not hard for me to find Henrik. He skates past, working a puck on the end of his stick. Making a sharp turn, he flicks it into the back of the empty net. Fuck, he's so beautiful. Even when all I can see is the bottom half of his face.

Next to me, Jayla hums. "You're different with him, you know?"

"Different how?" I say, not taking my eyes from him.

"You're more relaxed, I think."

I laugh out loud. "Yeah, right."

"You are," she says over me. "You seem more sure of yourself.

You've grown up, Teddy. Before, you were a boy. Now look at you—a husband, a daddy, a doctor. You're a man now."

I let her words sink in as I watch Henrik down on the ice.

She nudges me. "What are you thinking?"

"I've always felt like I was sort of blasting through life, you know? Taking risks, making mistakes."

She laughs. "We all make mistakes. It's called living."

I shake my head, still lost in thought. "No, I was . . . I think I was afraid to really live, you know? At least, I was afraid to live as me. I teased Henrik for compartmentalizing, but I did it too."

"How so?"

"I kept putting pieces of myself in boxes. Too loud? Put it in a box. Too emotional? In another box. I tried to be whatever people around me needed me to be. I did it so much, I think I forgot who I really was."

Her expression softens a little. "And now you've remembered?"

I smile. "Henrik helped me remember. And Karro. There's no such thing as too much Teddy for them. With Karro, I can be as loud and as silly as I want. I can bedazzle T-shirts and sing until I'm hoarse."

She loops her arm in with mine. "And Henrik?"

I watch him skate past, warmth glowing in my chest.

With one look at my face, she's pulling away with a huff. "God, forget I asked."

I laugh, keeping her pinned at my side. "Don't get me wrong, the sex is fucking epic. I mean, just the other day we were in the massage room at work and—"

"Nope. No way." She waves her hand in front of her face. "To me, you're still seven years old, wearing Superman pajamas, asking me how to make mac and cheese."

"It's not just about that," I say, still laughing. "In fact, it's not really about the physical stuff at all."

She glances up at me. "What do you mean?"

"I mean that with Henrik, for the first time in my life, I tried to build the relationship first, no sex. I think depriving me of sex was the key needed to unlock me. Does that make any sense?"

"Unlock you?"

"Yeah, like, unlock my personality. I was so afraid Henrik didn't want me sexually that it started to not even matter if he liked my personality. So, I just let it all out. He got the full Teddy treatment, with no filter."

"And he stayed?" she teases.

I shrug my shoulder in my bedazzled WAG jacket, recalling the sweet words he whispered to me in the massage room. "I think he might like me just as I am. Go figure, right?"

She hums, clapping along with the music as the lights in the stadium lower.

"What?" I say, raising my voice to be heard.

She just smiles, shaking her head. "Oh, Teddy."

"What?" I say again.

"I think he might love you."

"I thought you said we could get ice cream," Camila whines.

"We have to wait for your uncle Henrik," Jayla replies.

"But it's right there!" She stomps her foot, pointing to one of the concession stands, which has pictures of ice cream posted on the wall.

"They're shutting all these down," Natalie explains, holding hands with Evie as I push Karolina in her wheelchair. Now that her arm cast is off, she's using her crutches way more. But at these crowded home games, it's nice to have her safe in the buffer of a chair.

The game is over. Rays lost by two. Now we're working our way down the concourse towards the WAG room. "Henrik usually texts me by now. I don't know what's keeping him tonight."

My phone buzzes in my pocket with a new message.

POPPY: PRESS ROOM. NOW. HURRY.

"Oh no."

Nat looks over at me. "Teddy?"

"What's wrong?" asks Jay. "You look like you've just seen a ghost."

"Stay with Karolina."

"What?"

"I said, stay with Karolina. I've gotta go!" Not waiting for their reply, I take off down the concourse.

"Teddy! Hey! Where the heck do you want us to go?"

"'Scuse me," I shout, ducking around some drunk Panthers fans as they weave their way towards the stairs. "Outta the way!" I take the stairs two at a time, racing down for the lower level.

Majorie, the volunteer docent, stands watch at the press entrance as I sprint up. "My goodness. Everything alright, honey?"

I pat down my chest and all my pockets, trying to catch my breath. "I—can't find—fuck, my pass is missing." Groaning, I press a hand to my forehead. My arena pass is in the front pocket of my backpack, which is strapped to Karolina's wheelchair. "I don't have my pass. Marj, I don't . . . it's not here."

Oh my god, of all the times to not have my arena pass. Something is happening down there. And now I'm gonna miss it?

Marjorie glances around. "That's okay, honey. You go on through."

Just like that, the storm clouds clear. "Wait, really?"

She smiles, holding a finger to her lips. "It'll be our little secret."

Grabbing her by her bony, birdlike shoulders, I smack a kiss on her cheek. "Miss Marj, if I wasn't married, I'd get down on one knee!"

"Well, my heavens."

Ducking around the stanchion, I bound like a gazelle down the escalator. Landing at the bottom, I dart left and hurry down the hallway to where the crowd of press members wait. Looks like a full house tonight. It's always a full house when we play another Florida team. I weave my way through the back of the crowd, looking for a good view of the top table.

I think the press conference only just started. Coach Johnson is in the middle seat. DeGraw is to his left, Novy to his right. And there, next to Novy sits my Henrik. He hasn't done a press conference since the one where we announced our marriage. That feels like it happened a lifetime ago.

"Sorry we're running a little late, folks," Coach Johnson says into his microphone. "If you'll all find your places, we'll get started."

The first three rows of the press are all seated, while the cameras are clumped behind in two rows. Floaters with cameras stand around the edges, snapping pics, while ancillary staff like me stick to the edges.

Poppy catches my eye and waves, miming a relieved wiping of her brow. Then she points to Henrik and gives two thumbs-up. What, are we playing charades right now? What the heck is going on?

"Okay, folks," Coach Johnson goes on. "Before we get down to brass tacks and talk about the game, Henrik Karlsson is going to make a quick announcement."

I hold my breath as Henrik leans forward, his forearms folded on the table. Like the other players, he's fresh from a shower, dressed in his Rays warm-up kit. "Thank you, Coach." His deep voice is like a balm. "I felt it was time to break my silence about the events that have been unfolding for me personally over the last few weeks."

There's a shuffle amongst the press as they eagerly await the chance to snag a useful sound bite.

"At the start of the season, I announced my marriage to Doctor Teddy O'Connor," he begins. "I said then that I would only make one statement regarding our marriage, and I meant it. As an exceptionally private person, I consider any details about my life with my husband to be off limits for the press."

He looks slowly down the lens of each camera as he speaks, moving from left to right. "That you have tested this again, and again, crafting your baseless stories, making a mockery of us, even dragging our friends and family into your schemes, is inexcusable. I think I speak for every person in professional sports when I say that keeping our private lives from the press sometimes feels like a full-time job. A thankless job at that. And it's a job I've been failing at for weeks."

Finally, he catches my eye. Offering me a quick nod of reassurance, he looks back to the front row of the press. "You all seem determined to get a story out of me. But the truth is, I'm a painfully ordinary person. I work hard and have no time for hobbies. I eat overnight oats for breakfast every morning, and I go home to my husband every night. Ours is not a wild life of parties and drunken debauches . . . unless the parties are tea parties, hosted in our niece's closet with her dolls."

A few people chuckle.

"If you want a story that's really worth telling, I'm here to give you one. It's about a brave, compassionate, willful woman named Maria Karlsson . . . who just happens to be my mother. She also happens to suffer from dementia."

There's a new shift in the crowd as they all wonder where this is going. I'm wondering the same thing.

"I've never made this public before," he goes on. "With my parents' blessing, I do so now. I do it as a warning and a plea. You see, in your rush to print salacious stories about me, you all seemed to forget that I am someone's guardian, someone's husband, and someone's son. And my mother is in a precipitous decline. Anyone who has any experience with dementia knows what it's like to watch the person you love fade away before your eyes. She has not been immune to the gossip these last few weeks. How can she, when one of you crossed the line, going to our house and forcing your way in?"

There's an uncomfortable stir at this. Some of the press shift in their seats and start to look around.

Henrik continues to stare them down. "My mother no longer has the mental faculties to reason away the lies being told about me. So, to say these last few weeks have been devastating for us would be an understatement." Leaning into the mic, he looks right down the lens of the closest camera. "I pray you hear this message and heed it: Our families are not here for your entertainment."

"Well said," says Novy, tapping the table with his fist. Next to him, Coach Johnson nods.

"I am the public figure," Henrik goes on. "My husband is off limits. My niece, an innocent child, is most certainly off limits. And, yes, even my mother. Especially my mother. Anyone who meets her now cannot doubt that she has trouble with her memory. And yet, not two weeks ago, a member of the press forced their way into my family home, sat at my kitchen table, and used her. I will not forgive, and I will never forget."

An echoing silence follows his remarks.

He glances my way, and I nod. God, I'm so proud of him.

Leaning one last time into his mic, he keeps his eyes on me and declares, "In honor of my mother and the scarifies she's made to support my long and successful hockey career, today I announce that I've partnered with Ray of Hope, the new philanthropic wing of the Jacksonville Rays, to offer a matched donation of two million dollars for dementia care."

A gasp goes around the room as cameras flash. I'm smiling, radiant, so full of love for this man, I could burst.

"Two million dollars will be donated to the Alzheimer's Association," he continues. "We aim to offer grant funding for Florida-based families like mine in need of in-home care support. Poppy St. James intends to take over the management of this fund, with plans to grow it in the future through additional donations."

There's a smattering of applause at this announcement.

Henrik's smile for me is warm as he gives a nod. Then he looks back at the front row of press. "An additional two million dollars is being donated to assist in the building of Sweden's first dementia village. This is an innovative and thoughtful approach to memory care that prioritizes autonomy as a key measure of quality of life. Autonomous living has been the sole focus for my own family as we make necessary transitions, providing the best care possible for my mother."

Clearing his throat, he sits up and gestures to Poppy. "More details regarding these new partnerships will be made available by

Ray of Hope in the coming weeks. At this time, all further questions can be directed to Poppy St. James."

"That's me," Poppy calls from the corner, waving to the press.

Her exclamation pops the tension in the room. Most people laugh. There's a much more generous round of applause. Then everyone settles back into their chairs. To my surprise, Henrik nods once to Coach Johnson. Rising from his chair, he quietly leaves the stage.

Coach Johnson sits forward. "Right. So, were there any questions about the game?"

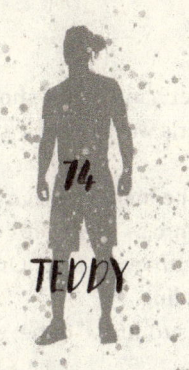

74

TEDDY

I don't stay for the end of the press conference. I know Henrik left to come find me. Slipping from the back of the crowd, I make my way through the tunnels, jogging towards the double doors that lead to the WAG room. Rolando, the security guard, waves me past the checkpoint with a nod.

I turn the corner to find Nat and Jayla standing with the girls in front of a brightly painted mural. A local artist crafted it to look like a watercolor painting of a school of rays on a coral reef. The girls are each exclaiming, pointing out the different fish.

Jayla sees me first. "Where did you go?"

Nat spins around, eyes wide with concern.

I jog up, smiling from ear to ear. "Sorry, Henrik was doing the press conference. I didn't wanna miss it."

Jayla's expression is wary. "Everything good?"

I nod. God, I feel like I have a pinball loose in my chest. It's pinging all around, making my heart flutter. And I can't stop smiling.

Nat grins. "Ted, what are you into? What did you do?"

Before I can reply, the door at the end of the hall slams open, and Henrik comes striding out, still in his Rays warm-up kit. Which, you know, thank god for whoever was in charge of picking the five-inch inseam on those uniform shorts. His tree-trunk thigh muscles flex as he jogs down the hallway.

"Hey, Henrik," Jayla calls with a wave.

"Can we still say, 'good game'?" Nat mutters at me.

I groan, shrugging her hand off my shoulder.

"We promised the girls we'd go get ice cream," says Jayla. "Hope you don't mind."

If Henrik hears her, he makes no sign of it. He only has eyes for me. His energy is volcanic as he sweeps down the hallway, determination thundering with every step. Once he's close enough, he smiles. My god, he's dazzling.

I hold out my hands to him. "Babe, that was amazing. I'm so proud of you—"

Henrik reels me in, kissing me breathless. Behind me, the nieces all squeak. His passion and excitement only fans mine. I'm gasping when he breaks the kiss too soon. Still smiling, he drops down to one knee.

"Henrik, what—"

"Marry me."

Behind me, my sisters shriek, and the girls fall apart in a fit of swooning giggles. My brain does a backflip while my stupid, boyish heart starts doing cartwheels. "I—babe, we're already married."

"I don't care." His gaze is steadfast, the blue of his eyes deep and warm. "Marry me again. Marry me properly. With flower girls, and photographers, and vows in English."

"And a kiss," Karolina squeals, bouncing in the seat of her wheelchair.

"And a kiss," he echoes.

I just shake my head. This is crazy. Too much is happening. There are too many unknowns. How can he think about us getting remarried while we're dealing with his family, and Karro's PT, and our work schedules, and this press-fueled nightmare with the case worker?

He searches my face, his brow furrowing slightly. "Why do you hesitate?"

I try to process all my thoughts and emotions to form one succinct answer. "Well . . . why now?"

Jayla steps in behind me, shaking my shoulders. "Are you crazy, Teddy? Just say yes!"

"*Shh.*" Natalie pulls her back. "I wanna hear his answer."

Slowly, Henrik rises to his feet. His heated gaze dances over the letters of my name, stitched onto the left breast of my WAG jacket. His number is on both my arms and my back. Our names are combined across my shoulders: "TEDRIK." Two halves of one whole.

"Why now?" I repeat.

He has to say it. I think I'll die if he won't.

Smiling, he cups my cheek. "Because I love you."

I close my eyes, leaning into the press of his hand. Behind me, my sisters and nieces squeal again.

"Look at me," he soothes, both hands now resting on my shoulders.

I blink my eyes open, ignoring my blurry tears.

"I love you," he says again. "You know I do. You knew it before I did. Before I could ever form the words, you already knew. I love you as a friend, as a lover, as the partner of my life."

"I hoped you did," I admit.

But he shakes his head. "No. You knew. You know me, mitt hjärta. No one has ever made me feel more seen than you. No matter what comes, we will be together, yes?"

I place both hands on his hips, anchoring myself to him as I nod. "Henrik, *yes*. I'm yours, you know that. I would have liked a second sink to prove your love," I tease. "But I guess this works too."

"You have to give him a ring!" Camila shouts from behind me.

"That's true," Natalie says from my left. "A proposal usually comes with a ring, Henrik. If you're doing this all again, do it right, honey."

Lips pursed with amusement, Henrik drops his hands from me and works the slender gold ring off his right pinkie. My heart officially fucking stops. He holds it up for my sisters and nieces to inspect. "Will this suffice?"

Jayla's eyes narrow on the band. "Is that real gold?"

I groan, but Henrik just chuckles. "It is. A Karlsson has worn this as a wedding ring for over one hundred years. It was my mother's. She gifted it to Teddy, the man who is my heart's fire, mate of my soul . . . Those were her words, correct?" he adds at me with a teasing smile.

It's all I can do to nod, tears ready to brim over.

"I've kept it safe for you, mitt hjärta. You told me to wait and give it to a partner I love, cherish, and adore." He holds it out to me. "Will you take it now? Take it, like you've taken my heart."

"Sweet lord," Jayla murmurs.

Nat elbows her. "Will you hush up? Let the man have his moment."

"Kneel down, Morbror," Karolina calls. "They always kneel down."

"Yeah, honey, do it right," says Jay.

I feel like I've swallowed a fucking rainbow as Henrik dutifully drops to one knee again, holding out the slender gold ring. He takes my right hand in his, pressing a tender kiss to my knuckles. "Theodore Malik O'Connor, make me the happiest man alive, and marry me . . . again."

"In English," Nat adds over my shoulder.

"Yes, in English," he agrees.

"And I'm flower girl," Karolina shouts.

"And we're all invited," Jayla adds.

"Of course." He gives a solemn nod. Then he looks to me. "So, will you? In front of our family and friends, will you vow to be mine for always?"

"Say yes, Uncle Teddy!"

"If you don't say yes, I will."

Henrik just waits, smiling only for me.

Feeling joyous and free, I nod. "Yes, Henrik. I'll marry you again."

Fingers trembling, he slips the thin gold band onto my right pinkie. We both stare down at it, finally at home on my finger. He brushes his thumb over the band. Leaning down, he kisses it. His lips sear my skin like a brand. It's a sacred act, a sealing of his intent. In this moment I decide: This ring is never coming off my finger again.

Grabbing him by the shirt, I pull him up to standing. My arms go around his shoulders and then we're kissing. The hallway erupts in cheers as our family loses it. I'm laughing and crying, kissing him again and again. "I love you," I pant, our hands everywhere as I claim his mouth.

"I love you."

"I'll marry you. God, baby, I'd marry you every day of the week."

He hums a laugh, holding me close. "Once more will be enough, I think."

Nat peeks around me, tapping us each on the shoulder. Then she pulls a scowl that could rival my mother. "Word to the wise? If Mama doesn't get to walk Teddy down the aisle this time, she'll probably burn this whole arena down."

Henrik nods. "Noted."

Leaning up on her toes, she kisses his cheek. "Welcome to the family."

"**W**hy didn't you tell me about all that stuff with the donations?" I say, my fingers woven with Henrik's atop the gearshift.

We're cruising home in the SUV. After our celebratory ice cream party, we dropped my sisters off at their hotel for the night. Camila and Evie begged us to let Karolina stay too. I've already denied them all so much time to bond as cousins. One look at my face, and Henrik quickly agreed. We've all made plans to have a big breakfast together tomorrow before I take them to the airport.

For tonight, I finally get Henrik to myself again.

"Poppy asked me not to," Henrik replies. "Not until everything was settled. And I didn't want to get your hopes up if it came to nothing."

"Well, so how did it happen?"

He keeps his eyes on the road. "Apparently, Poppy has been looking for an exit from public relations for a while now. She's been helping Mark Talbot build the scaffold of a new philanthropy foundation."

"Ray of Hope?"

He nods. "They had plans to announce it in the summer. She came to me with this idea, and they had to scramble to move up their timeline. But Talbot seems pleased. And Poppy is thrilled.

She'll be announcing her departure from Rays PR just as soon as they hire her replacement."

I lean my head back against the headrest. "Rays PR without Poppy St. James . . . it's like the end of an era."

He hums his agreement, taking a turn one-handed as he pulls us onto the street of our apartment building.

I turn my head to take in his profile, illuminated by the passing streetlights. "Announcing a major donation was an amazing idea. It's such an important cause. And you stated the case so well."

"You think so?"

"Totally. In the end, it's all about preserving human dignity. In their rush to print stories, the press seems to forget about the people behind them. These are very human lives they hold in their hands, and they have the power to crush us into dust with a few pointed words. Maria deserves more. Karolina definitely does."

Henrik just nods again.

"And Gunnar and Maria are really okay with it? Being in the press like this?"

He sighs, pulling us into the parking garage and coasting into our reserved spot. "Dad and I are both protective of Mom. And we Swedes are notoriously private people. But you're right—it's a matter of human dignity. That reporter knew my mother was unwell." He glares at the steering wheel, squeezing it tight. "He knew, and he pressed her anyway. It's unconscionable."

"It should be criminal," I mutter, mirroring his anger.

He glances at me. "It may not do enough to stem the flow of bad press." Lifting our joined hands off the shifter, he kisses my knuckles. "I will do whatever else is required to keep you and Karolina safe. I'll retire from hockey, or I'll get myself traded to a European team. The spotlight dims rather dramatically beyond the glare of the League."

Heart in my throat, I sit forward. "Henrik, no. All this bullshit aside, you're having an amazing season. Have you heard any rumblings from the team about trading you?"

"No."

"And this announcement tonight speaks of Talbot's willingness to support you on and off the ice. He's rolled you out as his first major partner for his flagship philanthropy foundation. I mean, that's no small thing."

He nods, his thumb brushing over the back of my hand.

"And the case worker came back," I add, trying to reassure myself now as much as him. "We have to trust she'll see through all the media drama and cut to the facts. And the fact is that Karolina is happy, healthy, and loved. None of this has touched her. We won't let it touch her. We can protect her, Henrik. You and me. Together. We can be everything she needs and more. We'll love her the way Petra would want her to be loved."

Reaching across the car, Henrik pulls me in for a kiss. "I love you," he says against my lips. "I know I don't deserve you—"

"Shut up," I growl. The stupid center console is blocking me from climbing into his lap, which is all I want to do in this moment. "Take me upstairs."

We kiss our way up the elevator and into the apartment. I kick off my shoes and am taking off my WAG jacket when Henrik reels me in by the wrists. "No, wait. Keep it on a moment longer."

Feeling drunk on anticipation, I drop my hands. "Why?"

"I need to show you something."

I lean away, eyes wide. "What do you need to show me?"

He takes me by the hand. "Come with me."

We pass through the living room. Gone are the boring white walls and furniture pointed at a lonely TV. Now, the space actually looks lived in—cozy blankets draped on the couches, art on the walls, framed pictures of us on the bookshelves. Karro's art box lies open on the coffee table, a mess of colored pencils left scattered atop her latest half-doodled masterpiece.

The results of our morning baking session sit on the counter in the kitchen. Karro and I made Swedish thumbprint cookies, dolloped with raspberry jam. The baking process was a sticky mess, but great PT to improve her fine and gross motor skills. And the results are passable. I may be a shit cook, but there's definitely potential for my baking.

"Babe, what—"

"Just come," he says, leading me down the back hall and into our bedroom.

I look around with narrowed eyes. Nothing looks out of place. The bed is made for once, and Henrik installed this floating shelf thingy that helps me organize my bedside table. The books I don't read are stacked on the shelf, while a charging station lets me plug in all my various electronics and hide them in the top drawer.

I frown. "Nothing's different."

He walks backwards, pulling me into the bathroom. "I had it in mind to propose to you in here. But when the moment came, I found I simply couldn't wait. Besides, I think it mattered to your sisters that they got to be involved this time."

"It did," I say, placing my hands on his chest. "It mattered so much. Thank you." I brush a kiss to his lips, feeling light and bubbly, like I swallowed a case of cola.

He smiles.

"What did you want to show me?"

Taking me by the shoulders, he turns me around.

I gasp as I take in the new vanity. It's a near match to the old one, but where there was once only one sink, now there are two. And next to the right side of the vanity, two new floating shelves hold all my hair- and skincare products. "Oh my god." I spin around, hands on his shoulders. "Babe, you got me a love sink!"

His smile widens. "I did."

"How? When did you do this?"

"Tonight, while we were all at the game. Tess let the delivery men in, and Ilmari installed the shelves."

I beam at him. "You're so sneaky. But I'll admit that I knew something was up when your phone was pinging yesterday. Your phone never pings unless it's from me. Between that and your silence over the media stuff, I was getting worried."

He shrugs, brushing his hands down his arms. "I wanted it all to be a surprise."

I turn in his arms, smiling at our reflection in the mirror. "I love it. And I love you." I wait, holding his gaze.

Pulling me in close, he kisses the crook of my neck. His arms unfold from around my middle, his hands coasting up the hard planes of my chest. "Jag älskar dig," he breathes in my ear. "Mitt livs kärlek . . . mitt allt."

"Min man," I tease, pressing into him.

He pulls aside the collar of my WAG jacket, sucking on the point where my shoulder meets my neck.

I fight a shiver, arching against him. "Why did you want me to leave the jacket on?"

He hums, still kissing me as he walks me forward. We don't stop until I hit the vanity, my hands bracing against my new sink. Our gazes catch in the mirror. His intensity makes my stomach flip. Reaching around, he strokes his hand down the column of my neck. "I'm going to fuck you against this sink while you're wearing nothing but my number on your back."

Watching him say the words hits even harder as I hear them whispered in my ear. "Henrik—"

Jerking me back against his chest, his other hand wraps around to slip inside the top of my pants. He cups my hard dick, nipping at my ear as he adds, "And you're going to watch every second of it in this mirror. You'll watch me fuck you and know you're claimed. My man wears my number and my cum. Only you, Teddy."

I whimper, dick twitching as he starts to stroke me. "Only me."

"My only love." His expression is adoring as he holds my gaze in the mirror and leans away. "Take your clothes off. Everything but the jacket."

My hands are at the top of my pants, ready to shuck them down, when I stop. Excitement bursts like little pops of fireworks in my chest as I smile. "Make me."

With a growl, Henrik folds me over the sink and jerks my pants down around my ankles. His hand wraps around to fist my hard dick, and I'm flying, rocking back against him. He's already panting, watching my face in the mirror as he strokes me. "Will you never just do as I say?"

I huff a laugh that sounds more like a groan as he circles his thumb over my tip. "Is that what you want tonight, baby? Want me to get on my knees and treat you like a king?"

His brain short-circuits as his brow furrows. I laugh out loud. He's just too damn easy. I spin around, ass pressed against the sink, my hands smoothing over his chest. "I'll tell you what. Tonight, I'll only be a brat until you get your dick inside me. Then I promise to melt in your arms and let you fuck me into oblivion. Deal?"

His frown deepens as he considers. "If you irritate me too greatly, am I free to spank you?"

I laugh again. "Like you even need to ask?" I kiss him, pressing my body against his. "Just you wait. We haven't even started to dip our toes into the pleasure pool. I've got toys that'll make you think your spirit was sucked out of your balls."

His eyes go wide, and I can't quite tell if there's a hint of interest mixed in with his shock. "Fine, we'll take it slow. No vibrating cock rings tonight." Tipping my chin up, I kiss him again. "We have the rest of our lives to learn and play together, find out what the other really likes. For now, we'll do things your way."

I turn in his arms and slip out of my WAG jacket.

In the reflection, Henrik glares at me. "Teddy . . ."

Feeling confident and in control, I shrug out of my T-shirt, leaving me naked and Henrik fully clothed. For good measure, I tug off the folded teal bandana that was holding my locs back, tossing it to the floor. Then I slip back into the jacket and bend myself over the sink. "I believe you wanted to fuck me with nothing but your number on my back?"

Groaning, Henrik folds himself over me, his hands smoothing up my naked torso. "I've never wanted anything the way I want you."

I rock back into each stroke of his hand on my dick, watching the possessive way he kisses and touches me in the mirror. I catch his eye and his hold on me softens. He flicks my hair aside and kisses the sensitive spot behind my ear.

"You have me," I assure him. "Forever."

75

HENRIK

Jacksonville Beach is swarming with families. It's the opening night of the annual Deck the Chairs event. Sponsors bid to decorate one of fifty lifeguard chairs. What follows is six weeks of concerts, parades, and events for the holidays. There's a musical light show and movies on the lawn. Food trucks provide dining options, while local businesses get to connect with members of the community.

My cold Swedish heart melts for Christmas, so I've always enjoyed attending—even before I had Teddy and Karolina *ooh*-ing and *aah*-ing on either side of me. She can finally bear weight on her leg. The cast is off, but she still has to wear a thick walking boot that wraps up around her shin, keeping the bone protected. She walks at my side, wearing a festive Christmas jumper and Santa hat, tugging at my hand every time she sees something fun.

Teddy and I are wearing jumpers too—at his insistence. His features a Christmas tree that actually lights up on the front. Mine has a glittery snowman. At this rate, I'll be brushing glitter from my beard until New Year's Eve.

We can't walk ten feet down the lane before someone from the team is shouting our name and waving us down. The Rays always sponsor a chair, and it's become tradition for the players and their families to take pictures with it each year. Many of the players use the picture as their Christmas card photo. I think that's why Teddy has us dressed up like this.

"Hey, Karlsson family!" A very pregnant Rachel Price walks up, wheeling a wagon behind her. Their son Jamie sits inside it, playing with a bubble wand. "Love the Christmas sweaters."

Caleb walks at her side, wearing the younger of their two boys in a sling. The toddler is crashed out asleep, mouth open. A mop of curly blond hair peeks out from the top of the baby sling.

"Hey," Teddy waves in welcome. "Have you seen the chair yet?"

"Yeah, we just left Jake over there," Rachel replies. "Poppy roped him into sticking around for a bit to take pictures with families."

"Is it epic?"

Poppy's been determined to win the chair-decorating contest for years, to no avail. Last year, our entry included an animatronic sting-ray that moved and sang carols.

Rachel shrugs. "Eh, it's pretty cool, I guess."

"We're a house divided this year," says Caleb.

"A house divided?" I repeat.

"Yeah, Out of the Net has a chair this year too," Rachel replies. "So, we gotta support our man."

"And our Tess," Caleb adds.

Rachel laughs. "Right? You'd think this contest was as serious as the Olympics for the way she's been running Ilmari ragged these last few weeks."

I glance around. "Where's their chair?"

She turns and points. "One row past the Rays chair, like five down on the left. You'll find Ilmari over there with the Langleys." She reaches out, placing a hand on my arm. "Just, whatever you do, tell Poppy you're voting for the Rays chair. You don't want her to swap out your Christmas cookies for lumps of coal."

Every year, Poppy hosts a party and makes enough desserts to feed a village—cookies and fudge, rum balls, macarons, coconut clusters. Every player and member of staff gets a thoughtfully organized tin of the most delicious treats. It's one of the highlights of my holidays.

Next to me, Teddy groans. "Man, I forgot about her cookies. She gave me a tin when I was an intern. I think I cried when I ate the last mocha truffle."

Rachel smiles. "Since you're both on staff, don't be surprised if you get two tins. We had to beg her to stop giving us four every year. It's too many cookies, and we could never eat them fast enough."

I cast Teddy a warning glare. "If you think I'm sharing any cookies with you, think again."

He crosses his arms. "If you love me, you'll let me have the whole tin."

Draping my arm around his shoulders, I kiss his brow. "Nice try."

Rachel and Caleb both laugh. "Hey," she says, one hand on her belly. "Do you guys have plans for the holidays? Henrik, I know you usually go back to Sweden if you can."

"Not this year," I reply. "Now that they've added the New Year's Eve game, there's just not enough time for travel."

She nods. "Yeah, Ilmari really wanted to get home to Finland this year too. But with the kiddos, it's just too hard—"

"And you're pregnant," Caleb presses with a scowl. "That's why we're not flying across an ocean to Finland. Because you're pregnant with our twins, Hurricane."

She just rolls her eyes. "These babies still have plenty of time to cook. I'm fine." She turns to me. "We were thinking of doing a quick trip up to my family's ranch in Montana. I wanted to make a party of it, take the private plane. My brother will meet us there with his husband and their girls. And the Langleys will come. You guys would be welcome too. I bet Karolina would love the snow."

Hearing her name, Karolina perks up. "I love snow!"

Rachel smiles down at her. "I knew you would. Do you know how to make snow angels?"

While Karolina explains her favorite memory of making snow angels in detail, I glance to Teddy. He just shrugs, casting a wary glance down at Karro. I know what he's saying without words. We thought we would hear something from her case worker by now. It was two weeks of chaos, then nothing, nothing, nothing.

Elin has advised us not to prod. There are processes for these things, and pushing our point won't make anyone rush. She told us not to go anywhere this holiday. We shouldn't be traveling with

Karolina until we hear from the court about any potential changes to the custody arrangement.

"You don't have to decide now," Rachel says. "There's time. Want to just let us know?"

"Can we?" Teddy replies with a weak smile. "There's just some stuff still up in the air."

She nods, reading between the lines. Then she glances at Caleb. "Babe, we should get going. Tess asked us to bring them back some coffee and donuts."

We part ways with the Prices, leading Karolina in the direction of the Rays lifeguard chair.

Teddy loops his arm with mine as we walk. Karolina walks in front of us, zigging and zagging to take in every sight and sound. "Montana would be fun," he says with a wistful sigh.

"It would be fun," I reply. "I'd love to be able to give Karolina a white Christmas, a little taste of home. But we should probably wait until we hear something."

"I know. It's just hard to turn down an offer to ride on Hal Price's private jet again."

I smile, patting his arm. "Next year."

We get through our photo shoot at the Rays deck chair, which includes approximately fifty poses, with Jake and Poppy acting as dueling set directors. The chair is designed to look like a coral reef with all these fish and rays swimming around it, all wearing Santa hats.

Karolina eats up every moment, posing first on the chair, then on each of our laps. Then we all stand in front of it. Then a shot with her on my shoulders, my arm around Teddy.

"Okay," Teddy calls, snatching my phone from Poppy. "I think we've probably got a good shot in there somewhere."

Jake helps me get Karro down from my shoulders while she whines that she can see all the chairs better from up there. I get her down to the ground as, next to me, Teddy gasps. "Ohmygod. Babe—" He shoves my phone in my face.

I take it, leaning away, wincing at the bright screen. "What?"

"Look!"

I look down at the screen, but I see nothing except the screen saver photo Hanna took of Teddy, Karro, and me at the beach a few weeks ago. "What am I looking at?"

He presses in next to me, grabbing my wrist to turn the phone. "I was just holding it, and it just buzzed in my hand. Babe, you got an email."

"Okay—"

"It's from Cheryl."

My breath freezes solid in my chest. "You're sure?"

He huffs, dropping his hand from my wrist. "Well, my god, check it and see!"

Noting something wrong, Poppy swoops forward and takes Karolina by the hand. "Karro, honey, have you seen the back of the chair yet? It's so cool. Come check it out." She tugs her a few feet away, exclaiming loudly about the lights and designs on the back of the chair.

Heart in my throat, I open my inbox and tap the new email from the case worker. Teddy stands at my side, both hands gripping tight to my arm. The anxiety is rolling off him in waves. "Well?"

I read the email twice through, making sure I miss nothing in the English-to-Swedish translation in my head. Then I let out the breath I've been holding for four long months. "She's ours."

Teddy cries out with relief, wrapping his arms around me. "Oh god, really?"

I nod, holding him to me with one arm, my other arm trapped between our chests, my hand still holding the phone. "She says we still have to follow through with the remaining protocols. But the judge has changed our status from temporary custody to full custody."

He presses a kiss to my neck. Then he pulls away and reaches for the phone, reading the message for himself. Just behind him, Jake has tears in his eyes. "I'm really happy for you, Karlsson."

I nod, my own eyes feeling misty. "I know it's what my sister would have wanted for her."

Jake smiles, glancing from Teddy back to me. "That's not quite what I meant, but I'm happy for all of it. You deserve good things." He holds out a hand to me.

I take it, clasping his hand in both of mine. "Thank you, Jake."

Teddy finishes the email and sinks against me, wrapping both arms around my waist, burying his face against my shoulder. "Oh god, babe, I felt like I couldn't breathe. I've just been borrowing air for weeks, feeling like I'm suffocating."

"I know." I drop Jake's hand, wrapping both arms tight around my Teddy. I kiss his temple, his cheek, the corner of his mouth. "Thank you," I whisper between each press of my lips.

"Thank you? For what?"

I lean away, cupping his face. "Without you, none of this would have been possible. Without you, they would have taken her from me. I'm not sure I could have fought it—"

"You would have," he assures me. "Henrik, you're so strong. She gets that from you, as much as from her mother. I see that now. You would have fought for her."

I smile. The love of my life is happy in my arms. His tacky blinking sweater is now dusted in glitter from the one I wear. I feel lighter than air. The only things keeping me tethered to the ground are Teddy's hands on me. "Now what do we do?"

He laughs, the sound joyous and full. "Now we finally get to make plans for our future, starting with Montana for Christmas. Then you're gonna marry me again."

I nod, relaxing my hold on him. "I was thinking something small."

"For Christmas? What, like a small present?"

"No, for the wedding. I was thinking we plan something small. You know, just Karolina, your family, and our close friends."

"Oh, honey." He lovingly pats my cheek. "That's why you're not planning it."

16

TEDDY

"**D**id you have fun tonight, lamm?" Henrik sits at the head of Karolina's bed, tucking her in, while I lie across the foot of it.

She gives a sleepy nod, still clutching the picture book we bought for her at Deck the Chairs.

"We have a surprise for you tomorrow," he says.

Her eyes blink open. "What is it?"

He smiles, smoothing her blankets. "You get to take the walking boot off."

She sits up, the book flopping to the side. "Really?"

"Yep, you're all healed," I say, propping my head on my hand as I stretch out on my side. "Are you excited, honey?"

She nods fervently. "Now I can do ballet, and surfing, and ride horses on the beach!"

I laugh, sitting up. "Easy, Supergirl. One thing at a time, okay? First, you gotta prove how strong you are by finishing up your physical therapy. We're gonna race Morbror in the swimming pool."

"And school? I can go now?"

Henrik nods. "You start at the new school in January."

She settles back against her pillows. After a moment, her tired smile turns into a pout.

Henrik brushes her hair back. "What's wrong?"

"I'll miss Mr. Torres."

"I thought you didn't like that he made you learn math," I tease.

Her pout deepens. "He taught me about the bees. And how the sun makes food for flowers."

Henrik considers for a moment. "What if we promise to have Mr. Torres over for dinner once a month? That way, he can learn all about your progress at your new school."

She nods, her pout softening a little. "And Hanna."

I step around to the head of the bed, placing a hand on Henrik's shoulder. "What about Hanna, honey?"

She glances between us. "If I don't have my casts anymore, will Hanna go too?"

I wince, catching Henrik's eye.

He recovers smoothly, taking her book and exchanging it for Teddy the Bear. "I already spoke with Hanna, and for your birthday, we're all going to Disney World together."

Karro squeals with delight, squeezing her bear tight enough to pop him. "Princess makeovers!"

"Oh, girl, just you wait," I say. "We're gonna do everything. Every park, plus the water one. Fireworks, animal safaris, all the shows. And Hanna will ride every ride with you. Morbror and I will too."

I don't miss the way Henrik's shoulders stiffen. Or the way Karro looks to him and stifles a giggle. "What?" I glance between them. "What's wrong?"

"Nothing," Henrik mutters, rising from the bed. At the same time, Karolina shouts, "Morbror is afraid of roller coasters!"

I slowly turn to face him, one brow raised. "Seriously?"

He crosses his arms, defiant in the face of my surprise. "They're a safety hazard."

I just shake my head. I did this to myself. I fell in love with a Capricorn and married him. This is my life now. There's no one else to blame, and there's definitely no turning back.

I'm standing at the sink shirtless, nearly done with my night-time hair- and skincare routine, when Henrik steps into the bathroom. He leans against the open door with his arms crossed, looking divine in a low-slung pair of house pants and a fitted grey T-shirt. "All good?" I say, adjusting the elastic band of my head scarf on my forehead. "She still asleep?"

He nods. "Yeah, she's out like a light."

"Good." I rub the last remnants of my loc oil into my palms, warming them with the friction. "How do you feel?"

He raises a brow. "About the custody decision?"

"Obviously." We walked around in a daze all night, looking at the rest of the decorated lifeguard chairs, playing carnival games, eating tacos from a food truck. Nothing felt real. We were just sort of floating. Then we came home. Now we're here.

Henrik considers for a moment. "Honestly?"

I pause, setting aside my little jar of under-eye serum. "Yeah, babe. Honesty always."

His brow furrows as he shrugs. "I suppose it feels a bit anticlimactic."

"Oh my god, right?" I turn to face him, leaning my hip against the sink. "*So* anticlimactic. Here I was, making worrying my entire personality. I was starting to dress to match my own frown lines. Like, what am I even supposed to stress about now?"

He chuckles, unfolding his arms and slipping his hands in his pockets. "I'm sure you'll think of something."

"I mean, yeah, there are already like five things." I give a distracted wave of my hand as I turn back to face the mirror. "We have to plan for Christmas and Karro's new school. We need to get her a backpack, folders, new colored pencils. Then there's the wedding, our trip to Sweden to see your parents for the bye week . . ."

As I talk, Henrik crosses the room, stepping in behind me. I'm dabbing my expensive gel serum under each eye with my pinkie as his hands go to my shoulders. I still as he starts to rub circles with his thumbs. I raise a brow at his reflection. "What are you doing?"

"Touching you."

I smirk, setting the little jar of serum down. "Don't start something you can't finish, old man."

He hums. "Old, am I?"

"Older than me," I tease. "And, apparently, afraid of rollercoasters?"

Stepping in close, he lowers his face to breathe in my skin, trailing the tip of his nose from my shoulder up the curve of my neck. I fight a shiver, hands dropping to grip the edge of the sink, as his lips press to the point just behind my ear. "Are you afraid I'm not exciting enough for you, mitt hjärta? Married to a boring old Swede who eats oats and drinks his coffee black?"

I shrug, leaning into his touch. "I already fixed the coffee thing."

He kisses my neck, his hands trailing down my sides. "Did you now?"

"Mhmm. Don't think I don't see you reaching for the milk every morning. You like it a little sweet, admit it—" I gasp as he wraps his hand around my neck and jerks my body back against his. "Hen, what—"

Reaching around me, he slaps something down on the vanity. I glance down at what looks like a little black remote. "What's that?"

"What does it look like?" he says in my ear.

I smile, pressing myself against him. "It looks like a remote. But to what?"

He nips the skin at my shoulder, making me groan. "Try it and see."

I pick up the remote, wholly distracted by his hands and lips on me. It's a simple thing with only a few buttons. I press the little On button. Behind me, Henrik jerks, his hands gripping tighter to my shoulders. He mutters a curse in Swedish. Then I hear a faint buzzing. My eyes widen as I stare at him in the mirror. "Babe!"

He groans, stepping in until I feel his erection against my ass.

I gasp again. "Henrik Karlsson, are you wearing a vibrating cock ring?" Spinning around, I cup his crotch. And, yep, there is definitely something wrapped around my man's junk right now. "Lemme see."

"Teddy—"

Grabbing the top of his lounge pants, I jerk them down, freeing his cock. It's half erect, growing harder. There's a thick ring of black silicone wrapped around the top of his cock and strapped under his balls. The ring buzzes and Henrik grunts, stroking his shaft. "Where the heck did you get it?"

He shrugs. "The internet. Do you not like it?"

I grin up at him. "The question is do *you* like it. How does it feel?"

"Good," he mutters. "Tight. Strange."

I just shake my head, unable to look away.

"What?"

"I am in awe of you, you know that? I never thought I'd see the day Henrik freaking Karlsson would surprise me with a vibrating cock ring."

He chuckles, stroking his hard cock again. But then he's grunting, his eyes closing. "I was going to suggest I fuck you while I'm wearing this, but now I feel a bit light in the head."

Scrambling for the remote, I turn the vibrations off. "Is it too much? Too tight? Do you want it off?" I reach for it, but he grabs my wrists.

"Give me a moment." He lets out a breath, staring down at the contraption. "Teddy, I want . . ."

His words trail away, so I twist my arms in his grip until we're bracing each other's forearms. "What, babe? You want what?"

He glances up at me, vulnerability in his eyes. I try to read his silence. "Do you want me to top you?" He nods, and I smile, letting out a breath of relief. "Oh, thank god."

"Why thank god?"

I just laugh. "You know me. My mind will instantly skip, hop, and jump right down into the dark place. I was ready to hear you say you wanted to be alone to play with your new toy."

"No, I want you with me."

"You wanna let go," I intuit.

He nods again.

I smile, leaning in to brush a kiss to his lips. "Don't even worry, baby. Between that ring on your cock and me riding your ass, you're gonna come so hard for so long, you'll think your soul was fucked from your body."

"Christ," he mutters.

"You're gonna have to call in sick tomorrow."

"Teddy . . ."

Laughing, I peck his lips again. Then I dart from the bathroom into the bedroom. He follows me out, leaving his pants abandoned on the floor by the sink. It's my soul that's gonna leave my body as, in the reflection of our floor-to-ceiling window, I watch him one-handedly tug his shirt off. He drops the shirt to the floor. Then he's standing naked in our bedroom, my cock ring–adorned Adonis.

"What are you doing?" he says, fisting his shaft.

"I get to play too, right?" Rattling open the bottom drawer of my side table, I pull out two vibrating butt plugs and hold them out to him. "Black or blue?"

His eyes go wide. "Christ, Teddy. You'll put these inside you?"

I hold out the more bulbous black one. "This is tricky to get in, but it hits the prostate like magic." I show him the blue one. "But this one vibrates so hard, you feel it in your teeth."

He hands me the black one.

"Good choice." I toss the other one back in the drawer and shut it with my foot.

Henrik steps in next to me, peeking over my shoulder. "What else do you have in there?"

"Wouldn't you like to know? Babe, get the lube."

While Henrik retrieves a bottle of lube from the bathroom, I strip out of my sleep shorts and crawl onto the bed. He comes back in to see me balanced on the edge, knees spread, my own fingers already wet with spit and prodding at my hole.

He crosses quickly to my side. With a hungry groan, he grabs my hips and tips me forward, his mouth descending. He licks and teases, rimming me like that's the job he gets paid millions to perform. I cry out, fisting the sheets, my erection going from excited to rock fucking hard in moments. "Oh my god."

I grind into the teasing of his tongue. With his mouth and fingers, he stretches me open. I almost miss it when he tosses the little black remote on the bed. I scramble for it, turning it on. He moans between my cheeks. Hearing the vibrations of his toy has me ready to come. "Get the plug," I pant. "Babe, lube it up. Put it in."

He does as he's told, generously coating the plug before prodding the bulbous end against my stretched hole.

"Fuck, just do it," I grunt, pushing back against the sting and pressure.

"Look at you." He strokes my ass cheek with one hand as he presses the toy in deeper. I feel it sink into place and let out a shaky breath. His hands continue to soothe as he kisses his way up my back. "Feel good?"

"Yeah. Feels so fucking good. Babe, turn it on."

He fumbles with the head of the plug, looking for the On button. Once he finds it, I rock into the sudden sensation. The vibrations shudder through me, warming me up. Henrik strokes his fingers along my taint, pressing up and in against the toy until I'm moaning. "I feel it," he murmurs. "I feel it inside you."

I push up with my hands, crawling to the side to make room. "You're about to feel me inside you. Get on the goddamn bed."

He drops down next to me. "How do you want me?"

"Are you kidding? You think I'm gonna miss watching a single second of my smoking-hot husband wearing a vibrating cock ring while he gets fucked? On your back. Grab your thighs. Show me what I want."

He rolls to his side, and I roll with him, getting myself between his spread legs as he stretches out on his back. The black silicone cock ring is stretched tight around his junk, still gently vibrating. His dick looks a shade darker than normal. A vein runs along the underside of his shaft, making it look angry and desperate.

He stretches an arm behind his head, smiling at me. "Better than a roller coaster?"

I can't contain my cheesy quip. "Baby, you know you're my favorite fucking ride." Then I duck down and suck his tip into my mouth, rolling back his foreskin with my hand. I feel the vibrations from the cock ring all down his shaft. I hum, adding my own all-natural sensation to his leaking tip. He curses in Swedish, something I always take as a good sign to continue.

This new angle on my knees changes the press of the plug on my prostate. I grunt, breathing through the delicious feeling of being overly full. Henrik's hands brush lightly over my head scarf before he grabs my shoulders. "I want you inside me."

I give the tip of his cock a last lick. Then I look up the length of his naked body, marveling at him all stretched out for me. "You gonna give me what I want?"

Huffing out a heavy breath, he grabs the backs of his gorgeous tree-trunk thighs and does a half curl, rocking back to expose his asshole for me.

"This is what we need a picture of," I tease, helping him hold the awkward crunch position.

He chokes on a laugh that turns into a groan as I wiggle my lubed fingers against his tight hole.

"Gotta relax if you want me inside you."

"How can you bear it?" he says through clenched teeth.

"Bear what, baby?"

"The vibration. I want to come so badly."

"Don't you fucking dare. Not until I'm inside you. Not until I say."

"Then hurry the fuck up."

Holding his gaze, I jam both my lubed fingers up inside him. I work them in and out as I reach for the remote. "You ready?"

"For what?"

I turn up his remote.

He rocks into the new vibration pattern. "Teddy—Christ—"

"My middle name is Malik," I tease.

He wraps his hand around his shaft and gives it a slow pull. "Need to come."

Being the brat I am, I slap his hand away. "When it's time for you to come, it will be *my* hand on your dick, not yours. Now lie back and think about how pretty you're about to look with my dick up your ass."

He groans in frustration, his knuckles white as he holds to both his thighs.

"Spread wide, baby. Make room for me." I have plenty of room, but I just love watching this man do as I say.

He drops his knees wide, opening his legs in a V. I grab a firm pillow and tuck it under his hips, giving him some support. Then I clench hard around my own vibrating plug as I press the tip of my lubed dick between his cheeks. "Bear down," I pant, holding my dick in place. "Baby, breathe."

Henrik lets out a deep exhale, and then I slip in. Grabbing his hips, I press in deeper, giving him another two inches. His head tips back, eyes closed, as he takes in the dueling sensations of the vibrating cock ring and my dick in his ass.

This moment should have me reeling too. Between the feel of the thick plug in my ass, my cock buried inside Henrik's wet heat, and his cock ring humming at the base of my shaft—god, I should be in sensory overload. I should be fraying apart. But all I can do is marvel at my husband. He's come so far. When this all first started, he flinched when I touched him. Now he's taking charge, experimenting with toys and letting me take the deepest parts of him. The trust he has in me is staggering.

"Look at me," I say, sinking in the last few inches. I rock against the cradle of his thighs, letting the base of his vibrating cock ring settle between us.

Henrik's pretty blue gaze locks on me. I used to look in his eyes and see deep wells of sadness, a loneliness that stretched on with no horizon. Now I see strength and purpose, love and loyalty. His gaze softens as he searches my face. "What, mitt hjärta?"

"I love you."

It's the simplest of phrases, spoken so many times, in so many languages. To love means to cherish, to value and adore, to prize above all else. That's what I feel for Henrik. All that and more. I love him, trust him. I ache to be near him.

He reaches for me with both hands, pulling me between his legs. His strapped cock gets pinned between us as he pulls me down, kissing me. "I love you," he says against my lips. "My only love. I want you with me always."

"Always," I repeat, rocking against him, burying myself in deep, as deep as I can get. "I never want to be parted from you. Love me. Keep me forever."

"Forever," he promises, sealing it with a kiss.

We keep whispering sweet lovers' words as we move together, taking our pleasure in each other. When I feel like I can't bear it another second, I wrap my hand around his shaft and set him free, whispering, "Come with me."

Crying out, we come together, awash in gratitude and relief. Nothing has ever felt as good as being in Henrik's arms. I mean to chase this feeling forever. Loving him, wanting him, trusting him in all things. With Henrik, I am seen. I am loved and cherished.

With Henrik, I am my truest self.

77

TEDDY

Three Months Later

"Okay, hair is almost done. Suit is pressed. Shoes are polished." Natalie runs through the mental checklist, ticking off each item with her fingers. "Oh—the flowers—"

"Already by the window," says Shae, busy fluffing Desiree's dress for the third time. The other flower girls bounce around the room, pretending they're princesses being chased by a dragon. Karolina wields a chopstick from our sushi lunch like a sword. Behind her, Camila holds a coloring book up like a shield.

Ignoring the chaos, Jayla stands behind me at the dressing table, her mouth full of pins as she tries to get the last few pieces of my twisted hair to lie just right.

"It looks fine," I say again.

"Ted, when I want your opinion, I'll give it to you," she mutters, her eyes narrowed at my hair's reflection as she meticulously moves another pin.

I just sigh. There's no use fighting her at this point.

"Okay," Bridget calls with a clap of her hands, striding into the middle of the room. She's the genius wedding planner Henrik hired to help bring my vision to life. "It's time to get our groom dressed!"

My sisters and nieces all squeal with excitement. Well, except for Jay, whose mouth is full of pins. "It just won't lie right," she grumbles.

"Did you try twisting it the other way?" asks Shae.

"You wanna come over here and try it?"

"Don't fight," I say, heading off a row. "Jay, it looks great. Better than great," I quickly correct, leaning away from her pointed glare. "It looks amazing."

It really does. She's twisted all my locs up into an elegant knot that sits high on my crown. The twists have movement and flow. Jayla is just a perfectionist.

She's also the only one of my sisters not dressed yet.

"Jay, you can't wear a bathrobe down the aisle," Natalie teases. "Girl, go get changed."

"Who's gonna finish this hair?"

"Let me."

We all turn as Mama strides back into the room. She left a few minutes ago to put her dress on.

"Oh, Mama," Shae sighs. "You look beautiful."

"You really do," says Nat.

Mama just shrugs. My sisters are all wearing cobalt-blue brides-maid dresses in different styles to match their body types. But Mama's dress is a soft slate blue with a sequined bodice and a chiffon skirt. It looks great with her darker skin tone.

"Granny, you look like a fairy princess," Camila calls.

"Cam, go get Granny her corsage," says Jay.

Camila bounces over to the table as Jayla sets down the last of the pins. "I can't get this part to lie right," she explains to mom.

"I got it," she replies. "You go get dressed."

Jayla hurries away, leaving us alone in the corner. Mom gets to work, fixing a few of the pins with deft fingers. "Are you ready for this, baby? Anything else you need?"

I smile at her reflection. "I'm fine, Mama. You've all taken such good care of me today."

She just hums, moving another pin. "You know, when each of your sisters got married, there was only one question I asked them. I would have asked you too, but—"

"Ask me now," I say over her. "This is my real wedding, Mama. The first one didn't count. We did it the wrong way, even if we did it for the right reason."

She glances over her shoulder to see Karolina in her flower girl dress, laughing on the couch with Camila and Evie. Their faces are glowing, like three little angels in fluffy blue dresses. "I see that now," she admits with a nod. "I see how right you are for them. You were made to make that little girl laugh, baby."

I smile, tears filling my eyes. "So will you ask me?"

She purses her lips, fighting a smile. "Even if I already know your answer?"

"It's tradition." I fiddle with the clasp of my watch. It was Henrik's wedding gift to me, my something new and blue. The lace appliques on my suit are old, taken from my sisters' wedding dresses. The cream ribbon around my bouquet is borrowed, something we found in Petra's old sewing box.

"Please ask me," I say again. "It won't feel like my wedding day if you don't ask."

"There," she hums, lowering her hands from my finished hair to my shoulders. "You're ready."

Reaching up, I place my hand over hers on my shoulder, holding her gaze in the mirror. "Ask me, Mama."

After a moment, she squeezes my shoulder. "Teddy baby, does he make you happy?"

Oh god, it didn't feel real until this exact moment. I'm getting married today. Somewhere just outside that door, Henrik is waiting for me. The tears spill over as I smile. "Yeah, Mama. He does. He makes me so crazy happy."

Sniffing, she blinks her own tears away. "Well, alright then."

"Ugh, you two are gonna be the death of me," Shae cries, sweeping forward to wrap her arms around Mom from behind.

"Teddy, we gotta get you dressed," says Nat. "It's game time, baby."

I smile at my own reflection, heart skipping with joy to see all the faces of my family smiling with me. "Okay," I say with a nod. "Yeah, let's do this. Let's get me married."

HENRIK

"Are you ready, my friend?" Lindberg asks in Swedish, patting me on the back. Ilmari and Novy stand just behind him in matching black tuxedos.

The music changes, and I nod, folding my hands dutifully before me. We're standing next to an altar, draped in spring flowers. I look out on the sea of white chairs set at the edge of this nature preserve. Trees tower behind us, making the natural beauty of the woods our sanctuary.

Teddy's dream was always to be married on a forest's edge at twilight. And my Teddy gets what he wants. When it comes to this second wedding, I've denied him nothing. Everyone from the team is here, including their children and partners. The support staff and their families are here too, even some of the volunteers who work at the arena. An old lady named Marjorie shuffled up to me moments ago and offered me a butterscotch candy.

I scan the crowd and see all the familiar faces of Teddy's other family and friends, including Colin, the PT for the Jaguars, and Doctor Brady and his husband, an imposing man with a thick mustache and scars on his face. Seated near them are the rest of the Prices and the Langleys. Ryan catches my eye and waves, giving me a thumbs-up. Tess sits on the end of the aisle, holding up a tablet. My parents have joined us via video call. She turns the tablet so I can see them and wave.

The crowd sighs with delight as the flower girls make their way down the aisle, led by Karolina in a pretty blue dress. Her hair is a crown of curls. Teddy's nieces, Camila, Evie, and Desiree, follow behind her, sprinkling their white rose petals on the soft grass. As the oldest, Desiree holds Evie's hand, keeping her from darting away.

Karolina hurries the last third of the way down the aisle to my side. I duck down and pull her to me, kissing her cheek. "Well done, mitt lamm. Now, go sit with Hanna, ja?" I point to Hanna sitting at the end of the first row. She smiles and pats the empty seat next to her. Karolina goes to her, taking the hand of her cousin Camila to bring her along.

The music changes again, and Teddy's sisters slowly make their way down the aisle. Each of them chose a different style of dress in the same color blue. Natalie winks as she passes me first. Jayla is already crying. Shae is the last down the aisle. She stops before me. "You'll be good to my baby brother?"

I nod. "As long as there is breath in my body."

Smiling, she leans in and gives me a hug. Then she takes her place as the matron of honor.

"Please, rise," the officiant calls.

Our sea of friends and family rise from their chairs, turning to face up the aisle. With the pressure off me, I glance down. I'm wearing a sleek black tuxedo with thin lapels. The top button of my shirt is open, no tie. Teddy surprised me by leaving a gift in my dressing room this morning. It was a pocket square made from a piece of blue satin he cut from his favorite head scarf. When I lifted it to my face, I could smell the faint hint of peppermint hair oil, a pure shot of Teddy right to my lungs.

I adjust the little square of satin in my pocket. Then the music changes to something soft and romantic. A gasp ripples through the crowd, and I get my first look at Teddy in over twenty-four hours. He and his mother turn the corner at the top of the aisle, and my heart stops.

"Holy shit," Novy mutters.

Reaching out, Lindberg squeezes my shoulder again. I hardly register the touch. I only see Teddy.

He's wearing all white, his hair up in a twisted knot. His outfit is a sleek white tuxedo with crisply pleated pants and a jacket. He's shirtless beneath the double-breasted jacket, which is accented at the lapels and on the sleeves with what looks like bridal lace. A sheer white veil is pinned at his shoulders, trailing behind him like a cape. He clutches a bouquet of flowers that Karolina helped him pick, which includes buttery yellow roses with sprigs of blue, a nod to our Swedish heritage.

In this moment, he's more beautiful than I've ever seen him. I called him the ocean before, deep and endless. But just for tonight, he is the sun. He's radiant and glowing, shining out like a beacon, calling me home.

His mother walks proudly at his side, her hand draped on his arm. Relations between us have improved over the last few months. I write her emails weekly, informing her about our life and my travels. I share pictures of Teddy and Karolina—at ballet practice and the pool, baking in the kitchen, making forts in the living room.

That's all his mother wants in the end, to still feel like part of his new life. I can give her that. And in return, she will give me the chance to show that I mean what I say: I will love Teddy until the end, until there is nothing left of me but ash.

Even then, the proof of our love will remain. Petra isn't gone. Not so long as Karolina draws breath. Not as long as we love her and honor her memory. My love for Teddy will be just the same. It's bigger than me, touching everyone in our lives, remaking us all.

Teddy stops before me, tears of joy shining in his eyes.

"Who gives this man to be wed?" the officiant asks.

Keziah looks to me and nods. Then she turns to the officiant. "His mother does." Kissing his cheek, she hands Teddy off to me, entrusting him to my care.

I take his hand in mind, pulling him forward. "You look beautiful, mitt hjärta."

"So do you," he replies, handing his bouquet to Shae.

The officiant gestures for the crowd to be seated, then she begins. I'm lost in a trance, unable to look away from my Teddy. His beauty is breathtaking, my man of sharp angles. The cut of his cheeks looks even more pronounced in this waning light. He feels my eyes on him and offers me a nervous smile, squeezing my hand.

Before long, the officiant is announcing the vows, asking us each to recite them. We already did this in Sweden. I promised to love and honor. I promised to shelter and defend. They were just words to me then. Now, I recite them as a sacred oath. I will love my Teddy for all my days. Honor him, yes. In all ways. I will shelter him and seek shelter in him. I will defend him with my life, with my dying breath.

"Do you, Henrik Johan Björn Karlsson, take this man to be your lawfully wedded husband?"

"I do," I declare.

His smile is blinding as he fights back his tears.

"And do you, Theodore Malik O'Connor, take this man to be your lawfully wedded husband?"

"Yes," he says on a breath. Blinking, he looks to the officiant. "Wait, I mean 'I do.' God, of course I do!"

The crowd laughs, and the officiant nods. Then she turns to Karolina. "Karro, do you want to come up here, honey?"

With a little nudge from Hanna, Karolina slips out of her chair and hurries over to us, taking one of our hands in each of hers. When we discussed getting remarried, this was always part of the ceremony that Teddy was adamant we include, much to my relief and delight.

"Karro, honey, your uncles have something they'd like to say to you." Turning to me, the officiant nods.

It feels strange to offer these words in English, but I made a promise to Teddy. Dropping down to one knee, I brush a tear off Karolina's cheek. "Mitt lamm, I've loved you from the moment you drew your first breath. You may not be my daughter by blood, but you are part of me, part of the soul of me. On this day, as I take Teddy into my heart and vow to make a home for him, I vow the same to you. I will love you always, mitt lamm. You will always have a home with me."

She cries, wrapping her arms around my middle. Ilmari leans around Lindberg, handing me the flower crown we had made for her. Smiling, I rest it atop her head. She lights up, eyes wide, as she brushes her fingers over the soft petals of the roses in her crown.

Wiping under his eyes, Teddy clears his throat, then takes her hand. "Karro, you know you're my best little friend. Becoming your uncle has been one of the great joys of my life. I believe we can pick our family and love them as fiercely as our own flesh and blood. And I pick you. I pick you to watch movies with, and bake cookies with, and watch hockey with. I will always pick you. I will always love you. And I will never leave."

She hugs him too. "I love you, Teddy."

Sighing, he drops to one knee and gives her a proper hug. "Oh, honey, I love you so much. Here—" He reaches behind him and his sister hands him his bouquet. He presents the flowers to Karolina. "These are for you. I'm so glad you finally got to be our flower girl."

Her joy and beauty are ethereal as she stands with her flower crown and bouquet. We keep her between us, me holding her hand, Teddy with his hand on her shoulder.

The officiant looks to me. "Henrik, was there anything else you wanted to say to Teddy?"

I nod, clearing my throat. Looking over Karolina to him, I hold his gaze. "Teddy, when we first married, it was under a cloud of fear and grief. You did it to help a friend. You saw me in need. But in Sweden you asked me . . . rather, you shouted at me on the side of a busy road with traffic whooshing by . . ."

"Oh god," he mutters to the soft laugher of the crowd.

"You asked me to name three things I knew about you. Just three things that would make you believe I cared for you at all." Slipping my hand in my pocket, I pull out a piece of paper and unfold it. "I know a few more things now."

He bites his bottom lip, trying not to cry.

"You listen to Norah Jones in the bathtub, Kendrick Lamar at the gym, and never the other way around."

The crowd laughs as Teddy shrugs. "True."

"You burn yourself every time you take something out of the oven. When you're stressed, you only want to drink Diet Dr Pepper. You have a strict eight-step skincare routine, and I'm not allowed to ask you any questions about it. If there's a risotto dish on the menu, you will always order it."

He smiles. "All true."

Folding the paper, I tuck it back in my pocket. "But those are just things, habits and patterns, the little routines you live by. I know more now. I know the rhythm of your breathing when you sleep. I know the catch of your breath when you hear something that surprises you. I know the furrow of your brow when you don't get your way. I think I could chart the pattern of the freckles on your cheeks with my eyes closed. They're more precious to me now than the stars in the sky. They are the constellation that guides me home. To you. Always to you. Only to you. My life and my love, my only one."

Tears trail down his cheeks and I reach out, wiping them away with my thumb. "We have a lifetime together to learn more trivia about each other. But the essential things won't change. I *know* you, Teddy. I know you and value you above all others, even myself. You married me once when I was drowning. You kicked for me, bringing me to the surface. In marrying me again, I vow to keep swimming, to keep trying to be worthy of you. I may not succeed, but I will always try. That is my vow."

Silence answers my words as half the crowd reaches for tissues to dry their eyes. I glance around, suddenly feeling self-conscious. "What?" I glance to Teddy. "Was that not correct for a vow?"

He chokes on a laugh, snatching the tissue his sister offers him. "Are you freaking kidding me?"

The crowd laughs as he dabs at his eyes.

After I nod to the officiant, she continues. "Okay, thank you, Henrik. And Teddy, was there anything you'd like to say to Henrik?"

He huffs, tucking the tissue in his pocket. "Sure, no problem. I'll follow that."

The crowd laughs again.

Cleaning his throat, Teddy reaches out and takes both my hands in his. "Henrik, I've loved you for six long years. I loved you before I really knew what love was. It was a fanciful, dreamy kind of love. The kind of love you get lost in while soaking in a bathtub, listening to Norah Jones."

There are a few chuckles out in the crowd.

"I had you up on a pedestal in my mind," he goes on. "You were perfect, my own masterpiece. I set up ropes and added alarms. I could look, but I couldn't touch. I think I was afraid that if I made you more human, you could hurt me. Worse, you could actually want me. Worse still, you could think you want me, learn more about me, then not want me anymore. I think that was my biggest fear, finally being seen by you . . . and having nowhere left to hide. Even once we were married, I hid pieces of myself away. I tried to play it cool and pretend like I wasn't dying inside every time you looked at me, every time you touched me."

His words hurt my heart, to know how he suffered in those early days.

As if he can read my mind, he glances out to the crowd. "Don't worry, this story has a happy ending." He gestures to me with a wave of his hand. "See? I got him. He knows everything about me, down to the freckles on my face, and he loves me anyway."

There are cheers and applause at this, all our friends and family smiling, delighted for us and our love.

Teddy turns back to me, his expression sobering. "No one else has ever loved me the way you love me. No one else has ever made me feel so safe to be myself, to be loud and messy and panicked and happy and stressed. You let me feel all my feelings out loud, all at once, all the time. Henrik, you are my safe place, my harbor, and my home. I never want to leave the comfort of your arms."

Lifting his hands to my lips, I kiss first the ring on his left hand, then the ring on his right. "I love you, Teddy."

"Oh god, I love you too."

The officiant smiles at us, nodding down at Karolina. I take Karro's hand as the officiant continues. "Nothing makes God happier than when people treat each other with kindness, love, and fairness. You've opened your hearts to each other and made a home for this girl you've vowed to raise together. We here stand witness to your vows and commit now to help you see them through. In return, we vow to be your community, your support, and your safe shore. Lean on us, as you will undoubtedly lean on each other."

"We will," Teddy says with a nod.

I squeeze Karolina's hand, smiling at them both. "I will."

The officiant nods, raising her hands. "Then, by the power vested in me by the State of Florida, I now pronounce you husbands. You may kiss, sealing the bond of your marriage."

With a squeak of excitement, Karolina steps back. Teddy trembles, his smile wide, as I pull him into my arms and kiss him soundly. No word of my vows was a lie. Tasting him on my lips is like coming up for air. I was drowning, and he saved me. I was lonely, and he brought joy and laughter into my life. I was lost, set adrift, and he found me. He reeled me in and moored me to him. We are bound now. Irrevocably. Teddy is my life and my love. To the end of my days, he is my home.

"I love you," he says, the words a brand on my lips.

Smiling, I kiss him again.

EPILOGUE

TEDDY

Five Years Later

Henrik and I make our way into the crowded auditorium. He has the flowers, and I have Karolina's coat. Before I can worry about trying to find our seats, a shrill whistle has us both turning. Ryan Langley stands about ten rows down, waving us forward. He looks dapper in a grey suit with no tie, his beach-blond hair flopping across his forehead.

"This way, babe," I say over my shoulder.

Henrik follows me down the aisle, where we're greeted by what looks like half the Rays. The Langleys are here, obviously. Tonight, Emma and Karolina are debuting as flower dancers in the Jacksonville Ballet Company's holiday production of *The Nutcracker*. Karro's been practicing hard for months. I feel like I have the steps memorized at this point too.

Paulie and his wife Maribel are here. Their daughter Beatriz is one of the Russian candy cane dancers, I think. Next to them are Rachel and Jake Price and their son Jamie.

"Where's the rest of the fam?" I say, patting her shoulder as I pass.

She smiles up at me. "Split efforts tonight. We wanted to be here to support the kids, while the others all went to watch Tuo's hockey game."

I grin at Jake. "Does it gall you at all? Your kiddo choosing to be a forward?"

He just shakes his head. "Not at all. Heck, I was a forward until I was fifteen. He's got time to change his mind."

"Maybe he'll be a goalie," I say with a shrug.

Jake smiles. "He's certainly got the genes for it . . . though his mom has two left feet."

She elbows him and he laughs. But Jake's not kidding. The older Tuomas Price has gotten, the more it's become clear exactly who his father is. The boy is only seven, and he's already the spitting image of Ilmari.

The St. James-Novikov-Morrows are here too. Poppy sits in the row one below Rachel, her daughter Fiona snuggled in her lap. Bennett sits between his dads, his eyes locked on the glowing screen of his tablet.

"Hey, Teddy." Poppy gives us a wave. "Oh, Henrik, those are gorgeous!"

He glances down at our bouquet of twelve long-stem red roses with a smile.

"We got flowers too," says Colton, pointing to the seat next to him where I see a pretty bouquet of winter florals.

I slip into the row in front of them, setting my coat on the seat the Langleys saved for us. "That's right. Grace is dancing tonight too, right?"

Novy leans back in his seat, arms folded across his chest in his sport coat. "Gracie is a snowflake. Act One. She's so fucking good. Our girl can arabesque like anything."

Poppy laughs, rolling her eyes. "She only demanded to audition because Emma and Karolina were auditioning. And she's complained every night we've taken her to rehearsals."

He narrows his eyes at her. "What are you saying?"

"I'm saying you may have to face the fact that, after five years, our daughter has fallen out of love with ballet. Now, all she talks about is wanting to be a drummer in a band."

I chuckle, sinking down in my seat.

Henrik sits next to me, leaning in. "There are many things I will abide in the name of Karolina's happiness, but a drum set—"

"I know," I soothe, patting his knee.

After two years in Henrik's old apartment, we finally moved into a bigger place closer to the beach. We're now only a five-minute walk from the Langleys. Ever since someone thought it would be a good idea to get Karolina a dog, it's a walk we make pretty much daily. "Sparkles bought you some good will," I assure him. "If she asks for a drum set, we'll just say he's allergic."

He snorts, carefully shifting the bouquet of flowers to under his chair.

Tess leans in over Ryan, squeezing my arm. "Is she excited? Did you see her all dressed and ready?"

I nod, grinning. "I took, like, a thousand pictures on my phone. I got some good ones of Emma too. I'll send them to you."

She gives me a thumbs-up as the lights go down.

Ryan leans around me to look at Henrik. "Hey, we're going out for pizza tonight to celebrate. You three wanna join?"

"Can't," Henrik replies, clapping along with the rest of the crowd as the lights flash on stage, illuminating the curtains.

"We can't?" I say, one brow raised. "Why not?"

"We've got plans," he replies, loud enough for Ryan to hear.

This is the first I'm hearing of post-ballet dinner plans. My Spidey senses start to tingle as I glance over at my husband. "What plans?"

He just places a hand on my knee, giving it a pat.

"I won't let up until you tell me."

"It's a surprise."

The overture starts, and I'm left dangling for the whole of Act One, wondering what plans he made without telling me. From the moment the "Waltz of the Flowers" begins in Act Two, Henrik and I are on the edge of our seats. I gasp as Karolina comes prancing onto the stage in her pale green tutu. I grip Henrik's arm. "Babe—"

"I see her." He takes my hand, weaving our fingers together.

"Wow, she looks good," Ryan says next to me.

Next to him, Tess is on the edge of her seat too, her mountain of red curls piled atop her head. A few strands frame her freckled face as she clutches to her phone, recording Emma, who is dancing two girls behind Karolina. My god, how could I forget?

"Babe, your phone," I hiss.

Henrik scrambles to get his phone, setting it to record, as we watch Karolina leap and twirl, her arms fanning. At ten, she's tall for her age. She's one of the tallest girls on the stage. Her icy-blonde hair has grown to her butt. She won't let us cut it. Her *Tangled* phase left too great an imprint on her psyche.

I was a proud papa bear watching Henrik help her braid it tonight. We got it pinned up in a crown and hair-sprayed it until it was practically a helmet. If that hair falls, it won't be our fault. She weaves between the other girls, prancing from stage left to stage right, hitting each mark.

Next to me, Ryan is muttering under his breath. "Tendu . . . pirouette into fouetté—*yes!*"

Emma and Karolina both nail landing in a lunge, back legs extended, chests open, arms extended.

Henrik's eyes are on Karolina rather than the screen of his phone. "She looks so beautiful."

Tears sting my eyes as I watch our girl go, owning the stage like she was born to dance. I don't often let myself dwell on the darkness of how we met, but in this moment, watching the power in her leaps, I can't help but think back to that little girl I met in Sweden, bruises on her eye, a fluffy pink sock on the foot of her broken leg.

She's come so far. She still loves drawing and watching movies. Math is her favorite subject in school. And she's pulled Henrik back into his love of photography. They want to set up a darkroom upstairs so he can teach her how to develop film. We all took surfing lessons together until Karro and I admitted we were too afraid of sharks to continue. This summer, we've planned a family trip to Peru to hike part of the Inca Trail.

"Doesn't she look beautiful?" His eyes glow as he watches her do her spins at center stage.

"She does," I murmur, a tear slipping down my cheek. "She's so beautiful."

The lights are up, and Christmas carols play over the speakers in the auditorium. All the families mill around, waiting for the dancers to be released from backstage.

"Did you like it?" I say at Bennett.

He just shrugs. "It was long. The rat dancers were kinda cool. Reminded me of *Ninja Turtles*."

I smile. Ah, the mind of an eleven-year-old boy. What a delightful and silly place.

Ryan has his back turned to me, laughing at something with Tess. The pair of them hold bouquets of pink roses as they wait for Emma.

"Your girl is really good," Novy says over my shoulder, patting Henrik's back. "How did she get so tall? Was your sister really tall?"

"I'd say she was average," he replies.

"I'm sure she'll start slowing down and let the boys catch up," I say. "My sister, Nat, was 5'11" by the end of middle school, but then she never grew another inch."

"If Karolina gets any taller, you'll have to try her out for volleyball," Poppy teases. "I always wanted to play, but I'm a bit too vertically challenged."

All at once, it's chaos as the dancers begin slipping out from the sides of the stage, trying to find their families in the crowd. Gracie Morrow comes prancing down the aisle, still dressed as a snowflake. "Did you see me, Fi?" she calls to her little sister.

"Baby cakes, you did so good!" Poppy hugs her daughter, passing her around from Novy to Colton. Bennett is the one to hand her the flowers. She takes them, giving him a side hug.

"Morbror, Teddy!"

I spin around to see Karolina darting through the crowd, hand in hand with Emma.

"Daddy!" Emma shouts.

"Hey, there she is!" Ryan sweeps Emma up into the air, making her squeal, as Tess smothers her with the flowers.

Karolina is more sedate as she hops like a bunny to come stand in front of us. "Well? Did you see me?"

Henrik hands her the flowers. "You looked so beautiful, mitt lamm."

She looks to me, smiling from ear to ear, clutching her giant bouquet of oversized red roses. "Teddy?"

Finally breaking, I let the tears fall and pull her to me. "You were fantastic!"

"Don't cry," she mumbles against my chest.

I snort a laugh that sounds like a sob. "Just try and stop me."

She pulls away, her smile shifting to more of a mischievous grin. She glances to Henrik. "Did you tell him?"

"I told him nothing," he replies stoically.

"Tell me what?" I glance between them. "Guys, tell me what?"

She clutches to her flowers, her cheeks blooming pink. "We have a surprise for you."

My brow furrows, even as my heart starts to race. "What surprise? It's not my birthday, and Christmas is still, like, two weeks away."

She bounces on the balls of her feet. "Should we tell him now?"

"Yes," I say as Henrik says, "No."

I groan.

"Get your stuff," he says at her. "We'll meet you right back here."

Shoving her flowers at my chest, she darts away in search of her lost duffel bag. She may not be mine by blood, but apparently the propensity to lose things is more a nurture-over-nature thing.

"I s dinner the surprise?" I say as Henrik pulls the SUV into the parking lot of High Tide. We've been playing the world's most unfun game of Twenty Questions, where I try to guess the surprise and they give me nothing.

"It's part of it," says Karro from the back seat. She's out of her costume now, dressed in a comfortable purple sweat suit set. But she still has her hair braided and her show makeup on. "Morbror said this restaurant was special to you."

I click off my seat belt as she says the words, sitting frozen in the front seat. My god, she's right. We haven't been here together since our first date. How is that even possible? I think I've been here a few times in the passing years. A birthday, maybe. And a work lunch.

But never with Karolina and Henrik. It's just far enough down the A1A that we never think to go here.

I slip out of the SUV as Henrik hands the keys to the valet. Karolina steps in behind Henrik, taking one of our hands in each of hers. She leads the way up the ramp, bouncing ahead to open the front door for us.

"Remember the photographer?" I say, pointing over to the patch of bushes.

Henrik smirks. "And the lady who was affronted at seeing two men holding hands."

I laugh. "Denise. God, how do I still remember her name?"

We step inside, and Karolina is already at the hostess stand. "We have a reservation for Karlsson," she says in her doll voice. "Three people."

The hostess smiles down at her. "Yep, I have it here."

We follow her through the first dining room into the far corner, where we're shown a table by the windows. During the day, this looks out on a gorgeous view of the Atlantic Ocean. The sun has long set, so now the view is now just a dark abyss. A candle lit on the table provides a warm glow that reflects off the large windows.

"Your server will be right with you," the hostess says, handing us our menus.

Henrik and Karro open theirs as if nothing fishy is happening. They both bury their faces behind the folds, leaving me to gape at them, my own menu ignored. "Guys, seriously? You have to tell me what's going on. It's not fair that you both know."

Before either of them can speak, the waiter comes over and takes our drink order. "He'll have an amaretto sour," Henrik tells him. "I'll have a pale ale, whatever's on tap. And we're ready to order. We'd like to start with an order of the mussels. Then we'll all split a branzino and a plate of the lobster and scallop risotto."

"Very good, sir."

The waiter takes the menus, and I'm left speechless. "You—but that—we ordered that on our first date," I finally blurt.

He smiles, sipping his water. "I know."

Snatching up my napkin, I stuff it under the table onto my lap.

"Okay, someone better start talking." I point across the table at Karolina, my eyes narrowed. "You. You're gonna tell me, aren't you?"

She glances up at Henrik. "Can we?"

He nods, and I sigh with relief, knowing my suffering is at an end. "We wanted to do something special for you for Christmas this year," he begins. "Karolina and I coordinated our gifts."

"But you both always get me such wonderful gifts." It's true. Last year they got me a lovely watch and a spa package. The year before, it was a family trip to Canada to go skiing.

"It's not so much something we can get for you," Karro explains. "More like . . . something we each want to ask you."

I glance between them. "Something to ask me?"

They both nod.

"Well, why are we doing this now? Why not wait until actual Christmas?"

"Because we wanted it to be just us," she replies. "Morbror goes out of town this week for games, then we'll all be busy with the trip to Montana. And we won't really be alone there . . ."

The Prices invited us to spend Christmas in Montana again this year. One week with twenty-five people trapped in one big ranch house. It's chaotic and fun, and she's right—we'll get no alone time.

The waiter delivers our drinks, and I take a sip of my amaretto sour. "Okay, so you say you have something to ask me?"

Henrik glances down at Karro. "You first, lamm."

Taking a deep breath, she reaches into the pocket of her purple sweatshirt and pulls out a folded piece of paper. Then she holds it out to me. "This is for you. I wrote it down."

At the look of nervous excitement on her face, I already know I'm about to freaking lose it. I take the paper from her, holding back my tears. She colored the front to look like a winter forest. In a scripty red font, it says, "Merry Christmas." Smiling, I open the handmade card. Inside, there's one line written in her slanted handwriting: "Can I call you Dad?"

I stare down at the words, heart racing. Slowly, I look up to see tears in her eyes, Henrik's hand on her shoulder. "You really mean it?" I say through my own tears.

She nods, sniffling. "Henrik will always be my morbror. It's all I've ever known, and we're happy. But I don't like calling you Uncle Teddy."

"Why?"

She shrugs. "You just don't *feel* like an uncle to me. I had a mom, and she was perfect. And I have an uncle," she adds, smiling up at Henrik. Then she turns back to me. "I think I'd like to have a dad . . . if you'll let me."

I set the card down, tears flowing. "Oh, honey, of course. I mean—is it okay with Henrik?" I look to him to see he's crying too. I choke on a laugh, grabbing my napkin off my lap. "Oh my god, look at us. The waiter is gonna kick us out of here."

They both laugh as they wipe their eyes.

I hold out my arms. "Oh, honey, come here."

She darts out of her chair and around Henrik, dropping into my lap with a soft sob. I hold her to me, my arms around her tight, trying and failing to keep my cool. I brush my hand up and down her back, slowly rocking her. "I'd be honored if you chose to call me your dad. Karolina, I love you so much."

"I love you." Her words are muffled against my chest.

"Can I call you my daughter? Is that what you want?"

She nods again.

I turn to Henrik. "Apparently you have something to ask me too?"

"I do." His expression is glowing as he reaches into the pocket of his suit and pulls out his own papers, folded long ways. Smiling, he extends his arm, holding them out across the table.

Still sniffling on my lap, Karro turns so she can watch me take them. Heart in my throat, I unfold the papers to see some kind of government document. "A name change application for the State of Florida? What, are we about to all go on the lam? Are we committing a crime before dessert?"

Karro grins.

"No," Henrik replies, his voice soft. "I'd like you to consider changing your last name."

"To what?" I reply, obviously in a daze.

The corner of his mouth twitches with a smile. "Well, I suppose that will really be up to you, but I was hoping you might add 'Karlsson' to the short list of options."

I gasp, dropping the papers to the table. "You want me to change my last name to Karlsson?"

He shrugs noncommittally. But I see the heat in his eyes. After five years together, I can read him like a book. He wants this. Desperately. "We're married," he reasons. "It's common practice for people who are married to take each other's name."

"We are married," I muse. I wear the rings to prove it. Heck, we did it twice, just to make sure it would really stick.

"And it's two against one," Karro chimes, pointing between her and Henrik.

"Oh yeah? Two against one, huh?"

"Yeah, 'cause our names are both already Karlsson. Yours could be too. I think it should be. Then no one can doubt that we're a family, that we belong together."

My heart flutters as I glance down at her. "You want this too?"

She nods.

I glance to Henrik. "Well, what if I want to keep my name? Would you consider changing your name to O'Connor?"

After a moment, he nods. "I already asked Elin about the process. Karolina and I can petition the Swedish Tax Agency to have our names changed if that's your preference."

I pick up the papers, flipping through them, trying to keep my tone measured. Meanwhile, my heart is racing. "But your preference is for me to become a Karlsson?"

"I have no preference," he calmly replies. "I'm merely offering you the options. If you don't wish to become a Karlsson, Karro and I will happily become O'Connors. We're ready, and we want this. We hope you do too."

Fighting my smile, I test it out, as if I haven't whispered it like a prayer a thousand times before. "Teddy Karlsson . . . it has a nice ring to it."

Henrik's gaze is molten. If we were alone right now, instead of in a crowded restaurant, he'd already have me in his arms, my body splayed across this table. The thought makes me sit up a little straighter. "Fine. I'll take your last name on one condition . . ."

He raises a brow, waiting.

I grin, playing my trump card. "You have to go to Burning Man with me next year. And, yes, before you ask, you have to wear the chaps. And the lace crop top."

He sighs as Karro giggles.

I glance between them. "What? What's funny?"

Henrik nods at her. "Give them to him."

Reaching in her pocket, she pulls out two small pieces of paper and hands them to me. I gasp as I see that she's cut them to look like handmade carnival tickets. On each one it says, "Burning Man: Limit One Entry." She even decorated the edges with cute little flames.

My gaze darts between them as I sputter. "But—I—*how*?"

Across the table, Henrik just smiles. "Because I know you, mitt hjärta. I know the soul of you. And I will wear your chaps at Burning Man next year. But first, you take our name."

My smile is so big it hurts as I set the papers aside and wrap my arms around my daughter, smiling across the table at my husband. "Dr. and Mr. Teddy Karlsson . . . Oooh, babe, that'll look so good on our return address labels."

He nods, sipping his beer. "Anything you want, mitt hjärta. Anything at all."

THE END

THANK YOU

I can't believe I'm here again. Book four is in your hands. I've said it before, but writing this series has changed my life. *You* have changed my life. Every reader who has taken a chance on this hockey romance series has added to my life being irrevocably changed for the better.

And how the heck did we even get here?? These books are too long, the plots are too thin, the characters are too silly, the titles are cringy, and what's the deal with all the zodiac nonsense? Trust me, over the last two years, I've heard it all. And through it all, I've stayed true to the voice of these characters. I've told their stories as they would want me to tell them. Are they perfect? No. But what art is?

At their heart, each of these books are about love and acceptance. As a queer person who came out later in life, it's become the story of *my* life. Casting aside my doubt, worry, and shame. Shaking off the shackles of societal correctness that tell me who I should be. Each time I write a character loving and accepting who they are, I accept a little more about myself too.

Teddy and Henrik are no exception. These men represent the best of me—my patience, my full heart, my careful reason, my commitment and loyalty. They also represent me at my worst—my fear and worry, my overworking tendencies, my cool distance, my inability to say what I truly feel unless it's written down and buried within the voice of a character.

Writing Teddy and Henrik's love pulled me out of the deep fog of depression. They brought joy back to my life. More than joy, they brought me hope, and I will forever be grateful to them.

Okay, enough of Emily crying over her own fictional characters. Let's thank some people!

To my alpha (Ashley) and beta team (Sam, Rachel, Alex, Joanne), thank you for being the first to know and love these characters.

To my ARC team, thank you for shouting about this series from the rooftops! It's the early work of my ARC readers that brought this series to where it is now. And to all my avid readers everywhere, I'm so grateful you're here!

To my PAs, Sam and Rachel, and my social media liaison, Jess, thank you for keeping me sane this past year as I juggled far too many events, preorders, and book launches (and Jess, yes, I just made up that title).

To my Patreon subscribers, thank you for going on this wild new journey with me. Special shout out to those in the Price Family Storage Closet: Amber, Kristina, Cait, Chelsea, Devjani, Elisa, Angie, Jenn 1, Jenn 2, Kaitlyn, Kelly, Miranda, Sarah, and Tonya.

To my Swedish language readers, Linnea and Micaela, thank you for helping me make Henrik sound unobtainably hot. And thank you so much for your insights into Swedish culture, especially baking and family dynamics.

To my sensitivity readers, Melan, Alexia, and Ciara, thank you for the careful attention you placed on reading both Teddy and Henrik. It matters to me that my stories resonate far beyond my own lived experience.

To my publishing teams at JABberwocky, Zeno, Tantor, Kensington, and Penguin Michael Joseph, thank you for taking a chance on me and this series and helping me bring the Jax Rays to a wider audience!

Lastly, to my family. This year really challenged us. Through it all, we've protected each other and loved each other, putting the safety and happiness of our little wolf pack first. Thank you for taking chances with me.

XO,

E Roth